CENHELM

Gaisel

MONTORI
SEA

Igna

KULA

SEA

Enta

ISLANDS

ALPRESORI SEA

The WORLD of the
GODS

RISE UP FROM THE EMBERS

Also available by Sara Raasch and Kristen Simmons

SET FIRE TO THE GODS

RISE UP FROM THE EMBERS

SARA RAASCH
& KRISTEN SIMMONS

BALZER + BRAY

An Imprint of HarperCollins*Publishers*

Balzer + Bray is an imprint of HarperCollins Publishers.

Rise Up from the Embers
Copyright © 2021 by Sara Raasch and Kristen Simmons
Map Illustration by Leo Hartas
www.epicreads.com

ISBN 978-0-06-289159-4

Typography by Jenna Stempel-Lobell
21 22 23 24 25 PC/LSCH 10 9 8 7 6 5 4 3 2 1
❖
First Edition

To those of us who must now
rise from the embers.

ONE

MADOC

MADOC HAD SAVED lives, altered thoughts, and drained the power from gods—but he could not stop the knife swinging toward his gut.

With a grunt, he twisted away, but the steel sliced through the side of his sweat-soaked tunic, a breath away from his skin, and came to a stop beneath his left arm, beside his pounding heart.

"You're not trying," Tor growled, his long, damp hair clinging to his jaw, his tunic stretching across his broad shoulders. He may have matched Madoc in size and build, but that was where the likeness ended. Tor was hardened by years of training; his reflexes were quick as flames. He was a seasoned Kulan gladiator—or at least he had been before his god was murdered.

Now he was an accused traitor, on the run from a vengeful goddess—Madoc's mother—just like the rest of them.

Madoc shoved Tor back and wiped the sweat from his brow with his forearm. They'd been training every day since they'd sailed out of

Deimos's war-ravaged capitol, Crixion, two weeks ago. They hoped to find refuge in the Apuit Islands with the goddess Hydra's people, who they'd heard had allied with Florus, the god of plants. But with the gods of fire and earth both dead and Deimos in the grip of Anathrasa, the Mother Goddess, they had no idea how they'd be received. For all they knew, Hydra would think them spies and send her warriors to destroy them.

That was, if Anathrasa didn't hunt them down first.

"This isn't working," he muttered. Though Tor had taught many fighters to use igneia, fire energy wasn't the same as the anathreia Madoc himself possessed. If he was going to be any use to Ash and the others, Madoc needed to learn how to effectively manipulate soul energeia. But whenever he'd used it before, he'd either lost control or nearly killed himself in the process. Even with Tor's lessons, Madoc was no more ready to face Anathrasa now than he had been when they'd fled Deimos.

"Excuses." Tor tucked his blade back into the leather sheath at his belt and wiped his palms on his reed leggings. "I've seen you make a seasoned gladiator cry for his mother. Rip the energeia from a god like a rotten tooth. If you're going to drain the Mother Goddess before she finds a way to claim the other five countries, you'll need to be ready for anything. You're holding back."

Behind him, the ship's rail bobbed against the horizon, churning Madoc's stomach.

He tripped over the hatch cover leading belowdecks as another wave hit the stern. The swells had been bigger the last two days, the air cooler. He could feel it now, needling each bead of sweat on his temple as the sun sank low in the pink sky.

They were getting closer to Hydra's islands.

"If this boat would stop moving, I could concentrate." He staggered to stand, glaring at Tor's steady, wide-legged stance. Maybe he had saved Madoc when Geoxus's palace had fallen, but Madoc was really beginning to hate him.

"Anathrasa doesn't care if you're on the land or sea."

"She'll care if he throws up on her."

Ash lounged on the wooden steps to the upper deck, waving five flame-tipped fingers in front of her face. Since Madoc had returned her igneia—transferred it through the conduit of his body with his soul energy—the fire she created was blue.

Like the dead fire god's.

Madoc had heard Tor whispering with his sister, Taro, and her wife. They thought Madoc had accidentally given Ash the power he'd taken from Ignitus.

He wasn't sure they were wrong. None of them knew exactly what it meant, but if anyone was strong enough to figure it out, it was Ash.

She was wearing two tunics to fight the cold, but her shins were uncovered, and his gaze had fallen to her bare ankles, crisscrossed by the leather straps of her sandals, when another wave knocked him sideways into the foremast.

She laughed, and he couldn't stop his grin, even as the small crowd that had gathered near the helm above her snickered. Every Kulan on this ship had their sea legs, but Madoc still spent every morning and night with his head over a bucket.

"I'm not going to throw up." *Probably.*

"Focus," Tor ordered. "Anathrasa will be ready. She'll have protection. Aera and Biotus were allies of Geoxus—they'll likely join her now that he is dead. And who knows how many of the god of earth's centurions will rise to her aid once they realize what she can do?"

Madoc shivered. His mother was cunning. She'd survived for centuries by tithing—sucking the souls out of the gladiators Geoxus had offered her. She would not be defenseless now. Those who stood against her would be tithed, and the rest would suffer in silent allegiance for fear that she'd turn on them next.

"You know my intention," Tor continued. "Now stop me."

"Maybe that's the problem," Ash said, snuffing out the blue flames in a closed fist. "You don't really mean to hurt him. When he used anathreia to fight before, there was always a threat to his life." Her dark eyes flicked to his. "Or mine."

Madoc's shoulders drew together as he thought of the Deiman guards dragging Ash out of the preparation chamber at the arena after Anathrasa had taken away her energeia. A new sickness twisted his stomach as he remembered the palace, the tithes—his hollow soul, needing to be filled. His mother had forced him to take Petros's power, even if it meant killing him, to make himself strong. He'd taken Ignitus's power next, then Geoxus's, and it had nearly destroyed him.

If he hadn't been able to give that power to Ash, it would have.

Now a hunger for those same feelings, for the taste of another's energeia, was with him all the time, pressing against his lungs with every breath. But he refused to give in, not when this ship was filled with people who'd risked their lives for him. Not when he knew what tithing had done to Ash. To his sister, Cassia.

If he was going to be strong enough to drain whatever power his mother—the mother of all gods—had left, he needed to find another way to sate this growing need.

"I have no problem making him bleed if that's what it takes," Tor said with a sharp smile.

Madoc winced in Ash's direction. "Has he always been like this?"

"Oh, no." She grinned. "He used to have a training room and full armory at his disposal."

Madoc sighed through his teeth as Tor drew his knife and advanced again, a driven look in his eyes that made Madoc suspect he hadn't been kidding about making him bleed.

He was close enough to strike, and Madoc raised his hands—empty, at Tor's insistence—to defend himself. As they circled on the deck, Madoc reached out with his anathreia, feeling for Tor's emotions, finding the same intense frustration as always.

But it was laced with something else. A thin, pulsing warmth that reminded him, with a jolt of pain, of Ilena.

He blinked back his last image of his adopted mother, holding his face in her hands, telling him they would see each other again, just before she disappeared into the riots outside the temple to find Elias, Danon, and Ava. It was better this way—the farther Madoc was from Deimos, the safer they were—but he worried for them all the same.

Tor's head tilted. "What was that?" When Madoc shook his head, Tor stepped closer, dropping his weapon to his side. "What were you just thinking of?" Warmth spread across the space between them, driving a new spear of hunger into Madoc's soul.

Madoc glanced to Ash, who was now leaning forward, elbows on her knees.

"Home," he said quietly.

He didn't feel comfortable discussing this with Tor—his family was his to protect, even from friends. But if mentioning it helped him control his anathreia, he would do it.

Tor breathed in slowly, his eyes lifting to the horizon. "When Ash was a child, we often traveled for matches and wars. She grew up on ships like this."

Madoc glanced at her, watching him with a confidence he didn't deserve. If she knew how much he wanted to draw that confidence out of her, she wouldn't be so steadfast.

"When she missed Kula, I would tell her that Kula had come with her." Tor stepped closer, resting one large hand on Madoc's shoulder. The warmth was undeniable now, separate from the igneia in his veins, and Madoc held his breath, not trusting himself to swallow the air without a taste of it.

"Home is here." Tor moved his hand to Madoc's chest, where he softly pounded his fist twice. "Not there." He pointed behind them, to the sea. "The things that matter live inside us, and we protect them as we protect any other part of ourselves, with the power we've been given."

Madoc thought of Ilena and Elias. Danon and Ava. Even Cassia. And Ash, because she belonged with them, too. Only now he didn't picture them fighting or running. They weren't being hunted by Anathrasa or tortured in some prison cell as he'd dreamed every night these past two weeks. They were surrounded by a wall higher than those outside the grand arena. One fortified with the hardest, heaviest stones Elias had ever moved.

He locked them safely behind his ribs.

"Igneia is pulled from flames. Geoeia from stone." Tor shook his head in wonder. "You already have a fine source to pull from—your own soul—you're just afraid to do it."

Anathrasa had told him he needed other energeia to feed his power. He'd felt it work when he'd taken energeia from Petros and when he'd warped Jann's mind in the arena. Though he thirsted for it now, he'd never considered taking anathreia from himself.

Whatever soul he'd possessed himself had been broken a long time ago by Petros's hands and Crixion's streets.

"Don't be afraid," Tor said, meeting Madoc's gaze.

When he breathed, he felt the fondness behind Tor's frustration, but he didn't take it. His hunger had changed; it solidified the walls around his fortress. A knot of muscle in his neck relaxed as his anathreia whirled to life inside him for the first time in two long weeks.

Without warning, Tor lunged, knife aimed at Madoc's heart.

Stop.

Tor's hand froze in midair. He looked at it as if baffled, just before the knife dropped from his grip and embedded into the deck with a *thunk.*

"Good." With a grin, Tor spun, reaching out a hand to draw igneia from a lantern posted on the ship's mast. The fire balled in his palm, then sliced across the air beside Madoc's left shoulder. The sleeve of his tunic was charred; the heat seared his skin.

Excitement raced through Madoc's limbs as he rolled aside, then leaped to his feet. The next attack came just as fast, but this time he was ready. Tor wasn't just coming after him, he was coming after Madoc's family, his home. This wasn't about fighting or training. It was about defending what was his.

Madoc raised his empty hands, clutching the cold air as the energeia raced through him, ready for orders. *"Stop."*

The red flames licking Tor's skin suddenly went out. He stumbled back as if hit by an invisible punch, then went straight over the side of the ship.

Madoc's anathreia retreated like a kicked puppy. For one second he gaped at a wide-eyed Ash before they both raced to where Tor had fallen. Madoc's fingers dug into the splintering wooden rail as he searched the white-tipped waves. A moment passed, and then Tor sputtered to the surface, his arms circling as he treaded water.

"Was that really necessary?" Ash asked, unable to hide her grin.

Madoc laughed weakly.

"Man overboard!" From the helm rushed a flock of sailors, including Taro, Tor's sister. She wore the same glare Madoc had come to recognize from her, though now her eyes sparkled in amusement.

"Can that soul energy of yours give you wings?" she asked. "Because you'll want to be somewhere else when he gets back up here."

Ash giggled, but Madoc only winced.

Following Taro's lead, he reached to grab a thick coil of rope lying on the deck. With the help of Ash and Spark, Taro's wife, they succeeded in dropping one end down to the ocean below and fastening the other around the nearest mast.

Tor grabbed the end and began heaving himself up. Madoc didn't need to see his face to feel the bolts of anger flying off him.

"Maybe we should leave him down there a few minutes to cool off," he suggested.

"Just delaying the inevitable," Taro said. "It was nice knowing you, Madoc."

He groaned as they laughed. They were joking, of course. Tor wouldn't really kill him.

He hoped.

"Get him up here." Behind them, Spark's voice had dropped. Her worry prickled against Madoc's skin even before he saw it etched into her face. He followed her gaze up to the crow's nest, where a Kulan sailor was shouting to the crew at the helm while he watched the horizon through his spyglass.

"What is it?" Ash tensed beside him, peering into the distance. The sun had dipped below the horizon now, painting the sky an angry scarlet. She snagged the arm of a sailor, a boy no more than fifteen, who was sprinting toward the mast.

"Ships on the port side coming on fast." The sailor's voice cracked. "Too fast for a mortal crew. They've got help."

Madoc's pulse quickened. "What kind of ships?"

Please be Hydra's or Florus's fleet, he willed. Surely the goddess of water had the ability to make her ships cut through the waves at an accelerated clip.

"Black and silver sails." The sailor slipped free of Ash's hold and raced toward the mast to uncoil the lines. "Three of them!"

Madoc turned to Ash, a roar filling his ears. Only one country boasted the black and silver flag: Deimos.

Anathrasa had found them.

Shoving past Taro, he grabbed the thick corded rope Tor was climbing and heaved, straining to get the older man aboard as quickly as possible. Taro and Spark took up the slack behind him as Ash raced to the quarterdeck to see what was coming.

"Next time," Tor ground out between ragged breaths. "Try to keep my feet on the deck."

Madoc managed an apologetic shrug.

"Deiman ships spotted on the port," Taro barked at her brother as he clambered over the deck. He was soaked straight through and shrugged off his tunic with a violent shiver.

"Can we outrun them?" Tor asked.

Taro shook her head. "They're coming on too quickly."

The mainsail cracked as it filled with air, and the Kulan ship sailed faster than an arrow. Madoc gripped the rail to hang on as sailors rushed around him, securing lines and shouting orders. Below him, the hull slapped against the waves, driving hard to the west, into the last smear of daylight.

Anxiety snapped through the air. It mixed with a cold, snaking dread that pressed through Madoc's skin, chilling him to the bone. He couldn't think with all the emotions screaming around him. He could no sooner drown it out than quiet the crowds in the grand arena during a war.

He caught sight of Tor exchanging tense words with the captain, then Ash, pointing behind them into the night. He carved a path around the twin masts toward her, peering into the failing light and focusing on the heat of Ash's skin as she wrapped her fingers around his wrist. Warmth rippled up his arm, through his chest, steadying him. Without thinking, he curved his other hand around the slope of her waist.

"There!" she shouted. "Do you see them?"

He squinted, and soon he could make out a flash of silver in the dark sky. As he stared into the gloom, another joined it. Then a third. Three Deiman ships, flying over the waves, the heavy hulls skimming the surface of the water as the sails above stretched to full capacity. The sight of them filled him with equal parts dread and wonder. He'd never seen ships move with that kind of effortless speed.

"How are they going so fast?" he asked.

"I don't know," Ash said. "Earth Divine sailors can't move a ship like that. They must be either Water Divine or . . ."

"Air Divine." Madoc blew a tight breath through his teeth. He'd once seen a gladiator with aereia create a tornado during a match—it wasn't a stretch to imagine one manipulating the sea winds to their advantage. If there were Air Divine sailors aboard those ships, that would mean that Aera, who had been Geoxus's ally before his death, had come to Deimos to join Anathrasa.

Ash nodded, her brows drawn with worry—not just about who the ships carried, but what trouble they might bring. He hadn't been the only one training these past two weeks. Her new igneia was different, more intense—she could pull the blue flames without a source but had trouble controlling them. This was the burden of possessing a god's power in a mortal body.

Sometimes he wondered how it hadn't killed her.

"Slow down!" called a sailor above them. "There's something ahead!"

They spun to search the darkness lying before them.

"Land?" Hope lifted Ash's voice. "Is it the islands?"

Ash and Madoc dashed toward the bow of the ship, past the captain at the helm. Tor was already there, shooting a stream of fire into the night to light the way. Spark and Taro stood beside him, squinting ahead, to where a gray, shapeless mass expanded in the distance.

"Fog?" The air had taken on a frigid chill, and the word puffed steam from Madoc's lips.

With a quick shake of her head, Ash lifted her arms and heaved a spray of blue flames ahead, twice as far as the others could manage. Taro, standing closest, fell to her side with a cry, the heat of the blaze too intense even for a Kulan.

The beacon illuminated a sparkling gleam ahead, rising into the sky, disappearing into the clouds. Fear raced through Madoc's blood.

Not fog. Ice.

A solid wall of ice.

"Stop!" Madoc shouted. "It's a blockade!"

The ship heeled as the captain turned hard to avoid the wall of ice. The change in course brought them closer still, and in dreadful awe, Madoc stared up at the gleaming wall, veined with a scaffolding of blackened vines. They'd heard that Hydra and Florus had created a barrier to anyone from the outside, but they'd assumed it was a barricade of ships, or dignitaries who would take their claims to the gods.

They hadn't expected a wall.

Ash's fire died as the starboard side scraped against the blockade, chunks of ice falling onto the deck. One hit a sailor, and with a stunted scream she toppled down the ladder.

"They're closing in!" shouted Spark. More calls rose around them, shifting Madoc's attention.

Then, snaking through the chaos, a golden thread of silence.

It pushed through the wood, through the cloth and flesh and blood. Through the night and the water. It lifted the hair on his arms and the back of his neck, and as he breathed it in, he knew this curiosity was directed at him.

Anathrasa.

"She's here," Madoc murmured.

Ash's fierce gaze heated the side of his face.

"Then we fight," she said.

He took her hand, squeezed her fingers in his. He wanted to look at her one more time. He wanted one more night of her sneaking into his bunk belowdecks, lying together in the quiet so they didn't wake the other sailors. One more frantic kiss behind the mast when Tor wasn't looking.

There was no time.

He'd known from the moment they'd left Deimos that his mother would come for him. He had what she wanted—the ability to drain the power from gods and transfer it, as he had with Ash. To give Anathrasa the energeia of the six gods and make them mortal so she could harness anathreia again and take over the world.

He needed to stop her before that happened.

"We fight," he said.

The ships were closer now. Their sails snapped in the wind. Their hulls smashed against the waves. Madoc made his way to port side, facing the closest ship that carved a line toward them, its silver bow like a battering ram, ready to shatter them against the monstrous wall of ice.

The captain was still trying to push the ship faster, but they'd lost the wind beside the blockade, and their speed had slowed to a crawl.

"Ready?" Tor called, somewhere to Madoc's left.

He tried to focus on his family, on protecting his home, but his concentration evaporated as Ash lit up the night with blue flames, revealing the old woman standing at the helm of the approaching ship, flanked by Earth Divine soldiers in silver armor and Air Divine warriors in pale, thin wisps of fabric.

Madoc's mother met his gaze, and even from three ships' lengths away, he could see her smile.

She would kill all these people—kill Ash—for him.

It didn't matter if he wasn't ready or trained. He couldn't let that happen.

Raising his hands, he drew every bit of strength from his own soul and reached toward her. His fingers, white with cold, shook as he forced the power rising in his veins to stretch across the water.

Stop.

She deflected his attack like a slap, and his focus crumbled. Beside him, Ash's flame faltered. Tor shouted his name, but he didn't listen. He anchored his hips against the vessel's rail and reached for Anathrasa again, pulling her into the net of his need. He would drain her like he had Ignitus and Geoxus, and then she would suffer a mortal's death like all those she'd taken as tithes.

Anathrasa's scream filled his ears, so shrill he nearly clapped his hands over them. It rose, silencing Tor's shouts for him to stop. In seconds, Madoc felt as if his bones were cracking under the pressure of that scream.

Panic twisted through his anathreia, freezing it like the wall that blocked their escape.

Then every frozen vein of his soul shattered, and the world went black.

TWO

ASH

UNPREDICTABLE IGNEIA DURING training was one thing—no one's lives depended on Ash countering Tor's moves. But in a battle, with Anathrasa's ships bearing down on them and the other Kulan sailors already streaking fire across the night sky—Ash's chest constricted with equal parts fear and dread.

She had been training for years. She could control her igneia.

Only this wasn't *her* igneia.

Ash shoved aside the thought and thrust out her palms. A funnel of blue arced over the waves. The heat in it came straight from her heart, stole her breath with the searing intensity of the white-blue flames.

From one of the Deiman ships, an Air Divine warrior let loose a column of wind that slammed into Ash's fire. She flinched and her fire arc missed the lead ship, slamming into the water with a hiss that clouded steam into the air.

Cursing, Ash shook her hands out by her sides and shot another stream of blue fire into the night, chasing the orange ones sent by the Kulan sailors. Sweat beaded along her hairline, racing in trickles down her neck. She focused on bending the fire stream toward the lead ship, toward Anathrasa.

Anathrasa, whose alliance with Geoxus had caused Ash's mother's death on the sands of Kula's arena, and who had drained Cassia of her energeia before Petros killed her, and who had drained Ash's own energeia.

Anathrasa, who would force Madoc to destroy the world—or force Madoc to murder her himself in order to stop her.

However demented she might be, Anathrasa was still his mother—and beyond that, *could* he even truly hurt her? Or would she just rip the anathreia from his body before he could do anything and leave him an empty, aching shell while she went about siring other Soul Divine mortal children who would actually obey her?

The fire pouring from Ash's hands wavered, then shot out even stronger. It burned so hot she saw the wood rail at her hip start to glow red. But it wasn't just the fire that was hot—it was *her*, her body, and if she hadn't been wearing fireproof Kulan reeds, she'd be bare in the night.

Ash clamped her eyes shut, every nerve aching with conflicting emotions.

Burn it all. Kill her.

Stop! It's too much—too much—

Then, a scream.

Ash peeled her eyes open. Images blurred in sweat, flashes of firelight, and movement on the Deiman ships.

Anathrasa, bent over on the forward deck, her lone figure flickering in the light from the Kulan fires.

Hope tasted bitter. Had Ash done that? Had she truly hurt—

But then she saw Madoc reaching for his mother, his face set with vicious intent.

He had been trying to take Anathrasa's soul. Were they close enough to each other?

Who had screamed?

Madoc's knees cracked onto the deck. He let out a strangled moan and Ash's resolve tightened.

There could be no more pretending that Madoc had given her her own igneia back. The night they'd left Deimos, Madoc truly had given her Ignitus's power. The fire god's body was gone, but his energeia lived on. It was why the Kulans were still able to use igneia—it hadn't vanished into nothingness. It was in *her*.

No longer did Ash have to pull igneia from a source. It was always just *there* now, inside her, ready. And she could make orange flames, sure—gold and yellow and scarlet. But the first one that burst out of her was always a startling turquoise flicker of scalding heat.

She had the god of fire's soul inside her now. She had power, and damn it all, she would *use* it.

It terrified her. It twisted her stomach into knots and had her choking down food she couldn't taste and falling into fitful sleeps, because she was *terrified* of what having this much power meant. What was she now? *Who* was she now?

But she was more terrified by how much it *didn't* terrify her.

And seeing Madoc on his knees, clutching his head, made all Ash's worries seem trivial.

This ended *now*.

Ash stepped up to the rail, her nails biting into her palms. The Deiman ships twisted through the obsidian waves, a trio of matching wooden bows. Their masts flew the flag of Deimos, a pearly column against a silver background, and the orange flashes of Kulan fire gave the flags a vivid glow. Across the decks, Ash caught sight of Deiman centurions with their fingers splayed, using geoeia to keep palm-sized knots of pebbles aloft, while the Lak warriors funneled coils of wind over their heads. All of them waited for Anathrasa's orders.

Anathrasa was now clutching the wooden rail. Was she gasping? Had Madoc done something to her?

She's weak, Ash's warrior instincts barked. *Attack!*

"Attack!" Anathrasa's gravelly voice filled the night air.

For weeks, Ash had been stacking rage like kindling in her soul. Cerulean fire streamed out of her, charging from the Kulan ship to the lead Deiman vessel. Anathrasa's face was pale in the coming light, and she dropped behind the rail as the scalding flames raced across the ship. The fire washed into the Deiman centurions and Lak soldiers behind her, who stumbled back.

Ash didn't hear their cries of pain. The sear and churn of the fire swallowed her up.

A lifetime ago, Ash had practiced with other fire dancers before performing for Ignitus, and she'd trained with her mother in igneia fighting techniques. She'd thrown fire whips and sustained flames and had spun fire in interlocking circles over and over and over, until she had complete control.

She didn't want control now. She wanted Anathrasa to cower knowing that Ignitus's energeia lived on. She wanted the Mother Goddess to know that, for all her centuries of planning her revenge against her murderous children, she could not extinguish Kula.

Sweat beads tumbled down Ash's temple as she bent her arms, remembering her dancing, all elegance; and her mother, all precision.

Her fire coiled around one, two, three remaining soldiers, and she squeezed. The flames contracted and her victims shrieked.

These weren't the screams she wanted.

Ash's concentration broke and she dropped the soldiers. Where was Anathrasa?

"The God Killer! Attack!" shouted one of the men she'd released. "Avenge Geoxus!"

Ash huffed an empty laugh. She remembered Geoxus's body dropping limply onto the marble floor of his throne room, the knife in her hand wet with his blood. She'd been suppressing her satisfaction at killing him just like she'd suppressed Ignitus's power. She'd thought she should feel guilt, or regret, or reverence for killing something immortal—but all she'd felt was glee.

God Killer. She liked the sound of that.

More centurions used geoeia to hurl rocks into the air. More Air Divine sent powerful winds to carry the rocks higher, faster. A wave of stones vaulted through the star-speckled sky, a shower of rocks as vicious as arrows.

Time slowed. There was only the burn of fire in Ash's limbs, the taste of salt and sweat on the air, the vague awareness of Spark tending to a barely conscious Madoc.

Ash's heart gave a hard lurch, horror almost yanking her to her knees next to him—it was only by sheer force of will that she kept her feet. Then that will turned to fury.

Anathrasa had hurt him.

Tor shouted something, but Ash couldn't hear through the noise in her mind.

She thought she'd feel some release after finally breaking the restraints she'd placed on herself. But the more igneia she poured out of her fingertips, the more a different need built. Pressure welled up in her throat, something that had sat under her igneia these past two weeks, waiting, waiting, waiting.

The stones came closer. Kulans across the deck sent up a cry.

Beyond them, Anathrasa sneered.

You will not touch him, Ash promised. *You will never touch him again.*

She lifted her arms. Her blue fire raged, hurtling up from the deck of the Deiman ship and washing through the air after the stones. Some of the rocks she could simply burn up before they did any damage; others she redirected with quick flashes of heat.

Fire and earth.

It made Ash dizzy, seeing the flames twist around the rocks. Each bump of fire against rock *hurt*. She could feel the singe, a sharp jab of awareness that made her recoil.

Ash sank back to her own body with a jolt and gulped scorched air. Her nerves felt deadened. She was raw and drunk and dizzy. It was so sweet, so simple, to use igneia—

But she wasn't using only igneia.

She could feel the rocks. She could *feel* the grit of porous sand-stone, the razor-sharp edge of shale. They were like fire, but they were nothing like fire, and Ash felt a part of her soul sigh, stretch, and burst forth.

"Ash!"

A voice, calling her. Something bucked beneath her—the very foundation of the earth.

"Ash—*stop!*"

The world pitched again. No—the ship.

Reality broke over her. Her heart hammered as though she'd run twenty laps around Kula's largest arena, and when she peeled her eyes open, she saw rocks.

Rocks all around her.

Boulders, chunks of marble, granite—they filled up the deck of the Kulan ship.

Tor's fingers bore into her arms. "Ash, you have to stop! You're sinking the ship!"

You're sinking the ship.

"No." Her mind tripped. "I'm trying to stop the assault—"

But as she spoke, a rock filled her open palms, then clattered to her feet. Another followed, and another, stones pouring out of her hands.

She was Fire Divine, not Earth Divine. She couldn't be—

The night they'd fled Deimos, Madoc had taken Ignitus's igneia—and he'd taken Geoxus's geoeia, too. Madoc had been nearly unconscious, unable to walk on his own, from the pressure of holding two gods' souls in his body. Then, belowdecks, he'd given Ash igneia. Afterward, he'd been his normal self.

No one had asked where Geoxus's geoeia had gone.

Ash's senses widened and she felt every grain of sand on the Deimos ships. Geoeia pulsed through her body, heavier than igneia, but in a sturdy, immobile way that Ash suddenly craved.

Impossibly, she felt herself smile.

She was the god of fire now, and the god of earth.

She had *both* powers.

Tor shook her. A look of horror crossed his face, and it was enough to break her out of her euphoria.

"You're sinking the ship," he repeated. "You have to get rid of these rocks."

Behind him, Taro and Spark knelt next to Madoc, the three of them gaping at her.

The Kulan ship groaned as the great vessel lowered, dropping closer and closer to the thrashing ocean waves. This boat was built for speed, not to bear the weight of stones.

Ash's mouth fell open. "I—I don't know how I'm doing this."

Burn it all—she had no idea how to use geoeia. Where had these rocks even come from, except her own subconscious will? Panic heated her body, and columns of blue fire surged out of her hands.

Tor wrenched back, hissing in pain as the fire licked his ankles. Only Ignitus's fire could burn a Kulan. *Her* fire. When she'd sparred with Tor in the past two weeks, she'd tried and tried to keep her flames away from his skin. Still, she saw red burns on his shins and arms. He had never mentioned it. Neither had she.

She buckled, dropping onto a boulder. "I'm sorry! I'm sorry—"

Her apology died. Sorry for *what*? Burning him? Sinking the ship? Tor's face was sympathetic but scared.

Their ship was in chaos, Kulan sailors hefting stones overboard, while in the distance, Anathrasa's ships sat still and watchful, likely confused as to why their prey was suddenly sinking.

Ash had doomed them.

Stomach clenching, she gagged and stared down at her traitorous hands, now wreathed in flame. She shook her fingers, curled them into fists.

Geoeia, she willed. *Control it, control—*

The ship lurched to starboard before rocking back to port. The crew wailed, grabbing for purchase on wood or stone as the ship rose through the water and came to a trembling stop.

They had been sailing for so long that the sudden immobility made Ash dizzy.

Had they hit the blockade? She and Tor stumbled for the rail and he shot fire over the water.

Not water now. Ice.

The whole of the ocean around the Kulan ship had solidified into a sheet of foggy ice that matched the barricade at their backs. Only the Deiman ships, rocking in angry waves, were still free. And Anathrasa, now upright again, was calling orders for her centurions to regroup.

"What happened?" Ash panted, her breath a cloud in the chilly air. Even with igneia living inside her, she was so cold here.

"Hydra," Tor guessed.

Madoc, now standing, shot his eyes to the wall of ice and vines. "Or Water Divine guards on the barricade."

Madoc. He was all right.

Ash lurched toward him, not caring about anything else. She had been furious at Tor for playing the role of overprotective father and for trying to keep her and Madoc apart on this voyage, as though she was a child who'd given her heart to the first boy she'd seen. She threw herself around Madoc now, Tor's glower be damned.

"What did she do to you?" she whispered against his neck.

His arms clamped against her back, weaker than usual, but still resolute. "I'm not sure. I tried to take her anathreia."

Ash stiffened. She wanted to tell him he shouldn't have done that, not yet, he wasn't ready. But how many other chances would they have? She would have done the same thing.

"And it hurt you somehow?" She touched the back of his head.

He shuddered. "I don't know—"

"What. Did you bring. *To my home?*"

The voice was melodic even in its obvious fury.

Ash twisted in Madoc's arms, unwilling to let him go just yet.

On the deck of their ship, amid the rocks Ash had summoned, was a woman who had to be the goddess of water. Behind her, Apuitian soldiers were climbing over the rail, dressed in glistening furs and skins, their arms wrapped in pulsing streams of water they could easily flick out in attack. And within that water, small particles glowed—some sort of algae, maybe? It gave off a subtle light that Ash's igneia couldn't touch, much like Geoxus's phosphorescent stones.

Ash had seen the water goddess long ago in Ignitus's palace. She had been only a face made of water then, as she'd been communicating with Ignitus from afar via her element, but Ash saw the same features in her now.

Hydra was tall and pale, with thin eyes that were narrowed in suspicion. She wore only a skintight layer of what looked to be sealskin around her torso and upper thighs, and her long black hair hung to her lower back, as shimmering and straight as an undisturbed pond. When the soldiers on Anathrasa's ships called out another attack, she flicked a long, slender hand at them and Ash heard a splash of water, followed by a mingled chorus of coughing and shouts.

Her attention jerked back to the fight.

Ash whirled, her body tense. Could she risk attacking again?

His arm still around her waist, Madoc tugged her closer. "Don't." His voice was gruff.

Ash looked at him. In the Kulan firelight, he was gaunt and gray, his eyes bloodshot. He was upright and conscious, but only just barely, and when her eyes met his, he exhaled and let his forehead drop against her jaw.

He'd tried to take Anathrasa's energeia—had she managed to take his instead?

Ash's heart kicked with dread. "Sit." She tried to lower him to the deck. "You should—"

"Hydra!" Anathrasa's voice cut across the waves. "My daughter. I have missed you."

Hydra went rigid and her glare cut to the Deiman ships. "Anathrasa?" Her lips barely moved.

"Surprise, darling," the Mother Goddess returned. There was a warble in her tone, almost as though she was in pain. "My death was a fiction created to protect me as I regained my strength. The time has come, Hydra. Tell your brother—this barricade you and Florus created will not protect you."

"From what?" Hydra scoffed, but Ash saw that the goddess's skin had taken on a sickly hue. "Geoxus's navy doesn't scare—"

"Geoxus is dead. Ignitus, too. And you have your brothers' murderers before you."

Ash's grip tightened on Madoc, protective, terrified. She would kill Anathrasa if she touched him again.

"Think carefully before you pick a side, daughter," Anathrasa said. "I will give you and Florus one month to show yourselves in Deimos and surrender to me. I'll even leave you these traitors—bring them with you when you return, or I will consider you complicit in their crimes."

Ash eyed Anathrasa's ship. Its sails snapped in the breeze, the wind curving the vessels around as Anathrasa limped across the deck.

She was leaving. Madoc *had* wounded her.

Any joy Ash might have felt dulled as Madoc's weight dropped heavier against her. She eased him onto the wood planks.

A rock clinked. Hydra flicked a small particle of gravel from a boulder to the deck, her nose wrinkling in disgust. Around her, the Apuitian soldiers seethed with eagerness to attack.

"Anathrasa. Two gods *dead*. A mortal who can use both igneia and geoeia." Hydra analyzed Tor, then a few Kulan sailors, before landing back on Ash.

Horror filled Ash's body. It stoked both the igneia and geoeia in her soul, and she had to clamp her jaw shut, her muscles wound to suppress the roiling power.

"So let me ask again," Hydra said. "What did you idiot mortals bring to my home?"

THREE

MADOC

MADOC FELT AS if he'd been taken apart and roughly shoved back together. His body ached in a dozen different places—his head, his back, his knees and eyes. Ignoring the pain, he stood and focused on Ash's hand centered between his shoulder blades, and on the goddess before them.

Hydra's pale eyes assessed them as she picked her way around the boulders on the deck. Her face and dark clothing were lit a pale blue by the glowing algae in her warriors' water. It was quiet enough to hear the soft groan of the wood beneath her steps, and the waves lapping over the ice that now cradled the ship.

"Speak!" she ordered, lifting a single finger. "But know that if any of you so much as thinks of using igneia, I'll sink this ship to the bottom of the sea. Is that clear?"

Madoc dipped his chin, as did the others. But Ash was trembling as she withdrew her hand from his back. Was she hurt? He tried to reach for a sense of her emotions, but his anathreia was raw and beaten. Guilt sharpened the pounding in his head as he glanced over her for injuries but found only scrapes and bruises. If he could have stayed on his feet, he could have helped her. She'd needed him—they all had—and he'd been useless.

Her voice faded in Madoc's ears, and he blinked back a wave of fatigue. He didn't know what had happened when he'd attacked Anathrasa. One moment, he'd been reaching for her soul, intending to wrench it free the way he had Geoxus's power. The next, anathreia had exploded inside him. Now he could barely keep upright.

"We came here to bring news of your brothers' deaths, goddess," Tor said, ignoring the wound that painted a thin, scarlet line across his tunic's chest. "To tell you that Deimos has fallen, and Anathrasa intends to claim the six countries as her own. We didn't anticipate her tracking us down before we reached you." He knelt, his head bowed. "This ship's crew and her passengers are not at fault for Anathrasa's attack tonight. The blame for that rests with me alone."

Ash opened her mouth to object, but Tor shot a glare her way, silencing her.

Tor would take the fall for all of them—for Madoc, though they'd known each other only a short time—in order to win Hydra's favor. Tension sharpened the pressure at the root of Madoc's neck. This man owed him nothing yet risked his life for him again and again.

Hydra stopped before him, one hand over her stomach. "How did my brothers die?"

"Geoxus killed Ignitus," Tor said, intentionally vague. "He was siding with Anathrasa."

Madoc's eyes briefly closed as he recalled the throne room at the palace. The boulders falling from the ceiling. The screams of the centurions and Kulans as they'd battled.

The manic glee in Geoxus's smile as he'd rammed a jagged shard of his throne through his brother's heart.

"She made them mortal?" Hydra glided fluidly across the boards, closer to Tor. "She didn't look very powerful to me just now."

Tor's jaw clenched. "I don't—"

His words were cut off by a choking gargle as water began streaming from the corners of his mouth.

"Tor!" Taro dropped to his side, slapping his back, but the water was leaking out of his ears and nostrils now. Madoc's heart kicked against his ribs.

"Please!" Ash lifted her open palms to the goddess. "We came to help you!"

"Then it would be a pity to drown on your lies now," Hydra said.

"I did it." The words scraped Madoc's already-raw throat. He refused to let Tor die protecting him. Not when he'd pulled Madoc out of the palace, where'd he'd been tortured by Geoxus, Petros, and Anathrasa. Not when he'd trained Madoc on the ship.

Not after he'd tried to save Cassia from her indentured servitude in Petros's villa.

It didn't matter that Tor and Ash had failed, or that Cassia was dead. Few people had stood for Madoc when he needed them, and he would not lose one of them now.

Ash's worried gaze met his, her hands fisted in the sleeves of her tunic.

Madoc sucked in a breath, hoping it would last if Hydra filled his lungs with water next.

Hydra stepped before him, her clear blue eyes aligning with his. After a moment, she blinked, and Tor gasped. He spread his hands over the boards as Taro ordered him to breathe.

Hydra assessed Madoc's dark hair and square jaw. "Why is a Deiman on a Kulan ship?"

"Half Deiman." Madoc squinted to focus on her flawless face as his vision wavered.

Hydra's brow quirked. "*You* rendered my brothers mortal?"

"Yes," said Madoc. "But Ignitus was an accident. I was aiming for Geoxus."

She huffed, a cold laugh that Madoc was sure would end in his drowning. But there was no point in hiding the truth now. It was just a matter of time before she learned who he really was, and if she didn't hear it now, from him, they would never earn her trust.

"And how did you do that?" she asked, amusement curling her lips. Around her, the Water Divine warriors shifted uneasily.

"Anathreia," he said. "Soul energy."

"Madoc," Tor warned.

Hydra's mouth flattened into a thin line.

"Madoc," she said tightly. "Only a descendant of Anathrasa herself would have soul energeia."

"She's my mother," Madoc explained. "We're not exactly close."

Hydra's chin lowered. Her hands flexed. Madoc siphoned in another quick breath, unsure what she would do next.

"So she's not just alive," the goddess mused darkly. "But mother to a mortal son."

Madoc nodded. "Geoxus had been feeding her human tithes in exchange for bearing a Soul Divine child—someone to help him take over the six countries. I was the only one who survived."

Hydra lifted one hand, and a drop of water rose from her palm, gleaming in the dull light. It was a tiny thing, barely the size of his pinky—but he didn't know what she intended to do with it, and that drove a spike of fear through his chest.

"Why should I believe you?" she asked. "If you can do what you say you can, you could destroy me right now."

The drop of water floating above her hand swelled and narrowed to the shape of a spear tip aimed at Madoc's eye.

"I wouldn't do that," Madoc said quickly.

"Why not?"

"You heard Anathrasa," he said. "If you don't surrender, she'll call for war—not the kind with gladiators. With armies. If you're going to fight her and win, you'll need me."

Hydra flinched, and the arrow spun in a glittering tornado into the shape of a clawed hand.

"Because you can defeat her?" Hydra huffed. "Then why didn't you do that tonight?"

He spread his feet. Lifted his chest.

"You lie, Madoc. And I detest liars." In a blink, the clawed hand had turned to an icy knife, which Hydra grabbed and held against Madoc's throat.

He went still, the sharp, frozen point digging into the thin skin over his jugular. Beside him, Ash cried out in surprise, but he held her back with an extended hand.

Believe me, he willed Hydra. *Trust me*. But she was as much a wall as her blockade of ice was. Too strong for his weakened power.

In desperation, he reached for the next best thing. The nearest Water Divine warrior—a man in a sealskin hide and a fur hood.

Help, Madoc willed.

The warrior twitched, the icicle in his grip dropping lower.

Now, Madoc screamed wordlessly to him as Hydra's knife nicked his throat.

The man shook his head. "Goddess . . . I think . . . I think he may be telling the truth."

Hydra blinked back at him in surprise. "You do, do you?" Her voice was ice and challenge.

As the other man's soul broke free from his hold, Madoc's breath came in a hard rasp.

"I'm sorry, Goddess." The warrior raised his weapon again, his eyes confused. "I don't know what came over me."

Hydra's teeth clenched as realization hardened her features. "I've seen these tricks before." She eased closer to Madoc until he could feel a trickle of blood sliding down his neck. "Maybe you are Anathrasa's son. Maybe you can sway a mortal mind. But my brothers were gods. If you did what you said, you would have absorbed Geoxus's geoeia, and Ignitus's fire. You would be a gladiator fit to take down Anathrasa."

He hesitated, unwilling to answer for fear of putting Ash in more danger, and in that moment, Hydra lunged.

"He gave them to me!" Ash cried, stalling Hydra's advance. "Ignitus's energeia. Geoxus's as well."

Hydra turned her glare on Ash.

"He *gave* them to you," Hydra repeated. "What a nice gift."

Ash wrung her hands before her. What was she doing? She had Ignitus's fire, but the geoeia had dissipated. He couldn't feel it in his blood anymore.

What had happened to it?

"I did this," Ash said, motioning to the boulders on the ship. "Madoc only intended to give me back the energeia Anathrasa took from me. But he gave me Ignitus's power. And he must have given me Geoxus's power, too."

Madoc eyed her carefully, wondering if this was the truth, fearing what it meant if it was.

With a forced swallow, Ash reached toward a boulder on the deck behind Hydra and shoved it away, knocking two men to the side as it tumbled off the broken side of the ship.

The icy knife at Madoc's throat turned to water, splashing down his front. He drew in a quaking breath.

Hydra straightened, the wall of ice gleaming behind her. She glanced from Madoc to Ash.

"A conduit who possesses anathreia," she said. "And a gladiator who can bear the power of gods."

"We can help you," Madoc said.

Hydra gave a thin laugh.

"Yes," she said. "I think you can."

She turned, and with a wave of her hand, the ice wall began to melt, a hole rising from the sea, growing broader and higher, until it made an arching waterfall large enough for a ship to pass through.

With a lurch and a loud crack, the ship began to move. Not just the ship, Madoc realized, but the entire block of ice it rested upon. The Apuitians lowered their hands and weapons, awaiting their goddess's instructions as the ship moved forward through the falls, into the night beyond.

"Look," Spark whispered, and Madoc glanced behind them, finding that the arch was already lowering into a solid sheet of ice again.

Madoc lifted his gaze to where a million tiny lights flickered in the distance. As they glided forward, the lights pulled into groups, and Madoc made out the vague shape of the mountains they outlined.

The Apuit Islands.

Soon they'd reached a dark dock, where a dozen more Water Divine soldiers waited in thick fur coats.

"Rest," Hydra ordered without looking back. "We'll talk in the morning."

With that, she lifted a bridge of ice from the sea below and stepped off the side of the ship, into the darkness.

Madoc woke in a fur-lined hammock to the sound of footsteps creaking across the floor. He jolted upright, remembering his sore body and pounding head too late.

Biting back a groan, he whispered, "Who's there?"

"Shh. It's me."

Ash's soft voice eased his nerves, and he swung his legs off the side of the hammock, his last memories returning in a rush. The Apuitian guards had brought them down the dock to a wooden lodge scented by smoke and salted fish. There, they'd been given water and food, and then been escorted to a series of huts along the shore. Ash had joined Taro and Spark in one. Madoc, Tor, and a few of the sailors were sharing another.

They hadn't had a chance to talk about what had happened with Hydra, or the fact that Ash appeared to have two energeias instead of one. Tor had probably wanted to wait until they were alone to discuss it.

"How'd you get in?" Madoc whispered. There had been guards posted outside the doors.

He could barely see Ash's silhouette creeping toward him, outlined by the moon's glow through a skylight. He wasn't sure how much time had passed—a few hours at most. The sky outside was still dark, with no sign of the impending dawn.

"Window," she said softly. He glanced across the room, past the hammocks hanging heavy with Tor and the other fur-clad sailors. They hadn't been permitted a fire in the central hearth due to Hydra's concern that the Fire Divine were hiding their true intentions, and though the cold bothered Madoc, he found it more manageable than the Kulans, who were used to scorching temperatures.

Her hand found his knee, sending a wave of heat up his thigh. He took her fingers, dragging her closer. He wished he had this hut to himself. If Tor woke up, he'd be lucky if he only tossed Madoc into the frigid ocean outside.

Tor still owed him for their training mishap earlier.

"Come with me," she whispered, her breath a warm cloud on the side of his face.

He pushed quietly off the side of the hammock and followed her through the netted beds, toward a closed window. She lifted the hatch and, after a quick glance outside, pulled herself up and over the edge.

He followed, less gracefully.

"Quiet!" she whispered as he picked his beaten body up off the ground.

Hand in hand, they ran down the rocky path toward another hut, this one smaller and unguarded. She pushed through the sealskin flaps over the entrance, clearly having already scouted out their path.

"What is this place?" he asked as she lit a small bundle of sticks on the floor with a blue flame from her fingertips.

"Storage, I think."

With the dim light flickering in the room, he could make out the stacks of furs and pelts and barrels of supplies lining the walls.

She stood, her teeth chattering despite her reed pants and extra tunics. Reaching for one of the furs, he wrapped it around her shoulders, then spread another on the ground in front of the fire. He sat on it and patted the space beside him.

With a grin, she sat, sliding close.

For a minute, they didn't speak. She leaned against his side, and he pressed his cheek to her hair, reveling in the feel of her warm body against his, even through the fur. But as they watched the flames, he thought of what had happened with Anathrasa, and how he'd failed Ash in the fight.

He'd been training so that she could count on him—so all of them could. But he'd fallen apart, like always. He could barely manage his own energeia, while she was somehow hosting two.

"Are you all right?" he asked.

She looked up at him, brown eyes sparkling. When her gaze dropped to his mouth, it took a moment to remember what he'd asked.

"I'm all right," she said.

"It doesn't . . . hurt or anything?" He couldn't help reaching for the silky ends of her hair and winding them around his finger.

She shook her head.

"How do you do it?" he asked. "When I had both Geoxus's and Ignitus's energeias in me, it felt like I was being ripped in half."

He could still feel his bones stretching, his blood too thick for his veins. He'd wanted to crawl out of his skin.

"I don't know," she said with a small frown. "Maybe Hydra has some idea."

His teeth dug into his top lip. Maybe the goddess of water would know of something to help Ash. Or maybe she'd try to exploit her, like Geoxus and Anathrasa had done to him.

"Do you trust her?" he asked. If Hydra had seen Ash fight with geo-eia and igneia, then surely Anathrasa had as well. It wouldn't be long before the Mother Goddess realized how Ash had become that way. A God Killer with god powers and a God Maker with soul energeia were even more of a threat than who'd they'd been before, and Madoc could not fathom what that might mean without Hydra's protection.

"I don't know yet." Ash shifted to look up at him. "Are you all right? You're not hurt?"

A scowl pulled his brows together. "Just my pride."

She chuckled.

He smirked, but the lightness inside him grew heavy again. "I thought I could take Anathrasa. Pull out her energeia like I did with the other two."

"It took six gods to defeat her before."

"And?" he said.

She smirked. "Good point. Why couldn't you kill her?"

He reached around and squeezed her side where he knew she was ticklish. He'd found that out last week, when they'd been sparring. It had been his favorite way to beat her ever since.

"Enough!" she squealed. In her attempt to get away, her leg had slid up his thigh, and it didn't matter how often they'd sparred, or kissed, or that he'd seen her nonstop for two straight weeks. Her leg made his mind go completely blank.

"You have that look again," she said.

"What look?" He tried to keep his voice even, but her foot was brushing the inside of his calf and he was starting to think about a lot of things that Tor would murder him for even considering.

"Like you like me." She bit the corner of her lip.

She had no idea what that was doing to him.

"That's strange, because I don't," he said.

Her grin widened. "Too bad. I was going to suggest sharing this blanket."

He cleared his throat. "Well, in that case, I like you very much."

With a snort, she pulled away, just enough to hand him the side of the fur, so he could wrap it around both of them. Inside that soft cocoon, he could feel her hand spread over his chest, her knee hiking dangerously high.

Tor will kill you, he told himself.

He lowered himself to his back, one arm behind his head. She curled up against him, her cheek on his chest, a perfect fit.

Just a little while, he thought. Then he'd get her back to her bunk. Tor would never know.

He willed the minutes to slow as he listened to her breathing, watching the rise and fall of her shoulder. She had to hear his heart thumping in his chest. His thoughts returned to the home Tor had told him about in training. The place he kept inside him to protect the things that mattered.

He wanted to protect Ash, but he had failed today. She needed to be able to depend on him.

He wasn't worthy of her otherwise.

With a frown, he pushed up to his elbow. He needed to get her back. Tomorrow would be a big day, and she'd need all her strength if she was going to prove her value to Hydra.

She looked up at him, her eyes sleepy, her hair a mess. "Not yet."

Tor and the gods be damned. Madoc wasn't going anywhere.

As he settled back, she pressed her lips to his collarbone, and then the slope of his shoulder. She kissed his jaw, and his breathing grew unsteady. He pulled her closer, pressing his lips to hers, for once glad that his anathreia didn't hunger for the power of her igneia, and that his own thirst wouldn't pose her any harm.

He kissed her slowly. An apology. A promise. His hands found her narrow waist and slid up her back, tracing each winged muscle over her shoulder blades. When his fingertips reached the nape of her neck, she gasped, and he had the sudden urge to kiss her there.

So he did. But there was a place she liked more, right beneath her ear, and when his teeth grazed that spot her moan speared him to the core.

Their pace quickened. Their hands grew more urgent. The past two weeks on the ship crashed through them—every stolen kiss, every knowing glance. The fear, the loss, the need, all overpowered by fighting, all coated with bruises. And then the chaos of the war was breaking through—gods and blood pushing them faster and faster, until her palms seared his side, and he could barely catch his breath.

She whispered his name and he was done. Done with arenas and war and the constant, infernal rocking of ships. Done with energeia he didn't understand. Done with everything but her.

He knew in some small part of his brain that he needed to slow this down. To think. They'd kissed and shared a few frantic moments, but this was different. He could feel himself on a precipice—one he wasn't sure she could see.

She needed to know she was safe with him. Even if he couldn't protect her in battle, he could make sure she felt safe now.

He pulled back. Kissed the long lines of her throat, her jaw.

"Is this all right?" he asked, his mouth on her collarbone.

She nodded quickly.

"And this?" His hand climbed the rise of her hip over her leggings, then down the lean muscled length of her thigh. Tracing the soft, warm skin beneath her knee, he pulled her leg over his hip.

She pressed against him in answer, and when her dark, hooded gaze held his, he felt anchored for the first time in weeks.

Another shift. Another question. "Yes," she told him, again and again, until she was over him, reaching into her pocket for a small pouch, which she emptied into her hand.

A dark-red powder spilled out, smelling vaguely of spice and earth.

"Taro gave me this a while ago," she said, her cheeks taking on the faintest blush. "It's . . . um . . . sellenroot. For—"

"I know what it's for," he said. Sellenroot was a contraceptive, meant to make a man temporarily infertile. Ilena had given some to him and Elias the day their voices had stopped cracking, along with a stern lecture about respect and not carrying on like cats in heat.

He sat up, enjoying the way her calves curled around him. "Are you sure?"

She nodded. Smiled.

His heart thudded in his chest.

"Are you?" she asked.

He wanted to tell her yes, but the word felt too small for all the feelings now raging inside him. He wanted to tell her he was honored she'd chosen him, and that she was the most beautiful thing he'd ever seen, and that if she changed her mind and wanted to stop, that was all right because holding her was enough.

He wanted to tell her that he'd be here tomorrow, and the day after that, and the day after that—as long as she'd have him. Because this wasn't the kind of infatuation that softened with time. She had wrapped herself around his bones. She'd become part of his home.

But he didn't say any of it. Instead, he reached for her hand and licked the powder from her palm, swallowing the bitter root and every last doubt that he wasn't good enough for her.

Her lips crashed against his, and soon the taste was on her tongue too. Their clothes were shed, their hands woven. And when the last barrier between them was past, he held her, shaking, and whispered all the things he'd been afraid to say before.

But he knew that for her to believe them, really believe them, he'd have to prove himself to her.

And somehow, starting tomorrow, he would.

FOUR

ASH

ASH WOULD HAVE slept forever if not for the thin sliver of light that cut under the sealskin door. It flashed over her eyes on a brush of wind and she burrowed deeper under the fur blanket.

Thoughts started to push through. Morning. She wasn't in her hammock—

Then the arm that was draped over her waist curled, dragging her closer to the cozy heat at her back, and rational thoughts drifted away.

Ash grinned and wriggled under the blankets until she was face-to-face with Madoc. He was still asleep, one arm bent under his head, the other now loose around her hip. His lips parted in slow, steady breaths, his brow furrowed in a dream.

Gods, he was beautiful.

Ash pressed her thumb to the wrinkle between his eyebrows. It softened, and she trailed her hand over his ear, down his jaw, reveling in the fact that she could touch him here, and here, and here, as much as she wanted. The muscles in his neck that had gone corded with exertion last night. The soft black hairs across his chest. The lines of his abdomen—oh, he had a truly striking stomach, and even though she had already traced these muscles over and over, the feel of them still made her body seize. Her fingers trailed lower, to his navel above another line of hair—

Ash looked back up at Madoc's face now, and he was smiling.

He cracked one eye open to peek at her.

"Hello," she said, as innocently as she could muster.

Madoc sighed drowsily and rubbed his thumb against her back. "What time is it?"

"Early."

He winced. "We should go back to our bunks."

But he made no move to get up, and neither did Ash.

She kissed his chest. His neck. Nipped at his earlobe, sucking it between her teeth, and his throat rumbled with a moan. He rolled her onto her back, pinning her against the fur they'd made a bed of, the top blanket wrapping them in a cocoon of heat and sweat and Madoc's mouth on hers, her arms around his torso, their legs knotted.

Ash arched up against him, pressing her bare chest to his, utterly consumed—

Just as a figure burst through the sealskin door.

All pleasure died. Ash actually felt it drop dead on the ground around them.

Instinct yanked her to her feet as she hastily held a blanket over her body.

Tor stood in the doorway, the flap peeled wide. Behind him, Taro and Spark were breathless—frightened, even.

She hadn't been in her hammock, so they'd been out looking for her.

Ash went immobile as she watched Tor take her in. She was holding the blanket up, but she was clearly naked—and Madoc was sitting behind her, pulling the bedding to cover himself.

"What—" Tor's mouth dropped open.

Ash had never seen his pupils so wide, his face so purple. A matching panic rendered her mind blank.

Tor waved his hands like he was trying to keep Ash from fumbling any explanation. "Get dressed," he ordered, his voice like iron. "Hydra summoned us half an hour ago."

He spun on his heels and marched out into the morning light.

Ash lowered to her knees, unable to support her own weight. Out of the corner of her eye, she saw Madoc fold forward, his face in his hands.

"Even when I was at the mercy of Anathrasa, Geoxus, *and* Petros," Madoc said into his palms, "I didn't feel as close to death as I did just now."

Ash sputtered with laughter. Madoc looked at her and gave an exhausted grin.

She pressed her eyes closed. "Get your clothes on before I build a stone wall around us and refuse to ever come out again."

Because apparently I can do that. Call stone as easily as fire.

And Anathrasa saw me do both.

Horror ripped a jagged hole in her joy.

Ash started to stand again when Madoc's fingers closed around her wrist.

She stared down into his dark eyes, speechless at the raw way he always looked at her. As if he was baring himself to her and her alone. Like he'd tell her all his secrets if she only asked.

"Whatever happens today, I'm with you," he told her.

She nodded. "And I'm with you."

Madoc kissed the inside of her wrist, then began searching through the furs for his clothes. Ash mirrored him, fighting hard to focus on the feel of his breath on her skin, but already the future was chipping away at her happiness.

Only Taro was still outside by the time Ash and Madoc were decent. She motioned toward a long, curved boat on the shore. Two Apuitian sailors stood within it.

"Tor left already," Taro explained as they took seats on a bench against the side rail.

Ash heaved a sigh of relief, instinctively reaching out to steady Madoc when the Water Divine flared their arms and the boat launched away from the shore.

Taro smirked at her. "Just focus on this meeting with Hydra."

"I plan to." But hesitation churned in her stomach. Doing so meant focusing on how she had both Ignitus's and Geoxus's energeias in her body. And on the fact that the last mortal who had had the power of gods inside them had been someone the six gods had united to create—and who they had used to combat the Mother Goddess.

Had Tor made that connection yet? Had Anathrasa? Was Ash the only one who was horrified at the prospect of standing before Hydra, knowing what kind of weapon she herself now was? What would the water goddess do with both Madoc and Ash as threats?

The boat followed the green-brown shoreline of the island where they'd spent the night. Huts littered the ground, not a tree in sight on the sloping rise of the otherwise barren hills. This was the northernmost island, closest to the ice-vine barricade, and from what Ash had found as she explored yesterday evening, not many Apuitians lived there. It seemed to be a docking place for outsiders, which until their arrival had only meant people from Florus's country of Itza.

Ash leaned into Madoc, half for his warmth, half just because she wanted to. As the boat turned south, she heard him gasp, and her eyes leaped to his face.

A look of pure wonder overtook him. Ash shifted to follow his gaze.

The waterway had opened up and was ushering them deeper into the Apuit Islands.

Any details that had been lost in the darkness last night were vivid now in the morning sun. Dozens, maybe hundreds, of islands dotted the ocean off into the horizon, large and small, flat and mountainous, stark and lush. Ash had seen glimmers of fire and candlelight in the midnight shadows last night, but they had looked warped somehow, like flames encased in multifaceted lantern glass. Now she understood why.

Unlike the visitors' island, every structure, from the houses to the docks to the grand, arching bridges that connected the islands, was made of ice.

Feathered ice arched to form a long tube-shaped house into which fishermen hauled crates of their catches. Walls of clouded ice made up clusters of villages, with smoke somehow puffing out of chimneys. Great ice spears vaulted up into the sky, holding delicate buttresses that supported bridges between the closer islands. Everywhere was green grass, brown earth and sand, and crystalline ivory-blue ice.

"This is incredible," Ash breathed.

"Do you notice what's missing?" Madoc asked. "Arenas."

She cut her gaze over the islands again. He was right. Not an arena in sight.

That was more disconcerting than the relentless cold, just because of how *unusual* it was, but Ash reminded herself that it was good. She and Tor had entrusted Kula's safety to Brand, another of Ignitus's champions, until they took care of Anathrasa—but for a moment, Ash saw beyond the impending war. She saw the sort of future she wanted for Kula, for every country.

Unease still grated against her heart, and she edged closer to Madoc.

The lack of arenas wasn't threatening—she knew Hydra and Florus were used to being peaceful. But in Kula, Deimos, Lakhu, and Cenhelm, fighting was ingrained in each person. What would those countries look like with no arenas, no outlet for that foundation of battle?

Ash pressed her lips together. Honestly, she didn't much care. Questions like that put the victims of this brutal world second, and *that* was what she and Madoc were truly undoing—stopping gods and bloodshed from taking precedence.

So let the rest of the world burn their arenas to the ground. They would find peace in the embers.

🔥 🔥 🔥

Hydra's palace filled a whole island.

Sheer columns of ice twisted into the air, showing people walking up and down ice steps within. Blue-white walls towered between clear ice balconies that must be alarming to actually stand on. Razor-sharp turrets gave subtle reminders that water could be wicked as well as lovely.

Their boat docked and the Apuitians led them ashore. Ash stared up at the glittering palace, and even though she had the power of two gods in her body, she felt small.

As they entered the towering halls she swallowed, steeling her expression. The air itself felt frozen, grating Ash's throat with each breath, and the floor was thankfully lined with a fur runner to counter the slipperiness. She tried to dredge up confidence. She thought of her mother, walking into arenas with her head held high. She thought of how it felt to use igneia. She thought of—

Madoc's hand found hers.

She clamped down on his fingers, both their hands frigid.

The God Killer and the God Maker, she thought. *What a doomed pair we make.*

The Apuitian guides led them through doors already open into a long, wide throne room. Either side of the ice floor was gone, showing lapping water. Courtiers gathered at the far end of the room around a throne sculpted of spears of ice every bit as deadly as Geoxus's obsidian throne back in Deimos, the same one he had broken apart to murder Ignitus.

Ash swallowed, unable to feel her hand in Madoc's anymore.

The moment they entered the room, Tor and Spark met them from the side. They wore the same layered tunics and furs as Ash and Madoc, desperately trying to stay warm while still having a range of motion. Tor adjusted and readjusted a cloak over his chest, refusing to look at Madoc.

The crowd around the throne parted. Hydra was seated on it, her hands on the armrests, her back straight. She pushed herself up to stand, showing the gown she now wore, a long, trailing cascade of blue silk lined with fur at the wrists, throat, and hem. Her black hair lay in a series of braids around her shoulders, a crown of ice atop her head.

She crossed the room halfway before stopping, her hands loose at her sides, her sparkling blue eyes going from Ash to Madoc to their clasped hands.

They both jerked apart at the same time. Too late, Ash realized they should have kept their relationship hidden.

"Goddess." Tor stepped up. "We didn't introduce ourselves properly last night, nor thank you for your interference with Anathrasa. I am Tor Tsea from Kula. This is my—"

"You talk too much." Hydra lifted her hand. Tor clamped his mouth shut, likely remembering the way she'd filled his lungs with water with only a glance.

Ash shot forward a step, panic welling. "Wait. Goddess, I'm Ash Nikau, of—"

Hydra flipped her hand in a circle. "Of Kula, daughter of Char Nikau, great-granddaughter of Ignitus, and so on and so on, and did you really think I wouldn't already have found all this out? Madoc, Anathrasa's son, also the adopted son of a poor stonemason family in Deimos; Taro and Spark, married, Undivine; a whole contingent of Kulan sailors with unimpressive histories but who are still being watched closely by my soldiers. And another of Ignitus's gladiators is in Kula trying to assert order in the chaos of Ignitus's absence—which I'm hoping is something you know about, and not another problem?" She waited only long enough for Tor to nod and mumble Brand's name. "Good. See how easy that was? Damn you mortals, for creatures with such short lives you sure do like to waste time with pleasantries."

Ash's mouth dropped open. "Well. All right."

Hydra whirled, banishing the courtiers. "The topics we're about to discuss aren't exactly common knowledge," she explained when they were gone. "Mustn't panic mortals when it can be avoided."

"With all due respect," Taro said from behind Ash, "the mortals are *already* panicked in the rest of the world."

Hydra ignored her and swept her gaze over their group. "The Mother Goddess is back. She's taken over Deimos, and soon enough Kula, you say? If Ignitus is dead."

Ash tried to object, to tell her that they had sent Brand to ready Kula's defenses to stop that very thing, but Hydra talked as quickly as water tumbling over a cliff.

"And I think it's a safe assumption that Aera and Biotus are either tied up in her plot, or soon to fall themselves? They always were predictable. Glory! Bloodshed! Riches! *Boring.* Now, what is your plan to defeat Anathrasa?"

Madoc pulled back his shoulders. "I'm her son. Soul Divine. I've been training to steal the rest of her anathreia. I—" He swallowed. How badly Ash wanted to take his hand again. "I tried to last night.

I think I injured her—or something happened, at least. We were hoping—"

Hydra frowned. "Why would you try to attack Anathrasa?"

Madoc's mouth dropped open. "To take her anathreia. To defeat her?" It came out as a question.

Hydra looked from Madoc to Ash and back again. "You have anathreia the same way all my Water Divine children have hydreia. They can control water, but their control of it poses no threat to *me*. Even in Anathrasa's weakened state, you could never actually kill her. You, born of her, will always be inferior to her as far as energeia goes. You can manipulate souls, which puts your power *slightly*"—she paused for emphasis—"above those of the six gods. But you are not equal to Anathrasa's power." Hydra pointed at Ash. "She is."

Painful silence gripped the throne room.

Ash's eyes peeled wide. She couldn't breathe. Couldn't blink. "I'm sorry," she managed, her throat dry, "what did you say?"

Hydra squinted at Ash, then at each confused, gawking mortal face in turn. "Wait an ice-cold minute." She smiled. *Chuckled.* "You mean to tell me you don't realize what she—Ash, is it?—what she is? You didn't do this to her *on purpose*?"

"Do *what* to her?" Tor growled the question.

"Do you know the full story of how we brought down Anathrasa the first time?" Hydra arched one thin eyebrow.

Ash's heart was tight in her chest. "Ignitus told us about the gladiator that the six gods used to defeat Anathrasa." Her mouth was still bone-dry; it hurt to talk. "By transferring pieces of their energeias into her."

"The same way Madoc transferred my brothers' energeias into you," Hydra finished.

Ash felt the blood drain from her face. She'd suspected it on her own, but hearing a goddess confirm it nearly pushed her unconscious, black spots dancing across her vision.

"What?" Tor frowned. "No. No, that isn't what—"

But his voice trailed off. Ash could feel everyone around her putting together these same realizations, their silence shifting to stunned horror.

"Do you think Anathrasa knows?" Ash whispered. Her whole body was numb.

"Of course she knows," Hydra threw out. "Why do you think she had her ships flee? I'm terrifying, yes, but I wouldn't have put up much of a fight to save you if they'd kept attacking. Not my battle—well, it wasn't at the time. No, Anathrasa ran because Madoc here must have surprised her with that anathreia attack—maybe she underestimates him?—and then you, Ash, rattled her while she was unexpectedly weakened. But I doubt that will last for long."

"How?" Madoc gasped the question. "I didn't turn Ash into anything!"

"You're lucky you didn't kill her." Hydra leveled a stare at Madoc. "When my siblings and I united to stop Anathrasa, we went through forty-seven mortals before we figured out how they can tolerate god powers. The rest—" She made a choking noise, her tongue out, eyes bulging.

Horror pinned Ash in place. Ignitus hadn't told her they'd had to murder people to find one who could handle their powers. And it made the fact that Ash *hadn't* died the moment Madoc gave them to her that much heavier.

"How am I alive?" Ash managed.

"Because you died," Hydra said matter-of-factly, "but someone brought you back."

"I think I'd remember dying and being resurrected."

"When we did it the first time, we were able to resurrect the gladiator through her connection to energeia. Did Ignitus rip you back from death after an arena fight?"

Ash spun a look at Madoc, and she knew he was thinking the same thing.

Elias had pummeled her with geoeia on the arena sands in Crixion just after Cassia's death. Ash had refused to fight him, even as he strengthened his attack. But Madoc had saved her.

"You didn't die, though," Madoc said, his voice thin. "You weren't . . . I didn't . . ."

He faltered, and Ash choked. Neither of them really understood what he had done to save her.

Had Madoc really brought Ash back from death?

Hydra smiled. "And then, either after or before, your energeia was taken? Figuring out *that* part was a complete fluke—when we practiced it on our gladiator, her goddess brought her back to life through their connection to the same energeia. It was tricky and terrible and damn near killed them both—but when it worked, the gladiator had no energeia at all. Which actually made her the perfect vessel for pieces of *all* energeias."

Tor huffed—whether in disbelief or fear, Ash couldn't tell. "You're saying that being brought back from death and drained of energeia is all it takes for a mortal body to hold a god's power?"

Hydra nodded, her hair flipping around her cheeks. "Yes. It blurs the lines between gods and mortals. Ash should be dead, but she's alive; she was made for energeia, but it was taken—you are exactly what we need to kill Anathrasa. Which I should be thanking *you* for, for not making me scramble to find some other way to avoid her war. In only a month! We'll need pieces of all the energeias. But for now, you're willing to fight her?"

Ash started. Was Hydra asking her? Could she actually say no?

She wouldn't, though.

She saw the future spiral out from this moment, one where she would need to embody not just fire and earth, but also water, plants, air, and animals. A future where she would become Soul Divine. Not like Madoc, who could control anathreia but couldn't hold other divinities in himself. No—Ash would have pieces of the six gods' energeias, Soul Divine like Anathrasa herself.

She would become the Mother Goddess to defeat the Mother Goddess.

"Yes," Ash heard herself say. It burst out of her from somewhere dark and wounded.

Yes, she wanted that. To know that she was more powerful than this cast-off Mother Goddess. Ash had seen what Anathrasa was capable of firsthand—she had watched her drain the geoeia out of Cassia's body in Petros's villa. She had sucked the energeia out of gladiators tithed to her by Geoxus. She had taken Ash's own igneia with a flick of her hand.

Ash wanted to watch Anathrasa cower and die for all the suffering she had inflicted. She wanted to know that Kula would be safe. Tor, Taro, Spark, everyone she loved—*safe*.

And Madoc wouldn't be the one to stand before his mother and deal the fatal blow.

"Yes," Ash said again.

Hydra faced Ash completely, her eyes piercing into the depths of Ash's soul. "Good. Then I want to try something. This might hurt."

She shoved her palm flat against Ash's chest.

A bolt of ice shot into Ash's body, freezing her inside out. She gave a startled gasp as the whole world crystallized into ice.

"What are you doing to her?" Madoc shouted. Distantly, Ash was aware of his hand on her arm, and him jerking back with a sharp yelp of pain.

All she could see was Hydra's face, blurring into a circle of color as her vision narrowed, a window clouding over with crawling tendrils of frost.

Hydra pulled back, her grin not dimming, even as Tor stood by with flames in his hands and Taro had a knife drawn. Tor must have pulled igneia from one of the fires they'd passed on the islands, arming himself. As if he could fight a goddess.

Ash's attention dropped to Hydra's hand. Age spots speckled her skin, and as Ash watched, more climbed her wrist, maturing her otherwise immortal flesh.

The same way Ignitus had had gray hair, and Geoxus had had wrinkles around his eyes.

Each time they gave pieces of their energeia, it drew the gods a little closer to mortality. And Hydra had freely given some of hers to Ash.

It instantly softened what remaining distrust Ash had toward her.

"You gave me hydreia?" Ash whispered.

"Ash, look at me." Madoc grabbed her arm. His other hand was at his side, clenching and unclenching against the fur lining of his tunic. The tips of his fingers were white with frost.

"What happened?" she managed.

Madoc shook his head. The frost was already dripping off his fingers.

He might have said something else, but Ash looked down at her own hands.

Water.

She splayed her fingers, and liquid spurted into the air before splashing against the icy floor.

No one responded. Madoc didn't let her go, and she felt his muscles tense, shocked fear radiating out of him.

"Three down," Hydra declared. "Three to go."

Impossibly, Ash felt her lips lift in a grin that matched Hydra's.

She had hydreia. She had never, in her wildest dreams, thought of controlling water.

In one hand, she pulled the heat from her chest and palmed a small blue flame. In the other, she focused on the chill in the air, on the ice beneath her feet, and an orb of water formed.

Oh, this would be *fun.*

Tor, fire still raging up his arms, stomped toward Hydra. "You have no right to put this on her. What will happen to Ash once she's as powerful as Anathrasa *and* has drained Anathrasa of her powers? Can a mortal—even one who can hold a god's power—endure all that anathreia? This could kill her. Or worse."

With a snap, Ash got rid of both the fire and water. "Whatever this might do to me, it's a risk we have to take. What's the alternative? Our plan to have Madoc face her wouldn't have worked."

Tor whirled on her. But after a moment of silence, he closed his mouth, resignation on his face as he put out the flames on his arms.

He shook his head, and Ash could see the strain on his face. "Florus may help us," Tor said softly, "but Aera and Biotus will side with Anathrasa if they haven't already. They won't willingly give Ash pieces of their energeias. What you did to her was unnecessarily—"

"I can get them."

Ash's heart jolted as Madoc stepped forward.

"I can get aereia and bioseia the same way I took Ignitus's and Geoxus's powers," he continued, confidence strengthening his voice. "If Anathrasa wants the energeia from all the gods, she'll probably be trying to get Aera and Biotus to Crixion too. Odds are good they'll both be there, so I can go back to Deimos and get aereia and bioseia"—he interlocked his fingers with Ash's—"and bring it to you, and you can . . . you can face Anathrasa."

"Smart," Hydra agreed. "That might work."

"No!" Ash shouted. She lowered her voice. "No—Madoc, you aren't going back to Crixion. Anathrasa has to know by now that you gave me igneia and geoeia. She saw me fight on the ship. It isn't safe for you to go to her—she'll kill you for betraying her."

Madoc licked his lips. "What if I'm the one who was betrayed? I'll tell her you tricked me into giving you Ignitus's and Geoxus's powers. I'll tell her that you and Hydra came up with this plan to defeat her, and once I heard it, I realized my error and ran back to her."

Ash blanched. "Madoc—"

"No, listen." He pushed closer to her, lightness in his lifted eyebrows, his half smile. "If I surrender to her and tell her I've rethought betraying her, I'll be at the center of her plans. I can get information, and I'll know exactly where Aera and Biotus are. Better than sneaking around Deimos—if I get caught doing that, there's no lie that will save me."

Ash *hated* this. She hated all of this.

"We'll get you on the first ship to Crixion," Hydra announced. "I'll have some of my Water Divine give you fast sailing waters. We can get you there in a few days."

"Wonderful," Madoc said, his teeth clenched, likely at the thought of being on a ship again.

"Won't Anathrasa be suspicious of how he got back so fast?" Ash tried.

"Tell Anathrasa you escaped when I sided with the Kulans," Hydra said. "Tell her you manipulated the anathreia in my Apuitians to get them to help you travel faster. Gods can't sense their people when they're being controlled by anathreia."

She spoke from experience, no doubt when Anathrasa had first tried to destroy the world.

"She'll still come for us in a month," Tor added. "We need to set up a meeting with Florus to get him on our side—how quickly can we get to Itza, or get Florus to come here?"

"Better that we go to him," Hydra said. "I'll tell him everything that's happened, but he'll want to stay in Itza and get his people ready. Not that I'm in any hurry to leave my *own* people, but I'll escort you to Itza, then pop back here as I need."

Tor looked doubtful, but he nodded. "We'll get Florus to add his floreia to our cause. Gather our armies and confront Anathrasa—all within her timeline of a month."

His eyes went to Ash. She noted how he'd said *get Florus to add his floreia to our cause* and not *get Florus to give his floreia to Ash.*

This scared him. It scared her, too.

Madoc nodded. "And I'll get aereia and bioseia in that time, too."

"We can aim to meet you in Crixion," Tor continued, his warrior side taking over. "You can—transfer over the energeias. Then Ash can—" He swallowed, his jaw tensing. "We can defeat Anathrasa."

Ash's lungs clenched tighter, tighter, driven by Tor's unease, by Madoc's odd confidence. She had never heard him sound so sure of himself, and it was about stealing energeias from gods *for her.*

"But—how will we know you're all right?" she asked Madoc, her voice small in her own ears. "When you're in Crixion, how will we know if something happens?"

Hydra waggled her fingers. Standing before them, her body changed from her solid human form into a translucent, rippling sculpture of water. "Goddess, remember?" A blink, and she was herself again. "I can pop in on him from time to time. And you have Ignitus's and Geoxus's powers too, so it's likely you can do the same—communicate and travel through fire and stone. I'll teach you. Are we decided, then? Good. I'll get a ship ready."

She spun away. Tor chased after her, arguing some other point Ash couldn't make herself care about. Taro and Spark, still lingering, were smart enough to give Ash and Madoc space.

They had barely had any time together. Running for their lives in Crixion, two weeks on a crowded ship, one stolen night in a storage tent. It wasn't enough, and as Ash turned into Madoc's arms, she felt a familiar sensation wriggle up her chest and heat her body with shame: loneliness.

She didn't want Madoc to go. She had Tor, Taro, and Spark, but none of them was the person she wanted to hold her when she was afraid or the one she trusted to always take her side. She had spent so much of her life secluded from other people out of fear of them discovering her disloyalty to Ignitus that she wasn't ready to let go of this. To let go of Madoc.

Ash shoved herself up onto her toes, locking her lips with his. She needed to feel his mouth on hers, his hands on the small of her back, arching her against his chest. She needed to remember this sensation in the coming days when war loomed and fear crept in and she woke up without him.

Because of course she would let him go. That was what this war demanded of her, and she would always do what was right, even if it killed her.

Freeing Kula had cost Ash her mother. It had cost Ash her god. It had chased her from her home and made her a target, and now it asked her to let go of Madoc, too.

A selfish burn singed her gut. How much else would this war take from her?

When would she get to start taking things back?

Ash pressed her forehead to Madoc's, their breaths mingling.

"You know Anathrasa won't hurt me," he said, "not if she thinks there's any hope that I'll get the gods' powers and give them to her."

"Like you're doing for me." Ash laughed brittlely. "Is this any better than her plan?"

"Yes." Madoc's response was instant and firm. "Let me do this. When I come back, we can be together. We—" He stopped, swallowed hard. "We won't have to worry anymore."

Ash's fingers curled into the short hairs at the back of his neck and she planted her other hand on his chest, over his heart, savoring the feel of it thudding against her palm.

They would both be fine. Anathrasa wouldn't hurt Madoc.

Because if she did, she would have to contend with the wrath of a goddess.

FIVE

MADOC

WITH ASH'S KISS seared into his memory and the freedom of the world on his shoulders, Madoc sailed home to Deimos to face his mother.

Propelled by a strong current created by a small crew of Water Divine sailors, the ship cut through the waves as it raced through the nights, pressing on too quickly for Madoc to succumb to his previous seasickness. Where the trip to the Apuit Islands had taken two weeks, the return voyage took only three days. Soon he found himself facing a fleet of Deiman ships bearing black sails, a hailstorm of gravel suspended over the hull of his boat, ready to sink him into the sea.

Furiously, he waved a white flag over the side of the deck, his eyes bouncing from the sky peppered with stones to the fleet five hundred paces away. As many times as he'd practiced this in his mind, nothing could prepare him for the horrific awe of this moment, and the gripping fear of what might happen if he never made it to land.

Barely two weeks ago, he had fled Crixion, half conscious, terrified for his family and with no idea of the effect Anathrasa's war had
on the world.

Now he was returning in much the same way.

"Come on," he muttered, sweat streaking down his face, burning
the sea salt on his chapped lips. The heat had increased dramatically
from the islands, and his tunic—the one shredded on the side from
Tor's training—clung to his chest. Hydra's people had offered him
new clothes, but he couldn't risk appearing on friendly terms with the
water goddess. It was better if he showed up in his Deiman clothes,
weathered as they were.

"It's not going to work," he heard a sailor whisper. They'd left
Hydra's lands with only three Water Divine sailors and a first mate to
captain the vessel. If they were going to make it look as though he'd
used anathreia to sway Hydra's people to sail him home, they couldn't
afford to have a fully crewed ship. Now they'd been waiting at the edge
of Deiman waters for over an hour.

Panic pressed against the edges of his control. Ash was counting
on him. He could not fail.

"They haven't attacked us yet," Madoc growled, waving the flag
harder. "They're stalling until Anathrasa gives her orders."

We surrender.

He focused on the words, willing them to stretch across the waves.
Willing his anathreia to save their necks.

Mother, I'm here.

A cool breeze lifted the hairs on his arms, climbing up his chest
to his throat.

Not a breeze—this came from inside him. A healing, the broken parts of his energeia fusing together in pulsing relief.

But there was something different about it. It was like spun sugar that was too sweet—good, but not quite right.

It felt like it had when he'd tried to take Anathrasa's energeia.

He didn't have time to wonder about it. He ignored it and concentrated on the nearest ship. With a focused breath, he reached across the waves, invisible strands of energeia seeking purchase on the souls, pulsing like lantern light on the crowded deck.

We surrender. Tell my mother I've come home.

"Look!" called one of the sailors at the helm. "They're pulling back!"

Madoc glanced up, huffing a sigh as the rocks overhead crumbled in midair, raining a harmless dust that stuck to his damp skin.

Madoc lowered the flag, keeping it hanging in sight over the side of the deck.

"Approach slowly," he called to his crew.

The Water Divine warriors lowered the sails, and as they carved a line through the waves toward the fleet, Madoc's pulse pounded in his ears.

The closer they got to the other ships, the more alive his anathreia became. It buzzed through him with no regard to his tense muscles or his wary thoughts. Despite their progress, a frown pulled at his lips. Even when he couldn't control it, his energeia had always been in sync with the rest of his body. But now it felt strange inside him, as if it wasn't entirely his own.

Like when he'd taken Petros's geoeia and felt it slipping through his veins.

He hadn't tithed on anyone. He hadn't even used his anathreia since four nights ago, when they'd been attacked at the barrier outside the Apuit Islands. He'd been trying to conserve his energy, rebuild his strength, so that when he faced Anathrasa he'd be ready. But something still felt wrong.

Dread mingled with his power as he considered whether this might have something to do with his proximity to the Mother Goddess. When they'd clashed on the water, something had happened. He'd felt gutted, broken—it wasn't the rush he'd experienced every other time he'd used anathreia, but rather the opposite effect. And now he was in Deimos, facing a fleet of her soldiers, and his anathreia was acting up again.

He shook his head. He didn't have time to worry about the unruliness of his energeia now. He had a surrender to fake, and two more gods to somehow siphon enough power from to turn Ash into a gladiator strong enough to defeat Anathrasa.

He felt a lot like the boy who'd stood in those fighting rings in South Gate—a fraud, boasting a power he didn't have. A kid with quick fists who could put on a decent show.

And just like he had then, he would let the crowd believe what they wanted, until he'd taken everything he'd come for.

The Deiman ships cleared a path for their boat, and as they steered toward the Port of Iov, Madoc lifted his chin to the sun, and to the lighthouse he thought he'd never see again.

His heart gave a hard lurch. *Home.*

Was Ilena safe? Had she found Elias? What about Danon and Ava? Without thinking, his gaze turned west, to the fields outside the city where the dead were buried to reunite their geoeia with the earth.

Pain rippled through his chest. Had they laid Cassia to rest in his absence?

The sailors remained silent, their wary gazes bouncing between him and the approaching shoreline, where a legion of soldiers were gathering. So many Deimans, already loyal to his mother. Their silver armor glinted in the sun, and Madoc didn't need to see them up close to know that stones and weapons were ready in each of their hands.

"You have no memory of what's happened since we left the islands," he called to the sailors as they slowed their approach. "If you're questioned, the last thing you remember was me telling you to board this boat."

He'd tried to use soul energeia to muddle their memories about their departure from the Apuit Islands—a precaution in case Anath- rasa captured and questioned them. But the closer they'd come to Crixion, the more unruly his power felt, as if it had been damaged in the attack on Anathrasa. He didn't want to risk hurting the sailors by losing control—he'd seen what had happened to Jann in the arena when he'd tried before. He hoped that they could act well enough to deter suspicion.

The sailors nodded in wary acceptance, but he could hear the water churning against the hull beneath them and knew that if it came to a fight, their instincts would steer them toward self-preservation.

He could not let it come to that.

As they passed the narrow peninsula hosting the lighthouse, his anathreia staggered his breath, pushing him onto the balls of his feet, and when he glanced down his hands were spread, as if prepared for attack.

The move had been unconscious, and he fisted his hands at his sides.

Be calm, he told himself. But the power in him said, *be ready*.

When the ship docked, they were boarded by two dozen centurions in full armor, ready with stones spinning above their hands. It felt like a lifetime ago that he'd fought the centurions off in the palace, and any confidence he'd had that he could turn their thoughts if needed evaporated into the dry air.

He pulled Ash into his mind and planted his feet.

"We surrender!" he shouted as they surrounded him and shoved him to his knees. "Please. Take me to Anathrasa. I don't intend any harm!"

He was dragged down the loading plank to the stone dock where the centurions waited in lines, staring at him uncertainly. Word must have spread about his part in Geoxus's defeat. He took some comfort in their fear, hoping it meant they would not be quick to attack.

Silently, the crowd parted, and his mother approached, her clean white gown fluttering in the breeze.

His stomach pitted.

"Madoc," she said, eyes narrowed. "I don't suppose you're here for the festivities."

He didn't know what she meant. His blunt nails dug into the callused heels of his hands. "I come to beg for sanctuary, and your forgiveness."

As she lifted her chin, his anathreia prickled inside him, feeding an anger that caught him by surprise. She stepped closer, and he saw, with some discomfort, that his onetime neighbor—an old woman they'd called Seneca—moved with more ease than he'd ever seen. Her back was straighter. Her skin, tighter, and flushed with a healthy glow. Even her white hair looked golden.

Instead of a woman nearing a century, she looked scarcely older than Ilena.

Tithes. That was the only answer. Anathrasa was feeding on innocent Deimans. Draining the energeia from their bodies, and leaving them as shells, like she had with Cassia and Ash.

He wiped any trace of revulsion from his face. She would not know his heart.

"Forgiveness," she said, even her voice clearer than he'd known when they were neighbors. "Sanctuary? These are powerful words, my son."

His stomach twisted. She may have been his mother by birth, but she had no right to call him *son*.

"The Kulan gladiators are beyond reason," he said as the Water Divine sailors disembarked in shackles. They blinked in confusion, seeming surprised that they'd come to Deimos—part of the plan that Madoc had devised. "I was wrong to trust them. I tried to convince them to turn back after that night at the blockade, but they wouldn't listen. They'll stop at nothing to avenge their god."

Anathrasa paused before him, close enough that he could reach out and wring her slender neck.

"And what of Hydra? What does the goddess of water say about this?"

Madoc shook his head, looking tired, torn. "She sided with them."

"Pity," Anathrasa said, as if she'd expected this. Her lips curled into a patronizing smile. She may have looked younger, but there were still shadows under her eyes and creases around her mouth. "How did you manage to get away?"

Madoc pictured Ash. Remembered the steadiness in her gaze when he'd left on this mission.

"I snuck out while they were summoning Florus. Convinced a few sailors to bring me back. My hold on the sailors' minds prevented Hydra from tracking them across the water."

A glimmer of interest arched Anathrasa's brows, but it was stifled by a hard glare.

"Or she chose not to follow you so you could spy for her." Fear chilled Madoc's blood as she stepped closer. "For all I know, she sent you to turn this legion against me and use the anathreia I gave you to make them do your bidding." She leaned closer, dropping her voice to a whisper. "We both know you'd like that."

He would. And he could do it. Tell the soldiers behind her to grab her arms. Those beside him to ram their spears through her heart.

"It would only delay the inevitable," he said, and it was true. "I want no part of Hydra's pact with the Kulans. Fighting you will just lead to more bloodshed. I've seen enough war."

"Oh, my dear," she clucked. "What you've seen could fill the palm of my hand."

Again, his anathreia pulsed with a strange, sticky-sweet urgency. *Fight*, it whispered. *Feed.*

Feed.

The hunger was returning, with teeth like knives. It rose in him like a wave, forcing his breath out in a huff.

He wanted to end this now.

He wanted to destroy her, so Ash would never have to fight again.

He shook his head, sweat burning his eyes. *No.* Hydra had told him he couldn't use his anathreia against the Mother Goddess, just as her Water Divine couldn't use hydreia against Hydra. That was why attacking Anathrasa on the ship had nearly broken him.

He had to stick to his plan. Join Anathrasa. Find Biotus and Aera. Give their energeias to Ash so that she could harness the power of the six gods and destroy the Mother Goddess.

"Even so," he said. "I pledge myself to you."

Her eyes narrowed. "You've pledged yourself to another, Madoc. A girl your fingers long to touch, even now."

Madoc's jaw clenched. He would not let her get to Ash—not until Ash was ready to kill her.

"She's made her choice," Madoc said, tension lacing between them, thin and brittle as ice.

Anathrasa cackled.

He willed the roar of his blood to settle. He could still make this work. He had sold hundreds of people on his performance as an Earth Divine fighter in the rings of Crixion. He could convince his mother he was on her side.

He dropped his chin. "She doesn't want me. Her only love is Kula. Is . . . *was* . . . Ignitus. I tried to get her to come, but . . ." He shook his head, looking crestfallen. "She would see the world burn, and dance on the embers."

Anathrasa assessed him long enough that he began to fidget.

"Then why didn't you change her mind?" she asked.

The thought of forcing Ash to do anything made him ill.

"Were you not strong enough?" Anathrasa pressed. "Did you not take Ignitus's fire? Geoxus's ability to manipulate the very earth we stand on?"

He could hear the test in her tone. She must have suspected he'd given those powers to Ash and was waiting to catch him in a lie.

If he didn't play this carefully, he'd lose his only shot at getting close to Anathrasa, and to Aera and Biotus. He wouldn't be able to give Ash the power she needed to defeat the Mother Goddess.

His head hung forward. "The gods' energeias were killing me. I couldn't hold them."

"And *Ash* could?" Her teeth pressed together over the name, like she'd bitten into bitter fruit. "How interesting."

Madoc reminded himself that Ash had Hydra and the Water Divine. She had Tor. And Taro and Spark and a crew of Kulan sailors that would rise to her defense if needed—but he still felt sick about siphoning this attention her way.

"She tricked me into giving them to her. I was weak." He swallowed, a blush rising in his cheeks. "She was . . . convincing."

"You expect me to believe your surrender is the result of a broken heart?" Anathrasa shook her head. "You take me for a pitying fool, Madoc."

Madoc went still. Anathrasa wasn't buying his story. With a wave of her hand, she spoke quietly to one of her guards, then turned to go.

He'd faced this moment a dozen times in street fights—the

moment when the act either became real, and his fate relied on his own fists, or the truth came out and everyone saw him for what he was. A liar.

He lifted his chin, clenched his fists, and fought.

"Wait!" he shouted as the guard drew his sword. "It's Hydra. She didn't trust me. She wanted me dead. If Ash hadn't helped me sneak out, I wouldn't be here now."

Anathrasa paused. Turned.

"Why would she want you dead?"

"She knows I am your son," Madoc said in a rush. "She thinks I'm loyal to you."

"And are you?" The sparkle in Anathrasa's eyes drove a stake of fear through him.

If he lied now, he was sure she would see it. But if he didn't, she might kill him before he had the chance to accomplish what he'd come to do.

"Does it matter?" He added a strain to his voice, a hunch to his shoulders. "I have nowhere else to go that she won't find me."

Anathrasa considered this for a long moment. "Now that their god has been brutally murdered, these soldiers belong to Geoxus's creator—me. I could have them cut you to pieces if you're lying."

"It is no lie."

She stepped closer, lifting her hand. Her fingers trailed down his cheek. Show or not, he fought the urge to jerk back; her touch revolted him.

"You should have considered that you might need me before you attacked me on that ship four days ago."

She wheeled back, faster than Madoc expected, and struck him hard across the jaw.

The slap stung his skin, radiating through his teeth and sending white sparks across his vision. His breath ripped through his dry throat.

But it was his mother who cried out.

Before him, Anathrasa's cheek stained pink, a perfect handprint appearing on her tan skin. She gasped in surprise, the sound that came from her lips a mixture of shock and pain. Stumbling back, she bumped into one of her guards, who caught her around the elbow. She shook him off, covering the mark on her face with her hands.

Had her power backfired? How had she injured them both by striking him?

Excitement doused his confusion, overriding his own physical pain. Up until this moment, they hadn't been sure they could hurt her without him draining what remained of her power, but now the proof was before him. Anathrasa could feel pain.

But could she die?

Around him, the other centurions erupted in confused shouts. Those nearest Madoc threw him to the dock. He blinked up at the sky, blinded by the pale circle of the sun for a moment, before a swift kick caught his gut. The wind fled from his lungs. He curled into a ball, but his back was exposed to the whipping spear shafts that rained down.

"Stop!" Anathrasa screamed. Fury and desperation crackled through the air like lightning.

The beating ceased immediately, and when the crowd cleared, Madoc found his mother on her hands and knees before him. Three soldiers tried to pull her up to safety, but she shoved them back. Her breath came out in a wheeze, and one hand was wrapped over her stomach, right where he'd been kicked.

Their gazes met, and a new wave of horror shook him as his stare moved to her still-red cheek.

She could sense his pain, and his own anathreia recoiled in empathy, an echo of the night at the blockade, when his soul had felt like it shattered.

It took another breath to realize there was no separation between her pain and his. They were one and the same—every welt, every gathering bruise.

Somehow, she'd hurt herself by hurting him. He didn't know what that meant, or how it was possible, only that this connection between them was very, very bad.

Ash was coming to kill the Mother Goddess. Would doing so kill him too?

Anathrasa grabbed a centurion's leg, pulling herself up only to lean against his side.

"Bring him to the palace," she snapped, her lips drawn back over her teeth. As he was dragged to his feet, her blue eyes seared with fury. "It appears he'll get a second chance to prove his worth to me after all."

She turned, with some effort, and was assisted off the dock, back toward land and the carriages that awaited.

In two weeks and four days, Madoc's home city had changed completely.

Through the carriage windows, he followed the routes he'd

walked all his life—streets that led to alleys that gave way to Market Square, where the great arena towered over the Temple of Geoxus.

Now the temple was in ruins, demolished in the violence that had ensued after Geoxus's death while Madoc was fleeing the city with Ash and Tor. The golden statue that had once stood three stories high had been knocked on its side and pounded by boulders of all sizes. The walls of the sanctuary were painted with goat's blood—signs saying *the gods are dead*, and *goddess pigstock*. Crude paintings of Geoxus crushed by a boulder, and Ignitus being defiled by a horse.

The market had once been filled with vendors and savory foods but now was empty except for a gathering of people all in white with chalk smeared across their mouths, chanting words Madoc couldn't make out. The carriage had to carve a path around boulders and rocks that had been pulled from the surrounding shops and apartments, half of which were blackened by fire.

I don't suppose you're here for the festivities. Had that been a joke? There were no celebrations here. Riots had destroyed the city.

Madoc moved to the edge of his seat, his heels drumming against the wooden floor. He pressed his palm against his jaw, feeling the edges of a bruise, and forced himself to think of this strange tie to Anathrasa, and not what had become of Ilena, Elias, Danon, and Ava in these harsh streets.

It seemed impossible, but Anathrasa's wounds had mirrored Madoc's, and his pain and hers had braided together into a single cord. He hadn't done this, at least not deliberately. But his anathreia had been acting strangely since returning to Deimos, or maybe since coming closer to her. For all he knew, he'd caused the mark on her face unconsciously.

She definitely hadn't done it to herself.

His mind kept returning to that night on the ocean outside the blockade—the connection he'd felt to her just moments before his world erupted. Had something happened between them then? Whatever tied them didn't seem to take effect until he'd come back to Deimos—until he'd tried to use anathreia again.

He wished he could talk to Ash about it.

But if he did, and Hydra found out, would they pull him out of Crixion? Think him a liability, too close to Anathrasa to do what he'd come to do?

His hands clasped together. Would he still be able to steal Aera's and Biotus's energeias now that he appeared to be linked to Anathrasa?

He'd have to find a way—he hadn't come here to fail. It wasn't just Ash depending on him, it was the entire world. If he didn't get the other energeias to Ash, she could never stop Anathrasa from overtaking the world.

The carriage slowed, tearing him from his thoughts. He looked out through the window again and sucked in a tight breath at the sight of the palace before him. The towers that had reached into the sky had fallen now, but here, at least, the structure had been rebuilt. The rubble in the gardens had been cleared away. The high walls had been widened into graceful, sloping balconies of white marble. No longer did murals of Geoxus tower beside the entrance. Now there were twin likenesses of Anathrasa—an even younger version than he'd seen at the docks—naked, holding her hands in a circle over her head.

He thought of the people in the market with the chalk on their mouths, and of the legion of soldiers that had accompanied her to the docks, and got a very bad feeling.

Madoc had assumed he'd be taken to the jail, a festering block of wooden cells, impenetrable by the many Earth-divine prisoners, on the south side of Crixion. He didn't know what she had in store for him here, and the uncertainty had his knuckles rapping against his thighs.

But when they reached the palace, he wasn't brought to Anathrasa, or to any holding cell. Surrounded by guards, he was led to a wide, new stairway and brought to the eastern wing of the palace—a private courtyard, surrounded by lounging chairs and tables already topped with decadent food. The circular balcony above led to open rooms, and through the doorways, past the fine furniture and art, Madoc could see the hazy skyline of the city.

His stomach growled as he registered the scent of honey bread. For the last three days, he'd eaten little other than salted fish, dried kelp, and seal meat.

"Madoc? Madoc!"

For the second time that day, Madoc felt the wind knocked out of him.

"Ava?"

The five-year-old girl came charging through the courtyard, her dark hair and blue ankle-length gown rippling behind her. Her arms lifted a moment before Madoc fell to his knees, and when she collided into him, he breathed in the scent of lavender water, and dust, and home.

He swallowed the emotion gripping his throat. Four guards still stood around him, though they made no move to stop his younger sister.

"Are you all right?" he asked urgently, suddenly fearing that she'd been brought here against her will, or worse, because Ilena was dead.

"Of course I'm all right," she said. "We've been waiting for you!"

"You've been . . ." He rose to his feet as a woman came running toward him, her black hair tied in a red wrap, her gown fine and expensive. Behind her was a younger boy of twelve, all limbs and awkward smiles.

"Ilena?" He couldn't believe his eyes. "Danon?"

"I told you," his adopted mother said, eyes glistening. "I told you we would meet again." She pulled him into a hug that crushed his shoulder and likely cracked a few ribs, but he didn't care. Tears streaked down his face. His heart felt too big for his chest.

"You did," he managed. Questions began catching up with him— how they'd come here, and why they'd been given such nice things. Ava had said she'd been waiting for him, but Anathrasa hadn't known he'd be coming.

Had she?

"I don't understand," he said. "How did you get . . . Why are you . . . here?"

"We're guests of the Mother Goddess," Ilena told him, and he didn't miss the tick of a small muscle in her neck as she said the words.

"Seneca—I mean, Anathrasa, of course—she wanted to thank us for caring for you all those years."

"I certainly emptied my fair share of her chamber pots," Danon added, earning a slap on the arm from his mother.

"She's letting us stay as long as we like," Ilena said. "Isn't that wonderful?"

It was wonderful that his family was alive and safe, at least for now. But Madoc knew Anathrasa, and she wasn't grateful for anyone or anything. The only reason his family had been brought here was because she had some hidden purpose for them, and based on their lack of surprise at his arrival, they had surmised the same. Whatever his birth mother wanted would come at a heavy cost.

His elation was sinking like a stone when the guards stepped back and retreated, and a steady clap of footsteps stopped behind him.

"It's about time you showed up."

Madoc turned and came face-to-face with his brother.

"Elias." The word was barely a breath, sanded down by fear and distance, and an anger he'd forced himself to swallow. The last time he'd seen his brother had been when Elias attacked Ash in the grand arena during the final fight of the war with Kula. He'd been unhinged, a tornado of grief and geoeia, ready to avenge their sister even if it meant losing his own life.

But those memories were overshadowed by others. The night they'd run from the centurions after cheating in a fight against Fentus in South Gate. Early mornings walking to work at the quarry. Late nights in their bunks in the quarter, laughing about something stupid that Danon had said.

The night they'd carried Cassia home from Petros's villa.

Elias stood before him now, older looking, as if years had passed instead of weeks. He was thinner than before, and his dark hair was trimmed like a man's instead of a boy's. The tunic he wore was tied with a belt instead of a spare piece of rope, and there wasn't a streak of mortar anywhere on it. Even his sandals were new, with silver circle buckles across the front of his shins.

He waited for Madoc to do more, looking uncertain, and that was all the apology Madoc needed.

He embraced Elias as he should have the night Cassia died. Maybe if he had, Elias would have known he wasn't alone in his guilt, and things would have been different. They stood there for some time, chest to chest, arms locked around each other's shoulders, while Ilena wept tears of joy, and Danon swung Ava onto his back and galloped around them.

But before Madoc drew back, Elias hooked one hand around the back of his neck and whispered, "Watch yourself, brother. The Mother Goddess sees all."

SIX

ASH

ASH HAULED HERSELF onto the raft, coughing frigid water across the salt-beaten wood. On her hands and knees, she glared across to where Hydra lounged on a wave she had morphed into something like a chaise, her head propped on one hand, her other arm draped over her curved hip.

"You're still trying to use hydreia as you do igneia," Hydra chastised in a singsong voice that Ash was really starting to hate. "But it isn't igneia. It is, in fact, hydreia."

"That doesn't get any more helpful the more times you say it."

Hydra lifted the arm from her hip. A separate wave rose behind her, a rippling sheet of blue and translucent white with an angry foam cap at the head.

Ash flew to her feet, hands out, body racking with an involuntary shudder. "Wait! Wait."

What other way could she deflect the water? Last time Hydra had thrown a wave at her, Ash had tried to divert it with a sharp shove to the left, but the water had simply risen higher and barreled over her. For the sixth time that morning.

Ash shook out her hands by her sides, flicking water on her bare feet, and tried to think of some other hydreia deflection method. But *gods*, she was just tired of being thrown into the sea in the tight sealskin suit Hydra's servants had given her. The material stopped midthigh and at Ash's shoulders, hugging her body so closely that she felt half naked in the icy air.

Despite the cold, she wished she could see Madoc's reaction to her in this outfit. She wished she could sneak into his room again wearing this, and pull him out of a groggy sleep back into the storage hut—

Heat climbed from Ash's stomach, spreading out to each limb and warming her cheeks. She sighed involuntarily, just glad to feel warm for a change, and that warmth pulled up memories she relived more often than was healthy.

That night with Madoc had been tentative. Neither of them had truly known what they were doing—Ash only knew from her own fleeting, private moments where Madoc should touch her and what motions snatched the breath from her lungs; she had found some of his places too, mostly by accident.

Spark had warned it might hurt the first time. She, Char, and Taro had explained a great many things to Ash, but all of it had been to help her avoid getting pregnant so as not to give Ignitus another Nikau Fire Divine gladiator to use in his arenas.

They hadn't told her how *good* it could be. Touches and kisses that Ash lost herself in like a dance. She moved, and Madoc followed; she swayed, and he bowed.

A water whip flicked Ash's nose.

She shuddered and blinked at Hydra.

"You're distracted," Hydra said.

Ash scoffed. "What do I have to be distracted by? My looming fight with the Mother Goddess, the deterioration of the godless countries, our ships preparing to sail to Itza tomorrow, the fact that Madoc is alone in Crixion doing who knows what—"

"I checked on him two days ago! I saw him arrive in Crixion—Anathrasa didn't see me, Madoc didn't see me, he's safe, *everyone's safe*. He's even back with his family. What more do you want?"

"I want—" Ash's voice cut off sharply. *I want to know how I'm supposed to do any of this*, she wanted to say, but she bit her tongue hard, until calmer words formed. "You said I could use Ignitus's or Geoxus's powers to communicate and travel through their energeia like you do with hydreia—I want to learn that so I can communicate with Kula, and with Madoc, and even Tor, who is just on the other side of this island. Not *this*." She waved at the sea around them, the water dripping off her hair.

Since Madoc had left five days ago, this was all Hydra had done. While Tor prepared the Kulans and some of Hydra's people to travel to Itza tomorrow, Hydra would drag Ash out at dawn, get her set up on this raft, and pummel her with waves and water whips and ice shards, all while spouting truly unhelpful advice like *Cold water feels pointy while warm water feels smooth*.

Yes, Ash now could call water into her hands the same way she could call fire and stone. But she'd learned from the first day of Hydra's training that she couldn't *do* much with water once she summoned it.

Just like she couldn't do much with stones, either, but who on this earth could teach her how to be the god of geoeia? That was the only spurt of regret she'd ever felt about stabbing Geoxus—that her best chance of learning how to harness geoeia was dead.

Hydra talked in circles if she let her, never getting to the point, a whirlpool lazily spinning. Ash was cold and tired of trying to get slippery, uncooperative water to listen to her.

"Will I even need to control hydreia to defeat Anathrasa?" Ash pressed. She tried not to scream, but she wanted to—she wanted to *rage*. "Don't I just need to combine all the energeias into one? Does it truly matter whether I can *control* each and every one?"

"And if you have to fight your way to Anathrasa?" The wave behind Hydra edged taller. Ash fought to ignore it and the dread that welled in her stomach. "The plan is to face her in Crixion. What if she has the whole of the city set against you, and our armies are falling, and all you have to fight with is igneia and unpredictable spurts of other energeias? What good will you be then?"

Ash glowered. "Well, none of this training will matter if I don't obtain floreia too. Can't you talk to your brother again? Have him travel here on floreia and just give me a piece of it, then he can go back to preparing Itza for war."

Hydra flopped back into her water-chaise with a dramatic moan. The water enveloped her and she sank down, the wave splashing over her. The movement rocked Ash's raft, and she widened her stance for balance.

A flash of foam, and Hydra materialized on the raft in front of Ash. Her arms were folded, one eyebrow curved, her lips puckered.

"I believe in you," she said, "but that doesn't mean Florus has to. If he's going to give you a piece of his *soul*, the least you can do is travel to meet him on his own land to do it."

Ash closed her eyes. She was being childish, but part of her was nothing but nervous energy, frail and shaking. "I know." She whipped her eyes open. "But if you taught me how to travel through fire, you and I could go to Itza instantly."

She was still pushing the matter, and the look on Hydra's face was indignant.

"Mortals, always in such a rush." Hydra rolled her eyes. "You need to sail there because you'll want your people with you when you meet him. Never underestimate the importance of support. Besides, this delay isn't just for us—Florus is making the same preparations I am, getting armies ready, yes, but also hiding those who can't fight, rationing food, building defenses of Itzan cities. Try to understand, this is the first we've heard of Anathrasa being back—"

"No, it isn't." Ash frowned. An unexpected surge of defensiveness straightened her shoulders. "Ignitus told you that he suspected Anathrasa was back. You ignored him."

Hydra jerked away with an exasperated snort. "Do you have siblings, Ash?"

She knew Ash didn't. She'd already found out everything about their group.

Hydra faced the shore and the rear of her palace stretching up toward the cloudy gray sky. Off to the side, part of the harbor was in view; ships bobbed in it, people bustling around them and on the docks, readying to sail to Itza with the morning tide.

"Anathrasa created Geoxus first," Hydra said to the distance. "Then me. Then Biotus and Ignitus, then Florus, and finally Aera. The dynamic of that—damn, Geoxus loved to taunt us about being oldest and strongest, as if that somehow earned him our loyalty. Biotus doesn't have a single independent thought in his head, so he was always happy to trail where Geoxus led. Ignitus *tried*, I'll give him that. He tried to make his own way, but one whiff of challenge from Geoxus or Biotus, and Ignitus couldn't resist rising to it. Florus only half pays attention to anything going on, so he and I spent many decades watching those three raze each other's countries and hurt each other's mortals."

She looked back at Ash. "So you'll have to forgive me for not acting on Ignitus's plea that I step in, because—and this was his message—*Geoxus is planning something with our mother.* Geoxus was always poking at Ignitus because he knew he could rile him up. And Anathrasa?" She snorted. "It sounded like empty nonsense. We'd sacrificed too much for her not to be dead."

Ash swallowed, rocking with the gentle waves. She could see why Hydra had ignored her brother's cry for help. Ash hadn't taken Ignitus seriously until the end, either.

"What about Aera?" Ash asked. "You didn't say how the air goddess fits into everything."

Something dark passed over Hydra's face, a shadow drifting across the surface of a deep-blue pond. "She's a pest. A mosquito who flits around Geoxus, Biotus, and Ignitus, pitting them against each other, darting away if they swat at her. She's a nuisance, and I should have told Madoc not to just take a piece of her aereia, but to drain her completely."

The rage that had built in Hydra's voice sent Ash teetering back a step. More than that, the sea around them had started to churn as though the water itself were boiling.

Ash eyed it, then turned back to Hydra, who had closed her eyes and dragged in a few slow, deep breaths.

"You know what?" Hydra rubbed a hand over her face. "I think I've been employing the wrong training methods."

Ash had to stop herself from making a sarcastic quip.

Hydra gave her a cruel smile. "You want to learn how to travel through fire? You want to learn how to listen to Kula? Focus on fire. Stretch your mind. Meditate. The sun's going down—maybe the extra cold will motivate you to get off this raft."

With a jolt of panic Ash realized what Hydra meant to do.

"Wait—"

But Hydra vanished, a cascade of water and foam, leaving Ash stranded on the bobbing raft.

"Damn you," Ash grumbled.

Ash spent an hour sitting on the raft, employing Hydra's vague suggestions.

Stretch your mind. Meditate. Focus on fire.

Traveling through fire proved far too difficult—the setting sun and falling temperature had Ash's teeth clacking together, and it was all she could do to pull a flame into her hand to keep herself from turning into an ice cube. It was easier to focus on the palmful of fire she called—something small yet intense.

Maybe Tor was near a fire, and she could talk to him, ask him to get a boat and come save her. Only she didn't need saving—didn't *want* to be saved—but she closed her eyes and hunched over the flame in her hand, giving herself a moment just to breathe in the smoke.

The smoke smelled like Igna. How long had it been since she'd been home? What was happening there now—surely Brand had spread the word about Ignitus's death? Were people mourning or rejoicing? In the palace, was—

She saw fires. Candle flames and lanterns spotted across a city. No—she knew that city.

Igna.

Her body surged into each flame, rebounding from one into another. A candle on a table in a kitchen; a lantern on a street post; a fire in a stove; a torch burning in someone's hand.

Stunned to silence, Ash let the fires pull her, afraid if she reacted too much or not enough this connection would break.

She was in Igna . . . in a way, her eyes and ears now each flame, a soul untethered yet bound to this flickering, feasting burning.

A bonfire drew her most strongly. It burned in the center of the city, a raging spurt of flame controlled by a ring of Kulan Fire Divine. People crowded the area around the fire, some holding hands, others weeping softly.

At the edge of the fire, someone started playing a harp. Lutes followed, and then voices swept in, and Ash's heart kicked with recognition—this was the song of the Great Defeat, the song she had danced to on the sands of Igna's arena so many weeks ago.

It had been Ignitus's favorite song and dance.

This was a memorial for him.

The shock yanked Ash from the fire. Her soul slithered out of the candle flames and torches, gathering back on itself and flooding into her body, where it sat, shivering, on the raft in the middle of the sea.

Gasping, Ash hugged her arms to herself. The people of Igna were mourning their dead god. Their cruel, bloodthirsty god, who had put so many of them in arenas, who had whittled away Kula's resources to the point of starvation, who had gotten Char *killed*—

And who had been willing to try to fix things in Kula. Who had admitted he was wrong and wanted to try again.

Tears fell. They instantly dried on Ash's cheeks and she scrubbed them away.

She wasn't crying for the loss of Ignitus, she told herself. She was crying for the loss of potential, for the memorial that should have been for her mother. For the wrongness of so much about their world's current situation and how she was supposed to fix it even though she couldn't get off this stupid *raft*.

The sun set fully, throwing Ash into darkness, and she wept into her empty palms, embracing the cold.

By the time Ash got back to the island, she was nearly frozen. As she finally collapsed on the frigid, rock-strewn shore, her muscles wailed in relief. She'd given up traveling through igneia and opted to move her raft using hydreia—which hadn't been any easier. But she'd caught an errant current for the last bit of the trip, otherwise she'd still be drifting aimlessly in the bay—she suspected Hydra had gotten tired of watching her painfully slow progress.

But even so, Ash *had* made progress. She'd gotten in a few solid, swift pushes with hydreia once she'd forced herself to sit and analyze why the water wasn't listening to her. Something Hydra had said kept coming back to her—*It isn't igneia. It's hydreia.*

Hydra never moved as Ash did, or as Ignitus had, all harsh jabs and forceful punches. Hydra's moves were subtle—flicks of her wrists, twitches of her fingers.

So Ash had done that. Embraced subtlety and softness. And she had *moved the water.*

She chuckled to herself on the rocky shore, utterly spent. Water and sweat mingled, trickling down her face, wetting the sand in the moon- and starlit darkness.

She needed to find Tor. She needed to tell him she'd been able to see Igna, that they were safe—for now—and she might be able to communicate with Brand and the other leaders there—

She felt a presence beyond her closed eyelids. Hydra.

"If you've come to gloat about how your methods worked," Ash started, smirking, "don't think I'll ever admit that you're the reason I finally got hydreia to listen to me. I don't—"

"I do not gloat."

Ash's eyes flew open and in an instant she was on her feet, the tide lapping at her bare ankles. The voice was thin and high, almost childlike, so she didn't instantly drop to the defense.

The moon shone light on a figure standing just back from her on the sands, a boy of no more than twelve or thirteen, thin but tall, with a soft face, wide green-brown eyes, and a feathery flop of brown hair. Twigs and leaves poked out of his hair and vines wrapped around his limbs—only Ash noted with a jolt that these plants were actually poking out of his skin. Tiny sprouts peppered his arms; one was growing out of his cheek.

"Florus?" Ash wheezed the name.

He tipped his head, an impish smile playing across his lips. "Ash Nikau."

Ash glanced up and down the shore. "You came. Did you talk to Hydra? Where is—"

"I understand you are hoping to meet with me. My sister wants me to give you floreia." His smile held.

There was a long moment of silence as he just stared at her on the empty beach.

"Yes." Ash drew out the response. Still, he was quiet, and she remembered what Hydra had said—if he was going to give her a piece of his soul, she needed to be worthy of it, to treat it with the respect such an act deserved.

She bowed her head at him, not sure if that was the right thing to do or not.

Florus's deep-green eyes didn't stray from her face. He was more youthful than the other gods Ash had seen, but now that she knew to look, there was the same agelessness in his eyes that she had feared so long in Ignitus—that irascible power that could level cities and snap mortal necks.

A prickle of unease started at the base of Ash's neck. "We *are* preparing to go to Itza—why are you here? Does Hydra know—"

"Centuries ago, we trusted Ciela, and she still failed."

"Ciela?"

"The first gladiator who fought Anathrasa. The one before you.

You don't even know your own history—how are you supposed to step into her place?"

Florus's words took up too much space in Ash's chest.

He was right—she hadn't heard the gladiator's name before. It had been easier when that person had been *the gladiator who fought Anathrasa*, some vague and distant mythical character. But she'd had a name, like Ash. She'd had a family. She'd had a *life*.

"I don't know," Ash admitted. "I'm trying. I want to face Anathrasa. I want to be ready to fight her—"

Florus shook his head, lips twisting. "Wrong answer. The correct answer is: it doesn't matter if you will step into her place. We were wrong about Ciela." His voice was worn with centuries of regret. "I don't want to be wrong again."

A splash made Ash turn.

Instinct clawed at her to get out of the way as a thick green vine shot up from the sea. But the vine still caught her, slamming into her chest and knocking her back into one of the tall boulders on the rocky shore. The angry, violent snake of writhing green wriggled and squirmed against her sealskin suit.

The impact sucked the air from her lungs. Too late, she realized she should pray to Hydra; too late, she got a grip on the vine and started to peel it off her chest—

But a flower grew from the top of it, close to her face. Bloodred petals peeled back to show a yellow core surrounded by an obsidian ring.

The flower convulsed and a burst of pollen clouded Ash's face.

"Florus!" Ash coughed. "What—what are you . . ."

The sea rippled. The sky went from black to pink to a swirl of yellow-red, and in that sky, she saw the god of plants, his youthful face set in a glare.

"We won't be wrong again," he told her, and the world fell into darkness.

SEVEN
MADOC

THAT NIGHT, WHEN the palace was quiet, Madoc snuck out.

A tray of food had been delivered earlier—crunchy bread and charred lamb—and though the aroma alone had been enough to make his mouth water and his stomach clench in hunger, he'd barely touched it. His mind was still churning with all that had happened at the dock—and the handprint that had appeared on Anathrasa's face when she'd struck him.

He could have imagined it—a shadow, or a blush in her cheek from the heat. But when he'd been attacked by the guards, she'd doubled over in pain, as if she'd been hurt alongside him.

There was something very strange going on, and he needed to find out what.

Lifting the tray with one hand, he pulled open the door of his quarters—a lavish room, with a bed twice the size of any he'd slept in before. Two guards waited outside, and at the sound, they turned, bracing their weapons before them.

Their tension moved over his skin like the legs of an insect. The need rose inside him to pull on it, to feed, but he held back. These soldiers were loyal to Anathrasa, and if she sensed he'd used soul energeia on them, what would she do to his family? To him?

He needed to be very careful. To only use enough anathreia to sway their thoughts.

"I can't eat this." The guards jumped back as he shoved the tray at them. "It's rotten."

The knife he'd been given with his meal was tucked into his pocket. He didn't want to use it, but knowing it was there made him feel slightly better.

The younger guard, a woman with a scar on her jaw, looked to her gray-bearded partner and grimaced.

"It looks fine to me," she said.

Madoc inhaled the smallest bit of their geoeia, hiding his sigh when it buzzed in his veins.

Just a little. Just enough so that they would let him leave. Breathing in their energeia made it easier to use his own power, a give and take, an ebb and flow. His thoughts shot to the ship, to Tor telling him to reach inside himself and use his own soul for fuel, but he couldn't focus on training exercises now. He had to figure out what was going on between himself and the Mother Goddess. And he needed to find Aera and Biotus so he could siphon off enough of their power to give to Ash.

"Look at it." He stepped closer, finding the man's thoughts

guarded by a hard layer of skepticism. The woman was easier to reach—her curiosity made her vulnerable, and he pressed an image into her mind.

"Maggots!" She jolted back, cupping her hand to her nose. "They're all over the meat!"

"A trick." The man examined the plate as Madoc's hand slid subtly over the knife. If this guard attacked him, he would have to defend himself. "Anathrasa said he might try something. I don't see any—"

"Look closer." Madoc pushed through the guard's uncertainty to the senses beneath. His own anathreia swelled, soothing and hungry for more. The man blinked, then grimaced.

"We'll take this back to the kitchen," the guard said. "Apologies, dominus. Our mistake."

Madoc nodded. He felt more in control than he had at the dock, when his anathreia had swirled inside him like a tempest. Maybe he'd been wrong to think he could tithe on his own soul to use his power. Maybe this was the way it had to be.

He pushed the thought from his head as the two guards walked away.

Keeping his steps quiet, he hurried down the breezeway in the opposite direction, staying close to the stone wall beneath the flickering sconces. The railing on his other side blocked a three-story fall to the courtyard below, where he'd been reunited earlier with his family. He hadn't seen where they'd been taken, but he had a good guess it was to the rooms on the second floor, where two other guards now stood watch.

He considered convincing them to abandon their post so he could have a word with Elias and Ilena, but he didn't want to draw unneeded attention their way.

Heart pounding, he made his way toward the stairs, jogging down the steps, then hiding in a shadow at the bottom as another guard walked by on his nightly rounds.

Anathrasa was keeping them well contained in this wing of the palace. Still, she would have known what Madoc was capable of. He couldn't help wondering if the ease of his escape was something she'd anticipated, even counted on.

Maybe this was a test Anathrasa had set up to see if he'd run—to see if she could trust him. For all he knew, she could sense that he'd left just as she'd felt that slap across her cheek.

He needed to find her and learn exactly what this connection between them entailed, but setting an intentional meeting would give her an opportunity to lie. If he could spy on her without alerting her to his presence, he might be able to gain valuable information for Ash and Hydra.

Geoxus's chambers had been in the northern wing of the palace, a tower that had fallen when he and Ignitus had fought. None of the rooms in this wing were grand enough for a goddess, and he didn't see any servants, so she had to be in one of the chambers above the throne room.

But as he set a course in that direction, he felt pulled another way, as if an invisible hook had caught his spine and was dragging him outside. Giving in to the strange sensation, he crept down a corridor lined with marble statues, remembering, with a chill, the way Geoxus had traveled through them. Now that Ash had his abilities, could she peer through stones the way he had? Could she come here, to Deimos, through the earth?

The thought of seeing her now, even for a moment, made his burden of fear feel lighter.

The hall opened to a marble staircase that descended into the palace gardens. From behind him came the scuffle of sandals—another guard, most likely—and Madoc rushed down the steps, ducking behind the stone railing. The pull was stronger now, unwieldy. His anathreia was responding to another call—coming to life without his bidding.

He was certain it meant the Mother Goddess was close.

When all was quiet, he continued on.

The gardens were as peaceful as they were haunting. Crickets chirped in flower beds, while carriage-sized boulders that had fallen from the towers during the battle lay half embedded in the scorched earth. He stepped through a vine-laced trellis, through trees toppled, their roots ripped from the ground and now reaching toward the half-moon. Everywhere he looked was a reminder of the power that had been, and the power that had destroyed it.

"Come closer, dear."

He froze at the woman's voice, hair prickling on the back of his neck. Ahead, he could see two figures. He recognized Anathrasa immediately, dressed in a fine white gown, standing beside a white marble fountain. She was motioning to a servant, a girl no more than fifteen, who complied with her goddess's will and knelt at her feet.

Realizing with some relief that he hadn't been seen, Madoc

ducked behind a boulder, flattening himself against the cold, jagged stone. Dread sank into his chest, the only anchor to his anathreia, which continued to whirl inside in a strange, unsettling way—like a power he'd taken from someone else and was holding in his body.

Anathrasa threw her head back, face turned toward the sky. She hadn't looked his way. For all Madoc knew, she didn't see him, but he could feel something happening. The quickening of blood in his veins. The rise of strength in his muscles.

Soul energeia.

She was tithing, and he could feel it.

He knew what would come next. The girl's power would be sucked out of her body. She would die, like Cassia had died. Like so many others must have for Anathrasa to look as youthful and strong as she did now.

Horror raked through him. He felt the urge to call out a warning, to tell her to run. But if he did, Anathrasa would know he wasn't loyal. The Metaxas might be punished. He wouldn't be able to get close to Aera or Biotus.

Anathrasa wasn't the woman Madoc had lived below in the stone-mason's quarter. She was already stronger, which meant she was a threat to Ash, even with the gods' energeias.

Every moment, his mother was growing more dangerous.

In a new wave of panic, a cold sweat dripped between his shoulder blades. If he could feel Anathrasa tithing on a Deiman woman, she would very likely feel him taking the power from a god.

He couldn't think of that now. He only knew he had to stop this.

Think.

He needed to create a distraction. To turn the girl's mind or alert a guard to interrupt. But his anathreia was still rising, whipping through him, and he couldn't direct it anywhere.

He couldn't stop her.

But he might be able to hurt her.

Silently, he slid the knife free from his belt and sliced a clean line across the palm of his hand. The sudden rush of pain had him gritting his teeth. Had his power roaring in his veins.

A shrill cry filled the night. As Madoc watched, Anathrasa stumbled into the edge of the fountain. She gripped her hand against her chest, a blossom of red staining the front of her gown.

It had worked.

Somehow, he and Anathrasa *were* connected. She'd bled when he cut himself. He'd found a way to hurt her.

Had he found a way to kill her?

The girl leaped up, forcing the dark thought from his mind. Sliding the knife back into his belt, Madoc locked his bleeding fist against his thigh. His heartbeat pounded in his temples. He hadn't thought of what would happen after he'd distracted Anathrasa, only that stopping her might save the girl.

But her fate had been sealed as soon as she'd stepped into this courtyard. To Anathrasa, mortals were only fuel. All he'd done was delay the inevitable.

"Goddess, are you all right?" The girl was terrified—more so than before. Her hands were clasped before her.

Anathrasa didn't respond. She rushed toward the palace, the girl on her heels begging for forgiveness.

Madoc jumped as a hand closed around his shoulder. He spun to find Elias crouched behind him, one finger pressed to his lips in an order to be silent.

Madoc's muscles tensed. What was Elias doing here? It wasn't safe. The Mother Goddess might try to tithe on him next.

Elias motioned toward the palace, and Madoc followed him in silence. He thought Elias meant to go back inside, but he skirted around the outside of the building, running to the back of the stables, where Madoc had once taken Ash after the ball so that they could sneak away.

They'd never made it past the gates.

Elias stopped and, breathing hard, leaned against the back of the barn, sinking into the shadows on the ground.

"What are you doing?" Madoc asked when his heart finally settled.

"Following you," Elias said. "You're not the only one who can sneak around this place."

Madoc didn't like this. It was one thing for him to risk Anathrasa's wrath. Another for Elias, who hadn't signed up for any of this.

"I made a hole in the floor of our room," Elias continued. "Now. You want to tell me what that was all about?"

He didn't know if Elias was referring to his spying or to the cut on his hand. It occurred to him that Elias didn't even know what Anathrasa had been attempting to do.

"She's tithing," Madoc said. "Feeding on energeia. It's making her stronger."

"I noticed. The old bat pulled me out of prison and said you were coming. That if we so much as tried to run you would suffer. She looked . . . *healthy*." He said the word like a curse. "I wasn't talking about that part," he added.

Anger spilled through Madoc's veins, mingling with the realization of what Elias meant.

He unfurled his palm, showing the already-scabbed line where he'd cut himself.

"Somehow, we're connected," he said. "When I get hurt, she gets hurt."

Elias's eyes widened. "What happens if *she* gets hurt?"

Madoc shrugged. He supposed the same principle worked in reverse, and it worried him to think that at any moment he might start bleeding as a result of her own experimentation.

"And if you die?" Elias pressed, his voice raw.

Madoc grasped his hands tightly. He didn't know the answer. If he could end the world's suffering with his own sacrifice—if he could save Ash's life by trading his—he had no choice but to do it. But he didn't know for certain that their connection went that deep. Anathrasa was still a goddess, after all, and had lived thousands of years. If he died and she survived, he would be of no help to Ash or their cause.

"I'm still trying to figure out how it works," he said.

"That's why you're here? To figure this out?" Elias didn't sound pleased with this plan.

"No. The connection—that's new," Madoc said. "I'm here because we found a way to beat her. I just need to get Aera's and Biotus's energeias first. Have you seen them?"

"They're here for the newest round of bloodshed," Elias said. "Aera eats men like us for breakfast. And good luck with Biotus. His arms are as thick as your chest."

Madoc scowled. He'd seen the god of animals from afar during wars between Deimos and Cenhelm and recalled thinking he was formidable. If there was a way to draw the energeia from him without a physical confrontation, that would be ideal.

"You're serious," Elias said, as if he'd been waiting for the punch line of a joke. "I heard rumors in prison about what had happened at the palace. I thought they were just stories."

Quickly, Madoc explained everything that had happened since they'd parted. The battle with Geoxus and Ignitus, how Ash had killed a god. The run through the city and the fight outside the ice blockade at the Apuit Islands. Their plan to make Ash strong enough to defeat Anathrasa.

"She can hold the powers of the gods within her." He pictured her standing in Hydra's throne room, water pouring from her hands. "She's going to use them to beat Anathrasa."

Elias considered this for a long minute, the crickets chirping in the grass around them.

"So . . ." Elias pulled a long piece of grass from the ground and wound it around his finger. "You came all the way back here for a girl?"

Madoc jabbed him in the ribs. "I came back to save the world, you idiot."

"Well," said Elias. "You're in deep."

Madoc was quiet, remembering the feel of Ash's skin, and the hitch of her sigh. The taste of sellenroot that had wound into their kiss.

The way he'd failed her on the ship with Anathrasa. The way he'd accidentally bound himself to his mother, making him unsure if he could even help Ash now without Anathrasa knowing.

Doubt weighed on him, slick and heavy.

He shook it off, changing the subject.

"Where's Cassia?" Her name brought a tension to his chest, and a heaviness between them.

"Anathrasa let me take her to the fields outside the city," Elias said. "Near an orange tree."

She'd always liked oranges.

"I put a stone on her grave for you. A big, ugly one, because it reminded me of you."

Madoc gave a watery chuckle. "Thanks for that."

Elias sighed, then rested his forehead on Madoc's shoulder. "I missed you, brother."

Madoc only nodded, because a knot in his throat made it impossible to speak.

Elias lifted his head, then pushed off the ground. He extended a hand toward Madoc and helped him up.

"Anathrasa's not taking any more of my family," he said, like a man twice his age. "If draining two more gods is how we take her down, you can count on my help."

Madoc stood, his lungs too big within his ribs.

But as they headed back toward the palace, he couldn't help thinking of his strange connection with the Mother Goddess and the unscratchable itch on his soul that told him that Anathrasa had not survived hundreds of years on tithes alone without considering just how she would exact her revenge.

They had to be ready for anything.

ꝯ ꝯ ꝯ

Madoc woke to a breeze blowing across his skin. It carried a soft, clean scent, like freshly laundered clothes, and behind his closed eyes, he saw the rocky western outlet of the Nien River, where everyone in the quarter went to wash their dusty tunics and robes. He sighed, thinking of how he had once carried the heavy, waterlogged basket home for Ilena, and how, after she'd hung the pieces to dry on the line, he and Elias would fling stones at them for target practice.

A high giggle made his eyes pop open.

There was a woman sitting on his bed.

Startled, he scrambled to the head of the mattress, dragging the covers over his naked chest.

"Good morning, sleepyhead," she said with a smile. "You had sweet dreams, I trust?"

She was as small as Ilena, with delicate curves and long hair like spun sunshine. Her dress—if that was what it was called—was pale blue, a single braid of fabric over her left shoulder that spread to a thin sheath over her breasts and ended just below the crux of her thighs.

His eyes widened involuntarily, and then his brain caught up with him.

The woman before him wasn't a woman at all, but a goddess whose likeness he had seen in a painting during the last war Deimos had had with Lakhu.

Aera.

Instantly, the power in him swelled, all gnashing teeth and sharp hunger—a response to the raw, god energeia surrounding her. His anathreia was reckless and primal, everything Tor had tried to teach him to control, and stole Madoc's breath. His gaze flicked to the three guards behind her, in the same small, wispy skirts. They were whispering to each other and ogling him in a way that made him very uncomfortable.

"So you're him," she said, her voice breathy and high, her pink lips parting around the words. His eyes lowered, but there was nowhere to look that he couldn't see skin. Bare shoulders, and wrists, and fingers, and legs. "The mortal son I've heard so much about."

He thought of Ash's legs, wrapped around his. Her hands splaying on his chest.

"Madoc," he said, his voice still rough with sleep. "Can I help you with something, goddess?"

"I can think of one or two things," said one of her guards with a quirk of her brow.

Madoc cleared his throat.

Aera leaned closer, her hand brushing Madoc's bare shoulder, teasing the swell of muscle. He had the distinct impression that he was being measured in some way. Evaluated.

"Anathrasa thinks you can help us," Aera said. "I hope, for your sake, she isn't wrong."

He nearly choked. Anathrasa didn't trust him. He'd been met on the docks by half the legion. His room was guarded, however lightly. His own family was being held prisoner.

But the glimmer in her eyes was filled with promise.

If he betrayed them, she would kill him.

His mind reeled. He could take some of Aera's power—if he was subtle, she might not even notice. He could hold it inside him until he took Biotus's energeia, then he'd find the Apuitian sailors and speed back to the islands.

This was what he'd come to do. This was what they needed to defeat Anathrasa.

But he thought of the cut on his hand and the blood that had risen on hers. Even if Aera couldn't sense what he was doing, would Anathrasa know? Would she feel it?

His family would be held accountable for his treason. Drained like Cassia. Killed.

But if he couldn't take Aera's and Biotus's power and give it to Ash, what good was he?

Panic pressed his teeth together as Aera slid closer on the mattress. The breeze that he'd felt before had come with her, a movement of the still air, threatening to calm his ragged senses.

"I came to wake you," she said, glancing out the window, to the gray sky now growing bright with dawn. "We're leaving soon."

"Where are we going?" he asked.

She rose and strode toward the door, her bare feet making no sound against the floor.

"To the arena," she called. "The gladiator games are about to begin."

She disappeared out the door, leaving him gaping in her wake.

Half an hour later, a carriage took him from the palace into the heart of the city, where people were already gathering on street corners and heading toward the arena. With a lurch, he remembered how fans had painted his name on their bodies when the gladiators had rolled through town. How girls had offered to meet him after a match. It was a game to them, just as it was a game to the gods.

Anathrasa's words echoed through his head: *I don't suppose you're here for the festivities.* Had she been talking about this? Elias had said the gods were here for *the newest round of bloodshed*, but Madoc had thought he'd meant the attack from Hydra and Florus, not gladiator fights.

He was almost glad his family had been left behind at the palace. Still, he didn't like being separated from them. The fact that they hadn't been invited today made him worry what was happening to them in his absence.

Sick with anticipation, Madoc leaned toward the window, breathing in a city that still reeked of smoke. It was better than inhaling whatever intoxicating scent floated around Aera.

He stole a glance at her, laughing at something one of the guards on her right had said. They fit together like woven strands. Two women on her left, another on her right. Geoxus's guards had always been solemn and cold, but these warriors clung close to their goddess, as if to make a shield with their bodies.

Madoc couldn't pick her energeia out from the rest if he tried.

"Who will be participating in these games? Hydra and Florus haven't sent anyone to fight, have they?" He tried to keep his voice steady, but nerves were cresting inside him.

Was Ash here? He wasn't ready. He'd been in Crixion for a night.

He wasn't even sure that Aera hadn't drawn him away from the palace to murder him.

"Don't you think you'd notice if Hydra and Florus had arrived?"

she said, laughing at something another guard whispered. They all looked at Madoc in a way that made him feel very awkward, as if he were wearing a lot less than the fine white toga that had been delivered to his room just after Aera's departure this morning. It reminded him of Anathrasa's gown last night, and he hoped that had been a deliberate choice the Mother Goddess had made. Whether she knew he'd been responsible for the cut on her hand or not, he hoped she still wanted him close.

The carriage slowed, then turned onto a narrow path that led to the gladiator entrance beneath the stands. Madoc had once ridden with Lucius and Elias here before he'd fought Jann, and before that, when he'd first met Ash face-to-face. That all seemed a lifetime ago now.

"Then which gladiators are fighting?" he asked, frustrated by her vague answers. "Earth Divine? Your Air Divine?"

His gut twisted at the thought that he might be made to fight. Was that what she'd meant when she'd said that Anathrasa had thought he could help them?

In that moment, he wished he'd never come home.

Aera registered his tone and met his gaze, her sky-blue eyes bright with amusement.

"Deimos. Lakhu. Cenhelm. We'll hardly stand a chance against Hydra's fleet next month with the city in shambles and half its people moping around, crying for their beloved god of earth." She walked her fingers over the bare knee of one of her guards as the carriage pulled under the archway, into the dusty belly of the massive stone structure. "We needed to raise an army. And what better way to determine the best fighters than by a trial on the sands of my brother's grand arena? Imagine it! No more elite gladiators—any Divine citizen can join the games, man, woman, child. We'll let them all fight, won't that be wonderful? And with a force made of the strongest mortals to subdue the rest, the world will be ours."

Horror rippled through him as the carriage pulled to a stop. Anathrasa was sending Deimans into the arena—children included—to determine the strongest fighters for her army in the coming war against Hydra and Florus. These weren't gladiators, they were common citizens. They would die, and if he tried to stop it, Anathrasa would punish him, and he wouldn't be able to do what he needed to in order to help Ash defeat her.

As he got out, the thunder of footsteps echoed from the seats above them, scratching Madoc's raw nerves. He could already hear the familiar cheers from the audience within.

He stuffed down his revulsion. He had to keep to the plan.

Aera. Biotus. *Ash.*

He needed to make Ash powerful enough to destroy the Mother Goddess, and to do that he needed to get close to the gods Anathrasa had sided with.

Bile rose in his throat as he and Aera were met by a team of centurions and led down a hallway. They traveled up a long, narrow flight of stairs lit by the phosphorescent green stones Geoxus had once installed instead of torches, to keep Ignitus's gladiators from accessing igneia. At the top, they crossed a wide corridor and came to a brightly lit box, already brimming with people.

Madoc stumbled as he crossed the threshold. The last time he'd been here had been with his gladiator trainer, Lucius, when he'd wanted to beg Geoxus for Cassia's freedom, and had instead been blocked by Petros.

He'd failed that day with Geoxus, but he was no longer a trembling boy who believed his god could save him. Mortals had no choice but to save themselves.

He spotted her, sitting on a white marble throne in the center of the box, surrounded by servants and fawning nobles. Her gown was white, like last night, and fastened around one shoulder by a silver circle.

If she noticed his arrival, she didn't show it. She took a drink of wine from a goblet and continued her conversation. But he could feel the strange pull of power in his veins and wondered if she, too, could sense him drawing near.

He was making his way over to a lavish table of food, from which he could watch the action in the box unfold from a safe distance, when a giant stepped before him, his shadow blocking the light.

"Have you met Madoc yet, brother?" Aera asked, sliding her arm around Madoc's.

The god of animals was a beast beside delicate Aera, his chest broad and bare, crossed by pelt straps, and his ship-mast thighs covered by a swatch of fur. Auburn braids of hair stretched to his muscular neck and shoulders, which flexed as he narrowed his black eyes on Madoc.

Madoc swallowed, feeling his bravery wither.

"Biotus." He bowed his head.

"Madoc." Biotus growled his name. "The one who drained my

brothers dry. You must be proud. It's not every day a mortal takes down a god."

He stared at Madoc in the way a predator eyes his prey.

Madoc's mouth was parched. He couldn't think of what to say.

"Leave him alone, Biotus." Aera slapped his shoulder playfully. "Madoc's on our side. Isn't that right?"

She smiled at him.

He nodded quickly. "I am, goddess."

With a hard look, Biotus shoved past Madoc, nearly knocking him over on his way to the box's exit. Madoc could feel the anger pulsing off him, the taste of copper on the back of his tongue that he knew was animal energeia. His heart begged to try it, even as his mind cautioned him to hold back.

His eyes flicked to Anathrasa, still talking with her servants.

"Don't mind him. He's just angry because his best soldiers haven't yet arrived from Cenhelm. Their ships are quite slow."

Her words reminded him of the way Crixion's ships had flown over the waves, aided by Air Divine sailors, when they'd attacked with Anathrasa at the blockade before the Apuit Islands. The tension behind his neck increased.

"Where is he going?" he asked, worried about his family, back at the palace, and Ash, even though she was over the sea. And anyone who might cross paths with the god of animals.

"To track the rest of his fleet, I'd guess," she said, her voice like a tinkling bell as she twisted a finger around a lock of her golden hair. It didn't ease his mind—he'd rather Biotus stay within sight, and the possibility of an entire Cenhelmian fleet's arrival in Crixion was daunting—but he couldn't follow him and not raise Aera's suspicion.

"This all must be very exciting for you," she said. "Have you ever seen an Air Divine warrior fight an Animal Divine *and* an Earth Divine at once?"

Three people in the arena together? In past wars, it had been only one champion against another.

"How many rounds are there?" he asked.

"Just one." She linked her arm with his and dragged him through the crowd of gossiping Deimans and Laks to the railing, where they could overlook the sparkling sand. Pots of flowers had been brought alongside it, and the sweet scent of jasmine and rose filled his nostrils.

His heart locked in his throat.

He could see the spot where he'd fought Jann below. Where he'd stood when Geoxus had chosen him for the Honored Eight. Where Ash had fallen when Elias had thrown all his geoeia at her.

The seats below and around them were filled to capacity. The spectators' voices rose like thunder, their excitement thick in the morning air.

"Anathrasa!" called an announcer positioned near the base of the arena, his voice magnified on the wind. "We honor you with this first of three tribute games—a battle of strength between our fearless Earth Divine, the Air Divine from Lakhu, and the mighty Animal Divine of Cenhelm! The best among them will receive the ultimate honor—to serve in your army." He paused, and the crowd roared their approval, but Madoc's heart sank.

"Now," the announcer continued. "Bring out the champions!"

EIGHT

ASH

THE WORLD BECAME a forest.

Thick brown trees shot up to support a fluffy emerald canopy that let shafts of golden light peek through. Ash stood on a bed of dew-laden undergrowth, watching leaves drift on a breeze in lazy spirals. The air smelled of moss and decay but also of life.

Everything was peaceful here.

Ash turned, watching the sunlight play in the canopy. The effect spun colors across the leaves—bright red and slants of butter yellow. It made her dizzy.

She was so dizzy.

She wanted to sleep.

"Ash, you have to wake up."

Ash turned, her arms drifting through the velvety warm air, and then she was dancing, a luxurious spiral from a lifetime ago. As she danced, she saw Char standing nearby, watching.

"Mama?" Ash giggled. "Mama!"

She stopped. Pulses of red and yellow and black throbbed around her. The decay smell was stronger now and Ash grabbed her head. She was so dizzy. Why was she so dizzy?

"You have to fight through it, Ash," Char said. "You know this isn't right. Wake up!"

Ash shuddered, not cold, not feeling much of anything.

"Wake up!" Char begged again, and Ash twitched, rubbing her eyes hard.

When she blinked them open, Char was gone; the forest, gone. Around her towered scarlet flowers with hypnotic yellow centers and black smeared across their insides, all of them swaying in a breeze.

Ash swayed too. She tipped over, crying out, and when her hands and knees dropped to the undergrowth, she felt only thorns. They stabbed her hands and blood fell, staining the leaves and rising up her arms—

Ash screamed, flailing, but the blood rose and rose into her mouth, salty and metallic.

She was still screaming when her eyes opened, and the flowers were gone. No forest, no Char, no thorns or blood.

She was curled in the corner of a bare room. Six hexagonal walls wrapped around her with a solid floor and ceiling—no doors, no windows. The only light came from gently pulsing spots on each wall—they flickered in and out, a yellow-green hue much like Geoxus's phosphorescent stones or Hydra's algae.

Ash held still for one full breath. Her head throbbed, an ache in the veins at her temples, and her tongue tasted like she'd licked sand. Where was she? She had the foggiest memory of Florus showing up on the shore. And thorns? No, a vine—

A vine with a red flower.

The bastard had poisoned her.

Ash rose, slowly finding her footing on the rough floor.

Florus had poisoned and captured her.

Her stomach roiled, and she forced herself not to vomit. She wouldn't think through the implications of this yet.

She would *get out*.

Gritting her teeth, she pulled blue flames into each hand and launched fire at the far wall. She pushed it hotter, as hot as she could handle; and even then, she gave it more. The floor and walls rippled in a scalding red glow as her heat sank into them, and still she pushed more, sweat breaking across her face and back, exertion tugging at the edges of her vision.

The entire room tipped upside down. Ash flipped, slamming against the far wall, the ceiling, the floor again. Embers from her escape attempt peppered the air around her as she spun, each toss ricocheting pain up her shoulder, her thigh, her skull.

"Florus!" Ash screamed. "Florus—*stop!*"

The room came to a halt, righted again—or maybe upside down now—but Ash crouched on the floor, shaking, her hair wild around her and the taste of blood in her mouth.

The god of plants materialized in the middle of the room, bringing with him the smell of earth, rich and heavy with life and fresh oxygen. It contrasted with how stale this room smelled, like a thousand years of neglect and rot.

Ash glared up at Florus. Should she attack him outright? Could she murder a god without Madoc first draining him?

The thought of his name broke her.

"Where is Madoc?" Ash gasped to the floor. "Did you side with Anathrasa? If you so much as—"

"Madoc? There's no one by that name here," Florus responded. "And I am *not* allied with Anathrasa."

Ash watched his face for any sign of a lie, but his eyes were wide and innocent, his lips soft in a half smile. Only a crease on his forehead showed he was at all distressed.

Ash bolted to her feet and lunged at him.

Instantly, a dozen vines shot out of the floor, knotted around her, and yanked her back. Her shoulder blades crashed into the rough wall and the vines held her against it, more of them squirming up to hold each limb in a locked, solid embrace.

"What are you doing?" Ash screamed. "Stop this!"

Florus shook his head. "No."

"I can break out of this," Ash threatened. Her skin started to burn, a blue flame on her hands and feet that crackled the vines. "I'll incinerate this whole prison."

That earned a thoughtful smile. "This prison was made for one such as you. You cannot escape." He stomped on the floor. "Petrified wood. It isn't alive, so no water to use; it isn't a stone, so no earth to use. It cannot be burned. It can only be manipulated by Plant Divine. And I will not give you floreia, Ash Nikau. You are not strong enough to save us."

She let her fire fall, let the vines keep her against the wall. Her chest beat in and out, and with rasping breaths she wanted to scream again, but she managed, "What do you want?"

Florus stepped closer. "I told you. We won't fail against Anathrasa again. I won't let us."

"You won't let us." Ash's heart sank into her stomach. "Where's Hydra?"

Had Hydra betrayed her? And where were Tor, Taro, Spark?

Ash felt her body heat spike again, but Florus shook his head. "Hydra will be quite upset when she finds out what I did. But she will get over it. We always do."

Florus flicked his wrist and a fan of razor-sharp leaves grew out of the floor, each as long as Ash's arm. Florus plucked one, testing its edge as one might a blade.

Ash bucked against the vines. "Florus." But her throat constricted. She couldn't breathe.

"Last time, our best efforts to kill Anathrasa failed," Florus started, still looking at the sharp leaf. "We only made it so she can't sustain her own anathreia. She can't retain the souls she draws into herself. She can't manipulate the emotions and thoughts of others—yet. But we tried with everything we had to accomplish more—we tried to defeat her, and we couldn't."

His eyes flicked to Ash.

"If she gets you, she'll have my brothers' energeias. She'll be at her full power again. And what will we be able to do to stop her then? We *can't* defeat her. We can only keep her in this weakened state."

"I'm going to stop her, Florus." Ash knew she sounded frantic, but she *was*. Her head still throbbed and each nerve tingled with desperate fear. "Ciela—that was her name?—I'm not Ciela. When I obtain all six energeias and become Soul Divine like Anathrasa, I'm going to kill her."

"Anathrasa survived Ciela."

"She won't survive me. I know Anathrasa's tricks. I know not to stop fighting until I'm *sure* she's dead."

"No." Florus pointed the leaf at her. "It won't matter. I won't risk the possibility of Anathrasa getting my brothers' powers from you. I'm ending this."

He leaned forward, his eyes scrambling over her face, her matted hair, a gash on her chin dripping blood onto her collarbone.

"Ignitus? Geoxus? Are you in there?" Florus whispered. "Can you hear me, brothers? I'm going to kill these last pieces of you. I've prepared for this moment—Hydra always thought you'd leave us alone forever, but I knew you'd eventually come and ruin everything. So I made you this prison. It will contain your igneia, Ignitus. And your geoeia, Geoxus. So don't try to fight me."

Ash gasped, a bitter sob. "Florus, Ignitus and Geoxus aren't here—it's just me. I'm—"

Florus put the tip of the leaf against Ash's lips. It sliced her skin and she tasted more blood, but she couldn't pull away, her head bound to the wall.

Florus met her eyes again, and Ash saw the insanity in him. She lost herself in it; even when Ignitus had been at his most unhinged, he had never been calm like this, and Florus's youthful face made it all the more horrifying.

"I'm going to kill this mortal shell," Florus told her. Told Ignitus and Geoxus within her.

Ash heaved against the vines. "Wait, wait—"

"It's the only way," he said, and he almost looked sad. "When the shell dies, my brothers' energeias will dissipate into the ether. They will be gone, and Anathrasa will never again be able to resume her full strength. This will all be over."

"No, Florus!" Ash fought, but more vines held her; she burned, but when one vine snapped away, another was there to take its place. "That won't stop Anathrasa! She'll still be here, terrorizing the world—I have to kill her, Florus! *Let me fight her!*"

"Shh," Florus cooed as though she was some tantruming child. "This will all be over soon."

He lowered the spiked leaf.

"Florus!" Ash screamed. "Florus, *don't—*"

He reared his arm back, shifted his weight, and drove the point of the leaf into her gut.

Ash choked. Before she could feel any pain, he stabbed her with another pointed leaf, and another, and another, until that was what held her body to the wall, not the vines.

Satisfied, Florus stepped back and folded his arms over his chest.

He was just going to stand there and watch her die.

Blood surged up Ash's throat and spilled down her chin, until all she felt was an iron tang of blood everywhere, consuming her senses.

She couldn't be dying. She couldn't *die* at all—Madoc needed her. Tor needed her.

A tear streaked down her cheek. She sputtered, gasping, and the act wrenched her body against the leaves, sending a spark of pain up her side. That pain lit others until her mouth cracked open, but she couldn't even scream; this pain was unbearable, unfathomable, an ache she couldn't put a name to because it was so beyond what a body should experience.

With one last effort, Ash pushed fire at the leaves that held her. They burned to the wall and she dropped, freed, only to collapse on the floor in a puddle of blood and broken vines.

"Really, Ignitus?" Florus chastised. "Die with honor."

"I . . . am not . . . Ignitus," Ash gasped, each word agony. She pushed herself onto her hands and glowered up at Florus. "I am not . . . Geoxus. I am . . ."

Pain seized her. She doubled over, wailing, her insides constricting in a spasm that shot stars across her eyes.

She rolled to the side, hands around her middle—

Her wounds.

Her wounds were healing.

The ones on her stomach. The gaping hole in her shoulder.

She writhed on the floor, half taken by the throbbing sensation of healing and half terrified as the holes made by Florus's leaves mended themselves.

Ash came to her knees, trembling, covered in blood and sweat and righteous fury. She looked up at Florus again, and his eyes were wide with realization.

"You have Ignitus's and Geoxus's energeias," he said, "and you have their immortality too, it seems."

Ash's chest heaved. She used the wall to pull herself to her feet. Her focus sharpened to a single point, something dark rising from the pit of her soul and hunching her shoulders, curling her fingers into fists, peeling back her lips in a snarl.

"I am more god than you," she growled.

"No," Florus told her. But his voice was clipped. She had rattled him; she had rattled herself. "Anathrasa will never find you. She will never resume her full power. It is still over."

When Ash lunged at Florus this time, she didn't want to burn him; no, she wanted to rip his head off and let him bathe in his own blood.

But before she'd crossed the room, Florus was gone.

Ash slammed into the opposite wall in his wake. She whirled, searching for him, but she saw only the vines, now withering away; the razor leaves covered in her blood; the stain on the floor of all the blood she had lost; and she knew she must look like death itself.

Ash beat her fists on the walls. Bruises formed, but she felt them tingle and heal. It was happening fast. She was a god. She couldn't be killed. She couldn't—

"Florus!" she screamed. "Florus! HYDRA!"

Ash reared back, gasping.

Hydra had briefly tried to teach Ash to travel like the gods. *Focus. Meditate.*

Ash knotted her fingers in her hair and turned in a circle, eyes shut, pulse hammering.

Hydra, she willed herself. *Get to Hydra.*

Madoc. Get to Madoc.

Madoc. If he took Aera's aereia or Biotus's bioseia without Ash there to receive it, the energeia would eventually kill him.

Ash sobbed. Her knees cracked to the floor, and she heaved, crying so hard she thought she might be sick.

Florus had tried to kill her. And that still might be her fate if she didn't get out of this prison.

If she didn't, no one would ever know what had happened to her. Tor, Taro, Spark—she would never see them again. Madoc—she would never touch him again, never feel the way he held her.

Her mind spiraled, thoughts and intentions too slippery to hold. All she could do was kneel there, weeping, half a god, half a girl, entirely defeated.

NINE
MADOC

THE GATES ON the south side of the arena, where Madoc him-self had once entered, opened, and a line of Deimans stepped onto the golden sand. These weren't the trained fighters Geoxus had trea-sured—most weren't thick enough to fill out the gladiator armor they'd borrowed. Some weren't even strong enough to lift their own weapons, dragging their swords on the ground behind them, or hoist-ing wobbling spears with both hands.

"They're all fighting at once?" Madoc asked. He'd assumed Aera had meant one champion of each country, but now it looked as if this was going to include everyone.

"Yes, isn't it exciting?" The goddess of air clapped her hands. "I heard Deimans were lined up in the streets all last week for a chance to appear in the arena. Everyone wants to be a hero and avenge Geoxus!"

A sheen of sweat coated Madoc's skin. In the box beside him, he heard an audible grunt of disgust, and when he turned, he saw Lucius, the gladiator trainer he'd once served. The man met Madoc's gaze, his eyes filled with anger, then looked away.

Madoc's mouth went dry. The last time he'd seen Lucius, he'd been training to fight as an Earth Divine champion. Surely by now the sponsor knew that had been a lie. Was he disgusted now at the very sight of Madoc? Did he know Anathrasa was Madoc's mother? He had to be wondering why Madoc was here, among some of the most powerful people in the world.

Regardless what the sponsor thought, Madoc felt his surprise settle into a tentative relief. There was at least one other Deiman displeased with Anathrasa's rule—even if Lucius's disgust was reserved for him.

Forty Deimans were on the sand now, but Madoc's gaze locked on the smallest among them—a boy with dark curls and a small wooden knife. He glanced again to Lucius. The sponsor never would have put a child on the sand, or any of these fighters for that matter. He'd taken only the best. The strongest.

Or at least those who'd appeared to be the strongest.

He had a sudden, desperate desire to talk to Ash, to tell her what was happening here. Did she know? Did Hydra look through the water to learn of the horrors about to take place?

Had Ash learned how to do the same?

No. She would have tried to contact him if she could. Still, too much time had passed since he'd left the islands. Was she all right? Had something happened? He wished there was a way that he could reach her, but how? He wasn't a god. They didn't even share the same energeia.

He was overcome by a wave of insignificance. This was the kind of thing they were fighting to stop. These people were risking their lives for the pleasures of the gods. And yet he was forced to stand by and do nothing.

Not nothing.

He was close to Aera. If he could figure out how to drain some of her power, they would be one step closer to ending these events forever.

"There they are!" The goddess of air squealed as the northern gate was pulled back to reveal another group—men and women with fair hair and skin, who carried thin golden shields and small handheld weapons. They moved over the ground like their goddess did—light on their feet, their gazes constantly in motion.

A moment later, seven warriors in fur skins stomped out of the far exit. They were braced for a fight, and even from the box, Madoc could feel the charge of their bioseia. As soon as the gate behind them had closed, the sand began to shift. At first, Madoc thought this was the work of geoeia, but as he watched, a trapdoor opened in the ground and a giant white mountain cat lunged up a hidden ramp. Two more followed, lithe beasts the size of horses, with paws as big as a man's head and claws like knives. When the last cat tried to pounce at the nearest Animal Divine fighter, it was caught around the neck by a metal collar and crashed to its side with a shriek.

The crowd went wild.

Madoc's gaze darted back to the Deiman boy, who clearly had no idea what he'd gotten himself into. This wasn't the gladiator fights of the old wars; this was a free-for-all—Earth Divine against Air Divine against Animal Divine. Like last night in the garden, the urge rose in him to stop this, but before he could say or do anything, the announcer raised his hands.

"Let the games begin!"

The audience screamed as the three divinities in the arena clashed in a torrent of wind and dust and clanging metal. Despite the unprepared look of the Deimans, they hurled themselves toward the Air and Animal Divine with a reckless bravery, and soon, a hundred energeias were heaving across the sand.

Madoc gripped the railing, sick to his core. He searched for the boy and found him near the outskirts of the fight, flinging balls of gravel into the fray before sprinting to a new position. As he neared the back of the arena, he came close to one of the jungle cats, and Madoc found himself yelling for the boy to move as the animal swiped at him with its monstrous paw.

The boy ducked just in time, but as the animal crouched to attack again, it twisted, its head ducked low in pain, and stumbled to its side. Behind it, an Animal Divine warrior lowered his hands from where he'd reached and drawn out the beast's life force, and he roared, bioseia flooding his veins.

Before he could attack, he was swept into the air by a Lak fighter and flung into the stands.

"Oh my," Aera giggled.

Madoc could feel the tingle of her victory dancing over his skin, and beyond it, the pulse of her energeia—a cool, invisible fog. It was different than this morning in the carriage. This was unchecked and unprotected, and as the moments passed, he became more aware of it, until his vision had fallen out of focus and he'd lost track of the boy in the crowd.

He eased closer to Aera, a dark hunger licking his soul. Everyone was distracted now. If the goddess of air didn't notice Madoc sipping the smallest bit of her energeia, would anyone else? Would Anathrasa?

Now might be his best chance to test how much, if any, he could take without her noticing.

Inhaling, he felt Aera's consciousness, light as a cloud. When he grasped for it with his anathreia, it slipped away. Drawing back, he steadied himself, then tried again.

Just a little, he thought.

He kept his eyes on the battle, vaguely acknowledging the four Earth Divine fighters who'd made a clay wall to block the attacks of the other two divinities. The Air Divine were picking off Biotus's warriors one by one, and soon had turned on the Deimans.

Madoc pressed against the threshold of Aera's energeia, invisible strands of his anathreia reaching for the goddess's soul. The sweet taste of spun sugar filled his mouth, then was gone a second later.

Aera flinched. She looked behind her, as if someone had tapped her on the shoulder.

"Wine?"

Madoc turned sharply to find Anathrasa standing beside him. She'd taken two goblets off a tray and was extending one toward Madoc.

He accepted it with a shaking hand but didn't drink. Had she known what he was trying to do? Was that why she'd interrupted him?

He tried to read her emotions, but his anathreia was unsteady from trying to tithe on Aera, so he searched her face for confirmation, only to find her staring at her reflection in the silver goblet with a frown.

"I've given you the finest bed in the palace in hopes that your good sleep will get rid of these bags under my eyes." She pulled gently at the corner of one eye, flattening the wrinkles. "I don't think it's helped, do you?"

The fight before him faded. Aera, who'd moved away to watch with her guards, slipped from his mind.

"So we are connected." He knew this—he'd seen it—and yet her confirmation made his chest feel as though it was filled with stones.

Anathrasa lowered the goblet, meeting his gaze with an unamused stare. "There are no accounts of mortals and gods who have been linked in this way before." Her chin lifted. "Then again, there are no accounts of mortals living after an attack on their god, either."

A shiver worked its way down Madoc's chest. So she did think what he'd done to her on the ship had caused this. He wasn't sure if that made him feel proud, or incredibly stupid.

She opened her hand, eyeing the scar across her palm. It had healed quickly—perhaps she was like Madoc in that way—but it still sent a new wave of fear through him.

She knew, or at least suspected, what he'd done last night.

"How does it work, I wonder?" she mused, her voice quiet amid the screams around them. "You didn't feel anything strange last night after you cut your hand, did you? Anything on your shoulder?" He flinched as she pushed open the collar of his robe, examining his right shoulder the way Aera had done this morning.

Wariness scrunched his brows. "Should I have, Mother Goddess?"

She moved the strap of her dress to the side, showing a red scab.

Had she cut herself as he had, to see if he'd bleed?

He was just starting to grasp what this might mean—that he could hurt her without being hurt in return—when she leaned down to a rosebush beside her and wrapped her fist around the thorned stem beneath a white blossom.

A pinch of pain ricocheted up his right hand, and when he looked down, he saw four points of blood beading on his palm.

"Interesting," she said, wiping her bloody palm on a servant girl standing behind them. "So why didn't it work last night? What were you doing?"

He'd been with Elias after the garden. Was it merely a matter of proximity, or had her attempt to hurt him not worked because of something else?

All he and Elias had been doing was talking. It didn't make sense.

"Nothing," he said. "I was in my room."

"No doubt plotting my demise," she said with a grim smile. "First a cut on the hand, then a knife to the heart, hmm?"

Again, a dark question penetrated his thoughts. If he died, would she die also? If he ceased to exist, this war could be over in moments. His family would be free. Ash wouldn't have to fight.

But he had to be certain it would work.

Frantically, he replayed last night's events. He and Elias had gone to the barn. They'd talked about Anathrasa. About Ash. It had been a welcome relief from the tension he'd felt since arriving back in Crixion.

Why hadn't her experiment worked, as his had? What had been different?

He'd been content with Elias. He'd felt *safe*.

Was that it? Was the difference as simple as the comfort of his brother's presence?

Straightening, Anathrasa turned to him, the sun glinting off her light hair. "Believe me, son, it will take more than your death to kill me. I've tithed enough souls to keep us alive a long, long time. Trying to end your life will only inconvenience us both."

He was equally relieved and disappointed.

"What do we do about this?" he asked carefully.

Her eyes met his, and a strange look crossed her face—something like hope, but more desperate. Though he was reluctant to believe it, part of him wondered if Anathrasa wanted his help.

He could use that to his advantage.

"We make ourselves strong," she said. "So that I can fix what has been broken."

"You mean so that you can rule the six countries." His tone had gone hard.

She inhaled slowly, locking her gaze on his. Even in this younger body, his old neighbor was still visible, looking at him as if she could see every unconscious desire that lurked within.

He bit the inside of his cheek, trying to remain steady. Trying not to think of Cassia.

"I was wrong to split my soul for these gods," she said quietly enough that no one, gods included, could hear. "When I made them, I thought they would love their children as I loved them, but they became worse than mortals. Fighting for power. Fighting for land. Turning on me, the one who made them." She made a sound of disgust that had his jaw clenching. "They're bent on destroying everything."

Aera and Biotus had turned on her in the past, as well, yet now they were preparing to stand beside her in war. Aera had even seemed to pity Anathrasa and her trusting nature. Perhaps she didn't know the Mother Goddess was speaking this way about her behind her back.

Or perhaps this speech was a lie, meant to lure Madoc in.

"So you'll destroy them instead?" he asked, wondering again where Biotus had gone when he'd left the grand arena. Was he truly investigating the delayed arrival of his people, or was he doing something for Anathrasa?

"Your mother's son, through and through." She inhaled slowly. "Yes. Help me, and you'll be free to do what you will."

"And the Metaxas?"

She smiled tightly. "We'll see how loyal you truly prove to be."

He froze, the shouts of the crowd drowned out by the buzzing in his ears. "What would you have me do?"

She faced him, leaning her hip against the railing. "Return the six gods' powers to me so that I can reunite the mortal world under one reigning goddess."

He scoffed. "You want me to take the energeias from Aera and Biotus?"

Anathrasa smiled, a look filled with dangerous promise. "Why do you think I called them here?"

He remembered the conversation with Aera earlier and was now certain she didn't know Anathrasa's true intent: to drain two gods, just as he'd come here to do.

"Biotus is very strong, and Aera, though she doesn't look it, is cunning. She'll be hard to pin down. You'll need my help." Anathrasa turned back to the fighting. "Which leaves the energeias you gave to the Kulan girl."

Ash. At the mention, Madoc's chest seized.

"We'll have to get them back when she arrives. It won't be easy. Not many are trained for the arena as thoroughly as your little gladiator friend," Anathrasa continued, motioning toward the fight below. "Clearly."

Madoc forced his eyes back to the fight so that he didn't give away his anger. His gaze found the boy just as he was hit in the shoulder by an arrow and thrown backward with a stunted cry.

Madoc felt as if the wind had been knocked out of him.

"Stop this," he said. "I'll help you, but please. These people aren't fighters."

"Neither were you," said Anathrasa, almost sounding proud. "The time has come for us all to be champions."

Below him, a Deiman woman sprinted toward the boy, her shoulders gleaming with ill-fitting silver armor, her hair shaved up one side and braided down the other. She grabbed the boy under the arms and dragged him aside, then sent a quake of sand toward two approaching Air Divine warriors, knocking them to the ground.

Half the fighters were strewn across the sand, bleeding and moaning, or fighting to stand. The cats were all down. One tossed its head in obvious pain. The others were drained, their lush white coats now clinging to their bones as if they'd been starved to death.

Only three fighters remained standing. Two Lak men, and the Deiman woman with the braid in her hair who'd helped the boy. They approached each other cautiously from three points of a triangle, their bodies heavy with fatigue but their hands raised and deadly.

"Please." Anger seared beneath Madoc's skin; it took all his control to keep his expression even. "If you truly want to win the heart of Deimos, you'll need more than just its finest fighters."

He couldn't watch this. He didn't know what he intended to do, but he couldn't stay here with her. He couldn't pretend this was all right.

Her chin lifted. "There is little room for mercy in times like these, Madoc."

He bit back a scoff. "There is no better time for mercy," he argued, aware now that he'd caught the eye of some of the others in the box, who were watching and whispering. "Tomorrow these champions will be forgotten, and the people who watched them fight will return to their broken lives—a life I knew well before I stepped into the arena." When she flinched, he stepped closer, but it wasn't her face he saw. It was Ilena, calling him *son* when his own father wouldn't. Cassia, who'd taken Madoc's hand and led him to what he would learn to call home. Elias, his brother in all the ways that mattered. Madoc knew he should be placating Anathrasa, earning her favor, but trust was earned with truth, and he was done standing by while gods used mortals as tools.

"Give them blood and they're yours for a day," he told her. "Show them mercy, and they're yours for a lifetime."

Without another word, he left the box.

🔥 🔥 🔥

It was a short walk to the Temple of Geoxus—not the sanctuary, where the fallen statue lay, but the sheltered area behind it, still enclosed by a singed wall. A guard at the arena, flushed with stress, had told Madoc that this was where the injured would be brought after the fight. The city hospital was already overrun with survivors from the riots, and the healers could not afford to leave those they were already caring for.

Madoc climbed the stone steps, blinking at the metal slot on the tall door where offerings were collected. He'd delivered his street fight winnings here, and once, long before, gotten his arm caught trying to steal coin to buy food.

He knocked twice, and when no answer came, he pushed the door inward. The courtyard was crowded with injured fighters—some propped against the walls or each other, others strewn out over the ground. Centurions and priests in white robes ran between them. Groans of pain filled the air, accented by crying and calls for help.

"No more room," a centurion snapped at him. "If there's anyone else, they're on their own."

"I'm here to help," Madoc said, chest tight.

The guard only shook his head and jogged toward the well, where a dozen people were fighting over a pail of water.

Memories clogged Madoc's throat. Inside these walls, he'd slept on bunks with dozens of other children—orphans, runaways, those who'd been shut out of their homes like he had. He'd been given food and water, and taught the proper ways to pray to Geoxus, with one hand on a stone and gratitude in his heart.

As he stepped into the dusty courtyard, a centurion shoved the wooden door closed behind him. The scent of blood and bile had him fighting the urge to gag. Pain was so thick in the air, he coughed breathing it in.

He shouldn't have come. He couldn't help these people. He'd healed Ash once, but that had been an accident. Maybe he could help clean wounds or bandage injuries—he'd worked as a stonemason long enough to know how to patch someone up after a stone broke or slid free from its mooring—but he didn't know where to start.

Biting back a surge of helplessness, he caught the arm of a passing priest—a young man whose lips were white with the chalk that had been smeared across his mouth.

"What can I do?" he asked.

The priest looked him over, brows scrunching in confusion at Madoc's fine cloak. They both knew this was not a place for privilege.

"Water," the priest said a moment later. "Make them comfortable. It's the least we can do before the circle is complete."

Madoc didn't know what this meant, but the priest was already gone.

Rolling up his sleeves, Madoc raced to the well. He filled a bucket with water and grabbed a ladle, then moved to a man with a mangled foot, offering a sip. Two girls, no more than seventeen, followed, blinking at the sky and prodding weeping cuts on their heads. He knelt beside a man in a dusty white robe who was crouched over a child with a puncture wound in his shoulder. Madoc recognized the boy from the arena—he'd been the one saved by the Deiman woman with the braid in her hair. His brow was pale and sweaty now, and he fought for air with quick, raspy breaths.

"I have water," Madoc said.

"He needs more than water."

Madoc's chin jerked up at the familiar rasp of the man's voice. "Tyber?"

The priest touched his jaw as Madoc's gaze lowered to the smear of white chalk over his mouth that had been mostly wiped away by sweat. Though his brows scrunched, he did not seem surprised at Madoc's presence.

"Much has changed since you were last here," Tyber said.

"You included," Madoc answered. It wasn't a question, but Tyber nodded anyway.

"The circle is loyal to Anathrasa's cause. We spread her message to the people."

"What circle?" Madoc asked tightly, his gaze falling again to the boy. "What are you talking about?"

"All priests of the Father God are recommitted to Anathrasa now," Tyber said. "We are part of her circle. The circle of energeia. Of life. The Mother Goddess is the bringing back together of all things, and we serve her to avenge Geoxus. Her return signifies a rebirth for the world. In the ashes of Geoxus's death, the Mother Goddess has returned to bring peace."

A bitter taste filled Madoc's mouth. "Forgive me, Tyber, but this doesn't look like peace."

"Peace is earned in sweat and blood," Tyber answered simply. "You of all people should know that, Madoc."

Madoc cringed, thinking of the ribs he'd been able to count when he'd lived here. Of the home he'd found with the Metaxas after Cassia had found him on the temple steps.

"This boy fought bravely to serve the Mother Goddess," Tyber said. "His wound is beyond the work of our priests. If his lung collapses, there's nothing more we can do."

Anger mingled with pity, turning Madoc's muscles to lead. This boy didn't deserve to die—not for Anathrasa, or any god. He was only a child.

Madoc's mind shot to Ash, who had watched her mother battle in the arena for as long as she could remember . She'd always known Char's fate would be to kill or die. He wondered if Ash had been told the same thing—that she'd have to fight bravely to honor Ignitus.

How easily he'd once believed Geoxus deserved such glory.

"Dying honors no one," Madoc said bitterly. Anathreia pulsed inside him, angry. Hungry. He could feel the tempest of emotions all around him, and the growing demand inside him to draw from their souls and soothe his own fury.

Shame rose in his throat.

The boy gave a rattling gasp, drawing Madoc's focus to a point. He dropped the water bucket beside him, the contents sloshing out onto the dusty ground. He couldn't look away from the boy's face, twisted in pain, and his trembling blue lips. The pain and fear rose in ragged waves, and Madoc longed to take it to comfort him.

To drain him.

No. He didn't want that. He wanted to save the boy the way he'd saved Ash.

Ash.

He'd healed her once, in the arena after Elias had attacked her. He remembered, with a twist of his gut, how Hydra had said Ash had been dead before that.

He shook the thought from his head. If he was strong enough, he could save this boy. But when he'd healed Ash, he'd used too much energeia and nearly died from the exertion. He couldn't risk depleting his strength and failing his task with Aera and Biotus just to save one person—one *stranger*—even if he wanted to.

If he could tithe on someone the way Anathrasa had once told him, he could be strong enough to heal this boy with soul energy. If Madoc could tithe on the boy's pain, maybe he could make himself powerful enough to heal him.

Shaking, Madoc swallowed and focused on the beads of sweat across the boy's pale brow. He reached toward him with his consciousness, the air shivering between them like the sky over hot sand. The boy's pain was a beacon, as bright as any emotion he'd ever sensed.

I won't hurt you, he willed the child to know, but the boy only squeezed his eyes shut and held his breath.

"Madoc?" Tyber asked, worry thinning his voice. "What are you doing?"

Carefully, Madoc inhaled, pulling that bright spot of pain away from the boy, into himself, until he could taste the sour bite of it in the back of his jaw.

His anathreia sighed in pleasure. It didn't care what part of the soul he fed on as long as it was sated, and Madoc gasped, feeling as though he hadn't truly breathed in weeks.

He exhaled and sent a warm wave of soul energy over the boy. It blanketed him, soaking into his pores like rain into parched earth.

The boy shivered.

Tyber gave a surprised grunt. "Madoc, what is this?"

Madoc blinked, finding the arrow wound in the boy's shoulder now gone. The boy took a steady breath. He sat up, and when he rolled his arm in a slow circle, he smiled.

Then he launched himself into Madoc's arms.

Whispers rose around them, excited murmurs and heated spikes of energeia, but Madoc didn't care. He'd done it. He'd healed someone without hurting them and was somehow stronger than before. When he looked up, he saw his own shock mirrored on Tyber's face.

"How did you do that?" Tyber asked as the boy ran off, telling everyone he passed what Madoc had done.

"By tithing."

Madoc's stomach dropped at the sound of Anathrasa's voice. He stood at once, finding the Mother Goddess making her way through the courtyard, flanked by centurions.

"That is what you came here to do, isn't it? Save these poor people?" As she approached Madoc, a circle formed around them. Centurions and circle priests, but others too. The injured began moving toward them—limping, dragging themselves closer. The Earth Divine seemed eager to do whatever she might ask, but he also saw Air Divine and Animal Divine, battered from the fight, who clung to the back of the group with wary looks on their faces.

Madoc was staggered by the sudden fear of what Anathrasa might do. He tried to tell himself to be calm, that even after all he'd said to her, he could not risk severing her trust. But if she intended to harm these people further, he would not stand by.

"At your wishes, Mother Goddess," he said carefully. "I know you didn't want anyone to suffer needlessly in these games."

A muscle in her neck twitched, and he braced for her wrath. Instead, she smiled.

"Tithing?" Tyber was standing now, too, and looked to Madoc, confused.

"Children of Deimos, Lakhu, and Cenhelm," Anathrasa interrupted, raising her arms. "The Earth Divine's beloved Geoxus may have been rendered mortal by Ignitus and murdered by the God Killer, but all is not lost."

At the mention of Ash—the "God Killer," as Anathrasa had named her—Madoc's knees threatened to buckle. He could still hear Anathrasa screaming about what Ash had done as the Kulans dragged him out of the crumbling palace, the raging power of both gods inside him.

Rendered mortal by Ignitus. He didn't realize Anathrasa was spreading that lie, but it made sense. Better to have the people think only a god could tear down another god, rather than a mortal like them.

"My son has been returned to me."

Madoc's teeth pressed together. He couldn't believe she'd just claimed him as her son. His gaze spun around the courtyard, wariness rising in him as he gauged the wide-eyed responses of those who listened. He couldn't help thinking of when Petros had done the same in front of Geoxus, and the gladiators he'd been training with at Lucius's villa had suddenly wanted him dead.

Anathrasa walked a slow circle around him. "Geoxus made my son a champion to show the people of Deimos how he would fight for your honor regardless of lineage. The god of earth protected Madoc, as he protected me, in the hope that one day Madoc would be embraced by his father's people." Anathrasa paused, giving Madoc a strange look of fondness that made him want to crawl out of his skin. "When the God Killer and Ignitus's gladiators stole my son from us, I thought him lost. But he persevered, just as he did in the great arena. He returned to fight for Deimos."

The relief Madoc felt at healing the boy was replaced by a bolt of panic. For all he knew, these people thought he was an Earth Divine gladiator—that was what Geoxus had said when he'd chosen Madoc for the Honored Eight to fight for Deimos in the war against Kula. But now they knew he wasn't what he'd claimed.

Whispers rose, prickling a defensive shield over Madoc's skin. He felt as if he were balancing on the edge of a knife, torn between running and holding his ground. But the people were nodding now, looking at him with wonder in their eyes, and when Anathrasa touched his shoulder fondly, they didn't flee.

He couldn't tell if that was because they bought her story, or because of the centurions now blocking every exit of the courtyard.

"I've sent Madoc here to continue his fight on the streets of Crixion," Anathrasa continued. "With the people he was raised to defend."

Madoc shuddered at her acknowledgment of his street fights with Elias. Anathrasa may have accepted his claim that he'd come here at her bidding, but it hardly relieved him. What was she playing at? One word, and her centurions could slaughter everyone in this courtyard. There was a reason she was going along with his claim, and he doubted it had anything to do with mercy.

Tyber hastened a woman to the front of the circle. She leaned heavily against another fighter, unable to walk, and based on the limp swing of her ankle, it looked as if her leg had been broken below the knee. Her tight grimace of pain tugged at Madoc's wariness.

"Will you help her, Madoc?" Tyber asked.

"I . . ." Madoc stumbled back a step. He glanced to Anathrasa, who smiled.

"I've heard this is the perfect time for mercy," she said quietly.

It was a trick, but he didn't know what else to do. His palms were sweating.

"Energeia is an unending cycle of give-and-take. I created Geoxus, and Geoxus created this woman. These people are all part of anathreia, and all part of you. This is the unending circle."

He glanced to Tyber, to the smear of chalk over his mouth. *Her return signifies a rebirth for the world. In the ashes of Geoxus's death, the Mother Goddess has returned to bring peace.*

"Pretty sentiment," Madoc said. "But why did you create something just to abuse it? Is that all we are to you—pigstock to feed off of?"

Again, Madoc could feel that hunger rearing inside him, gnawing at his control.

His gaze dropped to the woman, to the fear and hope in her eyes. He could help her. Even if Anathrasa was telling him to do it, it wasn't wrong. It had been his idea first. That boy was alive because of him.

"You'll tithe on her, just as you tithed on that child. Just as you tithed on Petros," Anathrasa said quietly, coming close. "Just as you tithed on the gladiator Jann in the arena when you pulled out his self-control. You took Ash's pain that day, Madoc. Her broken parts. You fed on them and left her changed. *Better.* Everything you think you've done has begun with extraction."

Madoc's gaze shot to Anathrasa. He'd felt this with the boy—the pull and push of energeia, like completing a circle.

"If you can't take from the willing, how will you do what you must with those who refuse? With those who now know what you're capable of?"

The threat whispered over his skin like the promising touch of a blade. She could pretend as much as she liked that he was her beloved son, but they both knew the truth. He was only as valuable as his ability to drain Aera and Biotus.

"The circle is unending," Tyber said, and other priests behind him took up the chant in an eerie, low tone. "The circle is unending."

Madoc reset his mind to the task she'd ordered. He looked at the woman, knowing his mind had already been made up. He would help her, and if Anathrasa wanted Deimos to think it was her idea, that was fine. Maybe it would prove his loyalty to her.

She would never suspect that the air and animal energeia he'd promised her would go to Ash.

He closed his eyes, and tithed on the woman's pain, finding it easier to take the second time. Healing her was easier too, and when it was done, he felt the thrum of power in his veins.

"You're a gift." Tyber clasped his hands together. "A gift from the Mother Goddess!" He bowed at Madoc's feet, the same man who'd once freed him from an offering box and smacked him upside the head for trying to steal. He and the other priests started herding the injured into lines to be healed.

This was good, Madoc told himself, even though something about it didn't feel right. He accepted the woman's thanks, and when she kissed his hand, he didn't object.

Beside him, Anathrasa smiled.

"The circle is complete," she said.

TEN

ASH

"ASH!"

Ash jolted awake, fingers splayed and body awash with cold sweat before she even knew where she was. Pinpricks of blue fire lit on her palms, ready to throw, ready to fight—

The speckled beige of the petrified wood walls came into focus. The floor was clean now; all traces of Ash's blood were gone, the broken vines and razor leaves removed. Florus must have come in while Ash was unconscious. At least he wasn't forcing her to stay trapped with her own carnage.

At that thought, Ash turned and vomited against the wall.

"Ash! Are you in there?"

She blinked, dazed, wiping one hand across her lips and swallowing, throat dry and sour.

That voice—it wasn't Florus. Was she drugged again? Part of her soul squeezed with the longing to be hallucinating. She had seen Char. She needed her mother right now, or Tor, or—

A fist pounded on the outside of the box. "Ash! ASH!"

Something heavier crashed against it, but the walls didn't so much as rattle.

Ash flew to the corner where she'd heard the voice. "Tor?"

How had he found her? She didn't even know where she was—

A pause, then the crash came again. "I'm getting you out of here."

His calm, collected voice dragged a sob from the pit of her lungs, forcing her to shove her fist against her mouth, quelling her need to scream.

"You're here," she managed, and a tear fled down her cheek.

Of course he'd found her. Of course he'd save her.

Another crash came, followed by the sounds of something shattering outside. "Damn it—what is this made out of? My igneia's doing nothing, and I can't break it."

"Fossilized wood," Ash said. "Fire won't burn it."

"Damn it," Tor cursed again. The noises of his efforts stilled. "What do you see in there? Can you—can you do anything with igneia?"

He meant Ignitus's igneia, but he didn't say it.

"I tried, but it didn't make any difference."

Tor was silent a beat. "You have Ignitus's powers," he said. "Maybe you can move like a god too? Can you travel through igneia?"

Another sob built, but Ash willed it down. Oh, she was a god, more than even Tor knew. She touched the spots on her tattered sealskin suit where Florus's razor leaves had speared her.

"All right," she said. "I'll try. Where are we? What's out there?"

"We're in Itza," he said. "In Florus's palace."

Panic turned her cold. "Is he here?"

"Don't worry about him right now. We're alone."

Alone? Florus didn't have her under guard?

Or had Tor killed everyone to get to her?

It didn't matter—what mattered was that she would *not* lose her chance.

Ash braced herself on her hands and knees. The tart smell of vomit was choking her, but she willed her mind to focus on the gritty petrified wood, on the weight of her own body.

How did the gods travel through the very ether using their energeias? Was it just a thought? When she'd managed to hear through fire and see Igna, it had been almost an unconscious will, just a focus and a wish—

Ash's fingers curled against the wood and she willed herself to dissolve into flames. She thought of Tor, standing just outside this box. If they were in Itza, in Florus's palace, did that mean the room was made of the same kinds of vines that Florus had dragged everywhere? Ash should have asked before she risked burning a hole through the floor. Hopefully they were on solid earth—

That word echoed through her mind. *Earth.*

The floor rose under Ash's palm.

She rocked back, gaping at the wood. It stayed in a slightly curved position before melting back to become flush with the floor.

Eyes wide, Ash waited, expecting Florus to appear. He had to have done that.

"Ash?" Tor's voice was pinched. "Are you all right? What's happening?"

"I—I think I moved the wood." Ash stared at the spot. "But it isn't *wood*, not really. How—is this a trick? Where is Florus?"

"He's not here, Ash. So whatever happened was *you*. What was it?"

"The floor. I think I made it move."

Tor was silent, and Ash knew what look was on his face—calculating, thoughtful, focused.

"It's fossilized wood," he said, "so no hydreia, no igneia. But . . . it has geoeia."

"No." But Ash hesitated. "Florus told me I couldn't manipulate it because it was only plant, that he'd taken all other energeias out of it to fossilize it."

"Touch it again. Try whatever you did before. Maybe there's more to this petrified wood than what Florus said."

Her breath held, Ash leaned forward and spread her palm flat on the wood again. She focused on the rough petrified wood, the long, thin fragments forever frozen together. It was mostly floreia, plant life suspended in time; she felt that and could do nothing about it.

But there was more to it. Tiny particles clinging to the once-wood that made her gasp.

This fossil wasn't quite anything—because it was pieces of *everything*.

It was air. She breathed, but aereia wasn't hers yet.

It had once been fire, heat and pressure bearing down on these trees to transform them. But the fire was long gone.

And, most important, it was stone.

Yes, this petrified wood was mostly plant—but Ash could feel grains of stone buried in the petrified wood. They didn't rage strongly like igneia did, but the geoeia was there all the same, quiet and steady and strong.

"Geoeia!" She kept her eyes closed, her voice tight with relief. "Tor—it's geoeia!"

"Open this box," he told her. "You have Geoxus's power now? Use it. Remember how he moved—thunderous but intentional, heavy and grounded."

Ash's brow furrowed and sweat popped up along her hairline.

She couldn't treat geoeia like igneia, just as she hadn't been able to treat hydreia like igneia either. Geoeia was in no hurry. It was content to wait and watch, so much of what Ash was not.

On a deep inhale, Ash called out to the stone particles around her. Some responded, tingling to life at the pull of her geoeia. One type of rock was strongest, shards of it all around her, humming at her awareness.

"Quartz," she said, half to herself, half to Tor.

"Ah—Geoxus loved quartz. Remember? He'd drape himself in it. Rose and white and gray and black. Make it listen to you. You are its god now."

Ash seized that thought. *I am your god now.*

Quartz was like a long-beloved pet of the earth god, and it reacted to Ash, thousands of slivers of it vibrating in every strand of petrified wood.

Ash contracted her fingers, each one curling slowly, steadily. She was in no rush.

Then she *pushed*.

The floor of the petrified wood prison trembled, bucking Ash backward.

"Good, Ash!" Tor called.

She held her grip on the quartz, forcing every particle of it to expand outward, dragging the plant and air particles with it—

The room quivered, and cracked, and exploded apart.

Ash tucked into a ball as pieces of the petrified wood prison erupted around her. When the last one stilled, she yanked her hands down and blinked through the dust and debris.

Tor was upon her in an instant, scooping her to her feet and sweeping her into a bear hug. She clung to him, arms knotted around his neck, hanging off the ground with the force of his grip around her waist.

He set her down abruptly and looked her over from head to toe, noting the smears of dried blood on her body, her tattered clothing. "Are you all right? Where are you hurt?"

Ash scrubbed the heel of her hand across her eyes, clearing her tears. "I'm fine," she lied, because physically, she was. Everything else about her, though—her mind, her heart, her soul—teetered on the brink of collapse. But she couldn't break down yet.

The space they were in was a kind of holding cell. A low ceiling and wide floor were covered in velvety moss of the softest, calmest shade of hunter green, and steps at the edge of the room led to an open iron door.

"What's happening?" Ash looked back up at Tor. He was outfitted for battle, no surprise, and his eyes were bloodshot, likely from lack of sleep.

"How long have I been missing?" she amended, though she wasn't sure she wanted to know the answer.

Tor's face was grim. "Over a week."

Ash rocked backward. A *week*? Gods, what had happened in that time—to Hydra, to their building army, to Anathrasa's own growing power, but mostly, to *Madoc*?

In response to the questions on Ash's face, Tor's lips thinned. "Hydra has been here, looking for you. I followed just behind with a Water Divine crew. Hydra sensed this box by means of the water in these plants, but she had me come for you—she and Florus are in his throne room." Darkness raced across Tor's face. "Biotus is here."

Ash blinked, stunned. "What? Why?"

"He's demanding they surrender to Anathrasa and come with him to Crixion."

"Anathrasa said we had a month before she'd make a move!" But the plea sounded childlike in Ash's ears. Of course Anathrasa hadn't waited; likely she'd said that after the battle in the Apuit Islands just so she could get away.

A low growl rumbled in her throat. *Stupid.* How could she not have foreseen this? Believing in Anathrasa's promise of a timeline had made Ash soft, made her *weak*—

Tor touched her shoulders. "We all believed her, Ash." His face softened. "We're going back to the Apuit Islands," he said, and took a step away.

But Ash stayed in place.

"And leave Hydra to face Biotus?" Ash shook her head. "She's earned my help."

"She's a *goddess*, Ash. She can handle this."

"We need Hydra to prepare for our own attack. And I need floreia."

That made Ash's chest swell. With all she had endured at the plant god's hands, she was *not* leaving Itza without his energeia.

And with Biotus here, she would make him give her bioseia too. She would get it all.

Ash pushed around Tor. "Take me to them or go back to the Apuit Islands yourself."

"Ash." Tor said her name, a warning. "We're leaving. You need to rest."

Instinct screamed for Ash to listen to him. The gods were distracted now—she could get back on the boat Tor had used and flee to the Apuit Islands. She could get as far away from Florus—and Biotus—as possible.

Her insides clenched with a desperate wail that she managed to choke down. She wanted to get away. She was tired and hungry and sore, and she was terrified still—so terrified that she was shaking before she could stop herself.

Fury overcame her, pushed down for the past hours—days?—beneath her terror. But it leaped at her call now, raging and ready to obey and destroy.

"I need," she said, running a tongue over her lips, "*floreia*."

The world dissolved in orange and gilded blue, and before Ash could stop herself, she was an inferno. The moss-covered room faded around her.

Hydra. Go to Hydra.

The next thing she knew, Hydra was shrieking.

"What the—*Ash*?" Her voice was sharp with shock and fear, but Ash barely had the sense to focus on that.

She'd done it. She'd traveled through fire. She glanced down at her body. Alongside the melted divots she'd made in Hydra's ice platform, her sealskin suit was entirely burned up, leaving only her fireproof Kulan underthings.

And she was in Florus's throne room.

A towering ceiling arched over a long, narrow floor. Like that storage room, every surface was covered in moss, but peppered with trees and branches and vines—Ash expected to hear the chirping of birds or the buzzing of insects, but the silence around her was thick. Not the peaceful silence of a still forest; the tense silence of a held breath.

Hydra stood next to her, tears in her eyes, hands to her mouth. Her watery eyes shot from Ash to the two gods beside her, and she looked like she was only barely restraining herself from grabbing Ash in a hug.

But Florus was here, too, sitting on a throne made of one solid piece of tree trunk, formed and curved to his body. He stared at her, his expression blank; Ash appearing here was probably the last thing he'd expected.

Right now, Florus was the least of Ash's concerns.

The god of bioseia towered next to Florus, clearly someone who was used to his size being intimidating enough to make everyone cower. Pelts of various furs were bundled over one shoulder, not for warmth, but more like trophies of kills, and he wore only worn fur wrappings around his muscular thighs. His pale chest was cut with swollen muscles, veins bulged up his rippling neck, and his dark eyes were filled with intensity beneath thick braids of red-brown hair.

He looked as though he'd been in the middle of yelling. His dark eyes locked on Ash, like an animal sensing prey.

His intensity took on a seductive air and he made a show of slowly analyzing her. "Well, well. Anathrasa mentioned I might run into you—Ash Nikau, is it? The mortal who thinks she can defeat gods."

Ash returned his look with a grim smile. "I *have* defeated gods."

His facade tightened. "I didn't come here to waste breath on a mortal girl," he spat. He looked back at Florus. "I'm done playing games. I'm taking all of you to Crixion. You'd be smart to come quietly, or I'll have fun laying waste to your islands with my creatures."

Ash noted then that the room was empty except for the four of them. There were surely mortals living in Florus's palace—had they gotten to safety? She had to hope so.

"That's all this is—you playing Anathrasa's servant?" Hydra stepped closer, hands on her hips. "Does she make you fetch her robe for her, too?"

Biotus growled. "Careful. I've broken you once, I can break you again."

Hydra's nostrils flared, her cheeks reddening. Ash didn't know what Biotus had meant by that, but she was ready to fight if Hydra moved.

The water goddess needed no one's help, though. Hydra surged toward Biotus, rising high on a small wave of water that shot out of the plants at their feet. She was level with his soulless eyes. "We both know you did nothing but obey Aera's orders just as you're obeying Anathrasa now. You are a chained dog, Biotus, and I will drown you."

She reared a fist back, but vines shot up from the floor and twisted around her wrist.

Hydra whipped a glare at Florus, who was now standing.

"We'll go with you, Biotus," Florus said. "Willingly."

Biotus swung on him with a manic grin.

Ash watched the plant god, who was looking straight at her, and wavered, the healed wounds from his attack aching.

"If," Florus added, "you can defeat my champion."

Biotus's grin tightened. "Your champion? Ha! I'll rip any Plant Divine to—"

But Florus pointed at Ash. "Not Plant Divine. Her."

ELEVEN

MADOC

"I DON'T UNDERSTAND why everything must be white," Ilena muttered as a tight-lipped servant fastened a silver circle brooch to the front of her pristine white gown. She and Elias had been sent to Madoc's room to prepare for tonight's ball, a celebration Anathrasa had announced after Madoc's visit to the temple, ten days ago.

"It will be stained before they even bring out the feast," she continued, worrying her bottom lip between her teeth. "Someone's going to bump into me and spill their wine and this beautiful gown will be ruined."

Elias passed Madoc a knowing look as he adjusted the belt over his own white tunic. Ilena had been making subtle jabs about the ball all week. At first she'd been careful not to say anything in front of the palace staff, but as the days grew closer, she'd become bolder with her complaints.

It wasn't hard to figure out why. After Anathrasa's announcement in the temple, word had spread of her mortal son—a human with the healing power of anathreia. Hundreds of Deimos's most influential citizens would gather to celebrate his return tonight, and Ilena, who had loved Madoc as her own since he was six years old, was not taking the news well.

She wasn't alone, either. It was one thing for Anathrasa to announce their connection to a courtyard of injured fighters, but entirely another to stand before the most powerful people in Deimos and admit that Madoc had not been the Earth Divine gladiator they'd once called champion. He shuddered to think what the gladiators he used to train with would say about that. Given Lucius's bitter expression at the arena ten days prior, he doubted the old sponsor would be too happy about it.

He paced toward Ilena, the servant backing away wordlessly to give him room. There was little they could say without being overheard, so he simply hugged her close, calmed by the steel grip of her wiry arms.

"You look lovely, Mother." It didn't matter who claimed him, or why. Ilena would always be his true mother.

When he pulled back, her lip trembled.

"I don't like this, Madoc," she said. "I don't like being this close to her. Not after what she did."

Memory punched into Madoc's chest. Every moment around Ilena brought thoughts of Cassia, and usually he managed to focus on other things to avoid the pain. But this moment, Ilena's closeness brought memories of Cassia raging up through his mind and heart, the ache of missing her like a scar on his soul.

"I know," he whispered.

"If she touches another one of my children, I . . ." Her hands fisted in his tunic.

Madoc squeezed her shoulders.

"I know," he said again.

Elias cleared his throat, gaze tilting to the servant who entered the room with a box of hairpins for Ilena. It was safe to assume Anathrasa's staff was listening to everything.

"We've hardly seen you this week," he said, changing the subject as he sat on the edge of Madoc's bed. "Where have you been?"

"Everywhere," Madoc answered, aware of the guards just outside the door, and the woman now trying to twist up Ilena's unruly hair. "We went to the poorhouses in South Gate. Then the stonemason's quarter. The shelters along the Nien River. I've been ti—" He swallowed the word, not wanting to worry his family. "Healing people."

After Anathrasa had seen the way the people responded to his work in the sanctuary, she'd prepared a tour around Crixion to earn the people's loyalty. It was a chance for Madoc not only to gain her approval—something he'd need if she was going to be aware of him taking Aera's and Biotus's energeias—but also for him to continue to test their connection in small, subtle ways.

When her focus was elsewhere, as it had been when she'd been trying to tithe in the garden, he could harm her. A small pinch to his arm or rib had her absently rubbing the afflicted area.

When she was agitated, as she frequently became at her guards and servants, he could prick her heel by stepping on a small rock.

When she was pleased with his healing, and with the gratitude of the people, nothing he did got to her.

It had to be a matter of distraction. Tor had talked about being strong, protecting the people and things that mattered with the power he'd been given. Anathrasa had tried to wound him after he'd interrupted her tithing—a cut to her shoulder that he'd never felt. He'd been with Elias then at the palace barn. He'd felt like he had before all this began—when it was just the two of them, taking on the brutes of the city in a street fight.

He'd felt safe, because Elias had his back.

At the gladiator games, the thorns on the rose Anathrasa had grasped had cut his hand. He'd been anxious about the fighting. When she'd been angry at him on the docks, she'd attacked him and felt the slap.

Every time they hurt each other they'd been upset.

If that vulnerability made them weak, then he needed to guard himself against it. Keep calm. Keep his temper in check. If not, she could injure him.

Maybe even do more. Apart from tithing on the servant girl in the garden, Anathrasa hadn't shown an ability to fully use anathreia yet, but she might not need it. If she didn't trust him, she could keep him in line through pain.

"Healing people." Ilena's huff softened the lines that had formed between his brows, pulling him back to the room with his family. "Is it working? Are you . . ." She motioned toward him.

He forced a smile, pushing his experiment with Anathrasa to the back of his mind. "Yeah. I'm pretty good at it, actually."

"Of course you are." Her lips curved, but her eyes stayed wary.

"And the people? They're pleased to see you?" Elias's pointed look said he meant Anathrasa, not Madoc.

"Of course," Madoc said. It wasn't like he could object when centurions shoved a man who'd called him a traitor into a carriage or removed a group of sick women who'd declined his healing from a hospital in South Gate. He had to stay quiet and look the part of the loyal son to gain Anathrasa's trust. If the Mother Goddess seemed healthier with each healing, he noted it in silence and kept his mouth shut. He could no sooner risk her sensing his true intent than he could deny the people of Deimos—people Geoxus had ignored—the help they needed.

And it wasn't like he was hurting anyone. Quite the opposite—for the first time in his life, he was doing something that mattered. Not just winning a few coins in some street fight to donate to the temple, but making real change in people's lives. Taking the cough from a baby. Watching a woman stand straight after removing the arthritis from her spine. Fixing a man's hands that had been burned in the riots.

He wanted to tell Ash about it. All of it—the smiles and relief. The rush of anathreia in his veins. The limitlessness of the power he was finally learning to control. Anathrasa wasn't the only one getting stronger; he was too. But Ash hadn't made contact with him since his arrival almost two weeks ago—Hydra hadn't either—and that worried him. He knew she was busy learning her new powers and preparing for war, but he couldn't help feeling as though something bad was happening. Something he could have helped her with.

He told himself he was being lovesick and foolish. That this was the price of loving a goddess. When they did talk, he'd tell her about all of it—all except his link with Anathrasa. Ash would be too concerned, and with good reason. If she told Hydra, she might see him as a liability. Pull him away before he could do what he'd come to do.

He couldn't let that happen.

He'd promised to help her. He'd vowed to be worthy enough to stand beside her.

He couldn't do any of that if he was deemed dangerous to their cause.

"Well, I hope you're still being careful," Ilena cautioned. "The city is not safe."

Like Elias, she was talking about Anathrasa. He nodded.

"You need to get dressed, dominus." A man in white robes carried Madoc's evening attire into the room—a black silk toga and silver-strapped sandals. It was almost exactly what he'd seen Geoxus wear at events during the war with Kula, and he was sure that wasn't a coincidence. Anathrasa wanted the people of Deimos to know that her son was still one of them, and that their beloved fallen god was not forgotten.

"Of course you get to wear black," Ilena said under her breath.

He reached for the clothing in the man's arms, taking the thin silver crown with a small sphere in the center off the top. An unending circle. People in the city were always talking about that when he helped them.

As he traced the circle under his fingers, warmth tingled under his collarbone. There was something soothing about that circle. The shape of it. The meaning behind it. It was like his anathreia, ebbing and flowing. He hadn't truly understood the nature of energeia before now.

Before Anathrasa had taught him at the temple.

"Madoc," Elias said, tearing his focus from the crown. His brother and mother were staring at him, grim expressions on their faces. He looked down again at the circle, but the metal was now cold in his hands.

What was he doing? Anathrasa wasn't helping him do anything to get closer to the other gods. This crown was a leash tethering him to her, nothing more. He had the sudden urge to snap it in half.

Gritting his teeth, he placed it on his head. Another time, another place, Elias would have laughed at him, but tonight he only looked away. Grabbing the black toga, Madoc stepped behind a screen, removed his tunic, and slid into the fine black silk. It slipped over his shoulders, cascading down his back. It was difficult to close—the knot in the sash at his waist wouldn't stay tied. He had the sudden fear that it would loosen while he was at the party, and when the toga fell open everyone would see him naked.

Ash would find that very funny, he imagined. The thought of her laughter settled him. He would have given anything to hear it now.

"Dominus? The ball is about to begin." The man who'd brought his clothes shifted nervously beside the door.

With a sigh, Madoc stepped out. Elias gave a huff at the sight of his silk toga, but Ilena shot him a withering look as she approached and fastened the sash into a tight knot.

"Keep your eyes open tonight," she said quietly.

He wanted to tell her this ball didn't mean anything. Anathrasa would never be his mother. But too many ears were listening.

He smiled. "You do the same."

She kissed his cheek and strode to the door, where four palace guards escorted them down the corridor and stairs toward the heart of the palace. He sensed their consciousness as they walked—it was as easy as breathing, after all the pain he'd tithed. A charged fog of worry wrapped around each of them, hidden behind their stoic demeanors. He hadn't felt this in any of the guards before—they'd been pleased to serve the Mother Goddess, as eager as any of the palace staff. But now, he couldn't help wondering if the guards, like Lucius, were wary of him.

Madoc's brows pinched together. He didn't like the idea of people being frightened of him. He wasn't like Anathrasa—he didn't want war, or for people to be needlessly hurt. But how could anyone see that? All week he'd been telling the people his aid was her idea.

He wanted to explain to them that he was different, that he was here to help them, but he couldn't do that without betraying Anathrasa.

Unless she didn't have to know.

He could rid these guards of their fear the way he had freed the people in the city of their pain. They didn't have to talk about it. He could tithe before they'd even noticed. What was the harm in that? If nothing else, it was good practice for when he would take Aera's and Biotus's powers.

Stepping closer to the front two guards, he inhaled, reaching for the tight tendrils of fear around their chests. Then he simply sliced the bands around them and set them free.

The guard on his right, a lanky boy with a ghost of a beard, stumbled, then straightened. His steps were lighter, his shoulders drawn back. The guard to his left blew out a slow breath, his stocky arms relaxing at his sides.

Elias gave Madoc a strange look, but Madoc only smiled.

Music reached his ears, a flutter of strings and a warbling flute. The beat of a drum put a bounce in his step, and as he entered the courtyard, the buzz of emotion was as constant as the voices from the crowd. Respected Deiman men and women were in attendance, along with Aera's entourage—a flock of beautiful, fierce people in barely there wisps of gauze and lace—and Biotus's leather-clad warriors, who seemed content to feast and ogle the Air Divine in the absence of their leader, who still had yet to return after leaving the arena during the fight.

But beneath the pulse of mingling energeias, Madoc felt the steady, familiar consciousness of the Undivine. Not just servants, but also attendees. Merchants in the harshly woven tunics of the working class. Esteemed tradeswomen in dresses no finer than Ilena's had been when they'd lived in the quarter.

He was certain Geoxus had never held a party that mixed Divine and Undivine guests, and as his gaze landed on Anathrasa, seated on a white marble throne beneath the starry sky, something bent in his soul straightened.

He felt himself smile at her.

She smiled back.

Guilt ate at him. But this was what he'd always wanted, wasn't it? Divine and Undivine on equal footing.

And Anathrasa had brought it about.

He didn't want to be grateful for anything she offered. He knew it was wrong. And yet . . . he was glad.

Perhaps she wasn't as completely rotten as he'd thought.

When she rose, the courtyard fell silent, as if everyone had been waiting for her to speak.

"Our guest of honor has arrived," she announced, raising her hands in his direction. A gap opened in the crowd, and he made his way toward her, returning the smiles of those he passed. Each one made his tense shoulders ease a little more.

"You all know Madoc Aurelius," she called as he took his place beside her. As every eye moved over him, he felt the heat creep up his spine. "Champion of Deimos. Beloved by our great Geoxus before his untimely death. He is a hero in every sense of the word, and I have spent the week proudly watching him attend to the sick and injured of our city as he would a beloved member of his own family."

Madoc scanned the crowd, finding Ilena and Elias still where he'd left them, on the far end of the courtyard. He could see that, despite her earlier complaints about possible stains on her white dress, Ilena held a goblet of wine in her hand, one she was making quick work of finishing.

"It is with great honor that I present the pride of Deimos, and my heart—my beloved, too-long-estranged son, Madoc."

Madoc had expected to feel rage. Disgust. To force a smile to cover the scowl he was sure would twist his lips. But as the crowd erupted in cheers, he felt none of it. That strange tingling that he'd felt when he'd relieved the guards' wariness on the walk over had returned beneath his breastbone, and he was almost . . . relieved.

These people weren't afraid of him, as he'd thought the guards had been. They were pleased.

He wasn't sure what to make of that. Were they happy with how Anathrasa had shaped their world?

Was he?

A centurion was waiting nearby, and as Anathrasa excused herself to speak to him, the crowd overran Madoc. Some simply wanted to make his acquaintance or say they'd cheered for him in the arena during the last war with Kula. Others wanted to thank him for healing their sister, or their father. It was overwhelming—all the gratitude and emotion pooling around him.

But it was also . . . nice.

Living with Petros as a child, he'd watched these parties from the back rooms, hidden because of his Undivine status. He'd been cursed at, and beaten, and had fully embraced his future as pigstock when Cassia had brought him home to live with the Metaxas. But even when he'd fought alongside Elias, he'd known he was a fraud—using Elias's geoeia to trick the crowds.

Now people knew who he was. They knew who his mother was. And they weren't afraid or disgusted.

A buzz filled his brain, headier than any wine could provide. He wished Ash were here. She belonged in a place like this—

A cool hand grasped his. Madoc looked up into a Deiman woman's face, her dark eyes lined with kohl and her lips curved in a sultry smile.

"Does our champion dance?" she asked, but it was more of a command—before Madoc could reply, she'd dragged him out onto the floor.

The woman entwined her arms around his neck, her body flush with his. Madoc went rigid, but music thrummed from instruments in the far corner, and as other bodies joined the dance alongside them, his tension again dissipated.

Madoc's hands settled on the woman's hips and she swayed against him, pulling him along to the music.

Everyone around him was smiling. Enjoying themselves.

Happy.

Anathrasa had made them happy.

Maybe he should talk to her. Maybe she wasn't fully set on the cruelty he'd thought—

"Madoc. You're needed."

He turned to see Elias standing too close to him. The woman looked at him with a frown that turned into a quick smile.

"You could join us," she purred.

Madoc expected Elias to grin back at her. She was his type— pretty, flirty.

But Elias grabbed Madoc's forearm. "Not likely."

And he dragged Madoc off the dance floor.

"What is wrong with you?" Madoc stumbled after him until they were both standing beside one of the stout white columns, where tables held suckling pigs and baked fish.

"What is wrong with *you*?" Elias shot back. "What do you think you're doing out there?"

Madoc swallowed a knot of guilt, realizing he hadn't looked for Elias and Ilena since the announcement had been made.

"Jealous?" he asked, trying to lighten the mood.

"Hardly," Elias muttered. "I think Ash might feel differently if she'd seen you dancing like that, though."

Madoc blinked, his mind clearing. Ash.

He shook his head. He'd danced with that woman—and hadn't thought at all about whether or not he *should*.

"Half the guests are props, you know," Elias continued. "Anathrasa probably told that woman to dance with you. Centurions pulled most of the people here out of their homes to put on a show tonight. Threatened to throw them in jail if they didn't display the proper respect. Look at that man over there dancing. Have you ever seen someone less happy in your life?"

Madoc followed Elias's gaze to a man dancing alone beside the musicians. He didn't look like he was in dancing shape—sweat dripped from his ruddy face, and he favored his left side—but his smile was as broad as the half-moon overhead.

So broad, it appeared forced.

But as Madoc focused on him, he felt only gratitude.

"If he was unhappy, I would sense it," he said, a frown pulling at his brows. People were talking all around, masking their private conversation, but he couldn't be too careful.

"Because nothing gets past you, is that it?"

Madoc hesitated. He wasn't claiming to know everything. But he had power—one that magnified the emotions of other people and was getting stronger by the day. He'd know if people were pretending for his benefit.

He could tell for a fact that Elias felt no such pressure.

Madoc looked for Anathrasa, but she must have gone somewhere

She wrenched out of Tor's grip. "What if they can't? Igna isn't equipped for all-out war. No city in this world is! They have no defense."

Hydra's eyes swam with concern. "Tor's right, Ash," she whispered, and Ash hated the sympathy in her voice. "Our armies move out in two days—you have to think of the bigger battle. But—" She glanced at Tor. "We could move out early. Go to Igna's aid."

"How long will that take?" Ash snapped. Her panic hadn't diminished, even as Tor and Hydra seemed to be settling into this plan. "Days, at least? I can be there instantly!"

"Ash." Tor lurched closer to her. He had rarely taken this voice with her, one of disapproval and command. "It's decided. Too much is at stake."

"I can fix this! I'm *immortal.*"

Saying it ached. Ash hated that it ached; she hated the fear that squirmed in her chest at the memory of Florus and his prison and his razor leaves.

And because of that fear, she would act. Goddesses weren't afraid.

"Your mother thought she was invincible too," Tor said.

Ash flinched, jarred out of her offense long enough to wheeze a gasping breath. "This is different. You *know* this is different."

"Is it?" Tor's voice had taken on a brittle quality. Was he close to tears? "Ignitus pushed Char just as ferociously as you are pushing yourself. You don't rest, Ash. You don't slow down. You don't let anyone help you."

"You mean I don't let *you* help me," Ash shot back. She couldn't acknowledge what Tor had said—was she just like Char? A plaything of the gods, trained to exhaustion, used as bait to foster bloodshed? "And what about you? You sent that messenger off to Kula without even consulting me. I'm supposed to save the world, but you still act like I'm a child who has to live with the decisions you make."

"Someone has to look out for you," Tor said through his teeth. His eyes shot to Hydra, accusing. "Someone has to make sure you take time to *breathe*."

"I can't afford to," Ash managed, a whisper. "This is my fate now. I shouldn't even be alive! Do you realize that? I should have died in that arena in Crixion. This life I'm living isn't *mine*."

That was where her fear was coming from. Her self-loathing. Her manic need to keep moving: her life, her body, her powers, weren't *hers*.

Tor was right. She was just like Char, a vessel used by gods. She would push herself, push and push, until nothing was left and the world was saved.

She spun away, pressing the back of her hand to her lips. "If we fail to defeat Anathrasa, I can at least fail knowing that Kula is secure enough to fend her off. This isn't—"

"*Stop.*" Tor barked the word. It echoed off the high, empty ceiling of the throne room, reverberating into silence when Ash just stood there, gaping at him.

"This is what I'm trying to prevent, Ash," he told her. "This war we're fighting will ask too much of you, but you don't have to bleed yourself dry, because you aren't the only one fighting it! Your mother never forgot that she had a team supporting her—you, and me, and

Taro and Spark, and others who were there to catch her and let her rest. She would be ashamed of the way you're behaving."

Ash jerked back like he'd struck her. Her eyes widened, shock falling over her like snow.

Tor's own eyes went wide. He could see he'd gone too far. "Ash—"

She fisted her hands, her body coiled. She wanted to attack him. She wanted to throw geoeia, hydreia, floreia, things she knew he couldn't control or deflect. She wanted to pummel him with all the fury raging inside, her frustration at how he could be so harsh, so cruel.

She whirled away, fists at her temples, and screamed. She screamed until fire swept up over her body, lighting her up like the sun, and she channeled her toxic feelings into one thought.

Igna. Find Brand, she willed, begging her strange new powers to comply. *Igna. Save my country.*

Other thoughts danced at the edges of her mind that she actively wrestled down.

Tor thought she'd changed. Had she? Was she wrong to want to help Kula?

No. Gods, *no*. She wouldn't let Tor make her doubt herself. Too many factors in the coming battle were out of their control—the least Ash could do was control what factors she was able to.

Ash's fire unfurled, and she was in Igna.

SEVENTEEN

MADOC

FOR THE SECOND time since his return to Crixion, Madoc found himself at the grand arena, only this time his body was not his own.

He could hear the thunder of stomping feet and the roar of the crowd as he waited in the tunnel along the northern entrance to the arena. When a servant handed him wine, he drank against his will, and felt the warm liquid slide down his throat. When one of Anathrasa's priests raised a piece of chalk to Madoc's face, he knelt, his legs ignoring his internal plea to run, so that white could be smeared across his mouth in honor of him spreading her word.

He could not stop any of it.

But a small part of him—an exhausted, beaten-down part—still fought. Still felt like *him*, locked in the prison of his controlled body. Maybe it was his soul energeia that shielded him. Maybe Anathrasa wasn't as strong as she thought he was. Either way, he was still *aware*, and could feel her presence creeping in on the edges of his consciousness, though he didn't know how to stop it.

The longer he was under her control, the weaker he was becoming. Stretches of time had begun to go missing from his memory. He knew Elias was somewhere in the palace, but he couldn't remember where. He couldn't recall where Danon or Ava had gone, or where the Metaxas' room was, though he knew he'd been there. He couldn't even say how he'd gotten here, to the arena.

He was disappearing, losing his hold on who he was. If he didn't figure out a way to fight off Anathrasa, he would soon be gone completely. Then Elias, and Ilena, and Danon and Ava would be lost. Ash would fail, because he had failed in his mission to get her the power she needed. And once Anathrasa used him to take the power from Biotus and Aera, and probably also Florus, locked in his glass bubble, the entire world was at risk. With the power of four gods, it was just a matter of time before she defeated Hydra.

A roar outside shifted his attention to the archway, and the gate, now opening onto the golden sand. Anathrasa took her position before him, her gown brushing his arm as she passed. Aera squeezed in beside her, and Biotus beside Madoc.

Hazy memories slipped through Madoc's consciousness of the previous day, when Anathrasa had made him kneel before the gods of air and animal life and tell them his escape from Crixion after Geoxus's death had actually been planned, and that transferring Geoxus's and Ignitus's powers to Ash had been an accidental side effect of trying to kill her.

Aera had been praised for reporting Ash's presence to the Mother Goddess, and it was decided that Ash's appearance in the palace only could have been an attempt at vengeance.

To show his loyalty, Madoc had kissed their feet.

The arena gates opened, and Madoc followed the gods onto the sand, before a crowd screaming their praises. His face smiled, his arm waved, but he controlled none of it.

Behind him, a red glass ball—the case holding Florus—slid into the light. The crowd hushed as it moved toward the center of the arena, carried by rolling grains of sand that the Earth Divine masters on either side manipulated with geoeia. When Anathrasa stopped and stepped beside it, Madoc's head turned, giving him a view of the youthful god and his wide, desperate eyes.

It had been almost a week since Madoc had first seen him in the dungeons. How long Florus had survived in his bubble before then, Madoc didn't know.

With a glance at the goddess of air, Anathrasa began to speak.

"People of Deimos." Her voice was not a shout, but barely a whisper. It came on a breeze, blown from the palm of Aera's hand. "And visitors from our beloved sister countries, Lakhu and Cenhelm. I have returned to guide you in Geoxus's absence. To unify our world, which has too long been at war."

Madoc's head bowed in reverence, along with the rest of the audience.

"But there are those who would oppose us."

A murmuring rose from the stands.

"Florus lured our allies from Cenhelm to join him in Itza under the guise of peace," she lied smoothly. "But along with the goddess of water, he attacked Biotus and his warriors." She paused as the murmuring grew to a dull roar and the wind carrying her words strengthened. "Florus is a traitor. A danger to our world. And I will tear down anyone who threatens to destroy our unified vision of peace and prosperity for both Divine and Undivine, be they god or mortal."

With this, the people cheered. *Madoc* cheered. But inside, he withered.

Anathrasa placed her hand on the red glass case. "As I speak, Hydra readies her army for battle. But whatever the goddess of water may bring to our shores will not be enough to withstand the fierce honor of Deimos."

Madoc's hands rose and clapped along with the spectators. His mouth shouted in approval that Anathrasa was their leader, the Mother Goddess, while his mind revolted at the words. Behind him, the Earth Divine knelt, pressing their hands into the ground and lifting the red prison to hip level on a column of sparkling sand.

"And let anyone else who might consider treason be warned what awaits them if they challenge the Mother Goddess. All energeia once belonged to me, and I will take it back from anyone who attempts to use it against me." She turned to Biotus. "Break it."

With a grin, he stepped to the thick glass and, with a roar, wheeled back and struck it with a hammering fist. The glass shattered in a spray of red dust, and though Madoc didn't move, he could feel a dozen pointed shards nick his face and arms.

The god of plants gasped, a horrible rattling sound, and his chest expanded with the first full breath he'd taken in days.

"Now," Anathrasa said.

Madoc didn't realize she was talking to him until his body turned toward the remains of the ball, and his hands reached over the jagged siding.

"Yes, my goddess," his mouth said, even as his mind screamed, *No!*

It was too late. Anathreia rose inside him like a torrent of wind, ripping through his soul, his flesh, his muscles. The hunger was sudden, absolute, and when he inhaled, he could taste earth and wood on the back of his tongue.

"Stop," Florus whispered, reaching for Madoc, but the god was weak from his days without breath, and the green branches that sprouted from his palms quivered, and then shriveled and turned black. With a guttural cry, Florus arched backward, chest lifted and toes pointed. Every muscle in his small body flexed to the point of snapping. His eyes bulged, staring desperately at the sky.

Madoc tried to shake himself free of his hold on the plant god. He tried to turn his shoulders, his head, any part of him away from the god of plants, but it was no use. Revulsion coursed through him, as potent as his own need. *I'm sorry*, he screamed silently. No one could hear.

Next to Madoc, Aera gave a quick gasp. From the corner of his eye he could see her hands fist. A wave of uncertainty peeled off her, but he couldn't make sense of it. She'd been the one to trap Florus in that bubble, breathless, in the first place.

She knows this could be her, he realized. Maybe he should have pitied her, but he didn't.

"More," Anathrasa ordered. "It was mine to begin with. It will be mine again, now."

Madoc reached deeper into Florus's soul, pulling at the twisting vines and roots of his energeia and yanking them free. Madoc could feel the pressure of the foreign power crushing him from the inside out—its heavy, living force sliding through his veins. His heartbeat pounded in his ears. His vision began to shake.

Florus collapsed in a heap, his breath shallow.

Madoc staggered. He blinked, and when he opened his eyes Anathrasa was before him. Her lips tilted in a smile as he took her hands, and maybe it was weak, but in that moment he longed for her help. Anything to ease this incredible burden.

How had he ever thought he was strong enough to help Ash?

"Complete the circle," she told him.

Her hands squeezed his, and when he exhaled, she siphoned the energeia out of his body. The screaming in his head quieted, the twisting of his joints released. He inhaled sharply, feeling a cool flood of relief. Too late he tried to cling to some small bit of floreia—enough to save for Ash—but it slipped away, drawn into Anathrasa's soul like a sprout opening to the sun.

Anathrasa sighed, her eyelids fluttering. When she smiled, not a single wrinkle lined her mouth. Her skin was flushed and smooth. Her hair was full.

"Thank you," she said quietly.

She released Madoc's hands, and he faced the crowd, disgusted with himself. Horrified by what he'd just helped her do.

"Itza belongs to Biotus now," Anathrasa told the people of Deimos, her voice carried again on the wind. The god of animals raised his chin and pounded his massive chest with one meaty fist. "The Itzan people are his, just as Hydra's Apuitians will soon be Aera's."

At this, the goddess of air lifted her hands and sent a blast of cool air across the stands, ruffling clothes and hair, delighting the crowd.

This was what Anathrasa had promised them, Madoc realized. This was why they sided with her—for power, for more people and more land.

They had no idea she intended to strip it from them the same way she had Florus.

"As for the god of plants, he belongs to Deimos now," Anathrasa finished. "Let's see how he fares among our fiercest fighters. The first one to bring me his heart will have their likeness cast in gold outside this arena."

No. Madoc glanced at the god of plants, so young and now so fragile, pushing himself to his knees in what remained of the shattered glass sphere. Madoc couldn't help thinking of the boy who'd been shot by an arrow at the first games—the child he'd healed at the sanctuary. He could offer Florus no such mercy now.

The Earth Divine who'd moved the glass sphere into the arena now exited the way they'd come, but Madoc and the gods did not follow. Before him, Anathrasa raised her arms, hands clenched, and the ground began to rumble. A moment later, dark roots burst from the sand, braiding together in a tightly woven staircase the stretched from the ground straight up to the viewing box.

The crowd screamed their approval.

Hand in hand, Anathrasa and Aera climbed, with Biotus just behind them, and Madoc trailing by a few steps, until they reached the marble ledge of the box and were helped down by their servants.

"Isn't that twig-armed grunt your brother?"

Madoc followed Biotus's pointing finger down to the sands, where more than thirty Earth Divine had emerged from the western gate to fight. Near the back of the cluster was a man in a red tunic, marked across the chest with an embroidered silver circle.

Brother—the word was only a whisper in Madoc's mind.

Madoc frantically realized that he'd nearly forgotten Elias. His brother was wearing the same clothing he'd worn to the party where Anathrasa had introduced Madoc as her son. How had Elias gotten here? The last thing Madoc remembered was searching for Ilena with him.

Ilena. Where was their mother now? And Danon, and Ava?

He couldn't lose his grasp on himself. He needed to hang on. To remember. To *fight*.

Elias wasn't holding any weapons, nor was he wearing any armor. His head moved, eyes roaming from his Deiman competition to the Air Divine filtering in from the opposite side of the arena and the horde of Biotus's warriors now spilling through the front gate. They'd brought more animals this time. Giant cats. Bears. Even wolves.

The ships from Cenhelm must have arrived, Madoc thought bleakly, remembering how few Animal Divine had fought in the last celebration. There were a hundred of them now, huge men and women with glinting steel weapons and leather armor.

In the center of it all, a small mortal who'd once been a god lifted a shard of red glass to defend himself.

Madoc looked again for Elias. *What have I done?*

"A Deiman not loyal to my mother is no brother of mine," he told Biotus.

The god of animals snorted, then gave a laugh. He slapped Madoc on the back hard enough that he nearly went over the railing.

"Then he'll be meat for my warriors," Biotus said. "But not before they take my brother's heart."

Madoc's consciousness trembled with what rage he could still muster. He hoped Anathrasa did use him to drain Biotus, just so the god would suffer.

Not yet, Anathrasa warned in his head. *We still need the loyalty of the Air and Animal Divine to defeat the water goddess and her little pet.*

When Madoc pictured Ash, he could feel Anathrasa's laugh rumble through his chest.

Below, Elias crouched, picking up a fistful of sand and rubbing it between his hands. He was passed by another fighter, who offered a quick word before moving on. He looked the part of a Deiman gladiator—his armor fit well, and he was big enough to fight off any of the Animal Divine.

Lucius, Madoc realized. He remembered the trainer's disgusted expression at the last fight. Maybe he'd decided he couldn't stand by and had entered the games himself.

Maybe, like Elias, he'd been forced into the ring.

"There's my little soul stealer." Madoc felt two hands slide around his waist, and a female body press against his back. He breathed in and was overwhelmed by Aera's floral scent as she rested her chin on his shoulder. "Finally learned your place, have you?" She giggled. "What you did down there was quite impressive. I'm glad you didn't get the chance to do it to me."

His eyes lifted to the shattered red prison, and disgust reeled through what remained of his soul.

"Never, goddess," Anathrasa said through his mouth.

Aera smiled against the back of his shoulder. "How about a wager? If a Deiman wins my brother's heart, I'll come to your room tonight. But if it's a Lak?" She nuzzled her nose against the side of his neck and, inside, he trembled in powerless rage. "You'll come to my room, lover."

Push her away, he told himself. *Tell her no.*

His body didn't listen. He covered her hands, splayed across his chest, with his own, and lifted his chin so she could kiss his throat.

She likes you, Anathrasa whispered. *That will serve us well when we drain her.*

The games began with the blare of horns and a wave of black and silver flags, and soon all the warriors were struggling to get to Florus in the center of the arena. The boy was fighting them off with handfuls of dirt and a spear he'd taken from someone, but the effort was weak and inconsequential. He disappeared beneath a crowd of bodies, only to be tossed into the air by a powerful, aereia-controlled burst of wind. When he landed, a Cenhelmian took him to the ground, but they both were soon knocked aside by an earthquake sent by one of the Earth Divine fighters. Madoc tried to follow Elias, but his eyes kept roaming, controlled by Anathrasa, who was seated on a white marble throne at the back of the viewing box.

The next time Madoc saw Florus's body, it was being thrown through the air, limp and bloody. A Lak fighter screamed that she had his heart, but she was immediately speared through the chest by an Animal Divine.

Soon Florus's body was forgotten, and the game became who could hold the heart of a god.

Biotus shouted for his warriors to draw blood, and they did not disappoint. Four Animal Divine warriors surprised a group of Aera's fighters, rallying around the bloody heart with a net, trapping them to the ground. Taking advantage of the move, Lucius buried them in a wave of gravel, only to be blown against the perimeter wall by another Lak man.

The fighters appeared to be attacking as though their lives depended on it. There was no sign that Anathrasa was controlling them, but if she could take over Madoc's body, she could do the same to others. Make divine men and women more skilled and powerful with their energeia than they'd ever been.

A new terror pressed down on the edges of his consciousness.

Finally, Madoc's gaze returned to Elias. His brother's back was against the wall—a choice, Madoc realized, that was serving him well defensively. Those who attempted to attack were forced to come straight at him, and Elias warded them off in droves with tidal waves of gravel and dust.

Stay standing, Madoc willed him. He didn't know if Anathrasa would end this battle before people died again, or if those who'd lost would be healed. He suspected Elias would not be so lucky. With another shock of helpless terror, Madoc remembered the first-round winners from the first games in the palace dungeon, and feared Elias would meet the same fate.

"My fighters still hold the heart," Aera sang. Her cool lips slid down the tendons of his neck, and he was revolted again by the pleasure she took in her brother's brutal death. "I think that means I'm winning."

Madoc could feel competitiveness take him by storm. It wasn't his choice, but rather Anathrasa's enjoyment whipping through his blood. He wanted nothing to do with these games, but as Lucius knocked down two Cenhelmian fighters in one battering swing of his spear and stole the heart for himself, his excitement grew, and soon he was cheering along with the other gods.

You're enjoying yourself, Anathrasa told him.

His body turned back to face the Mother Goddess. Smiled.

You're *enjoying this*, he wanted to respond. But she either didn't hear him or didn't care.

And after a moment, he didn't care either.

EIGHTEEN

ASH

IN IGNA, ASH was near the harbor. She faced the bulk of the city, its sprawling obsidian structures speckled with windows in a rainbow of hues. The sky was gray with low-slung clouds and the air had a twist of humidity, thick like a storm had come or was about to come.

She was relieved—only for a breath.

Then grief hit her, a piercing feeling of absence: Ash hadn't been to Igna since her mother died.

She had the sensation of being underwater again, her senses muted as though she was submerged, noises muffled to a dull roar, her breath a grating rumble alongside the thudding of her heart. Each blink was languid and painful, flashing with memories she had been able to ignore for several weeks.

Char taking her to Igna's markets. Idly shopping with her, whiling away time and money on trinkets and smiles to combat the horror of Char's life as Ignitus's champion.

Char and Tor arm in arm as they walked along the waterfront. Her mother, smiling, her teeth a blinding white and her face soft.

Char trying a dish at a tavern, then spitting it out and laughing through tears at how spicy it was.

Everywhere, Ash saw her mother. Everywhere, Ash heard her voice, her all-too-rare laughter.

She hadn't felt Char's absence so strongly since she'd watched her mother die.

Wheezing, Ash stumbled around and faced the sea.

Everywhere, Kulans were running. Innocent citizens were fleeing in terror; warriors, their bodies awash in flame, were positioned strategically around the bay.

And out in the water, charging through the surf, were half a dozen Deiman ships.

The breath went out of Ash's lungs.

Around her, screaming voices pushed through her fog.

"Ignitus!" They had seen her fire. They had watched her appear in a flare of blue and gold. "Ignitus! Our god has risen!"

But they turned, and they saw *her*, not Ignitus, and the cheers became confused cries, and Ash couldn't deal with an explanation right now.

"I haven't been to Kula in decades."

Ash glanced over her shoulder to see Hydra behind her, shifting out of her water form.

"I'm not leaving Kula with you," Ash told her.

Hydra locked eyes with her. "I know."

That was it. Just acceptance, and Ash realized with a jolt that Hydra had come to help her. Or at least to make sure Ash didn't get herself irreparably hurt.

Ash nodded, surveying her surroundings. She and Hydra were on the path in front of a naval building on the largest military dock. As she turned to leap up the steps, a man shot out of the doors and drew up short at the sight of her.

"Ash?" Brand's face contorted. Ignitus's former champion looked behind her, to Hydra, and his frown deepened. "How did you—"

"What is happening?" Ash demanded.

He took the steps two at a time to stand in front of her. The last she had seen the cocky champion, he had been gaunt and stricken by Ignitus's death. That, and his short time in Kula explaining Ignitus's fate, had seemed to mature him. The flighty confidence Ash had hated in him was gone. A rough line of stubble made him look unkempt and tired. He was wearing Kulan reed armor, but it was dented and well-used, not ceremonial in the slightest.

"Deimos sent a message ahead of their ships," Brand told her. "They've come to take the Fire Divine to fight in Crixion's arenas. It's a *privilege*"—he spat the word—"and the winners will become part of the Mother Goddess's circle. Whatever that means."

"She sent centurions to capture Kulans," Ash said, half to herself. Just as Anathrasa had sent Biotus to take Florus.

"Not just centurions," Brand said.

Ash frowned.

He pointed at the ships. "If you look through a spyglass you'll find rows of armed gladiators on those ships. If she's taking Kulans to fight in her arenas, and using the victors—"

"She's building an army of gladiators." Hydra was the one who finished the thought. Brand gave her an odd look, like he recognized her but couldn't place her, and nodded grimly.

"An army made of the fiercest fighters in the world," Ash said. She felt ill. "Such a force would quell any unrest."

Hydra blew out a breath. "Anathrasa would have complete control of the world."

Ash faced the sea, the coming ships. Anathrasa may have gotten Deimans, Laks, and Cenhelmians to obey her, but no Kulans would join her army.

Brand echoed her unspoken sentiment. "The Mother Goddess seems to think she can *make* Kulans bow to her, but after what Geoxus did to our god, any supporter of Anathrasa will find only bloodshed here!"

He shouted the last words and punched a fist into the air. All around him, frantic warriors and cowering citizens alike responded with a cheer.

But Ash watched Brand's face. His eyes showed none of the conviction in his voice.

He sobered and bent closer to her. "Many of our warriors deserted when they learned of Ignitus's death," he whispered to her. He kept his focus on the passing soldiers, the ones who were scrambling to set up a defense as the Deiman ships drew ever closer. "They fled the city, seeking shelter in the wilderness outside Igna. They think the world is ending."

He paused, eyes sliding to her in an unspoken question. *Is it?*

"We know how to defeat Anathrasa," Ash told him.

Some of the tension in Brand's face subsided. He cast his eyes to Hydra, this time with purpose. "Did you bring help from the Apuit Islands? Or Itza?" He looked down at her again, confused. "How did you know we were in trouble?"

"I heard you," Ash said. "And I did bring help. This is Hydra."

Brand's mouth fell open. For a moment, his body twitched as though he might drop to his knees in reverence.

But Hydra waved him off. "Ash is more powerful than I am."

Brand's jaw went slack. "What?"

Ash didn't respond. She was still watching the ships and could barely make out moving shapes, rocks shifting and lowering as centurions—gladiators—prepared their attack.

Such an army would destroy this city at Anathrasa's command and drag Kulans into her war, to be drained of their igneia if they refused to fight for her.

Ash would die before she let Anathrasa touch any of her Kulans. Because they were just that—*her* Kulans, *her* compatriots.

Anathrasa would not take anything else from her.

"Hydra," Ash said, taking slow steps toward the water. "With me."

Brand followed them. "Where is the army? Who did you bring? We have soldiers stationed around the—"

"Call them back," Ash told him.

"What? Are you insane? We can't leave the bay undefended."

"Call them back," she said again. She cut her eyes to him, and the strike of her glare rendered him silent. "Clear the bay. Now."

Brand faltered a step, but he nodded and started shouting the order. It caught, tentatively, and Ash watched the small specks of Kulans peel back from the water. Or maybe she just sensed it through her connection to them, the thrumming of her igneia beating stronger now that she was in Kula, surrounded by Kulans.

"You'll need to get closer," Hydra told her. "You'll have more control of your energeias if you can see what you're attacking and where."

Ash continued walking, closing the distance to the shore. When she reached the lapping water, she paused, whipping a look to Hydra. "*I'll* have control? You're not going to help?"

Hydra had matched her pace and was next to her. "You wanted to save your country? You're a god now. So get out there and act like the god of Kula."

Ash's hands shook. Blame was heavy in Hydra's tone. If something happened to Ash or Hydra—if Anathrasa captured them or injured them somehow—it would be Ash's fault, because she hadn't waited, because she was impetuous.

She was also a goddess, and Kula was hers, and she would defend it.

Ash started walking again. Small pillars of water lifted to meet each footstep as she headed out into the bay.

The lead Deiman ship had just reached their waters.

Ash stopped a few paces back from its bow. Hydra was beside her, hovering on a similar pillar.

A man onboard saw them.

"Turn around and sail back to Crixion," Ash told him.

The centurion laughed. "Not likely."

He noted their position, standing on the water. He noted Ash, especially, smoke like steam gathering around her and flames licking her face.

Fear broke his confidence with a flinch.

"Leave Kula," she said. "Now."

"We have our orders. Kula's god is dead. The Mother Goddess wishes to bring his lost children into the fold of her guidance—"

"I will kill the Mother Goddess," Ash promised. "Just as I killed your god of earth."

That made the centurion's unease shift into anger. "God Killer! We will not leave until all able-bodied Kulan warriors have surrendered to the superior might of Deimos. We will not leave until we have taken from you what you took from us tenfold!"

"Are you going to let him keep talking?" Hydra whispered. *"Attack."*

Ash felt the flames on her arms waver.

"High ground," Hydra prodded. "Rise up."

Attack. High ground. These were all things Ash knew from her arena training. How to fight. How to *win.*

She lifted her arms and a thrashing wave carried her into the air. The commotion on the Deiman ships paused as everyone watched her.

She saw the rows of immobile gladiators now. Their heads lifted as one, their eyes on her empty and unseeing.

Ash realized with a jolt of horror what Anathrasa had done. She was building an army of warriors wholly given over to her control. This was what she wanted from the world—utter, explicit obedience.

"The circle is unending," the gladiators began to chant. "The circle is unending. The circle—"

Panic swelled in Ash.

"She did this before." Hydra's voice came from the droplets of water on Ash's ears, the raging waves thrashing beneath her feet. "Forced people to obey her. It's disgusting."

"She's stronger than we thought." Ash felt sick.

"Steady. You can do this. They know you can control hydreia now. Attack where they won't expect it."

Yes. Ash could do that. The unexpected.

She called all manner of ocean plants up from the depths, and they squirmed and writhed around the thick hulls and up the wooden rails. The igneia was still alive within her, even as she used floreia. Fire sparked off the tips of her hair and the ends of her fingers and glowed from every muscle on her body. Water spewed foam and froth around her as it held her aloft, and the plants that scurried to do her bidding grew in great, powerful surges of green life.

"There are rocks on the ships," Ash said to Hydra, and she laughed. Didn't these stupid mortals know who they had come to fight?

"Get to them," Hydra told her, "before the Earth Divine can use them. Call on plants and fire also—I'll handle the water."

"I thought you weren't going to help?"

Hydra gave Ash a sardonic look. "Don't make me change my mind."

Ash laughed again. "Kula already has a god, Anathrasa," she told the Mother Goddess. She knew Anathrasa wasn't there, but she was listening through these people, and Ash's voice resounded out of the rocks onboard every ship. "And I am Deimos's god too."

Ash clapped her hands together.

The plants slammed into the wooden planks of the ships, snapping them like twigs. Hydra sent water gushing over the rails and pouring into the cracks. Ash called on flames to lick at rope and barrels, bright bursts of light and heat that singed hands and served as warnings. And when the centurions cried out and dived for their precious rocks, Ash used those, too; she lifted every stone into the air and crushed them to shards that she then showered down on the Deimans.

It wasn't enough. Ash pushed the shards of rocks outward, flinging them like projectiles. They met skin, dug deep; she pushed, the shards burying at her command as screams rose—

"Ash!" Hydra's voice pitched high. "Ash, *stop*! You don't need to kill them!"

"They'd kill my people!"

"Stop," Hydra pleaded. "Stop the bloodshed. Let them live."

Ash could so easily sink these ships to the depths of the bay.

But she felt Hydra, felt her intention tug gently on Ash's control of hydreia. The goddess would always control water, even while Ash manipulated it.

With a snarl, she relented.

The ships were damaged, not destroyed. The crews sprinted for order, but there was no order.

There was only Ash.

She had spared the crews' lives. She had given them a second chance. That was more than Geoxus had let his gladiator give to Char. More than Ignitus had given to Rook after his son had died. More than Anathrasa had given to Madoc. That was more than any god ever gave to any mortal, and for that, Ash would be known not only as God Killer, but Merciful.

"This world does not belong to you, Anathrasa," Ash said. "Ready your armies. I am coming for you."

She lifted her arms higher, pulling the wave she stood on up, up, up, before she dropped all her weight and plummeted into the water. The force of her surge propelled the Deiman ships hard and fast for the open, stormy waters of the Hontori Sea.

The bay churned and rocked. Ash hovered in it, watching the ships to make sure they wouldn't try to charge back. But their crews scrambled to turn sail, fighting the cracks Ash had left in their vessels.

Only the gladiators were not panicked. Ash thought she saw them smile.

Ash turned to Hydra, expecting to see the water goddess looking as triumphant as Ash felt.

But the water goddess scowled at the horizon.

"You look like you think we lost the battle," Ash said, gasping as her body trembled with the aftershocks of the fight. "Look what we did! We—"

Hydra lifted her hands. "We protected Igna, but at what cost? You were a threat to Anathrasa before, but you are deadly to her now. And with your Madoc currently in Crixion . . ."

Ash recoiled. Her body still hummed with the power she had unleashed, a ripe, resilient flurry that made her feel . . . *everything*.

Every particle of sand on the shore. Every thudding heartbeat in the crowds watching her. Every sparking flame in the hands of the Kulan warriors. Every splash of water.

Everything but the fear she should feel, knowing she had endangered Madoc even more.

It should have consumed her, that fear. She should have been frantic to talk with Tor and find some way to salvage it.

But all she could think of was whether or not Madoc had gotten aereia and bioseia yet. Had he given them to Anathrasa, or was he fighting her off to save them for Ash? She wanted those missing pieces. How much swifter would her defense of Kula have been if she had been complete?

"He'll be fine." Ash looked up at Hydra. "He'll get the other energeias for me—"

Hydra's eyes narrowed. "That's it? You just made your lover even more of a target, and you don't have any reaction? Any guilt?"

"I defended what's mine!" Ash whirled, a wave cutting up around her. Fire streamed along each arm, holding there in threatening flickers.

From the shore, a chant started. Ash thought she heard Brand's voice kick it up first.

"Goddess! Goddess!"

"Do you hear them?" Hydra snapped. "Do you hear what they're calling you?"

"Goddess!" the Kulans cheered. "Goddess!"

"How does that not terrify you?" Hydra's eyes teared. "Look at the gods of this world. Look at what has happened to them. All of them, all of *us*, are murderous and cruel. This is what you want to become?"

"Maybe it's what I already was," Ash said. "Cruel. Selfish. Untethered. Maybe this power just set me free to stop cowering and embrace that I've had this strength in me all along."

Hydra shook her head, tears clouding her eyes. "This isn't strength, Ash. There can be power in unbridled selfishness to a degree, but you need to learn those limits."

The water goddess sank into the bay, a ripple of sea-foam on the surface. Ash stared down at it, her shoulders heaving and her muscles aching while the crowd chanted *goddess* all around her and the sky raged a stormy gray above.

She screamed, and fire shot out from her hands into the roiling sky, and she fell into the flames.

NINETEEN

MADOC

MADOC'S CONSCIOUSNESS REVIVED in stages.

A breath of cool air on the balcony in his room.

A bite of sour yogurt with breakfast, Aera giggling with Biotus, all at a table together. Panic seized his mind when he realized he'd lost time—how long had it been since the fight? Where was Elias? Had he been injured?

The last he recalled, Aera had made a wager about whose people would win—a Lak or a Deiman—and whose room she and Madoc would later meet in. He prayed he hadn't followed through on that bet. That Anathrasa hadn't let him be used in that way.

Before he could find out more, he grew foggy and slipped away.

Days passed—he could feel them ticking down in his mind like notches in a wall, though he could never grab hold of any one moment long enough. He was so tired, drawn so thin.

He rested. He didn't know what his body was doing.

And then—the low light of a sheltered corridor, leading toward a stairway. He had to duck as he walked down the steps so he didn't hit his head on the ceiling. He felt as though he was waking from a long sleep and couldn't quite get his bearings.

He was following Anathrasa.

He became alert in a rush.

He was conscious. He would *stay conscious—*

Yes, stay awake, my son, Anathrasa told him. *I want you to watch this.*

He tried to lash out at her. He tried to fight—but fog overcame him and he started to slip away again. He relented, panicked.

She was still in control.

Where were they going?

"To prepare our winners."

Madoc didn't have to see Anathrasa's face to know she was gloating.

Would they tithe on them? He couldn't even summon the energy to be disgusted. He was so tired from fighting her. It was like standing in a room with Aera, feeling the breath pulled out of his lungs.

At the bottom of the stairs, they turned, the path twisting into a broad hall. The fighters were crowded in cells, lined with metal bars easily manipulated by the Earth Divine, but reinforced by a line of soldiers standing shoulder to shoulder. A quick glimpse told Madoc these people suffered from the same affliction that those in the palace dungeons had—their eyes were blank, staring mindlessly ahead. Their skin was paper-thin, showing shadows of sinew and bone beneath.

There was something very wrong with them, and Madoc

wondered if that's what would happen to his body should Anathrasa be left unchecked in his brain.

The winners were being held like prisoners. They'd suffered a few scrapes and bruises but seemed all right overall. Circle members in white robes tended to them, carrying jars of water slung over their shoulders.

Elias? He tried to look inside a cell, but his head wouldn't turn the right way. He could only catch sight of Lucius, sneering in his direction, arms threaded through the metal bars. Madoc could see the dark stains on his hands and remembered with another turn of his stomach that he'd last seen Lucius raising Florus's heart in his fist. Had he won? Madoc hoped not, now that he had seen what Anathrasa did to Deimos's fiercest warriors.

"Looks like you're a champion after all," he spat as Madoc passed. "How does it feel, son of Petros, to cheat your way into the company of gods?"

At the mention of his father, Madoc felt sick.

"Bring Lucius," Anathrasa said, without slowing. "The fight's victor will be the first."

Regret pinched the base of Madoc's neck.

"Or perhaps I'll be the last," Lucius tossed back, a clear threat to end the Mother Goddess's reign. "Why don't we meet in the arena? We'll see how your soul energeia withstands the power of an Earth Divine gladiator."

Madoc didn't watch the centurions beat the man, but he heard the grunts of pain.

"Madoc?"

He managed to turn toward the sound of his name and found Elias pushing through the winners to get close to the edge of the cell. Madoc's body didn't stop, so Elias had to keep moving to match his pace.

"Madoc, you have to stop her. She has—"

"That's enough," Anathrasa said.

Madoc lifted a hand, and Elias's words were cut short by a surge of anathreia. Elias scratched at his own throat, his eyes wide.

Panic strangled Madoc's relief at finding Elias alive. He focused all his energy on loosening his hold on his brother, and thankfully, Elias crumbled to the floor a moment later.

Had Madoc done that? Or had Anathrasa simply grown bored with hurting Elias?

They were escorted to the end of the hall, to a room like those Madoc had once prepared for matches in. Inside, the low light pulsed, and the decadent scents of meat and fresh bread wafted from a table against the far wall.

"Mother Goddess." One of Anathrasa's priestesses brought her a goblet of wine, the smear of chalk on her mouth already thinned by sweat. "Are you ready to begin?"

Madoc's consciousness rippled with horror as he recognized the woman.

Ilena.

She wasn't dead. She was here. She was . . .

"Mine," said Anathrasa. "Yes. She's mine, as are you, Madoc. You didn't really think I'd dispose of her completely, did you? She still has much to give."

Ilena didn't look at Madoc. She didn't look at anything. Her hands stayed slack at her sides as she awaited further instruction.

What will you do? Madoc's silent demand echoed through his soul.

"What I must," Anathrasa said, then patted Ilena's head and sent her from the room. "We need a suitable army to defeat Hydra and Florus's Plant Divine, do we not? The strongest fighters in Deimos?"

He thought of the people who'd been called to join the celebration games. It didn't matter if they'd been trained as gladiators—if they were strong, they were welcome, regardless of age or ability.

Two centurions appeared in the threshold of the door, carrying a limp Lucius between them. His head hung forward, his short hair matted with blood.

Despite everything, Madoc pitied him.

"You were right when you said I meant to take over the six countries," Anathrasa continued, stalking toward Lucius. She extended the goblet of wine at her side, and Ilena raced in from the doorway to take it. "But it's not as simple as sailing off and claiming them. As long as people have power, there will be those who mean to destroy me."

The gods, he thought.

"Not just the gods, Madoc. Those the gods created. The Divine."

Panic trembled through him. She meant to destroy the Divine?

Anathrasa glanced back at him, a patronizing smile on her lips. "Come now. You of all people should recognize the danger they pose. A god's power was never meant to live in a mortal body. I see now what a failure this Divine experiment truly was. They were always meant to be fuel for our own energeia, nothing more."

Madoc didn't understand what she was saying. She couldn't drain all the Divine in the world. There were too many of them. They would rally against her.

"They'll be too busy fighting among themselves," she said. "It's already begun. The most powerful Deimans, Laks, and Cenhelmians have already volunteered to join our cause. Look at how much happier they are to serve." She strode to Lucius, grabbed his hair, and jerked his head back. With a moan, his eyes blinked open, focusing unsteadily on Madoc.

Anathrasa was using her gladiator games as a way to rid the world of Divine. She pretended to honor them, raised them up in Geoxus's name, then she turned them into what Madoc had seen in the dungeons.

Empty soldiers. An army that would fight without fear, without emotion. Without their *souls*. She would tithe the entire world, becoming more powerful by the moment, and when all were shells, she would use them as she pleased—by controlling them with anathreia.

Anathrasa didn't just want to take over the six countries; she wanted to destroy them.

Ash. She had to hear this. She had to know.

He tried to focus on her in his mind, but he couldn't see her clearly. He couldn't remember the shape of her eyes or the sound of her laugh. He couldn't remember the last thing they'd talked about.

He couldn't remember anything they'd talked about.

He tried to hide his thoughts too late.

"Oh, she knows, my dear. The first wave of my army has already attacked Kula. I hear she mounted an impressive defense, but it did not save all her Fire Divine brothers and sisters. Aera tells me your Ash is gathering a sad little army, meant to face me." A smile. "She will find more resistance than she expected here."

This was bad. He needed to stop Anathrasa. He needed to . . .

"What?" she asked, dropping Lucius's head. With another groan, he attempted to stand, but he stumbled into one of the men holding him. "You need to what, Madoc?"

Help you.

He needed to help his mother.

"Yes," she said with a smile. "And soon, the Divine will be gone, just like you always wanted. You won't be that awkward boy fighting his way through the stonemason's quarter any longer. The Undivine will flourish. You'll be their champion, and I'll lead them all, a true Mother Goddess. The only one responsible enough to yield the power of energeia."

He watched as Anathrasa placed her hands on the sides of Lucius's jaw and sipped in a steady breath. Lucius struggled—quietly first, but then with the desperate movements of a man on the brink of death. He screamed and thrashed as he fought the guards.

Madoc did nothing to stop it.

The woman raced from the door, dropping to her knees beside Lucius. "He's ready, Mother Goddess."

Madoc blinked, and her face came back into focus with a sharp bite of clarity.

This was his mother. Not Anathrasa. *Ilena.*

"Complete the circle," Ilena said in a flat voice, controlled by Anathrasa's soul energeia. "Complete the circle."

He forced himself to focus, not to fall to Anathrasa's control. He willed Ilena to look at him. He reached for his anathreia, trying to force her to comply. Was she locked inside her body as he was inside his? The thought sickened him.

With a breath, Anathrasa lifted her hands, and Madoc could feel the surge of power in his own veins. Her mouth opened. Her eyes rolled back.

Lucius went still. He straightened. With renewed horror, Madoc watched as Lucius blinked and stared ahead with wide, blank eyes.

"Ah." Anathrasa lowered her arms. When she smiled, not a wrinkle lined her mouth. "Look at that. Isn't he wonderful?" She strode toward him, the use of her power not slowing her down in the slightest.

"Wonderful," said Ilena.

Madoc looked at Lucius again, at his pale face and slack mouth, and his head grew blissfully silent.

He couldn't remember where he'd seen this man before.

"Wonderful," Madoc said.

"They'll fight without fear," Anathrasa said. "The ultimate soldiers. Unafraid of death. Only willing to do what I ask."

"Wonderful," Madoc said again.

"This is how we win," Anathrasa said. "How we beat the Divine. By turning their strongest into true believers."

"The circle is complete," said Ilena.

"Go get Elias," Anathrasa told Ilena. "Bring him in next. He'll make a fine subject for Madoc's first attempt."

Elias.

Elias was his brother.

The last remaining shreds of Madoc's consciousness dug into his soul. He was losing himself, he could feel that now. There was little time left before he was completely Anathrasa's.

He had to protect Elias, but how? He couldn't move his body. His thoughts were betraying him. He was slipping into a black hole.

Ash.

Ash would pull him out of that hole.

He forced himself to rally. Ash was the goddess of fire and earth. She could help him.

But how? She was so far away.

The shame piled on him, weighing him down. Ash had always been a better fighter. Stronger. Smarter. She'd been able to hold the power of gods when it had nearly killed him. He'd thought that if he could help her, she'd see his worth. She'd keep him. But he'd always known it was just a matter of time before she'd see the truth.

He couldn't help her.

He couldn't even help his own family.

The things that matter live inside us, and we protect them as we protect any other part of ourselves, with the power we've been given. The words came from far away. An echo, already fading.

They lit one final spark of hope inside him.

He was still Deiman. Still that pigstock boy, fighting in street matches with lies and luck, fighting for Geoxus's blessing to keep him alive. Going to the temple. Kneeling before the golden statue. Touching the stones in the hope that the Father God would hear him.

Now Deimos had a new god.

With all his might, he wrenched his body toward the nearest wall.

Automatically, his hand lifted to brace against the stones. Then he did the only thing he had left to do.

He prayed.

Ash, if you can hear me, help Elias and Ilena. Protect them from me. Save them.

And then his grip faltered, and he lost his hold on brother and mother. On Danon and Ava. On the stone yards where he'd once been a mason and the arenas where he'd fought on the streets. On Petros, and Cassia, and Tor, and finally on Ash.

It all slipped away until there was nothing. Until he had no name but servant, and the shell of his body belonged to the Mother Goddess.

TWENTY

ASH

THREE DAYS AFTER Anathrasa's attack on Kula, Ash had actively shut her mind to the onslaught of prayers in her name. The city of Igna had embraced her as their new goddess and set her up in Ignitus's dormant volcano palace. Day and night, servants and staff and warriors funneled into the grand receiving hall to swear fealty to her. Brand, who had once been a champion devoted only to Ignitus and to bloodshed, rarely left her side, overseeing her transition as Kula's ruler with surprising skill and allegiance.

Her display against Anathrasa's navy had been more than enough to turn the country's loyalty to her. But by the time Hydra left to join the fleet of Water Divine and Plant Divine sailing into Igna's harbor, Ash felt no more ready to face Tor again than she had right after their argument.

She stayed long enough on the shore to let her Fire Divine warriors see her accept the fleet as friendly, not threatening. Then she nodded at Brand, who would organize the chaos of coordinating the

Apuitians' and Itzans' lodging. Not that they would be here long—they were all due to depart to attack Crixion at dawn.

Before Tor could disembark from the lead ship, Ash vanished in a flare of blue flame.

She reappeared in the bedchamber she had taken, a massive room carved into the dormant volcanic rock. The walls were roughly cut, following the natural divots and texture of the black obsidian, and the floor was covered with a vibrant orange-and-gold rug. The bed sat just next to an open balcony, letting in a salty breeze from the Hontori Sea.

Moments alone had been rare the past few days, but for each minute of solitude Ash had salvaged, all she could bring herself to do was lie on her bed, stare up at the canopy as it rippled in the sea wind, and ache.

Hydra hadn't really spoken to her since the attack, and her last words to Ash resonated as strongly as Tor's—all doubts and reprimands and horror at how Ash was behaving. She'd thought Hydra, of all people, might understand that Ash was simply accepting what she was now, but even the water goddess had pulled away.

So while armies converged in Igna and time ticked down to Ash's confrontation with Anathrasa, she was in a room in Ignitus's place, alone.

And she would walk into that final battle, alone.

And if they defeated Anathrasa—*when* they defeated Anathrasa—Ash would leave that victory alone too. She would still have this strange power inside her, and it would still cause a rift between her and Tor, between her and Hydra. Would Madoc see the same flaws that they saw? Would he cringe away from her?

Ash squeezed her eyes shut. She'd missed him every moment since he'd left, even when she'd seen him in the library and been in his arms. She felt like she was forgetting who he actually was, and all these worries would vanish if they could just be together without fear of attack or intrusion—

Ash.

She bolted upright, eyes darting around her room. But it was empty; even the sea breeze still for a moment.

Ash, the voice said again.

Ash stood. The scarlet gown she was wearing brushed her ankles, her black hair loose and curling against her shoulders as she tipped her head.

Maybe she *was* going insane. Because that voice sounded like . . .

It sounded like Madoc.

If you can hear me. His voice was rough and desperate and exhausted, as though he was using the last vestiges of his strength to speak to her.

Gods. He was *praying* to her. He was Deiman, and he was praying through stone.

"Madoc!" Ash didn't know how to talk back to him. The only reason she could hear him was because she *was* geoeia now, but there were no rocks in this room that obeyed geoeia—in any room in this palace, thanks to Ignitus's paranoia.

Ash spun in a circle. How had she listened through fire before? She hadn't practiced any more with stone—

—*help Elias and Ilena*, Madoc told her. *Protect them from me.*

"Madoc!" Ash stopped, eyes welling. "*From* you? What do you mean? What is she doing to you?"

Save them.

"Madoc!" Only silence followed. Ash gasped, tears sliding down her cheeks.

She said his name again. She shouted it, and she heard her warriors in the hall thundering toward her cry.

The door burst open. "Goddess? Are you all right?" one asked.

Ash drew in a shaky breath. She pressed the back of her hand to her lips and willed herself not to disintegrate.

Madoc had prayed to *her*. Not to Ash, who was the goddess of Kula—just Ash, who had powers he knew of but didn't shy away from.

And in that moment, that was all she was. The layers of her power stripped away, her destiny pooling at her feet. She was just a girl who loved a boy who needed her to save him.

She replayed Madoc's message.

If you can hear me, help Elias and Ilena. Protect them from me. Save them.

A familiar defiance almost had her launching away to help him right then.

But she stopped herself.

Breathed.

"Bring Hydra and Tor to the receiving room," Ash told her guard. "We're accelerating our plans."

There were only a few warriors and servants bustling about the receiving room when Ash entered through a side door that put her right next to the throne Ignitus had often sat on.

It was beautiful. Carved entirely of Kulan glass, the seat jutted out from a fanning back of opalescent scarlet, orange, and yellow. It looked like a fire that had been frozen somehow, each twisted strand of glass mimicking a shoot of flame.

Once, Ash had chastised herself for thinking anything Ignitus touched was beautiful.

Once, she would have scowled at the throne and ordered it shattered, as though doing so would avenge her mother.

Ash hesitated, her hands fisting at her sides. Through all the pomp and reception she had endured the past few days, she had stood, thanking everyone who swore themselves to her cause. She had purposefully put Ignitus's throne at her back so she didn't have to think about it.

But now Ash crossed the space to the throne and stood before it, looking down at the seat that had only ever held the god of fire.

The receiving room hung silent. Or maybe that was her own pulse deafening her, the rush and surge of blood through her veins making her want to run.

She turned and sat, hands on the armrests, back rigid.

Goddess.

Part of her reveled in the title, but part of her wanted to be exactly what she had been when Madoc had prayed to her.

Just Ash. Just a girl.

Sitting on Ignitus's throne, she couldn't help but wonder if the other gods ever wished for that. Mortals certainly dreamed of being godly; did gods dream of being ordinary?

Could she ever go back to being *ordinary* again?

The door at the far end opened. Tor rushed in, walking fast without quite running, Taro close behind him. The two of them pulled up short when they saw Ash on Ignitus's throne.

They said nothing.

A trickle of water cascaded down one of the obsidian pillars on the edge of the room, and Hydra materialized, leaning one shoulder against the glassy rock. She eyed Ash, her jaw tight.

Ash's fingers dug into the armrests. Tor, Hydra, Taro—they were all forced to look up at her on this raised dais. Forced to remember who she was now, as though they could forget. A god in a mortal body. A warrior who would save the world. An angry, violent girl.

"I'm sorry," she said, her voice cracking.

The servants and warriors must have felt the tension, because they dissolved into the shadows, giving her privacy.

Hydra pushed herself off the pillar, scowl shifting into surprise. "Are you?"

"I have become capable of more than I ever thought possible, but I was wrong to think that meant I was invincible." Ash could only look at Hydra as she spoke. Her chest ached with Tor's focus on her, and his final words to her still cored her out.

Your mother would be ashamed of the way you're behaving.

She swallowed and leaned forward. "I'm sorry I haven't been listening. That I've acted rashly. I don't—" She dropped her focus to her hands. The backs of her eyes burned. "I don't know how to do the things I have to do, but I'm trying. And I need your help."

"That's what I've been trying to tell you, Ash—" Tor started, but Ash snapped her eyes up to him.

"Madoc prayed to me," she said. "I heard him through the stone in Deimos. He said he wants me to protect Elias and Ilena—from *him*."

"What?" Taro's voice pitched. "What does that even mean?"

"Anathrasa is overtaking his mind," Hydra whispered.

Ash nodded. She knew her eyes were glassy with tears, but she was angry, too, and she let that anger build. "He wouldn't have asked me to intervene unless it was urgent. I think that prayer was his last attempt to contact me before she—" She couldn't finish. Her words fell and her eyes dropped too, landing on the floor. "We need to move. Now. Anathrasa is confident enough in her army that she sent them to attack Kula. She has Madoc under her control. We need to go to Crixion *now*."

There was a long moment of silence. When Ash looked up, Tor was watching her, frowning.

"Why didn't you go to Crixion yourself?" he asked.

Ash bristled. "I'm trying to think of the greater effects my actions have on this war."

Tor took a step toward her. "I meant it as a compliment. Thank you for coming to us first."

Ash ground her jaw.

"My people have barely started to disembark," Hydra said. "We can easily load back up and make for Crixion."

"Your Water Divine won't be too exhausted to accelerate the trip?" Ash asked.

Hydra gave a grim smile. "Who said they'll be giving us the fast trip? You and I will be traveling with them, and goddesses don't tire. Do we?"

Ash couldn't help but return Hydra's grin. "No. We don't."

"We'll get to Crixion and confront Anathrasa's army," Tor said, down to business. "If Madoc is under her control, how will we defeat her? We can't wage war indefinitely."

Ash pushed herself up off the throne. "Maybe we don't aim to defeat her with this attack."

Tor's brow furrowed.

"Maybe we just salvage what we can," Ash continued. "We save Madoc's family, and Florus too. We get as many innocents out as possible and we regroup. We take away her leverage."

Planning to do this without Madoc felt wrong. As though he was already lost.

But no—Ash would figure out some way to save him, too, once she got his family to safety.

"We'll need time to search for everyone." Hydra folded her arms. "Anathrasa could have Florus imprisoned anywhere—he might not even be in Crixion anymore. And I'm not leaving without my brother."

"We need a distraction," Taro offered.

"Something to keep Anathrasa diverted while we get Florus and the Metaxas out of Crixion," Ash said.

"And other innocents," Tor clarified.

"And other innocents." Ash worried her lip.

What would most distract Anathrasa? What would she *have* to respond to, for her own honor, for her own protection?

Ash paused. How had the gods been causing distractions for

centuries? By using their arenas.

"I know I can't defeat Anathrasa yet," Ash breathed. "But *she* doesn't know that."

She looked up, catching Hydra's eyes as a new thought formed.

"What if I appear in Crixion's grand arena and challenge Anathrasa?" Ash formed the words slowly. "We let Anathrasa think that Madoc already got me aereia and bioseia, and that I have everything I need to defeat her. We keep her occupied there while our armies free anyone still fighting her, and then we fall back to Kula. For now—"

"This is victory enough." Tor's face was a mask.

A wave of nausea surged through Ash's body. She nodded once. Again.

"Let's go to war," she said, the words tasting of dust and decay.

Hydra vanished, presumably to pass on orders to the Apuitian and Itzan ships. Taro whispered something to Tor before walking toward the door.

But Tor remained, hands at his back, staring up at Ash.

"You're not pleased with this plan?" she asked.

He flinched. "I didn't say that."

"But you're still here. So you must disapprove of something I've done."

A sigh, and Tor's shoulders deflated. He looked as if he might disagree before he shook his head. "Do you remember when we first met?"

The question threw her. She eased back to sit on the edge of the throne and shook her head.

Tor shrugged. "Not surprising. You were about four, maybe five.

Char and I had been together for a few weeks. Her mother had just died in an arena."

Ash shivered, not from cold, but from the mention of the grandmother she couldn't remember. Char hadn't spoken much of her mother after she'd taken her place as Ignitus's champion, carrying the name of Nikau into arenas, fighting for him.

Char had hated it and did everything she could to keep Ash from the same fate.

A lot of good that did.

Ash shivered again.

"She brought you to my house the day after Ignitus declared she would be his next champion," Tor said. His voice wavered, warmer than Ash had heard from him in a long time. "You tried to pull a ball of flames from the fireplace and nearly set fire to my kitchen table."

Ash felt her lips twitch. "That sounds like me."

Tor smiled, his eyes gentle. "I showed you some toys I'd gotten for you, and while you were playing, Char asked me to take care of you if anything happened to her."

"What? She never told me that."

Tor took a step forward. "I have sworn many oaths in my life. Most to Ignitus, so they meant little. But what I promised your mother that day is the beacon I have lived by. To be someone worthy of being trusted with such a precious gift. It's an honor I would rather die than break, taking care of Char's little girl. I shouldn't have brought her into our argument when you heard Igna was in trouble. I'm sorry."

"I'm not that little girl anymore." Ash's voice was barely a whisper.

"No." His smile fell. "No, you aren't. I've been trying to come to terms with that for years."

Ash couldn't hold Tor's gaze. She looked at the obsidian floor, but it blurred in the tears rimming her eyes.

"I've been trying to do right by your mother," Tor continued. He was closer to her. She still didn't look up. "Trying to do right by you, not just as Char's daughter, but as"—his voice caught—"as *my* daughter."

Ash squeezed her eyes shut, but tears still fell. She stood and closed the space between them, throwing her arms around Tor's shoulders, burying her face into his neck. He caught her with a startled huff and wrapped his thick arms around her, holding her in Ignitus's empty receiving room.

Igneia burned in a chandelier high above them, and Ash wondered if, somewhere, Char could see them.

If she knew that Ash still had Tor to lean on.

If she had known, all those years ago, what an unshakable foundation she was leaving for Ash when she brought Tor into their lives.

TWENTY-ONE

MADOC

"VERY GOOD." THE Mother Goddess examined the woman before them, staring into her vacant brown eyes. The woman was empty. Soulless. Brought to this state by Anathrasa's command and by his own power. But even though anathreia swelled inside him, he was only vaguely aware of it. A fly buzzing in the corner of a room he occupied.

"You're getting the hang of it. She barely struggled," Anathrasa noted, pride in her voice.

He couldn't remember the woman struggling at all. He couldn't remember anything before this moment. If there'd been others. If he'd hurt them. If they'd suffered.

He felt nothing.

He saw only what his goddess wanted him to see. The four dusty stone walls of this room. The centurions with their dull eyes. A vaguely familiar woman in white standing at the back of the room holding a tray.

He did not know how long he'd been here, or where he was.

It didn't matter.

With a smile, Anathrasa sent the girl into the hall, and immediately another Deiman was brought in. A man with a gray beard and tears in his eyes.

"Please," he was saying. "Please. Not this."

The Mother Goddess sighed. "It's difficult to see their pain, isn't it? How wrong we were to give them such a wide expanse of emotions. Their soft minds clearly couldn't handle it."

"Please!" the man begged.

"You'll make an excellent soldier," Anathrasa said slowly, loudly, as if the man would otherwise fail to comprehend. "Find solace in the fact that you will soon do your part to take back my world from the selfish gods who would put you in this kind of anguish." As he trembled, she slapped his cheek lightly. "Your fear will be over soon. You'll be in my care, as you were always meant to be."

"I'll do anything," he begged.

"Yes. You will." Anathrasa waved a hand. "Now, if you don't mind, hold still. My son must tithe to stay strong, as he did with Florus. Hydra will be here soon, and there is much work left to do. Isn't that right, Madoc?" She grinned at him.

Madoc.

The name was familiar. He knew it, the way he knew water would ease a parched throat, and a gray sky meant rain. But he didn't know how he knew it, or why he was called it, or what kind of man this Madoc was.

His hands lifted. Again, his anathreia swelled. Fed. But he felt no relief as the man went still in the grip of the soldiers.

The man walked from the room of his own accord. His hands loose at his sides. His stare dull.

"I need some air," Anathrasa said, stretching her arms out to the sides. "Shall we see how the training is progressing, my love?"

He followed her out of the room, down a dark hall lined with cells filled with Deiman men and women. They called out in anger. In fear. Some cried.

He felt nothing.

Sunlight cut a sharp line across their path, and he followed the Mother Goddess through the stone archway onto the yellow sand. An arena stretched before him, an oval as deep as the palace, surrounded by empty stands.

Before them, lines of Deimans stared straight ahead, set in place like chess pieces by centurions in silver and black.

"One!" a centurion commander called from the front of the arena.

As one, hundreds of men and women lunged forward, extending their right hand in a thrusting punch.

"Two!" Their left hands followed.

"Three!" A hard kick.

An old woman in the front fell but continued to kick from the ground in silent compliance. A centurion righted her, but her hips buckled, and when she fell again, the soldiers dragged her off to the side. She continued to kick while they moved her.

"Four!" The lines returned to a ready formation in a cloud of dust.

"Impressive, isn't it?" Anathrasa asked. "Did you ever think you'd be capable of such great things?" She laughed as he stared forward.

"I did. To think that Ilena would have had you moving stones in the quarry, like some kind of Undivine animal."

At the name Ilena, he twitched, a reaction he didn't understand.

Anathrasa took his hand in hers and pet it gently.

"You are so much more than anything she could have seen."

A light flickered inside him, a tiny spark in the gloom. A question, outside the silence of his mind.

"What am I?" he asked.

Anathrasa looked up at him, her eyes gleaming, her mouth tilted in a smile.

"You are my servant," she said. "And that is all you need to be."

TWENTY-TWO

ASH

THEY LEFT IGNA before sunset.

Ash took one of the lead ships while Hydra captained the other, and together, they launched their fleet across the Hontori Sea. A journey that would normally take a week sped by in mere days, and their ship thrashed at the edge of Crixion's waters just as the sun was coming up behind them two days later.

She wasn't tired, but Ash panted all the same, sweat dampening her skin and sea spray sticking her hair to her cheeks. She was already wearing Kulan reed armor, the kind made for battle, not ceremony, and as the water stilled, she was grateful that she didn't have to worry about getting ready. If she paused, she might not do what she needed to do. She might just find Madoc and whisk him away and do something to force Anathrasa out of his head. Instead, she had to be steady, and patient, and careful.

The water around their ships solidified. Not ice, just Hydra holding them steady while they took stock of Crixion, spread out before them in the rising pink-gold dawn.

Anathrasa was ready for them.

All of Crixion's ships sat in a blockade before their harbor, waiting, laden with centurions and soldiers. Beyond, who knew what the city would be like?

A cold hand slid into Ash's. She met the water goddess's blue eyes.

Before they'd left Igna, Ash and Hydra had talked about how goddesses could fight differently than Divine mortals.

This was one large way.

Ash closed her eyes as Hydra did. Together, on the deck of their ship, as their people adjusted to being here and moments from battle, their two goddess leaders looked in on Crixion.

Hydra would take every waiting vessel of water—ponds and wells and pools. Ash would jump through fire. Together, they could make a feeble map of the city, who was where and what obstacles they might face.

Ash exhaled, let her shoulders relax, and widened her awareness. No one in Crixion was praying to her, unsurprisingly; a few Kulans on the ships were saying idle prayers for safety, but Ash pressed on, peeking through every flame in the city, every fireplace, every simmering coal.

There weren't many. Few houses had flames lit, few storefronts nursed fires.

Ash pulled back into herself, heart thudding.

"It's quiet," Hydra said beside her.

Ash nodded. "I didn't sense Madoc or his family. Or Florus. Did you?"

Hydra shook her head.

Worry made Ash go slack. Madoc's final plea had been to keep his family safe. What if she was too late?

"That doesn't mean anything, though," Hydra tried. "We knew Anathrasa would prepare for us. They're probably hidden somewhere—"

"Wait." Tor came up to them, hands slack on the jars of combustibles around his hips, things he could light with igneia and use in the attack. His eyes were on the line of Deiman ships, and he squinted in confusion. "What is that?"

Hydra and Ash turned. The lead ship in the Deiman blockade was in the process of raising something into the air. Two tall wooden poles, with a flag between them—

Ash retched, hand to her mouth.

Not a flag. A body.

A body with a gaping hole in its chest, rib cage torn open, gore and blood on display.

"Who is that?" Hydra asked the question that Ash couldn't bear. A hundred possibilities surged through her mind as Tor took a spyglass from a nearby sailor and lifted it.

He frowned. "A boy?"

Hydra snatched the spyglass.

The moment it touched her eye, she swayed.

"No," she said, and a wave arched out of the water in front of their ship. "*No*," she cried, and the wave rose, rushing for the Deimans. "*NO*," she screamed, and the wave blocked the ships and the city from view.

Ash grabbed Hydra's arms. "Stop! Who is—"

Hydra whirled on her, blue eyes feral, fury and agony ripe on her face. "Florus. It's *Florus*."

Ash went still. Her fingers turned to vises on Hydra's thin arms and she couldn't move as Hydra dropped the spyglass to the deck. It shattered at their feet, and Hydra screamed.

The wave slammed into the lead Deiman ship. Distantly, Ash heard centurions shouting, their cries buried in drowning garbles, but she found she couldn't care.

"Anathrasa killed the god of plants," Ash said, because she needed to see how that fact fit into this world now.

She hated that, selfishly, she felt vindicated. Her torturer was dead.

But if Anathrasa had killed Florus, then either she was strong enough to make him mortal on her own now, or she had forced Madoc to drain him as he had drained Geoxus and Ignitus.

In a final roar of foam and froth, Hydra made the sea swallow the ship whole, leaving the rest of Anathrasa's fleet unharmed, if horrified by what they would have to face.

Tor's head dropped to his chest.

Around Ash, their mostly Apuitian crew went silent, watching the wave decimate the Deiman ship. But on their other ships, the ones carrying Florus's Itzan warriors—the crews began to shriek. Not screaming in pain or wailing in grief; it was a screeching battle cry, a chant Ash couldn't make out, but the feel of it caught her chest like wildfire. The chant was agony, and it was power, and it was misery, and Anathrasa would regret having killed Florus and displaying his body in that vile, taunting way.

Ash pulled Hydra close. She didn't mourn Florus on her own, but she mourned for Hydra's loss. "She will pay for this."

Hydra sobbed hard, once. She pushed back from Ash, face red with tears, and growled. "I'm coming with you."

Ash inhaled as deeply as she could. Her part of the plan was to appear in the main arena and keep Anathrasa distracted. Tor would lead their fight here, keeping Anathrasa's army at bay.

Hydra had been meant to sneak through the city to find Florus and the Metaxas.

The Metaxas still needed saving. Ash eyed the sea where the ship with Florus's body had so recently sat, letting her mind calm, letting it calculate.

What other cruelty did Anathrasa have planned?

"All right," Ash said. She looked at Tor. "Hydra's with me. As soon as you break into the city, send groups scouting for the Metaxas and any other innocents who want to flee."

"Should the water goddess stay here?" Tor cocked his head at the remaining Deiman ships. "If you can so easily take down one vessel—"

Hydra shook her head. A grim smile twisted her lips and she nodded at the sound on the air, the chanting Itzan warriors. "You won't need me. The Itzans will be ruthless now."

Tor looked around. He met Ash's gaze and his own sobered, dark and purposeful.

"Be careful," he told her.

She smiled, but it didn't reach her eyes.

They would get out of this. They would survive to attack again.

And together, they would all see another dawn.

"Let's go," Ash told Hydra, and she burst into flames, one thought pulsing in her mind: *the grand arena.*

Last time she had been there, she had been dead on the sands from Elias's attack. Madoc had had to save her. Then Anathrasa had taken Ash's igneia, and her world had been chaos ever since.

So when Ash appeared in Crixion's main arena, she had a moment of painful nostalgia. The only thing different about it was the decorations. Banners fluttered from the high balconies, displaying an ivory circle instead of Geoxus's symbols. All signs of him were gone, his signature stones and gems, his onyx decor.

Ash stood in the center of the arena's fighting pit, staring up at the banners, and breathed.

The decorations were truly the *only* thing that had changed since she had been here last.

The stands were full. Full as though the audience that had watched her fight Elias had never left, waiting to see her bleed again.

Next to her, Hydra hissed in a breath. "What did we interrupt?"

Ash turned, eyes flicking from person to person, pulse roaring in her ears and sweat already dripping down her back. There were no gladiators midfight. And the crowd wasn't cheering or booing; they didn't even react when she and Hydra appeared. They sat in the seats, quiet, observant. It was eerie, as if the dead were watching them, and Ash's hands started to shake even as she pulled blue fire into her palms.

"I don't think we interrupted anything," Ash said. "I think she knew we'd come."

This was why the city had been empty. Everyone was *here.*

Hydra grimaced and matched Ash's fire with palmfuls of ice crystals. "Shit."

What had they walked into?

After a steadying breath, Ash screamed into the stands, "Anathrasa! Face me!"

The crowd didn't react. They looked like the gladiators on the ships that had attacked Igna.

"She's controlling them," Hydra whispered. She twisted so she and Ash stood back to back, ice and fire at the ready. "We're too late."

She felt Hydra deflate, just a little, just enough to spear Ash in the gut with panic.

"We are not too late," Ash told her. "We are not too late until Anathrasa rips the geoeia and igneia from my body."

She felt a rumble in Hydra's back—morbid laughter. But it gave Ash strength.

"Anathrasa!" she shouted. "I have what I need to defeat you. Come out and face me. You are not the only Mother Goddess anymore!"

As one, the crowd started to stomp. First one foot, then the other, a slow, thunderous build that wound the tension. It played the wrongness like a taut string.

Ash and Hydra spun in a slow circle, each eyeing the stands, searching for some sign that Anathrasa had heard her—

When a door opened in the wall ahead of Ash.

She stopped. Hydra turned, looking over Ash's shoulder.

A shadowed figure walked out, feet sliding through the arena's golden sands. The moment the morning sun's light caught on his face, his armor, the weapons at his sides, Ash went slack.

Hydra spun, grabbing Ash's wrist. "Ash, it's a trick."

"Madoc." His name slid out of her mouth and she almost sobbed. She lifted her hands, snapped the flames out. "Madoc."

When she'd seen Florus's body on display, part of her had been certain Madoc was dead too.

He was still alive. He was *here*, and—

"*Ash!*" Hydra shook her. "It's a trick. She's trying to distract you, like she did to me with Florus." Her voice cracked on her brother's name.

Hydra was right, and it broke Ash's heart. Anathrasa had planned this too.

Madoc kept walking across the arena toward them.

Ash took Hydra's hand. "With me." It was a question. A plea.

Hydra squeezed her fingers in unspoken confirmation, and they began walking, mimicking Madoc's steady pace.

He didn't look at Ash, didn't react to her being here. His movements were stiff and unnatural, and Ash wanted to scream.

Panic made Ash's chest buck.

Had Anathrasa overtaken him? Were they truly too late?

Ash almost collapsed on the sand, but she made herself stand tall. She wouldn't play Anathrasa's sick game.

She and Hydra stopped walking. Madoc did the same, close enough now that Ash could see his eyes. They were vacant and dark, his face void of expression, just as much a shell as the thundering crowd around them.

This was the world Anathrasa wanted: one she controlled in every way.

"Madoc," Ash tried. "I heard your prayer. I heard you, and I'm here now."

He didn't move.

Ash noted his armor. It was fighting armor, not ceremonial.

Her pulse sped up. "Madoc, please. I don't know how to help you. Give me some sign that you're still there. Let me—"

"Oh, he's not there, sweetie."

Ash's muscles went utterly rigid. Next to her, Hydra whirled around. Such a look of fury overcame her that Ash knew who had spoken before she even turned.

The goddess of air hovered a hand's width above the sands, arms behind her back, golden hair flowing in a gentle breeze. Behind her, shifting from eagle form back into a man, was Biotus.

Aera's round, childlike face twisted in a manic smile that only grew as she lowered all the way to the ground. "At least," she continued, taking delicate steps through the sand, "not the parts that matter to *you*. He's better now. Just as Anathrasa will make us all better."

"You killed Florus," Hydra growled. Her hands balled into fists. Spikes of ice flared up her arms, and Ash knew she should try to calm her, but she didn't. There was no calming this situation. No stopping this fight.

It was building and building, and they couldn't escape it.

Aera cut a wide circle around Ash and Hydra, then came to stand beside Madoc. "I did no such thing," she cooed. "My group lost. Yours did too, didn't they, Biotus? It was one of the Deiman gladiators who got Florus's heart."

Biotus hadn't followed Aera, putting Hydra and Ash directly

between them. It sent an uncomfortable itch up Ash's back.

Hydra went so still Ash thought she'd turned to ice. "What?"

Biotus folded his arms across his beefy chest and grinned wickedly. "Gladiators ripped Florus's heart clean out of his chest. After that one"—he pointed at Madoc—"made him mortal."

Hydra was now panting, shoulders heaving. Ash felt her fury on the air, electric and contagious, and she faced Madoc, wanting to burn this stadium to the ground. More than that, she wanted to run. To grab his hand and run and forget all the horrible things that had led them here.

That wish sparked from what felt like a lifetime ago, in Crixion's library. They should have run that night.

Ash's hands fisted, wrenching tighter when Aera traced her finger along Madoc's jaw. The only solace was that, while he didn't shove her away, he didn't lean into her touch, either.

"Anathrasa let Florus die," Ash said, more for Hydra's benefit, reminding her who the real villain was. "We didn't come to fight you. Where is she?"

"Are you sure you don't want to fight him?" Aera looked at Ash, ignoring her question as she wrapped her fingers around the tense muscles of Madoc's forearm.

"We're not playing these games," Ash growled. "Where is Anathrasa?"

"He's very impressive now," Aera said. "Unhindered. A real *champion*. The Mother Goddess has used this vessel for tremendous feats now that he's wholly given over to her."

Ash almost cried out. Aera's words struck like a knife to her soul, confirmation that Madoc wasn't himself. Not anymore.

"Shut *up*!" Hydra spun, flaring ice shards in the sand at Aera's feet. "Where is our mother?"

Her question echoed off the stands, the crowd still stomping.

Aera pouted. She'd launched herself up to avoid the ice but lowered now and put her hand on Madoc's shoulder. "Are you going to let her speak to me like that, lover?"

Ash called on igneia and had a ball of fire in her hand before she could think not to. Arm lifted, she aimed to hurl it at Aera—

But Madoc intercepted.

He grabbed Ash's wrist, twisted, and threw her across the arena. Ash went flying, only gathering her wits enough to vanish in fire and reappear on her feet before she hit the wall.

This wasn't him. She told herself that, held it against the agony that cut her.

Ash looked back at Madoc, gasping.

He was crouched for a fight. And then he was running at her.

Behind him, Hydra hurled water whips and ice shards at Aera and Biotus. Dark shadows of birds and hawks pinpricked the sky as Biotus called animals to his defense while the arena's sands caught up in funnels of Aera's aereia.

Madoc was closer. Closer still. The tendons in his neck stretched and he leaped at her.

Ash had no choice.

She wouldn't leave him. Even if it meant she had to fight him.

TWENTY-THREE

MADOC

THE GOD KILLER attacked with a vengeance. Blue flames spouted from her raised palms, a wave of heat searing his side as he dived to the sand. He coughed as his throat filled with dust. From the corner of his eye, he saw her lunge toward him, and he shoved himself back, sputtering.

"Stop!" she shouted at him, as if she hadn't just attacked him. "Madoc, can you hear me?"

Madoc.

He didn't know a Madoc. He only knew Anathrasa. His only purpose was to protect the Mother Goddess. He was her soldier. Her servant.

From the opposite end of the arena came a howl of manic laughter, magnified on the whipping wind. A tornado was ripping apart the southern stands, tossing bodies and hunks of stones into the air and over the ledge of the arena. Aera stood behind it, dress and hair dancing wildly. She shot another blast of aereia toward Hydra, who was fending off a giant lion behind a defensive dome of ice.

Anathrasa's servant shoved to his feet, then stumbled when the ground began to shake.

"I don't want to hurt you," the God Killer said, wiping the sweat from her brow with the back of her wrist.

He wanted to hurt her.

He needed to kill her.

With a roar, the servant sprinted toward the God Killer, knives bared. She threw another bolt of fire at him, but he dodged it, then dropped low to sweep her legs. She fell hard on her back, a huff of breath parting her lips, and when she screamed, the air hummed with a chilling vibration. He glanced up, searching for her next attack, only to find beads of water flying across the sands from all directions, congealing into a blast of hail that scraped his skin.

In his distraction, she leaped to her feet and charged toward him.

Drain her. The Mother Goddess's order resounded through his body.

He threw himself toward the God Killer, hooking her ankle. She tripped, but when he reached for her calf, a black root shot from the ground, snaking around his arm. Another hooked around his back. Instantly they tightened, cutting off his circulation, stifling his breath. He gasped, panic roaring through his blood.

"Stop fighting me!" The God Killer's voice trembled. Her eyes were glassy with tears. Her hair, pale with dust, was plastered to her cheek. A screech filled the air as a small black bird dived toward her. She batted it aside with a wave of water, but soon another followed, and another. An entire flock of birds sacrificing themselves at

Biotus's command, pelting her with sharp beaks and pointed claws. She raised her hands, blocking them with a weave of roots, and the pattering sound of their bodies bouncing off the hard surface filled the servant's ears.

Get up, the Mother Goddess ordered.

The order was not meant just for him. The ground began quaking as the bodies in the stands rushed to the edge of the arena, driven by Anathrasa's call. They jumped over the railings, landing on the sand, sprinting toward him, and toward the goddess of water, still battling her siblings.

He tried to peel off the vines, but they were too tight. His gaze shot to the God Killer fending off a wall of Anathrasa's soldiers. They fell in droves, then piled over one another to get closer to her. With a scream, she swung her arms in a wide arc, and a high wall of flames drew a hot, blue-tinged circle around her. The soldiers barreled into it, unafraid, but this was no ordinary fire. The moment a mortal body touched it, it burned them to ashes.

As the servant continued to struggle with the vines, some of the soldiers cut to the back, to where the circle of flames was not yet closed. The God Killer shoved them away with a blast of ice, but they were too many. A man fell against the servant's back. The soldier was broad-chested. Deiman. His eyes were like black coals, unfocused and empty, and the back of his tunic was still aflame.

A thought slipped through the servant's mind, too slick to cling to. A villa atop a hill. A sponsor shouting orders to his prized fighters. *Lucius.*

The thought was gone.

"Cut me free," he told the Deiman soldier.

The soldier, ignoring the fire that ate at his clothes, pulled a knife from his belt and hacked at the vines. Before he could sever them completely, a root tore from the earth and wrapped around his chest. It lifted him like a doll and threw him through the haze of smoke, out of sight.

Rushing to beat the God Killer's next attack, the servant ripped through the last threads of the vine holding him and hurtled toward her, tackling her to the ground.

Geoeia. Igneia. Floreia. Hydreia. He could feel it all raging inside her. His anathreia hungered for it, its sharp teeth biting at the shell of her soul. He would tithe it from her, split open her soul and drink its power like spilled milk.

"Stop!" She writhed beneath him, then twisted, her chest to his. He locked her hands over her head and dropped his forearm to her throat. Her lips parted on a gasp.

The heat was more intense now—sweat blurred his vision and made his grasp slick. The circle around them had been closed, a wall of flames blocking them from the war beyond.

He inhaled, drawing the power out of her like poison from a wound. His teeth bared with the effort. Blood pulsed in his temples.

"Madoc, please!" she managed.

Take her powers. End this. Beyond the flames, he could see a shadow rising at a dozen different points, and knew the army was attempting to climb over the barrier.

He pressed harder. Reached deeper.

"You know me," she wheezed.

Lies, the Mother Goddess hissed.

"We met here, in this arena . . ." She swallowed a breath, fighting harder. His muscles clenched as energeia surged through his body. It fought against the seams of his soul, threatening to tear out of him. Pain ricocheted down his spine and limbs.

Draining her would kill him.

It didn't matter.

"We fought just like this . . . ," she gasped. "No energeia. Which was good because . . . you didn't have any."

Pigstock.

He shook his head, the crackling flames warring with the thunder of his heart. That wasn't the Mother Goddess's voice. It had come from another place. A locked room in his memory.

"We danced," she said. "Do you remember? At the palace. The night we found Stavos."

He flinched, his arm loosening around her throat and wrists. He could see a body just as clearly as if he'd been laid out on the ground beside them. *Stavos.* The champion had stumbled through the palace gates, arrows in his back. Someone had murdered him.

"You remember Stavos," she said, blinking. "Do you remember Jann, too? You beat him here with anathreia."

He knew Jann—he could hear his taunts before their fight. Could see the gladiator curled into a ball, weeping, after they'd fought.

"And afterward, Tor and I told you . . ."

"Tor," he whispered.

The God Killer's powers sizzled across his nerves.

She nodded. "Yes. Tor. We told you we needed your help to take down the gods. And then we went to Petros's villa . . ."

He jerked his arm away from her throat.

He could see Tor, lunging across a ship's deck at him, knives and fire in his hands. *The things that matter live inside us, and we protect them as we protect any other part of ourselves, with the power we've been given.*

Lies, screamed Anathrasa. *End this!*

The shadows were climbing—the soldiers had nearly reached the top. One went over, but was seared by the flames on the way down, and with a stunted scream turned to ash.

"You called me," the God Killer managed. "You prayed to me through the stones to help you. To save Ilena and Elias."

He stopped pulling her energeia. His hands were shaking. The God Killer's energeia inside him was too much. Her words were illusions.

Don't listen to her, Anathrasa screamed. *She's nothing. She is no one.*

"I came back for you," the God Killer said. Her eyes were glassy, her fear thick. But there was more there. More he didn't want to feel. Hope and grief and longing.

Love.

He looked into her eyes, and he remembered.

The curl of her fingers over his on the ship's rail. The feel of her smile against his lips. She'd once said his name sounded like a bird call.

One memory returned at a time. One brick placed after another, and another.

Ilena. His mother. Scolding him for growing too fast. Kissing his forehead before he fell asleep.

Elias calling him brother.

Cassia bringing him home.

Him carrying Cassia home.

Brick by brick by brick, until he had a wall pushing back Anathrasa's howling screams in his head. Until he could breathe.

He was still there. He was still Madoc.

"Ash?" he whispered.

Tears spilled from Ash's eyes. Her nose scrunched as she gave a watery laugh. "Yes."

He gritted his teeth, more memories pouring back.

Home is here, Tor had told him, his hand on Madoc's chest.

Madoc forced his trembling hand off Ash's wrists and to his own damp chest. Screams from outside punched through the flames. He couldn't see Aera, but a burst of her power blew the flames in a sudden slant, singeing his skin. They went out in a hiss on one side, but before the wave of bodies, charred and burned, could press into the circle, he held out his hand and whispered, "No."

The soldiers went still. Watching. Waiting.

You disobey me? Anathrasa roared. *You are nothing without me.*

You're wrong, his own voice echoed inside his head, stronger than he'd expected. He was Madoc Aurelius, born of a goddess and a monster, survivor of the streets of Crixion, loved by a family whom he loved in return.

One brick followed another.

He was a champion of war, a gladiator trained in trickery and anathreia. A brother. A defender. A healer.

The walls rose until they became a fortress. He pushed himself back to his knees, holding Ash's stare as she rose on her elbows.

He loved her.

He couldn't remember the moment it had happened. All he knew was that he'd tripped when he'd first seen her in this arena, and after that nothing had been the same. She'd opened his eyes to the treachery of the gods, and the vastness of the world. She'd shown him the true meaning of bravery, and that honor could still exist, even in a city torn apart by greed and power.

"Ash," he said again. The name was familiar on his tongue.

Crawling to her knees, she took his face in her hands and kissed him. Her lips were soft but unforgiving, punishing him for forgetting, making him pay for every second they'd been apart.

He took it all. Her anger. Her fear. Her love. He breathed her in and remembered what it was like to be home.

Enough, growled Anathrasa. She wrenched Madoc's arm back like a puppet's, ready to drive his fist through Ash's chest like a spear.

No.

Madoc caught Anathrasa before she could follow through. His hand stopped, trembling over Ash's rib cage. He focused all his efforts on holding it there, forbidding his muscles from driving their full strength into her.

Anathrasa's scream filled the arena—not just in his head, but outside it.

The Mother Goddess was here.

"Go," he muttered to Ash. His arm was shaking. He wasn't sure he could hold Anathrasa off much longer, and he didn't want to hurt Ash.

She shook her head, rising to her knees. "No. You can fight her off. I'm not leaving."

She placed her hands on Madoc's chest, and his breath ripped free in a staggered gasp. The warmth of her fingers bled through his sweat-drenched tunic. His heart thundered against his ribs.

"Fight her off," Ash demanded again, a fierceness in her gaze that he'd come to know well.

Madoc closed his eyes, trying to drown out the fighting around him, trying to swallow the screaming voice in his own head.

He had a source of anathreia to pull from. He didn't need to tithe to use it—the well inside him was already full.

Don't be afraid, Tor whispered in his memories.

They were running out of time. Anathrasa was here—he could feel her consciousness punching through the synchronized pulse of the army she'd created.

The hunger inside him warred with the charge of the energeia he'd already taken from Ash. His anathreia was desperate, roiling like a shaken jar of wine. But the fortress he'd built around his soul held steady.

He opened his eyes and turned the hunger in on himself, giving it a source on which to feed: Anathrasa.

Do not—she began, but her demand broke off into a cry of panic.

His energeia swallowed her screams in his head, scraped her out of every crevice she'd lodged into—the gaps between his bones, the hollow of his throat, the spaces between his thoughts. It fed and fed, and it roared in satisfaction when she cried.

And when she was gone, before his hunger turned on the energeia he'd stolen from Ash, he pressed his hand to her stomach and forced it back into her body. Hot tendrils of fire. The solid strength of earth. Water slipping through her veins and the rootedness of living plants.

She gulped a breath, her head tilting skyward.

Then she fell into him.

He caught her, holding her tight. His chin dipped into the crook of her neck and he breathed in the warm, familiar scent of her skin.

"Are you . . . ," he started.

"Yes." She pushed back, wonder in her eyes. "You're back."

Her lips curled into a smirk as he pulled her up.

Again, the ground began to quake, and they braced against each other as a deafening hiss filled the air. The soldiers Madoc had stilled with anathreia were suddenly knocked aside by a slithering flash of red. A snake, as thick as the pillar holding up the palace roof and covered with glittering scales, circled them, strangling the flames Ash had raised beneath its massive body. It lifted its head, a black tongue darting out as milky poison dripped from two fangs the size of Madoc's arms.

A rumbling hiss echoed from its throat. "Traitors."

"Biotus," Madoc realized, horror flooding his veins as the snake's body coiled tighter, scraping over the sand. Before he or Ash could defend themselves, they were caught in the vise of his body, crushed together with a crack of bones and a gasp of breath.

With a scream of frustration, Ash tried to use her power, but was smothered by another rope of scales. Madoc struggled to move his arms, push them free with his legs, but his ribs were popping under the pressure.

His vision compressed. In the black smoke that rose around them, Anathrasa's army suddenly appeared, slack-jawed and single-minded. They stumbled toward Madoc and Ash, climbing over Biotus's coils, sending a new bolt of panic down Madoc's spine.

He couldn't breathe. Ash's knees dug into his thighs, her arms locked against his cracking ribs. They couldn't move.

His gaze lifted through the smoke to the stands, where a goddess in white stared down at him.

Anathrasa.

Fury rose inside him, hotter than Ash's flames and twice as potent. Anathrasa had done this—made this army, caused this war. Killed his sister and taken his mother.

He would not let her take anyone else.

He closed his eyes, drowning out the wind and screams and hisses, quieting even Ash's voice as she whimpered his name. Madoc drew on his strength again, on the power that made him *him*, and reached through the snake's thick skin with cool spikes of anathreia. Biotus's energeia was raw and bitter, and the taste of blood in Madoc's mouth made him gag, but he didn't stop.

The coils loosened, but he didn't stop.

Ash broke free, fighting off the army, but still, Madoc drank.

The snake shriveled. Writhed. It broke into the form of a human. Biotus's skin lost its luster. His muscles thinned. His mouth fell slack. He begged—*We can help each other, set me free.*

Madoc didn't listen.

Only when his power was completely gone did Madoc release his hold.

He staggered to one knee as Biotus crawled away through the waves of soldiers that were still pressing in. Madoc's vision was blurred by the thick, wild power inside him. He blinked, forcing his pounding head to focus, and frantically looked up to the box.

Anathrasa was gone.

"Madoc?" Ash helped him up. Touched his face. Blood was smeared across her cheeks. She cradled her left arm against her chest.

They were surrounded by a wall of rapidly crumbling stone—a fortress of Ash's creation. Already soldiers were knocking down the stones in a spray of dust.

He didn't have to ask if she was ready; she'd been born for this.

Trembling, he pushed Biotus's energeia into her the way he had Florus's power into Anathrasa. He sensed no resistance in her, only a welcoming warmth. She took it all, lips parted and eyes open, and when he was done, her teeth set in a vicious smile.

"One left," she said. "We still need Aera's power if we're going to beat Anathrasa."

"We don't have much time," he managed. The Mother Goddess had to have seen what he'd done. If Aera didn't know already, she would soon.

The goddess of air wasn't hard to spot. She had Hydra pinned at the top of the arena, throwing stones and sand at her with pummeling gales.

"Once she figures out what I'm doing, we won't have long," Madoc said.

Ash nodded. "I'll be ready."

"If you can hold her, I can drain her."

"We need to catch her by surprise," Ash said.

"No problem."

Madoc spun to find Elias. Dust coated the side of his brother's face, and his shoulder was weeping blood down his chest.

Madoc threw his arms around him, pulling him close. He'd never been so happy to see him in all his life.

When Elias pulled back, he was grinning.

"Did you know I can throw a dust wave across this entire arena?" Elias asked.

"Unfortunately, I did," Ash answered, making him cringe. He turned to Madoc.

"You know the sign," he said.

Madoc huffed. "You'd better be ready."

"I'm always ready." With a smirk, Elias grabbed Ash's forearm and dragged her away. They fought their way through the soldiers coming through the stones, leaving Madoc alone, clinging to hope.

He sprinted toward the side of the arena, pushing back those closest with a wave of soul energeia. He shoved off two of Aera's guards and one of Anathrasa's soldiers who attacked with a severed hand. When Madoc was close enough for a clear view of the goddess of air, he ducked low.

He focused on the strength inside him, and his anathreia surged and struck out toward Aera. Silver slivers of light cut across the gold sand. Her power darted away from him, the same uncontainable wind he remembered from the palace library.

She spun, fury painting her face. "Madoc!" she screamed. With a punch of her hand, she sent Hydra flying toward the far side of the stands, where she fell in a heap and did not rise.

Madoc aimed his anathreia at her again, but she spun, the wind whipping her a spear's throw to the left. He adjusted, tried again, but she was gone.

He heard her laughter behind him and twisted just in time for a breeze to cut beneath his knees and knock him to his back.

"Sweet Madoc," she cooed. "Did you really think it would be so easy?"

He scrambled up, and she jabbed a hand toward him. The air fled from his lungs in a hard cough, leaving him wide-eyed and gasping.

"It's a pity," she mocked, striding close enough that he could see the dark veins branching out like lightning beneath her eyes, and the jutting bones of her cheeks and bare shoulders. "I would have enjoyed playing with you for a few decades."

He tapped his fingers against his thigh.

"Sorry to disappoint," he rasped.

The ground shook, and twin waves of gravel three times his height rose on either side of Aera. They slammed into her with the force of two galloping horses, drawing a surprised scream from her throat.

"Now!" Ash cried from his left. To his right, Elias threw another wave of sand against the goddess of air.

Madoc couldn't see Aera in the cloud of dust, but he could feel the hum of her aereia, and struck out for it. With her power focused on Elias and Ash's attack, she couldn't siphon the air from his lungs or play her games. Cool fingers of anathreia locked her in place. Once he'd trapped her soul, he inhaled her energeia in gulps, the rise of wind rushing through his blood, raising the hair on his arms.

In a whirlwind, she broke free, forcing back the waves of dust that Ash and Elias struggled to throw at her. But before she could turn her attack to Madoc, she was lifted off the ground in a funnel of water, spinning and twisting against the self-contained current.

"Hold still, sister," Hydra growled, standing below her.

"Madoc, now!" Ash screamed.

He didn't delay. He pulled and pulled, teeth bared, feeling as though his skin would rip from the mounting pressure beneath. He drained Aera until she writhed in her prison of water. He drained her until her aereia was his, and her beating heart sounded no different than any other mortal's.

"That's enough," a woman ordered.

He fell to his hands and knees, dizzy with power. When his chin lifted, he saw Anathrasa standing beside him. Behind her stretched a wall of emerald vines, peppered with white flowers and bodies.

Ilena's body. Ava's. Danon's. Anathrasa had even managed to pull Elias away from the fight with Ash. They were held so tightly they couldn't even struggle.

Terror coursed through him.

Lunging forward, Ash struck out toward the wall with a burst of her own floreia—twisting ivy that shot toward Madoc's family. But before it reached them, the plants withered and ripped free from their roots in Ash's hands. With a shout of pain she staggered to one knee.

"You may know a few tricks," Anathrasa snapped at her, waving aside Ash's rescue attempt. "But you are not the goddess of plants."

"Finish this!" Elias shouted at Madoc, just before a vine twisted around his mouth to silence him.

"Give me the aereia, Madoc," Anathrasa said, carefully making her way toward him. "Give it to me, and they'll live. Drain the God Killer and give me the rest, and your family goes free."

He glanced at Ash, who was staring at Anathrasa, uncertainty in her eyes. At Hydra, who'd dropped the quivering form of her sister and turned her focus to the horde still closing in around them.

"The aereia," Anathrasa snapped. "Or Ilena is the first to die."

The vines pushed Ilena's body forward, revealing a thorned tendril that wrapped around her slender neck. She stared blankly ahead, still under Anathrasa's power, the white chalk on her mouth making her lips look pale and sickly.

Madoc quaked from aereia. From the terror twisting his soul. He could not lose Ilena. He couldn't lose any of them.

But he would if Anathrasa lived. She'd never let his family be free. As long as he was a threat, they would be used against him. He glanced to Hydra, fighting off the people still under Anathrasa's control. All of them had families too. All the world would suffer as long as she lived.

She would destroy the Divine and crush the Undivine into submission.

His gaze found Elias's, steady and knowing.

"I'm sorry," Madoc muttered. He tore himself away from Elias. From his mother, and sister, and brother, who he could no longer protect—who he never had been able to save.

He stumbled toward Ash. The last hope for his family. For Deimos. For them all.

"I love you," he said, and kissed her.

TWENTY-FOUR

ASH

ASH GRIPPED MADOC'S shoulders. The kiss was more pain than pleasure, his lips rough and insistent, bruising her mouth. Power poured from him into her, a whipping, violent tornado that thrashed from Ash's head down to her toes and sucked the air from her lungs. Air only surged back in as Madoc pulled away, transferring his breath to her.

He trembled, gasping, and Ash held him up as she felt him start to droop. His hooded eyes lifted to hers and he gave her a sad, aching smile.

"The last type of energeia," he said. His face darkened. "Get her."

Ash eased him to the sand. He knelt at her feet, one knee up and his forearm across it like he was bowing in reverence to her, not falling in exhaustion.

Ash looked down at him, shaking, her lips still hot from his. Her fingers splayed in front of her and she stared at them as though they would be different, some instructions scrawled across her skin as to what she should do now.

Aereia was the last piece. It fought for room in her body, churning winds and wild gales that were tempestuous and ever changing and never satisfied.

Bioseia was a constant growl in the back of her throat, an animalistic sharpness that took hold of her senses, heightening sight and sound and smell. The arena stank of body odor and metallic blood, of fear that smelled acidic and grief that smelled sooty and pain that smelled like bile. She could see everything, everyone, and hear the thrum of their heartbeats, a swelling whir like the agitated wings of a hummingbird.

Aereia and bioseia clicked into place with the floreia, hydreia, geoeia, and igneia.

Six energeias that had once been one.

Ash felt them unite inside her. She felt the aereia breathe life and the bioseia form it and the floreia grow it and the hydreia water it and the geoeia build it and the igneia detonate it. One energeia, one sprawling blanket that connected every part of her body and every person on this earth, Divine and Undivine and god.

Tor had worried this much power might kill her. Ash knew now that it was a foolish fear—this power was life. This power was death. This power was everything, and she understood now why a mortal had to die before holding such infinity.

A tear tracked down Ash's cheek. How had all the gods grown so far apart? How had they forgotten how much they needed each other?

How had Anathrasa corrupted the crystalline beauty of anathreia?

Ash turned. Barely a moment had passed in her revelation, all of time holding its breath as it waited and watched a new Mother Goddess form.

Off to Ash's left, Aera lay in the puddle of her water prison, screaming in fury. Hydra was fending off the soldiers.

There were no gods to worry about now.

Except one.

Anathrasa matched Aera's frustrated howls. "You fool!" she cried at Madoc. "You will watch your family die!"

She contracted her hand and the vines squeezed. Ava screamed in terror while Danon wept and Elias squirmed, his cheeks purpling. Only Ilena still didn't react, her face wearing that delicate sheen of controlled acceptance.

Ash lifted her hand. *Stop.*

The vines froze solid, the water deep in their pores quickly setting.

A flick of Ash's arm, and every vine withered, sliding Madoc's family to the soft, churned golden sands.

Anathrasa's eyes were wide and manic, a sign of how close she was to the edge even as she laughed. "You think you can challenge me, mortal? I am ageless. I am eternal. I will be here long after your bones turn to dust and you—"

Ash flared her hands palm-out and sent a whip of fire snapping into Anathrasa's chest. It threw her back against the swelling press of the army still bent at her command. Hydra was holding off the worst of them, but people poured in from every doorway, filling the arena, pulled by Anathrasa's call.

No more.

Ash closed her eyes.

No more.

She heard their minds. The same thought connected each soul to Anathrasa, like a tapestry fraying out its threads from a single point. Anathrasa's command fueled them: *Stop the God Killer.*

She had forced herself on these people. They were mortal and hadn't had a chance against a goddess.

Ash opened her eyes and released the hold Anathrasa had on them. *You are yourselves again.*

Instantly, raised weapons paused. War cries tapered to nothing. People blinked and looked around as awareness seeped back into them. Ilena was one of them, gathering her children into her arms.

Ash heard weeping from every direction, cries of confusion, pleas of surrender. But she smiled.

Anathrasa could not control these people anymore.

And now Ash would kill her.

Anathrasa righted herself from where Ash had thrown her. She bellowed in rage and the ground began to shake—great, mighty oaks burst up through the sand, pulled by Anathrasa's will. Their branches were jagged and sharp and skewered whoever happened to be in their wake, eliciting wails of pain and horror.

Ash punched her hands in two directions, one to push the floreia away from Madoc's family, and one to keep him and Hydra safe as well. She couldn't react fast enough to save everyone, and screaming dug into her ears, breaking past the battle-ready fog of concentration that was keeping her heart beating.

The roar of the growing trees settled, and where the arena had once been was now a deadly forest. Soldiers from the former army struggled to extract themselves from the twisted limbs and sharp branches. Blood dripped from the trees, falling like leaves.

Ash couldn't spot Anathrasa.

The screams of agony cut through the stillness that a forest couldn't help but bring. It was a nauseating contrast, peaceful floreia and so much pain.

"Ash." Hydra ran up to her and grabbed her arms. "Where did she go?"

"I don't—"

"Use the anathreia," Hydra coaxed.

Ash shuddered, wrapping her arms around herself. The trees blocked out the sun. They blocked out the sky. There were people impaled on their branches.

She couldn't break. She couldn't get distracted, not now.

She had to kill Anathrasa.

Eyes pinched shut, Ash pushed out the shouts and blood, the thundering of these hundreds of abused hearts and the fear in these innocent souls. She widened her awareness.

There was so much *pain* in this arena. It had already been a place of death, and agony was soaked into every particle of sand.

Ash grimaced and tore her eyes open. "I can't! We have to help everyone here—I can't see past the suffering."

She yanked her hand and sent a tree back into the earth, freeing the people stuck in it. Anathrasa had the bulk of Florus's floreia while Ash only had a small gift of it, but she would still be able to send this forest away, tree by tree.

Hydra grabbed her shoulders. "Not now. I need you to be

single-minded Ash again. I need you to be action-first-questions-later Ash. You can take care of this entire forest once you stop her. You need to find Anathrasa and eliminate her *now*."

Ash writhed, gasping. Anathreia was so much. It was all too much. The beauty in it was blinding, too bright, too expansive. There were thousands of people in Crixion alone, and they were hurting, scared, and Ash could feel it *all*—

"Let me."

A warm body pressed against Ash's back. Hydra released her as arms came around Ash's stomach, tightening, Madoc holding her to his chest.

His forehead rested on the back of her head and he looped one arm across her chest while the other kept her hips pinned against his. She could feel his anathreia, the essence at the core of him. He was scared, yes; he was tired; he'd been wounded somewhere on his side. But beneath all that, he was resolute, and he wasn't letting go of her.

She leaned into him, her body arching back so her head fell against his shoulder, and she knotted her fingers around his wrists.

"Breathe," he whispered. "Build a wall in your mind. One thought, then another, things you can use as anchors in the noise."

One thought. She just needed one to start.

She reached—and a searing pain came from one of the soldiers in the trees. She winced, shaking her head, whimpering. "No—it *hurts*, Madoc, it all hurts—"

"I know." He pulled her tighter, taking her weight. "Think about Tor. He's your anchor. Think about Taro and Spark. Think about Igna.

Think about—" His voice hitched, breath hot on the side of her neck. "Think about us, Ash. I'm not leaving you. I love you. Think about that, and anchor yourself to it, and use it to come back to yourself. Remember? We'll always come back to each other."

Ash reached up to touch Madoc's cheek, her fingers slipping down to hold his neck.

She loved him, too. She loved him, and that had saved her through this war, time and again.

It would save her now.

Ash stretched her mind. Anathreia swelled, bubbling up and out and scrambling across the arena.

Souls cried. People *wanted* and they *ached*—

Ash bit down on her tongue. Madoc. Madoc holding her, and his heart beating against her back.

Her anathreia searched and searched, scrambling through souls.

"When I find her," Ash started, her tongue dry and gritty, "what then?"

"Then you take the energeia in her body. Take it until there's nothing left. It's a hunger." She felt him swallow. "And it must be fed."

And then? Ash wanted to ask. What happened once she had Anathrasa's power? What did she do with so much anathreia?

Her awareness caught on someone behind her.

Ash's eyes flew open.

She whirled and shoved Madoc aside as Anathrasa charged out from behind one of her trees. A wave of vines carried her, one tendril licking the air ahead of her with a talon-like thorn at its head.

That thorn stabbed the space where Madoc had just been. Ash

spun her hands and cut the vine in half, letting the two pieces fall harmlessly to the sand.

Anathrasa kept charging. Ash braced her feet and planted her arms up so when Anathrasa reached her, the two of them slammed to a halt, Ash with her hands on Anathrasa's chest, Anathrasa snarling and spitting down at her.

"You will not take my victory!" Anathrasa shrieked, and then she *pulled.*

The energeia in Ash's chest rebounded, banging inside her as it fought against Anathrasa's incessant call.

Ash growled and fisted her hands in the collar of Anathrasa's gown. "This is not your victory," Ash spat back and scrambled through the Mother Goddess's body for the final remains of her soul.

Anathrasa felt Ash pulling at her energeia and redoubled her efforts. Her eyes strained, veins bulging in her face, sweat beading. Her smooth skin wrinkled and aged before shifting to become young again, a warring tangle of power and weakness as they each pulled the other's energeia.

An oily, horrifying thought wiggled into Ash's mind—she wasn't strong enough. Anathrasa may not have had her full power, but she was ancient and resilient all the same, and Ash barely knew how to use the power she had just gotten.

One of her feet slipped, sending her lurching back through the sand. She gritted her teeth and pulled at Anathrasa's energeia, harder, with everything she had—everything that still wouldn't be enough.

"Take it!" Ash heard a cry behind her. Hydra? "Madoc, take my hydreia and give it all to her, *now!*"

A hand touched her back, and water gushed through Ash's body. Cool and refreshing, it chased the other energeias in her soul and infused the hydreia already waiting there with extra power.

Something else came, too. Something still and sturdy and familiar. Madoc was giving her his own anathreia.

She wanted to tell him not to. She wanted to stop him, but it filled her before she could protest, an effervescent burst of anathreia. It was small against the power Ash had—but it was enough.

Like the final surge of a wave against a weakening tide wall, Ash threw the extra power at Anathrasa.

A moment of tension, and then it gave. It gave and gave until Anathrasa's soul went limp and surrendered to Ash's grasp.

Ash stumbled back. Everything was sunlight. Golden rays cascaded over the arena, the forest, the world, threads of connection, pulses of energeia.

All she could see was golden power.

The knowledge came, sure and strong: no one had ever been this powerful. No being, no mortal, no god. Ash was something bigger than all of that. Something darker, and brighter, terrible and wonderful all at once.

She could rule it all. The world would bow to her, and those who wouldn't bow in honor would bow in fear. She was a goddess of goddesses and she was *everything*.

Ash breathed too fast and her heartbeat thundered.

Anchors in the noise.

Tor hugging her. Taro and Spark, smiling at her. Madoc, his lips on hers, his laugh.

To Marie

THE HIGHEST POINT IN THE COUNTY
IS MARKED BY MYSTERY.
IT IS SAID THAT A MAN DIED THERE IN A
GREAT STORM, WHILE BINDING AN EVIL
THAT THREATENED THE WHOLE WORLD.
THEN THE ICE CAME AGAIN, AND WHEN IT
RETREATED, EVEN THE SHAPES OF THE
HILLS AND THE NAMES OF THE TOWNS
IN THE VALLEYS CHANGED.
NOW, AT THAT HIGHEST POINT ON
THE FELLS, NO TRACE REMAINS OF WHAT
WAS DONE SO LONG AGO,
BUT ITS NAME HAS ENDURED.
THEY CALL IT —

THE WARDSTONE.

Contents

MEG
SKELTON

This is a tale that must be told; a warning to those who might one day take my place. My name is John Gregory and I'm the local Spook; what now follows is the full and truthful account of my dealings with the witch Meg Skelton.

THE FIGHT WITH THE ABHUMAN

For five years my master, Henry Horrocks, had trained me as a spook, teaching me how to deal with ghosts, boggarts, witches and all manner of creatures from the dark. Now my apprenticeship was completed and I was fully qualified, still living at my master's Chipenden house and working alongside him to make the County a safer place.

Late in the autumn, an urgent message came from Arnside, to the north-west of the County, begging my old master and me to deal with an abhuman, a foul, monstrous creature that had brought terror to the district for far too long. Many families had suffered at

5

its cruel hands and there had been many deaths and maimings.

Henry Horrocks's health had been deteriorating for quite some time, and three days before the message arrived he'd taken to his bed.

'You'll have to go on ahead, lad,' he told me, struggling for breath, his chest wheezing as he spoke. 'But take care – abhumans can be very strong. Keep it at bay as I've taught you, using your staff, then stab it through the forehead. If the job looks too dangerous, keep watch from a distance. As soon as I'm fit enough, I'll follow you north. Hopefully tomorrow . . .'

With those words we parted, and carrying my staff and bag, I set off for Arnside. Had I been going to face a witch, I would have borrowed my master's silver chain, but there were doubts about its effectiveness against abhumans, which have varying levels of resistance towards such tools of our trade as rowan wood, salt and iron. No – a blade was the best way to deal with such a creature.

I visited Arnside village and a few farms to gather as

much information as possible concerning the nature of what I faced and where I would find it. What I heard did little to boost my confidence. The creature was immensely strong and had attacked a farmer only a week earlier, ripping his head from his shoulders while the terrified milkmaid watched from her hiding place in the barn. After killing her unfortunate employer, the abhuman drank his blood, then tore the raw flesh from his bones with its teeth. It had now made its home in a tower and usually went hunting for prey soon after midnight. People for miles around were living in fear; no home was safe.

I came down into the forest at dusk. All the leaves had fallen and lay on the ground, rotten and brown. The tower was twice the height of the tallest trees, like a black demon finger pointing up at the grey County sky. A girl had been seen waving from its solitary window, frantically beckoning for aid. I'd been told that the creature had seized her for its own and now held her as its plaything, imprisoning her within those dank stone walls.

First I made a fire and sat gazing into its flames while I gathered my courage. It would be better to wait for Henry Horrocks to arrive; two of us would have a far greater chance against the creature. But despite his assurances I had no confidence that he would join me. His condition had been steadily worsening rather than improving. Besides, the creature would probably kill again this very night. It was my duty as a spook to deal with it before then; my duty to the people of the County.

Taking the whetstone from my bag, I sharpened the blade of my staff until my fingers could not touch its edge without yielding blood. Finally, just before midnight, I went to the tower and hammered out a challenge upon the wooden door with the base of my staff.

The creature came forth brandishing a great club and roared out in anger. It was a foul thing dressed in the skins of animals, reeking of blood. Almost seven feet tall, with a chest like a barrel, it was a truly formidable opponent. I am a spook and trained to

deal with creatures of the dark, and I was strong then and in my prime, but my courage faltered as it attacked me with a terrible fury.

At first I retreated steadily, but I released the blade from its recess in my staff and waited for my chance to counter-attack. Jabbing repeatedly at the beast to keep it at bay, I whirled to the left in a rapid spiral and drew it away from the tower into the trees. Twice that massive club smashed against tree trunks, missing my head by inches. Either blow would have shattered my skull like an eggshell.

But now it was my turn to attack. I whacked the creature hard on the side of the head, a blow that would have felled a village blacksmith, but it didn't even stagger. Then I managed to spear it deeply in the right shoulder so that, within moments, blood started to run down its bare arm and splatter onto the grass. That brought it to a halt and we faced each other warily.

As it bellowed in anger and prepared to attack again, I flicked my staff from my left hand to my right and drove it straight into the creature's forehead with all my strength. The blade went in deep and, with a gasp and then a terrible groan, the abhuman fell stone-dead at my feet.

I paused to catch my breath, looking down at the creature. I had no regrets about taking its life, for it would have killed again and again and would never have been sated.

It was then that the girl called out to me from the tower, her siren voice luring me up the stone steps. There, in the topmost room, I found her lying upon a bed of straw, bare-footed and bound fast with a long silver chain. With skin like milk and long fair hair, she was by far the prettiest woman that I had ever set eyes on. She told me that her name was Meg and pleaded to be released from the chain; her voice was so persuasive that my reason fled and the world spun about me.

No sooner had I unbound her from the coils of the chain than she fastened her lips hard upon mine. And so sweet were her kisses that I almost swooned away in her arms. It was a night that was to change my life. My first night with Meg.

I awoke to see sunlight streaming through the window, and spied the toes of Meg's shoes peeping out from under a chair in the corner of the room. They were pointy; pointy shoes. My heart sank within my chest. My master had warned me that pointy shoes were often a strong indication that the wearer might be a witch. Worse was to come, for as Meg dressed, I saw her back clearly for the first time and my blood froze cold within my veins. She was one of the lamia witches, and the mark of the serpent was upon her. Fair of face though she was, her spine was covered with green and yellow scales.

'Witch!' I cried, reaching for the silver chain. 'You're a witch!'

'I harm nobody!' she cried. 'Only those who wish *me* harm!'

'It's in your nature to practise deceit,' I said angrily.

'Once a witch, always a witch – your kind are not even human . . .'

I threw the chain that had previously bound her, and the long hours I'd spent casting against the practice post in the Chipenden garden paid off. The chain dropped over her head and shoulders, binding her fast so that she could neither walk, speak nor move her arms. Filled with anger at her deceit, I carried her, thus bound, back to Chipenden – where a terrible shock awaited me.

CHAPTER 2
HARBOURING A WITCH

To my sorrow and dismay, I found Henry Horrocks dead and cold in his bed. He had been a good master and eventually my friend, and it grieved me sorely to lose him.

Leaving the witch safely bound, I buried my master at the edge of the local churchyard. Although a spook is not permitted to be interred in holy ground, no doubt some priest might have been persuaded to pray over his body, but Henry Horrocks had already told me that he didn't want that. He had lived a blameless, hard-working life defending the County against the dark, and felt capable of finding his own way through the mists of Limbo to the light.

That taken care of, it was time to deal with the witch. First I dug a pit for her in the eastern garden, then had the local mason and blacksmith construct its lid, a stone rim with thirteen iron bars. Once she was in the pit, I would drag the lid into position.

By now my anger had abated somewhat. I had left Meg chained to the side of the house, where she had been soaked to the skin by a heavy downpour of rain. She looked a pitiful sight, but despite her bedraggled appearance her beauty still captivated me. My heart lurched with pity and I had to harden my resolve.

When I released her from the chain, she struggled so fiercely that I barely overcame her and was forced to pull her by her long hair through the trees towards the pit, while she ranted and screamed fit to wake the dead. It was still raining hard and she slipped on the wet grass, but I carried on, dragging her along the ground, though her bare arms and legs were scratched by brambles. It was cruel but it had to be done.

We reached the edge of the pit, but when I started

to tip her over the edge, she clutched at my knees and began to sob pitifully.

'Please!' she cried. 'Spare me. I can't live like that – not trapped down there in the dark!'

'You're a witch and that's where you belong,' I told her. 'Be grateful you're not suffering a worse fate—'

'Oh, please, please, John, think again. Can I help it that I was born a witch? Despite that, I never hurt others unless they threaten me. Remember what we said to each other last night? How we felt? Nothing's changed. Nothing's changed at all. Please put your arms around me again and forget this foolishness.'

I stood there for a long time, full of anguish, about to topple over the edge myself – until, at last, I made a decision that changed my life.

She was a lamia witch and such creatures have two forms. Meg appeared to be in the domestic, near-human shape rather than the feral one, in which form the creatures become savage killers. So perhaps she spoke the truth. Maybe she did only use her strength in self-defence.

There was hope for her, I thought. So why not give her a chance?

I helped her to her feet and wrapped my arms about her and we both wept. My love for her was so sudden and all-consuming that my heart almost burst through my chest. How could I put her into the pit when I loved her better than my own soul? It was her eyes that captivated me: they were the most beautiful I'd ever seen – along with her voice, which was sweeter and more melodious than any siren song.

I begged her forgiveness, and then we turned together and, hand in hand, walked away from the pit, back towards the house that now belonged to me.

It was a fateful night and sometimes, despite my faith in free will and my firm belief that, minute by minute, second by second, we shape our own futures, it does seem to me that some things are meant to be. For had Henry Horrocks still been alive on my return, Meg would certainly have gone into a pit.

But I was captivated by Meg and she became the

love of my life. Beauty is a terrible thing: it binds a man tighter than a silver chain about a witch.

We lived happily together for almost a month in my Chipenden house, Meg and I. My fondest memories are of the times we sat together on the bench in the western garden, holding hands and watching the sun go down.

However, things soon started to go wrong. Unfortunately, Meg was very strong-willed, and against my wishes she insisted on visiting the village shops. Her tongue was as sharp as a barber's razor, and right from the start she began to have lively arguments with some of the village women. These disagreements had small beginnings: one woman pushed in front of Meg in a shop, as if she wasn't there. Another called her an 'incomer', and she sensed hostility from all the women to an outsider who was certainly prettier than any of them. A few of these disputes quickly developed into bitter feuds. No doubt there was spite on both sides.

'Meg, let me do the shopping,' I suggested to her. 'You're drawing too much attention to yourself. If it wasn't for me being a spook and you living at my house, they'd have already accused you of being a witch. You'll end up in the dungeons at Caster Castle if you're not careful!' I warned.

'I can take care of myself, John,' she replied, 'as you well know. Would you want me to be confined to this house and garden just because some shrews in the village insist on making trouble? No, I must fight my own battles!'

Eventually, being a witch, Meg resorted to witch-craft against her enemies. She did no serious harm to the women. One suffered nasty boils all over her body; another exceptionally house-proud woman who worshipped cleanliness had recurring infestations of lice and a plague of cockroaches in her kitchen.

At first the accusations were little more than whispers. Then one woman spat at Meg in the street and received a good hard slap for her discourtesy.

It would probably have stopped at that, but unfortunately she was the sister of the parish constable.

One morning the bell rang at the withy-trees crossroads and I went down to investigate. Instead of the poor boggart-haunted farmer that I had been expecting, the stout red-faced parish constable was standing there, truncheon in his belt and hands on his hips.

'Mr Gregory,' he said, his manner proud and pompous, 'it has come to my attention that you are harbouring a witch. The woman, known as Margery Skelton, has used witchcraft to hurt some good women of this parish. She has also been seen at midnight, under a full moon, gathering herbs and dancing naked by the pond at the edge of Homeslack Farm. I have come to arrest her and demand that you bring her to this spot immediately!'

'Meg no longer lives with me!' I said. 'She's gone to Sunderland Point to sail for her homeland, Greece.'

It was a lie of course, but what could I do? There was

no way I was going to deliver Meg into his hands. The man would take her north to Caster – where, no doubt, she'd eventually hang.

I could see that the parish constable wasn't satisfied, but there was little he could do about it immediately. Being a local, he knew not to enter my garden for fear of what he might find there. Generations of spooks had lived and worked at Chipenden, and the villagers believed the house and its surroundings were haunted by denizens of the dark. So he went away with his tail between his legs. I had to keep Meg away from the village from that day forth. It proved difficult and was the cause of many arguments between us, but there was worse to come.

Egged on by his sister, the constable went to Caster and made a formal complaint to the High Sheriff there. Consequently they sent a young constable with a warrant to arrest Meg. I was told about his imminent arrival by the village blacksmith, so I was ready. I needed to get Meg away as quickly as possible.

My former master had bequeathed another house

to me: it lay on the edge of brooding Anglezarke Moor. I had visited it just once and found little about it to my taste. Now it could be put to good use. In the dead of night, very late in the autumn, Meg and I journeyed to Anglezarke and set up home there.

It was a bleak place, wet and windy, with the winter threatening long months of ice and snow. The house had no garden and was built in a ravine, right back against a sheer rocky crag that kept it in shadow for most of the day. It was big, with ten bedrooms, including an attic, and a deep cellar; but even though I lit fires in every room, it was cold and damp – not a place where I could safely store books. However, we made the best of it and were happy for a while. But then there was an unexpected development that made my life much more difficult.

Unbeknown to me, Meg had written to her sister, giving her our new address. When the reply arrived, she became agitated. I found her pacing up and down in the kitchen, the letter clutched to her chest.

'What ails you, woman?' I demanded.

'It's my sister, Marcia,' she admitted at last. 'Unless we help, she'll be killed for sure. Can she come here to us?'

I groaned inside. Her sister? Another lamia witch!

'Where is she now?'

'Far to the north beyond the boundaries of the County. She's being hidden and protected but it can't go on for much longer or those who guard her will be in danger themselves. There's a quisitor in the area and he's already growing suspicious. A thorough search is being carried out. Please say she can come here,' Meg begged. 'Please do. She's my only relative in the whole world . . .'

Quisitors worked for the Church, and hunted down and burned witches. I had no love for such men – they would burn a spook too if they got the chance. Often they were corrupt and colluded with jealous neighbours to burn women who were totally innocent of witchcraft. Afterwards they confiscated their land and grew rich.

'She can come for a while until the danger is over,' I

said, relenting at last. I was too much in love with Meg to deny her anything.

Meg wrote back, and later that week a reply came. Her sister was travelling to Anglezarke by coach. We were to meet her on the Bolton road at the foot of the moor.

'She's coming by night,' Meg said. 'It'll be safer for her that way . . .'

CHAPTER
3
JUST A PUSSYCAT

So it was that just after midnight we waited shivering at the crossroads for the coach that would bring her sister to stay with us. There was still snow on the ground, but there had been no fresh falls for over three days so I was reasonably confident that the road would be open. At last, in the distance, we saw the coach approaching, the breath of the team of six horses steaming in the cold night air.

I waited for Marcia to alight from the coach, but instead, the driver and his mate jumped down and began to unfasten the ropes that bound something large to the back. They carried it towards us and laid it at our feet. It was a black coffin . . .

Without a word the two men climbed back up onto the coach; then the driver cracked his whip, brought the horses about and off they went again, back the way they'd come. I felt cold inside. Colder than the air freezing my forehead and cheeks.

'Don't tell me this is what I think it is . . .' I said softly.

'My sister is inside. How else could she have got here undetected?'

'She's feral, isn't she?'

Meg nodded.

'Why didn't you tell me?'

'Because you would never have allowed her to come here . . .'

Cursing under my breath, I helped Meg drag the coffin back up the slope towards the house. Beautiful though she was, Meg was extremely strong, and once back in the house she wasted no time in tearing off the lid with her bare hands.

I stood back, my staff at the ready. 'Can you control her?' I asked.

'She's just a pussycat.' Meg smiled, stepping back to allow Marcia to scuttle from the open coffin.

It was the first time I'd seen a lamia in the feral form. My master had described them to me and I'd read entries from books in the Chipenden library, but nothing could have prepared me for the actual thing.

Marcia was far from human in shape: she balanced herself, as if ready to spring, on four thin limbs which ended in large hands; each finger had a long claw. Her back was covered in green and yellow scales and her hair was long and greasy, falling over her shoulders as far as the ground. Her face, which looked up at us each in turn, was like something out of a nightmare, with gaunt features and heavy-lidded eyes.

Marcia first took up residence in the attic, and this worked well enough for a week or so. A feral lamia can summon birds to her side, where they wait in thrall, unable to fly off, until she finally devours them. The attic had a big skylight and I would hear the birds gathering on the roof; then their cries of terror as she pulled off their wings and, too late, they realized they were food for a lamia.

Then there were the rats. She could summon them too. I would hear them squealing in excitement as they climbed up the drainpipes, finally using the same route as the birds and dropping through the skylight to scamper across the floorboards. Every evening I would hear Marcia scuttling about as she chased them, and Meg would look up from her weaving and give me a warm smile.

'She likes a juicy rat, that sister of mine. But the chase is as good as the eating!'

Every week Meg would bring Marcia raw meat from the butcher's to supplement her diet. She looked after her sister well, regularly sweeping the attic floor clean of feathers and rat-skins. I wasn't happy, but what could I do? I didn't want to lose Meg. And I reasoned that a feral lamia was better off safe in the attic of my house than roaming free and threatening the County.

But then, one dark moonless night, Marcia got out through the skylight, went up onto the moor and killed a sheep. There was a bloody trail leading back to the house where she'd dragged the carcass behind her. Luckily a fresh fall of snow before dawn obscured the tracks so the farmer was none the wiser. I imagine he put the loss down to wolves or the wild dogs that sometimes ran in packs on Anglezarke Moor during the winter.

Meg gave her sister a good talking to and told me that she'd promised never to do it again.

It was just a few weeks later that Marcia first came downstairs . . .

I had been sitting next to Meg, facing the fire, when I heard unexpected sounds on the stairs: the clip-clop of shoes. I turned and saw Marcia peering at us from the doorway. It was as if a savage animal, a predator, had suddenly dressed itself in human clothes; a creature that was breathing too rapidly and noisily and still hadn't learned how to stand properly.

'Come here, sister, and sit beside us. Warm yourself at the fire,' Meg invited.

I was shocked by the change in her appearance.

Lamias are slow shape-shifters, and the weeks Marcia had lived at the house and the long hours she'd spent in the company of her sister had altered her form significantly towards the domestic. She was wearing a pair of her sister's pointy shoes and one of her dresses: the garment's hem was knee-length and cut away at the shoulders, and I could see how Marcia's arms and legs had fleshed out. Her hair had been cut neatly too, and her long deadly claws were the only visible aspect of the feral that remained. Her face was almost fully human, with a wild, savage beauty.

Marcia sat herself down and looked at me out of the corners of her eyes; she licked her lips before giving me a twisted smile.

'We could share him, sister, couldn't we? A man between us. Why not?'

'He's mine!' Meg retorted. 'I don't share my man with anyone – not even my sister!'

I think that was what hardened Meg against Marcia; what spurred her to alert me to danger in the middle of the night.

'Marcia's not in the attic!' she told me breathlessly. 'She's gone out onto the moor, looking for food.'

'Not another sheep,' I groaned, swinging my legs out over the edge of the bed and starting to pull on my boots. It seemed that Marcia, despite her changed appearance, still had much of the feral lamia's inner urges.

'No. It's worse than that. Far worse. She's after a child. One she spied at the farm when she killed that sheep. I thought I'd talked her out of it!'

'How long has she been gone?'

'A few minutes at most. I heard a noise on the roof and went up to the attic and found her missing.'

Marcia's tracks were easy enough to follow across the snow-clad moor. Meg went with me, offering to help as best she could.

'If she kills a child, they'll find her eventually. She'll never get away with that and we'll have to move again,' Meg complained.

'That may well be true, but we should be thinking of the poor child. The child and her family!' I retorted angrily, increasing my pace. Would we be too late? I wondered with sinking heart.

The footprints led through the farm gate and into the yard. Then we saw Marcia crouching in the shadow of the barn, looking up at a window – no doubt the bedroom of her intended prey. I breathed a sigh of relief. We could still save the child.

'No, sister, you're going too far!' Meg called out, keeping her voice low so as not to disturb the household. 'Come back with us now!'

But blood-lust held Marcia in its grip; she was beyond words. She hissed at us, then looked up at the bedroom again. Suddenly she kicked off her pointy shoes, surged forward and scampered straight up the sheer wall of the house, her finger- and toenails gouging into the stone.

She smashed the glass with her left fist, then seized the window frame and plucked the whole thing, wood and remaining glass panes, from the wall and hurled it down into the yard, where it fell with a tremendous crash. She climbed into the bedroom and I heard a child cry out with fear. The next moment she jumped out through the window again, down into the yard, and landed facing me, carrying the child under her arm. It was more baby than toddler and it was screaming its lungs out.

'Give the child to me, Marcia!' I commanded, my left hand targeting her with the blade of my staff, my right reaching out towards the baby.

She hesitated, and maybe she would have done as I instructed. But all at once the farmer burst out of the front door brandishing a big stick, his wife at his heels wailing as loud as a banshee. He went straight for Marcia, but she swiped him with the fingers of her free hand, the talons laying open his forehead to the bone. He fell to his knees, blood running into his eyes, while his wife screamed even louder and started tearing at her hair.

Seizing her chance, Marcia raced off across the farmyard and I immediately gave chase. She started to climb, heading up towards the moor tops. She seemed to be pulling ahead even though I was running as fast as I could. I glanced back. Meg was quickly catching up with me. When she drew level, I shouted out angrily.

'If your sister kills that baby, I'll put my blade through her heart! Do something now or she's dead!' I warned, and I meant every word.

In response Meg began to surge ahead of me. I was slowing because of the deepening snow, but she was starting to close on her sister. I lost sight of them as they passed beyond the brow of one of the lower slopes. When they came into view again, there was a series of blood-curdling yells and screams.

They were fighting: clawing, biting and scratching so that blood sprayed out onto the snow. But where was the baby?

To my relief, I saw that it lay on the ground to one side, still crying loudly. My first instinct was to pick the child up and get it away from the danger of that furious fight. But then the two witches broke apart and I saw my chance.

With a flick of my wrist, I cast my silver chain towards Marcia; it was the one I'd inherited from my master – though I also had the one that had once bound Meg in the abhuman's tower. It was a good shot and it dropped over Marcia's head and bound her tightly, bringing her down into the snow.

Meg wiped the blood from her face, went over to pick up the child and started to whisper in its ear. I don't know what she said, but it was effective: within seconds it became silent, closed its eyes and nestled against her neck.

I hefted the bound Marcia into position over my left shoulder and headed back towards the farm. When we arrived, the mother cried louder than ever at being re-united with her baby, but they were tears of joy.

'Thank you! Thank you! I never thought I'd see my little girl again!' she said between sobs. 'My poor husband though – he'll be scarred for life!'

I wondered how grateful she'd be if she knew that

I'd been harbouring her baby's abductor in my own house? So with Meg walking silently at my side, I trudged back to my house, deep in thought. Once inside I told Meg what I intended.

'Down in the cellar there are graves and pits ready for boggarts and witches. So far they're all empty. My master, Henry Horrocks, had them prepared for the work he was doing locally. But after staying here for a while he decided that he didn't like this house, so they've never been used—'

'No! Please, John, don't put my sister in a pit. Don't do that . . .'

'I'll give her just one chance to avoid a pit, and one chance only. There are rooms on the upper levels of the cellar. She can stay in one of them – she'll be comfortable enough there. The iron gate on the cellar steps will give us extra security, so effectively she'll be sealed behind that gate and the neighbourhood will be safe.'

So that's what we did. A lamia has more resistance to iron than other witches, but the gate was very strong;

Marcia was in a secure place. Of course, Meg insisted on seeing her sister every day. They chatted in her room below the gate, and Meg often took her fresh meat and offal from the butcher. Marcia couldn't summon birds down there, but she ate a lot of rats – as I could see from all the skins Meg had to clear up.

The winter moved on and the days began to lengthen. I did a few jobs locally, including moving on a trouble-some hall-knocker boggart and slaying a ripper with salt and iron. I realized that there was a lot of work to be done on Anglezarke Moor, but Chipenden also needed my help. Could I leave Meg here while I paid the village and its surroundings a short spring visit?

Eventually the decision was made for me, but in a way I didn't expect. It began in a similar fashion to the difficulties in Chipenden. A few words were exchanged between Meg and the local women. This time the constable didn't get involved because the people of Adlington had a strong sense of community and believed in sorting things out for themselves.

Meg still liked to go shopping, but I'd employed the local odd-job man, Bill Battersby, to bring me bulky supplies of potatoes and other vegetables up from the village to save her the trouble of carrying them. It was he who gave me warning of what was happening. To begin with it was nothing that I hadn't heard before: accusations of using curses – a woman suffering night-terrors; another too afraid to venture beyond her own front door. But then there was something new . . .

'She's after someone's husband. The villagers won't stand for that. Your Meg has gone too far!' Battersby warned.

'What do you mean? Make yourself clear!' I demanded, my heart already torn by his words. I knew precisely what he meant but couldn't bring myself to believe it.

'She's taken a fancy to Dan Crumbleholme, the village tanner. His wife, Dolly, spied them together. And there are reports that they've been seen kissing behind the tannery. Folks won't stand for it. They think she's used witchcraft to turn his head. If it happens again . . .'

I sent Battersby away with bitter words, still unable to believe that Meg would betray me by seeing another man. But I'd noticed that she'd taken to shopping later, when the sun was about to go down – something I could see no reason for. So the following afternoon I resolved to follow her.

I noticed that she had put on a pair of pointy shoes that she'd only bought the previous week. It was the first time she'd worn them and I remember thinking how attractively they set off her ankles. I kept my distance but was always in danger of being detected. A seventh son of a seventh son has a certain immunity against the powers of a witch, but Meg was exceptionally strong and I had to be vigilant.

Meg did her shopping, being the last customer at each shop she visited, and I began to feel better. No doubt she just shopped late to avoid the throng of local women and the opportunity for quarrels and disputes. But my relief was short-lived. She went to the tannery last of all. Worse, rather than knocking at the front door, which was already locked for the night, she went to the rear of the premises.

I didn't wait long before following her. I had hardly gone round the corner when the back door slammed and I saw Meg walking towards me.

'What are you up to, Meg?' I demanded.

'Nothing. Nothing at all,' she protested. 'I wanted some soft leather to stitch myself a new bag, that's all. The shop was shut but I knocked on the back door and Dan was kind enough to take my order even though his business has just shut for the night.'

I didn't believe her. She seemed flustered, which was unusual for Meg. We quarrelled bitterly, and following the heat of our exchange, a coldness came between us to rival that of the winter top of Anglezarke Moor. It persisted, and three days later, despite my protests, Meg went shopping again.

This time the village women resorted to violence. Over a dozen of them seized her in the market square. Bill Battersby told me later that she'd fought with fists like a man, but also scratched like a cat, almost blinding the ringleader of the women. Finally they struck her down from behind with a cobblestone and, once felled, she was bound tightly with ropes.

Only a silver chain can hold a witch for long, but they rushed her down to the pond and, after breaking the ice with stones, threw her into the deep cold water. If she drowned, they would accept that she was innocent of witchcraft; if she floated they'd have the satisfaction of burning her.

Meg did float, but face down, and after five minutes or so became very still in the water. The women were satisfied that she had drowned and didn't really have the stomach for burning her anyway. So they left her where she was.

It was Battersby who pulled her out of the pond. By rights she should have been dead, but Meg was incredibly tough. To his amazement, she soon began to twitch and splutter, coughing up water onto the muddy bank. He brought her back to my house across the back of his pony. She looked a sorry sight, but in hours she was fully recovered and soon started to plot her revenge.

I'd already thought long and hard about what needed to be done. I could cast her out; let her take her own chances in the world. But that would have broken my heart, because I still loved her. And I had to make allowances because it wasn't all Meg's fault. You see, she was an exceptionally pretty woman and it was natural that men should be attracted to her. The temptations for her were consequently greater than for most women, I told myself.

My knowledge of a special herb tea seemed to be the answer. It is possible to administer this to keep a witch in a deep sleep for many months. If the dose is reduced, she can even walk and talk – though it impairs the memory, making the witch forget her knowledge of the dark arts. So this was the method I decided to use.

It was very difficult to get the dosage right, and painful to see Meg so docile and mild, her fiery spirit (something that had attracted me to her in the first place) now subdued. So much so that, at times, she seemed a stranger to me. The worst time of all was when I decided to leave her alone in my Anglezarke house and returned to Chipenden for the summer. It had to be done lest the law catch up with her. There was still a danger that she might be hanged at Caster. So I locked her in a dark room off the cellar steps in so deep a trance that she was hardly breathing.

'Farewell, Meg,' I whispered into her ear. 'Dream of the garden at Chipenden where we were so happy. I'll see you in the autumn.'

As for her sister, Marcia, despite my former promise to Meg, I hired a mason and smith and had her bound in a pit in the cellar. I had no choice. I could not take the risk that she might eventually break through the iron gate. Without human companionship or contact with a domestic lamia, she would slowly shift her shape until she became feral again. And she wouldn't starve. She would never run out of rats – they could always be relied on.

I left for Chipenden with a heavy heart. Although I'd

experimented through the winter, I still worried whether or not I'd got Meg's dose of herb tea right. Too much and she might stop breathing; too little and she could wake up alone in that dark cell with many long weeks to wait until my return. So I spent our enforced separation riddled with sorrow and anxiety.

Fortunately I had calculated the dosage correctly and returned late the following autumn just as Meg was beginning to stir. It was hard for her, but at least she didn't hang, and the County was spared the harm she could have inflicted.

But a lesson must be learned from this, one that my apprentices should note carefully. A spook should never become romantically involved with a witch; it compromises his position and draws him dangerously close to the dark. I have fallen short in my duty to the County more than once, but my relationship with Meg Skelton was my greatest failing of all. This is a tale that had to be told and I'm glad the telling is over.

Always beware a woman who wears pointy shoes!

DIRTY DORA

My name is Dirty Dora Deane and I'm a dead witch.

Some call me Dirty because I spit thick slimy gobs of spittle to mark my territory. But I'm bad, not mad; have a reason for all I do. When I sniff that spit, I know I'm home and safe in the dell. Sniff it in the dark, I can, when I'm crawling back on my hands and knees.

Although I'm cold and dead now, and live under the rotting leaves in Witch Dell, I'm still strong enough to leave it and I want to tell my tales while I still can. Most nights I hunt for blood, but once or twice a week I go back to our cosy cottage, where my sister, Aggy, still lives. We chat together about the old times while my damp clothes steam in front of the fire; then, after Aggy has combed the beetles out of my hair, I spend a bit of time jotting down my memories. It's not easy because I find it difficult to remember what happened and I want to get it all down before it's all gone out of my mind – or I can't write no more. Don't know which will happen first. Never can tell with us dead witches. Sometimes the mind goes completely. Then again, it could be my hands that drop off so that I can't hold a pen. More than one dead witch crawls round the dell with pieces of her body missing. One ain't even got a head!

Now I only remember three things properly. Three chunks – that's all. The rest has gone.

CHAPTER 1
MY SABBATHS

I'll start by telling you about my sabbaths. The ones I enjoyed as a girl and a young woman.

The four main ones are Candlemas, Walpurgis, Lammas and Halloween. They're the nights when the Pendle witches meet. Not together, mind. The different clans don't see eye to eye; they gather in different places. We Deanes usually meet on the outskirts of our village and build a big fire. The thirteen members of the coven form a circle around it, warming their hands. Other witches from the clan stand further back, according to their age and power.

We kill a lamb first, slitting its throat and covering our hands and faces with its warm blood. Once its carcass has been thrown into the fire, we start with curses, shrieking them up into the sky to fly out towards our enemies or make their bodies wither and rot. Exciting, it is. Loved that more than anything when I was young.

But Halloween was always my favourite sabbath because that was when the Fiend sometimes paid a visit. Got lots of names, he has. Some call him Old Nick, but people who ain't witches usually call him the Devil.

Didn't stay long, but it was good just to get a glimpse of him. Most witches want to see the Fiend at least once in their lives. Big, he was. Very big, with a tail, hooves and lovely glossy black hair all over his body. And what a lovely stink he gave out – ranker than a tom-cat. He'd appear right in the middle of the flames, and the coven members would reach out their hands to touch and stroke him, not caring about burning their arms.

I remember the night it all went wrong though. The night when an enemy stole into our gathering. Nobody saw it coming. Nobody sniffed it out. The Fiend had just appeared in the flames and all our eyes were on *him*, not on what was dashing out of the darkness straight towards the fire.

It was a wild woman, her hair flying behind her as she ran. She carried three blades – one in each hand, the third gripped between her teeth. She burst right through to the edge of the flames before anyone could stop her, and threw a blade straight at the Fiend. I heard him scream, a shriek that split the sky above with forked lightning and made the stones groan beneath our feet.

But she wasn't satisfied with that. Twice more she threw her blades. I wasn't close enough to see, but they told me later that all three reached their target: the first one stuck in his chest, the second in his throat, and the third went up to the hilt in the left cheek of his hairy arse. The latter would have been the worst for sure, but he turned away at the last moment.

Why he didn't kill her on the spot nobody knows – certainly not we Deanes. The Fiend simply vanished, and the fire died down and went out in an instant, plunging us all into darkness. That was how the mad knifewoman made her escape.

We raked three blades out of the embers of the fire. Each one was tipped with silver. We used our best scryers, but we couldn't find out who the madwoman was or where she'd gone. She'd cloaked herself in powerful magic.

Later we sent assassins after her, three in all, over the space of a few days. Not one of them came back, and then the trail went cold and even the best trackers couldn't find her. The Fiend didn't appear to us for five years after that. It was a bad time. Really bad. Our magic was weak or didn't work at all, and some of our coven died of wasting diseases. They say it was the Fiend taking his revenge on us because we hadn't taken enough precautions against an intruder; we hadn't kept him safe.

Why she did it nobody knows – at least, perhaps some do but, if so, they ain't saying. Got a glimpse of her face as she passed me sprinting towards the fire.

She was young, hardly more than a girl . . . somehow, I felt I knew her. Seen her somewhere before. Almost had her name. Almost. It was on the tip of my tongue . . .

They were good times until then. I miss being part of that big happy group. Most of all I miss the cursing and seeing the Fiend. Who knows, if I'd lived long enough, I might have become one of the coven and got to stroke the Fiend myself. But that wasn't to be. The mad girl spoiled all that.

And there was something else. Didn't see it coming, but my life was almost over.

CHAPTER 2
MY DOOM

We are all fated. All doomed. What is written will be. We witches can sniff out the future, see dangers approaching. But few of us see our own doom coming. I certainly didn't . . .

Over seventy years ago, even before my mother was born, a quisitor called Wilkinson arrived in Pendle. Wanted to deal with the clans once and for all, so he brought priests, wardens and thirty special constables. And they were all armed to the teeth and keen to kill witches.

Made his base in Downham, he did, and started to arrest suspected witches from all three clan villages – Goldshaw Booth, Roughlee and Bareleigh. Not all clan members are witches though, and he tried to sort them out using different tests. He swam a dozen of them. Three drowned and another died of fever afterwards. Another three sank but were dragged out barely alive. The five who floated were tried, found guilty and hanged at Caster Castle. But swimming never works, and only one of them was really a witch. Not that it bothered Wilkinson much anyway. He was a nasty, greedy man. He seized their houses and possessions, sold them and kept the money.

After that he arrested lots more – mainly Malkins. Tested them with a bodkin this time; jabbed its sharp blade into their flesh until he found what he called 'the Devil's Mark', a place where he said they couldn't feel any pain. All nonsense of course, but they say that he enjoyed his work.

However, the clans weren't going to stand for that. Not them. So they banded together in a temporary truce and collected their dead. Buried them under the loam in Witch Dell with the others. Somehow Wilkinson and his men were tricked into passing through the dell. Don't know how they did it. Nobody seems to remember that.

It happened after dark, as they were travelling back to Downham. The dead witches were lying in wait, desperate for blood.

Wilkinson survived, but over half his party were slaughtered. Their bodies were recovered later – but in broad daylight, of course, with the bright sun over-head. All the dead had been drained of blood and their thumb-bones were missing.

The quisitor was in fear for his own life, so he made a hasty retreat from the district. But they weren't finished with him yet, were they. The Malkin clan used a powerful curse, and within thirteen months every last one of Wilkinson's men was dead, including him. Some died in accidents; others just vanished from the face of the earth – probably victims of witch assassins. Wilkinson's own death was particularly horrible. His nose and fingers fell off and his ears turned black and withered away. Scared of dying but scared of living, he was too. So he tried to hang himself but failed when the rope gave way. Driven mad with pain, he drowned himself in a local pond. So the clans' revenge was complete. Didn't think anyone would ever try it again.

Became too sure of ourselves, we did. All of us – me included. Well, I paid the price for that and no mistake. Didn't see my own doom coming, did I?

One morning I was begging at a farm gate on the outskirts of Downham. This was the third time I'd been back in less than a week and I'd scared that old farmer good and proper – threatened to make his crops fail and his livestock be struck down with foot and mouth. The first time I'd just asked for eggs; the second, a leg of lamb; but this time I'd come for his hoard of coins.

Farmers are always moaning and crying poverty, but most of them have got something squirreled away. 'I want money this time,' I told him. 'Nothing less will do . . .'

'I have no money,' he protested. 'I can scarcely make

ends meet. You've already taken the food out of my children's mouths . . .'

'Ah, you have children,' I said, giving him a wicked grin. 'I do hope they thrive! How many have you?'

At that his hands began to shake and his bottom lip to tremble like a withered leaf in an autumn gale. I could tell that he really loved those children of his.

'Two girls,' he said, 'and another child on the way.'

'You're a bit old to be a father. Got a young wife, have you?'

There was a movement in the doorway and a woman came out into the late evening light and started to peg out her washing. She was less than half his age but a bit of a dumpling and not at all pretty.

'Give me your money or it'll be the worse for you,' I threatened.

The farmer shook his head, his expression a mixture of despair and defiance. He was on the fence now and didn't know which way to jump, so I made up his mind for him.

'Wouldn't want anything to happen to that little

defenceless unborn your wife's carrying in her belly, would you? And what about her? Is she strong? What if she were to die in childbirth? How would you manage this farm alone as well as raising young children?'

'Be off with you!' he cried, raising his stick.

'Give you a chance, I will. Be back tomorrow at the same time. Don't want all your money – I'm not greedy. Half will do. Have it ready or suffer the consequences!'

Should have sniffed out what was coming. A stinky wind blows from the future, but I didn't even get a whiff.

Next evening the old farmer was waiting for me at the gate but his hands were empty. Where was my bag of coins? I wondered angrily.

'Made a big mistake, you have!' I warned him, curling my lip. 'Got a nasty curse ready for you, old man. I'll make the flesh drop off your young wife's bones . . .'

He didn't reply. Not only that, he didn't even look

scared. Well, maybe just a bit nervous, but not what I'd expected. I opened my mouth to begin the curse, but suddenly heard footsteps behind, running towards me. I turned and saw half a dozen big men with clubs approaching, spread out in a big arc and cutting off any hope of escape.

Right! I'd show him. I leaped the gate and ran past the farmer towards the house. His wife was inside – and, even better, his children. I'd take them hostage; use them to make my escape. I slipped my sharp knife – the blade I used to take thumb-bones – down my sleeve into my left hand to be ready. Let 'em know I meant business. I'd almost reached the back door when I was brought to a sudden halt.

A man was standing just inside; behind him lurked another one holding a large stick. Swaggering confidently, they both came out into the yard in front of me. By then other men were climbing over the gate behind me, and within moments they'd surrounded me. I tried to fight, I really did. I spun and slashed at them with my knife, but there were too many of them and the blows they dealt were savage. One of the first knocked the knife from my hand; then they rained down on my back and shoulders. I crouched low, trying to cover my head, but they found it eventually. There was a flash of light and then darkness.

I was the first they captured that day. In the end five of us were tested down at the pond. By chance I'd chosen to beg from that farm on the very day that a witchfinder had called at Downham; the first such visit to Pendle by a quisitor since the days of Wilkinson. The farmer had gone to warn him and then they'd set their trap and awaited my return.

How come I chose that day and that place? It was my doom. It had been fated to happen.

Swimming is terrifying. We witches can't cross running water but lakes and ponds are usually no problem. I'd even been known to kneel at the water's edge and wash myself once in a while. Not in winter though – far too cold then. Dirt keeps out the winter chills.

But it's very different when your hands are tied to your feet. I was the third they swam that cold January afternoon. The first woman floated. She was just a clan member and lacked the craft, but that didn't bother them: dragged her out of the pond, they did, and threw her up into the back of a wagon.

The second one sank like a stone – and she was a real witch; one of the Malkins. The Fiend didn't bother to save her, did he? Told you swimming don't work. They took their time getting her out of the water. By the time they did she'd stopped breathing, so they chucked her body back into the pond, where it sank for a second time.

Then it was my turn. Two of them swung me back and forth before letting go. I hit the water hard. Was going to try and hold my breath, but that cold water was too much of a shock. I gasped and opened my mouth. The dirty water rushed in. I seemed to sink, but must have been floating face down. I could see the dead witch below me through the murk, hair drifting over her open mouth and bony nose, dead eyes staring up at me. I choked for a while but then it didn't hurt any more. Gave up, I did. I was going into the dark. Well, why not? I'm a witch. That's where I belong.

Next thing I knew, I was lying in the mud, pond water gushing out of my mouth. Then I was sick as a dog over one of the men's boots. Gave me a good kicking for that, he did, before bundling me into the back of the wagon.

They called three of us witches and rushed off towards Caster. Weren't going to risk the wrath of the clans this time, were they? Wanted to get us away from Pendle and into the safety of Caster Castle.

Thrown into a dark dungeon, I was. And all alone. Not that I wanted the company of the other two. One was a Mouldheel, the other a Malkin – clan enemies. Dark and damp, it was, down there, with water dripping from the ceiling and just a bed of filthy straw to lie on. They couldn't even leave me in peace to enjoy my misery though. Came for me at midnight. Dragged me along a corridor and into a room with a big wooden table. Clamped my wrists and chained my arms. Weren't satisfied with testing me once.

'Before we kill a witch, we have to be doubly sure she *is* one,' said the quisitor. 'We've used swimming. Now it's time for pricking!'

Really loved his work, that one. Matthew Carter was his name, and he smiled as he stuck that long pin into me. The more I groaned and flinched and shrieked, the more he loved it. I fainted more than once. Soon my body was hurting all over and I couldn't tell when he was jabbing me and when he'd stopped. Said he'd found the Devil's Mark then. True enough, I'd a birthmark just below my knee. About the same size as a copper coin, it was, and this was where he said the Devil had touched me; a place where the Fiend protected me and I couldn't feel pain. It was enough for him. I was proved a witch twice over.

They were going to execute us just after dawn – that's what he told me – and I spent the long night in that dungeon shivering with cold and fear. Couldn't face being burned. Not that. Please not that! The pain was supposed to be terrible. And a witch can't come back after burning. She has to stay in the dark for ever then.

They took us out into the yard at first light. It was a miserable morning with heavy drizzle falling out of a grey sky. I remember there were three seagulls on a nearby roof – one for each witch about to die. But then my spirits lifted because I saw what awaited us in the far corner of the castle yard. It wasn't a fire. It was a gallows. They were going to hang us. That meant I'd be able to come back . . .

Can't say it was pleasant though. Not nice to be swinging on a rope, panting for breath, with your face going purple and eyes bulging. That's the last thing I saw: the Mouldheel witch hanging next to me, gasping out her last breaths. Then my sight dimmed and every-thing went dark. All I could hear was my own heart thudding. At first it was going so fast that the thumps all merged into one. Then it grew tired. It was faltering . . . slowing . . . missing beats.

Funny thing, dying. Strange the last memories you have. I saw the madwoman run past me again on her way to throw her knives at the Fiend. Suddenly I recognized her. Knew her name! It was . . .

But then I died.

CHAPTER 3
MY REVENGE

The Deane clan collected my body from the castle yard and took it back to Pendle. They buried me in a shallow grave in Witch Dell and covered the bare earth with rotting leaves. Then they left me to enjoy my new existence.

I remember sensing something above, so I stretched up my arms into the chill night air. I sat up and my head burst through the covering of earth. The dell was lit with a silver light: I was looking up through the branches of a tree towards a yellow orb. It was the full moon. That was what first summoned me back to this world.

My next need was blood. Never had I felt so

hungry. I began to crawl through the dell, sniffing for prey. There were no humans within range but I soon caught a few juicy rats and a field mouse. The rats took the edge off my appetite. Very small, the mouse was, hardly a mouthful, but I couldn't remember anything tasting so delicious. I was a bone witch but had drunk blood before – though none tasting like that. It's so much better when you're dead. You don't need ordinary food any more. What good are potatoes and cooked meat to a dead stomach?

That food, little though it was, gave me strength. Now I could stand ... walk ... maybe even run? So how would I feel if I managed to catch a man, woman or child and drink human blood? Some dead witches ain't that strong and the most they can ever do is crawl. I felt sure I'd be one of the stronger ones.

So I slid under my covering of leaves again and lay on my back for a while, just my nose and eyes peeping up through them. Lying there, I suddenly noticed just how much my head itched. I kept having to scratch it. That's the problem with spending so much time close to the ground and hiding under dead leaves. Things get into your hair and make their homes there.

You get lots of time to think when you're a dead witch. And my first thoughts were of revenge. At first I decided just to kill that farmer and his dumpling wife; the children would be really juicy. But that would be too easy. There was someone else I really owed for what had happened. Matthew Carter had tortured and murdered me; brought my happy life to an end. I wouldn't enjoy sabbaths no more; would never get to stroke the Fiend.

Deserved the same back, he did, and more. But how could I get to him? I now knew he was based in Caster. It was a long way there – could be done, but surely there had to be a better way . . .

Didn't take me long to work it out, so I set out for Downham right away. I was going to have a serious talk with that old farmer.

I still wasn't as strong as I'd have liked but I made my way slowly north, keeping Pendle Hill to my left. Just before dawn I managed to catch a couple of rats and settled myself down under a hedge to while away the daylight hours.

It was long after midnight the following night before I arrived at the boundary of his farm. The first thing I did was kill one of his pigs. It was a small plump pink thing, and it squealed almost until the moment it died. That started the farm dogs barking: must have been chained up or they'd have caught my scent. Pity, that. I could have managed to drain a dog or two. But I have to tell you that pig blood is quite tasty. Next best thing to draining a human.

That little squealer made me feel a lot stronger. I walked up to the front of the farmhouse and pulled the door right off its hinges. Somewhere above, a child started to cry; it was soon joined by another, and it wasn't long before the old farmer came to the top of the stairs in his nightshirt, the stub of a candle in his trembling hand. He saw me standing in the open doorway, gave a cry of terror and ran back into the bedroom. I heard him slide a bolt into place. Not that it would do him much good.

I followed him upstairs and leaned hard against the door until, with a creak and a crunch, it flew open. By then his wife was making more noise than her children, who were still screaming from the next bedroom.

I went in, sat down on the edge of the bed and stared hard at the pair of them. They were sat straight up, blankets pulled up to their chins, arms around each other. Couldn't tell which one was shaking the most. I grinned at them and scratched at my itchy head. A worm dropped out of my hair and began to wriggle around on the coverlet.

'Might let you both live,' I told them. 'Might let your children live too. But you've got to do exactly what I say . . .'

'Don't hurt us, please,' begged the farmer. 'We'll do anything. Anything at all . . .'

I smiled. 'All you have to do is get Matthew Carter

to come here again. Make sure he arrives after dark, mind. Must be after dark – that's important. Round about midnight would be best. Just tell him another witch has been bothering you. And you need him here to sort her.'

'What if he won't come?' asked the trembling farmer, his eyes wide with fear.

'Well, in that case don't bother coming back. Because if you do, you'll find your family dead.'

He left before dawn, but I stayed close to the house and buried myself under a pile of straw in the barn until it was dark again. Just the tip of my bony nose was sticking out.

At dusk, that's where the child found me. The eldest daughter – no more than five years old, she was; plump little thing too. I could smell blood pumping through her warm body, and it took all my will power to let her live: I didn't want to have the mother in hysterics again. She had to be calm and peaceful when Matthew Carter arrived.

'When it goes dark,' said the child, 'my mother turns all the mirrors in the house to the wall.'

'Then she's a wise mother. That'll stop witches spying on you and your family.'

'But you're a witch and my mother says I should keep away from you,' said the child.

'Mothers know best,' I told her, 'so perhaps you should.'

'What's it like being a dead witch?'

'Itchy, child,' I told her, scratching at my head. 'Very itchy.'

'I could comb your hair if you like . . .' the child offered.

She ran off, and five minutes later came back with a comb. I had planned to kill her and the rest of her family eventually, but as she was combing the worms and insects out of my hair, I relented. I'd just kill the old farmer.

'Go back to your mother and tell her to take you and your sister as far away as possible from here,' I told her. 'And don't come back until well after dawn. Tell her to go right away. It's the only way to save your lives.'

I watched from the doorway of the barn as the mother took her children to safety, waddling like a duck as she set off on her little legs. Now I had to get myself ready. This time I would be the one waiting in ambush. Firstly I lit the entrance and the stairs well, using half a dozen candles.

A dead witch slowly loses her control of dark magic. But I hadn't been dead long and I had enough left for what was needed.

I heard the men approaching the front door. The old farmer had done well. I guessed that two would be planning to wait inside the house, like last time. I wasn't disappointed: luckily Matthew Carter was one of them. He came through the doorway first.

I smiled at him from the top of the stairs. 'Why don't we two have a little chat, Handsome Matthew?' I suggested pleasantly, giving him my sweetest smile. 'Just you and me alone together in the bedroom . . .'

As he started to climb the stairs towards me, his

tongue was hanging further out than a hungry dog's at the sight of fresh meat. Below, his companion looked very disappointed at not being invited into my company.

I was using the dark magic spells *glamour* and *fascination*, of course: the first could make even a dead witch appear extremely attractive; the second would have made him climb those stairs anyway.

'Come and sit next to me on the bed,' I bade the quisitor, closing the door behind us. 'Why don't we start with a little kiss?'

He did as I suggested, but just before his lips fastened on mine, the eager expression on his face turned to one of dismay. He'd smelled the real me: the stench of rot and decay, of dark damp loam and mouldy leaves. Then I uncloaked myself from the spell and his dismay turned to terror.

As I started to feed, that Matthew Carter screamed louder than the little pink pig I'd killed the previous night. I plunged my teeth deep into his neck and drained him with great hungry gulps. I felt the throb of his blood start to become erratic. Soon his heart stopped beating. Now he was Dead Matthew, and no longer of any interest to me.

I killed the second man in the doorway. The third and fourth were hiding in the barn, but I soon sniffed them out. There were others but they ran off in panic. Only the old farmer stayed. He thought his wife and children were still inside the house.

I'd had more blood than I needed and was full to bursting. Even so, I passed close to the old farmer as I walked across the yard – close enough to start his knees knocking.

'I've decided to let you live. But next time a witch begs at your gate,' I warned him, 'give her what she asks for.'

Then I was gone, heading back south towards Witch Dell.

There's something else I forgot to tell you. After I'd died I couldn't remember the name of the madwoman again. Strained my dead brain but it just wouldn't come. Now I'm a lot weaker and can't walk any more. Even a dead witch doesn't last for ever. And though my memories are slipping away fast, odd fragments keep coming back.

I can see that daft girl now as she's running past me on her way to knife the Fiend. And now I've remembered she was a Malkin and her name's on the tip of my tongue . . . the very tip. If only I could remember! I'd write it down then and our clan would seek her out for sure. She can't hide for ever. There are too many of us and she can't defeat us all.

It'll be light soon, so I've got to crawl back to the dell. Maybe I'll remember and write it down tomorrow night. That's if my fingers haven't dropped off. And if I can still remember the way here . . .

GRIMALKIN'S
TALE

My name is Grimalkin and I fear nobody. But my enemies fear me. With my scissors I snip the flesh of the dead; the clan enemies that I have slain in combat. I cut out their thumb-bones, which I wear around my neck as a warning to others. What else can I do? Without ruthlessness and savagery I would not survive even a week of the life I lead. I am the witch assassin of the Malkin clan.

Are you my enemy? Are you strong? Do you possess speed and agility? Have you had the training of a warrior? It matters nought to me. Run now! Run fast into the forest! I'll give you a few moments' start. An hour if you wish. Because no matter how hard you run, you'll never be fast enough, and before long I'll catch and kill you. I am a hunter and also a blacksmith skilled in the art of forging weapons. I could craft one especially for you; the steel that would surely take your life.

All the prey I hunt I will slay. If it is clothed in flesh, I will cut it. If it breathes, I will stop its breath. And your magic daunts me not, because I have magic of my own. And boggarts, ghosts and ghasts are no greater threat to me than they are to a spook. For I have looked into the darkness – into the greatest darkness of all – and I am no longer afraid.

My greatest enemy is the Fiend – the dark made flesh. Even as a child I disliked him; saw the way he controlled my clan; watched the way its coven fawned over him. That growing revulsion was something instinctive in me; a natural-born hatred. I knew that unless I did something, he would become a blight upon my life, a dark shadow over everything that I did.

But there is one way in which a witch can ensure

that he keeps his distance. A method that is very extreme but ensures that she is free of his fearsome power. She has to be close to him just once and bear his child. After he has inspected his offspring, he may not approach her again. Not unless she wishes it.

Most of the Fiend's children are abhumans – evil creatures that will do the bidding of the dark. Others grow to be powerful witches. But a few – and it is rare indeed – are born perfect human children untainted by evil. Mine was such a child.

I had never felt such love for another creature. To feel its warmth against my body, so trusting, so dependent, was wonderful beyond my dreams; something I had never imagined or anticipated. This little child loved me and I loved it in return; it depended upon me for life, and I was truly happy for the first time in my life. But such happiness rarely lasts.

I remember well the night that mine ended. The sun had just set and it was a warm summer's night, so I walked out into the garden to the rear of my cottage, cradling my child, humming to him softly to lull him to sleep. Suddenly lightning flashed overhead and I felt the ground move beneath my feet. The Fiend was about to appear and my heart lurched with fear. At the same time I was glad, because once he saw his son he would leave and never be able to visit me again. I would be rid of him for the rest of my life.

I was not prepared for the Fiend's reaction though. No sooner had he materialized than, with a roar of anger, he snatched my innocent baby boy and lifted him high in the air, ready to dash him to the ground.

'Please!' I begged. 'Don't hurt him. I'll do anything but please let him live . . .'

The Fiend never even looked at me. He was filled with wrath and cruelty. He smashed my child's fragile head against a rock. Then he vanished.

For a long time I was insane with grief. And then thoughts of revenge began to swirl within my head. Was it possible? Could I destroy the Fiend? Impossible or not, that became my goal and my only reason to continue living. I was still young – just turned seventeen – although strong and tall for my age. I had chosen to bear the Fiend's child as a means to be free of him for ever, and once I'd decided to pursue that course of action, nothing could stop me. Nothing would stop me now.

Wearing my thickest leather gloves, I forged three blades, each one tipped with silver alloy. It was painful for me even to be close to that metal which is harmful to all who have allegiance to the dark. But I gritted my teeth and did the work to the very best of my ability. Next I had to find my enemy – but that was the easy part.

The Fiend does not visit on every sabbath; some years he does not come at all. But Halloween was the most likely, and for some reason he particularly favours the Deanes at that time. So, shunning the Malkin celebration on Pendle Hill, I set off for Roughlee, the Deane village.

I arrived at dusk and settled myself down in a small wood overlooking the site of their sabbath fire. I was not too concerned about being detected. They would all be excited and distracted by their preparations, and besides, I had cloaked myself in my strongest magic, and such a thing as I planned would come as a surprise to them, to say the least. Most witches would consider it insane. The Deanes are not generally known for their imagination and are the least creative of the three clans.

Soon the witches began to gather and, combining their magic, they ignited the fire with a loud *whoosh*. Most of the fuel used was wood, but at its heart was a large pile of old bones, those no longer useful for dark magic. Most people call such a blaze a bonfire, but that name is derived from the word that witches use – *bone*-fire. The coven of the thirteen strongest witches formed a tight circle around its perimeter; their lesser sisters encircled them.

Just as the stink of the fire began to reach me, the Deanes began to curse their enemies. With wild shrieks and guttural cries, they called down death and destruction upon those they named. Someone old and enfeebled, or a witch grown careless might fall victim to such curses, but mostly they were wasting their time. All witches have defences against such dark magic. But I heard them name Caxton, the High Sheriff at Caster. He had arrested one of their number recently and now they wanted him dead. I knew that he would be lucky to survive the week.

As they finished cursing, there was a change in the fire: the yellow flames became orange, then red. It was the first sign that the Fiend was about to appear, and I heard an expectant gasp go up from the gathering. I stared towards the fire as he began to materialize. Able to make himself large or small, the Fiend was taking shape in all his fearsome majesty in order to impress his followers. The flames reached up to his knees, revealing that he was tall and broad – perhaps three times the size of an average man – with a long sinuous tail and the curved horns of a ram. His body was covered in thick black hair, and I saw the coven witches reach forward across the flames, eager to touch their dark lord.

I knew he would not stay for long. I had to strike now!

I left my hiding place in the trees and began to run as fast as I could, straight towards the fire. The witches would not see me approaching out of the darkness. Neither would they hear the pounding of my feet, distracted and excited as they were by the monster at the heart of the flames.

I had a blade in each hand; the third gripped tightly between my teeth. There was great danger here, but I hated the Fiend and was quite prepared to meet my death, either blasted by his power or torn to pieces by the Deanes. I cast my will before me; I had the power to keep him away but I did the reverse: I wished him to stay.

I ran through the gaps between those witches on the fringe of the gathering. As the throng became denser, I pushed them aside with my elbows and shoulders, and saw surprised and angry faces twisting towards me. At last I reached the coven and threw the first dagger. It struck the Fiend in the chest, burying itself up to the hilt. He shrieked long and loud. I'd hurt him badly and his cry of pain was music to my ears. But he twisted away in the flames so that my next two blades did not quite find their intended targets; even so, they buried themselves deep within his flesh.

For a moment he looked directly at me, his pupils red vertical slits. I had nothing with which to defend myself against the power that he could marshal: I waited to die. What was worse, however, he would, I well knew, find me after death and inflict never-ending torments on my soul.

Now I was willing him away. Would he go? Or would he destroy me first?

To my relief, he simply vanished, taking the flames of the fire with him so that we were all plunged into darkness. The rule had held. I had carried his child, so he could not be in my presence; not unless I wished it.

There was confusion all around me, shrieks of anger and fear; witches running in all directions. I slipped away into the darkness and made my escape. Of course, I knew that they would send assassins after me. It meant I'd have to kill or be killed.

I ran, heading north and passing beyond Pendle Hill, then curved away west towards the distant sea. I knew exactly where I was going, having planned my escape far in advance. On the flatlands, east of the river Wyre's estuary, was the spot where I would make my stand. I had wrapped myself in a cloak of dark magic, but it would not be strong enough to hide me from all those who followed me. I needed to fight in a place where I might gain an advantage.

There is a line of three villages there: Hambleton, Staumin and Preesall, aligned roughly north to south, joined by a narrow track that sometimes becomes impassable because of the tide. On all sides they are surrounded by soggy moss. The river is tidal, with extensive salt marshes, and north-west of Staumin, right on the sea margin, is Arm Hill, a small mound of firm ground that rises above the grassy tussocks and treacherous channels along which the tide races to trap the unwary. On one side is the river; on the other, the marsh, and nobody can cross it without being seen from that vantage point.

I waited for my pursuers, knowing there would be more than one. My crime against the Deane clan was terrible indeed. If they caught me, I would die slowly and in great pain. The first of my enemies came into sight at dusk, picking her way slowly across the marsh grass.

As a witch, I have many skills and talents. One of these proved very useful now. As an enemy approaches, I instantly know her worth: her strength and ability in combat. The one crossing the marsh towards me now was competent enough, but not of the first order. No doubt her talents as a tracker and her power to penetrate my dark magical cloak had brought this witch to me first.

I waited until she was close, then showed myself to her. I was standing on that small hill, clearly outlined against the fading red of the western sky. She ran towards me, a blade in each hand. She did not weave; made no attempt to make herself a difficult target.

It was me or her. One of us would die. So be it!

I pulled my favourite throwing knife from my belt.

This one was not tipped with silver alloy but that wasn't necessary; it was sufficient to slay a witch. I hurled it at my attacker and it took her in the throat. She made a little gurgling noise, dropped to her knees and fell face down in the marsh grass.

She was the first human being I had ever killed, and I felt a momentary pang. But it quickly passed as I concentrated on ensuring my own survival. I hid the witch's body under a shelf of grass tussocks, pushing her down into the mud. I did not take her heart. We had faced each other in honourable combat and she had lost. One night that witch would return from the dead, crawling across the marsh in search of prey. As she was no further threat to me, I would not deny her that.

I waited almost three days for the next to find me. There were two and they arrived together. We fought at noon, the late autumn sun painting the slow tidal ebb of the river blood-red. I was strong and fast, but they were veterans of such fights, with a repertoire of tricks that I had never encountered. They hurt me

badly, and the scars of those wounds mark my body to this day. The struggle lasted over an hour, and it was close, but at last victory was mine, and the bodies of two more Deanes went into the marsh.

It was almost three weeks before I was fit to travel, but in that time they sent no more avengers after me. The trail had gone cold and it was unlikely that anyone would have recognized me that night when I attacked the Fiend. I thought long and hard about what had happened. I had hurt the Devil. Would he try to kill me in some way? Or might I find a way to destroy him first?

I consulted a scryer. Her name was Martha Ribstalk, an incomer from the far north. She did not use a mirror to see the future; her method was to peer into a steaming blood-tainted cauldron, one boiling up thumb- and finger-bones to strip away the dead flesh. At that time, before the rise of Mab, the young scryer of the Mouldheels, she was the foremost practitioner of that dark art. I visited her one hour after midnight, as we had arranged. One hour after she had drunk the blood of an enemy and performed the necessary rituals.

'Do you accept my money?' I demanded.

She nodded, so I tossed three coins into the cauldron.

'Be seated!' she commanded sternly, pointing to the cold stone flags before the large bubbling pot. The air was tainted with blood, and each breath I took increased the metallic taste at the back of my tongue.

I obeyed, sitting cross-legged and gazing up at her through the steam. She had remained standing so that she was higher than me, a tactic often practised by those who wish to dominate others. But I was not cowed and met her gaze calmly.

'What did you see?' I demanded. 'What is my future?'

She did not speak for a long time. It pleased her to keep me waiting. I think Ribstalk was annoyed because I had asked a question rather than waiting to be told the outcome of her scrying.

'You have chosen an enemy,' she said at last. 'The

most powerful enemy any mortal could face. The outcome should be simple. Unless you wish it, the Fiend cannot approach you, but he will await your death, then seize your soul and subject it to everlasting torments. But there is something else; something that I cannot see clearly. An uncertainty . . . another force that may intervene. Just a glimmer of hope for you . . .'

She paused, then stepped closer and peered into the steam. Once again there was a long pause. 'There is someone there . . . a child just born—'

'Who is this child?' I demanded.

'I cannot see him clearly,' Martha Ribstalk admitted. 'Someone hides him from my sight. And as for you, even with his intervention, only one highly skilled with weapons could hope to survive. Only one with the speed and ruthlessness of a witch assassin. Only the greatest of all assassins – more deadly even than Kernolde – could do that. Nothing less will do. So what hope have you?' she mocked.

Kernolde was then the assassin of the Malkins. A fearsome woman of great strength and speed, who had slain twenty-seven challengers for her position – three each year, as this was the tenth year of her reign.

I rose to my feet and smiled down at Ribstalk. 'I will slay Kernolde and then take her place. I will become the witch assassin of the Malkins – the greatest of them all.'

I turned and walked away, listening to the scryer cackling with mocking laughter behind me. But mine were not vain boasts. I believed that I could do it. I truly believed.

Three pretenders to the position of Malkin assassin were trained annually, but this year one place remained to be filled. No wonder – for most believed it was certain death to face Kernolde. The other two witches had been in training for six months. Thus half a year remained before the three days assigned for the challenges. That was the time left for me to gain some of the skills necessary. Barely time for most to learn the rudiments of the assassin's trade.

The training school was in a clearing in Crow Wood.

My first day there filled me with dismay. The other two trainees had no confidence, and death was already written on their foreheads. I grew more and more disgruntled with every hour that passed.

At last, just before dark, I spoke my mind. We three were sitting cross-legged on the ground, looking up at Grist Malkin, our trainer. He was droning on about blade-fighting. Behind him were two sour-faced matriarchs of our clan, both witches. They were there to ensure we did not use magic against our trainer.

'You are a fool, Grist!' I snapped, no longer able to control my irritation. 'You've already prepared twenty-seven defeated challengers before us. What can you teach us but how to lose and how to die?'

For a long time he did not speak but simply locked eyes with me and glared, his face twitching with fury. He was a big man, a head taller than me and heavily muscled. But I was not afraid and met his gaze calmly. It was he who looked away first.

'On your feet, girl!' he commanded.

I stood slowly and smiled.

'Take that grin off your face. Don't look at me!' he barked. 'Look straight ahead. Have some respect for your teacher. Listening to me might just save your life . . .'

He began to circle me slowly. I watched him out of the corner of my eye as he disappeared behind my left shoulder. Suddenly he seized me in a bear hug, trying to squeeze the breath from my body. I felt a sharp pain as one of my ribs cracked.

'Let that be a lesson to you!' he cried, throwing me down into the dirt.

But I made sure that he did not speak again: I was on my feet in an instant and broke his nose with my left fist, the punch knocking him to the ground.

The struggle between us was over quickly. I did not let him get close to me again. My blows were swift and executed with precision. Within moments one of his eyes was swollen and closed. Seconds later, his forehead was split open and blood was running into his other eye. Unable to see, he could offer little defence and I quickly administered a chop, bringing him to his knees.

The two crones knelt at Grist's side. One was his mother, and I saw that tears were streaming down her cheeks.

'I could kill you now,' I cried, 'but you're just a man and hardly worth the trouble!'

I began to walk away, but before I entered the trees I turned. I had one last thing to say.

'I'm leaving this place,' I told them. 'But I'll return to face Kernolde.'

There is one thing that I have not yet told you. Grist had trained my older sister, Wrekinda. She was Kernolde's fifth victim: one more reason to kill the witch assassin.

It was fortunate that I was already skilled in the ways of the forest and crafting weapons. Fortunate too that, as the third accepted for training, I'd be the last to face Kernolde. Even in defeat the other challengers might weaken her, or at least drain some of her strength.

So I trained myself. I worked hard; invited danger; ate well; built up my strength; swam daily to increase my endurance for combat – mile upon mile despite the winter cold. I also crafted the best blades of which I was capable and carried them in sheaths about my body, which grew stronger and faster by the day. I ran up and down the steep slopes of Pendle to improve my stamina, readying myself for the fight to the death against Kernolde.

In a forest far to the north, beyond the boundaries of the County, I faced a pack of howling wolves. They circled me, moving ever closer, death glittering in their hungry eyes. I held a throwing knife in each hand. The first wolf leaped for my throat; leaped and died as my blade found its throat first. The second died too. Next I drew my long blade, awaiting the third attack. With one powerful stroke I struck the animal's head from its body. Before the pack turned and fled my wrath, seven lay dead, their blood staining the white snow red.

At last the time to face Kernolde arrived and I returned to Pendle. Did I say I hoped the other challengers would weaken the witch assassin? My hopes were short-lived. She slew each with ease; both were dead in less than an hour. On the third night it was my turn.

The challenge always takes place north of the Devil's Triangle, where the villages of the Malkins, Deanes and Mouldheels are located. Kernolde chose as her killing ground Witch Dell, where witches are taken by their families after death; taken there and buried amongst the trees to rise with the full moon, scratching their way back to the surface to feed upon small animals and unwary human intruders. Some of the dead witches are strong and can roam for miles seeking their prey. Kernolde used these dead things as her allies – sometimes as her eyes, nose and ears; sometimes as weapons. More than one challenger had been drained of blood by the dead before Kernolde took her thumb-bones as proof of victory. But she often triumphed without these allies. She was skilled with blades, ropes, traps and pits full of spikes; once her opponents were captured or incapacitated, she would often simply strangle them to death.

All this I knew before my challenge started; I had thought long and hard about it and had visited this dell many times during the previous months. I had gone there in daylight, when the dead witches were dormant and Kernolde was out hunting prey in distant parts of the County. I had sniffed out every inch of the wood; knew every tree, the whereabouts of every pit and trap.

So I was ready. I stood outside the dell in the shadow of the trees just before midnight, the appointed time for combat to begin. High to my left was the large brooding mass of Pendle, its eastern slopes bathed in the light of the full moon, which was high in the sky to the south. Within moments a beacon flared at the summit, sparks shooting upwards into the air, signalling that the witching hour had begun.

Immediately I did what no other challenger had done before. Most crept into the dell, nervous and fearful, in dread of what they faced. Some were braver but still entered cautiously. I was different. I announced my presence in a loud, clear voice.

'I'm here, Kernolde! My name is Grimalkin and I am your death!' I shouted into the dell. 'I'm coming for *you*, Kernolde! I'm coming for *you*! And nothing living or dead can stop me!'

It was not just bravado, although that played a part. It was the product of much thought and calculation. I knew that my shouts would summon up the dead witches, and that's what I wanted. Now I would know where they were.

You see, most dead witches are slow and I could outrun them. It was the powerful ones I had to beware of. One of them was named Grim Gertrude because of her intimidating appearance, and she was both strong and relatively speedy for one who had been dead more than a century. She roamed far and wide beyond the dell, hunting for blood. But tonight she would be waiting there: she was Kernolde's closest accomplice, well-rewarded in blood, for she helped to bring about each victory.

I waited for about fifteen minutes – long enough to let the slowest witch get near. I'd already sniffed out Gertrude, the old one. She'd been close to the edge of the dell for some time but had chosen not to venture out into the open: she had retreated deeper into the trees so that her slower sisters could attack me first. I heard the rustling of leaves and the occasional faint crack of a twig as they shuffled forward. They were slow, but I didn't underestimate them. Dead witches have great strength, and once they fasten onto your flesh, they cannot be easily prised free. Soon they begin to suck your blood until you weaken and can fight no more. Some of them would be on the ground, hiding within the dead leaves, ready to reach out and grasp at my ankles as I sped by.

I sprinted into the trees. I had already sniffed out Kernolde. She was where I expected, waiting beneath the branches of the oldest oak in the dell. That was her tree; the one in which she stored her magic; her place of power.

A hand reached up towards me from the leaves.

Without breaking my stride, I unsheathed a dagger from the scabbard on my left thigh and pinned the dead witch to a thick, gnarled tree root. I thrust the blade into her wrist rather than her palm, making it more difficult for her to tear herself free.

The next witch shuffled towards me from my right, her face lit by a shaft of moonlight. Saliva was dribbling down her chain and onto her tattered gown, which was covered in dark stains. She jabbered curses at me, eager for my blood. Instead she got my blade, which I plucked from my right shoulder sheath, hurling it towards her. The point took her in the throat, throwing her backwards. I ran on even faster.

Four more times my blades sliced into dead flesh, and by now most of the other witches were left behind – the slow and those maimed by my blades. But Kernolde and the powerful old one waited somewhere ahead. I wore eight sheaths that day; each contained a blade. Now only two remained.

I leaped a hidden pit, then a second. Even though

they were covered with leaves and mud, I knew they were there. At last the old one barred my path. I came to a halt and prepared myself to attack her. Let her come to me!

I looked at Grim Gertrude, noting the tangled hair that came down to her knees. She was grim indeed and well-named! Maggots and beetles scuttled within the rank curtain that obscured all of her face save one malevolent eye and an elongated tooth jutting upwards over her top lip almost as far as her left nostril.

She rushed towards me, kicking up leaves, her hands extended to rend my face or squeeze my throat. She was fast for a dead witch; very fast. But not fast enough.

With my left hand I drew the largest of my blades from its scabbard at my hip. This was not crafted for throwing; it was more like a short sword, with two razor-sharp edges. I leaped forward and cut Grim Gertrude's head clean from her shoulders. It bounced on a root and rolled away. I ran on, glancing back to see her hands searching amongst the pile of rotting leaves where it had come to rest.

Now for Kernolde. She was waiting beneath her tree. I saw that ropes hung from the branches, ready to bind and hang my body. She was rubbing her back against the bark, drawing strength for the fight. But I was not afraid – she looked more like an old bear ridding itself of fleas than the dreaded witch assassin feared by all. Running directly towards her at full tilt, I drew the last of my throwing knives and hurled it straight at her throat. End over end it spun, my aim fast and true, but she knocked it aside with a disdainful flick of her wrist. Undaunted, I increased my pace and prepared to use the long blade. But then the ground opened up beneath my feet: my heart lurched and I fell into a hidden pit.

The moon was high, and as I fell I saw the sharp spikes below waiting to impale me. I twisted desperately, trying to protect my body, but to avoid every spike was impossible. All I could do was contort myself so that only one spike speared into me, inflicting the least damage.

The least, did I say? It hurt me enough: the spike pierced right through my thigh. Down its length I slid until I hit the ground hard and all the breath left my body, the long blade flying from my hand to lie out of reach.

I lay there, trying to breathe and control the pain in my leg. The spikes were sharp, thin and very long – more than six feet – so there was no way I could lift my leg and free it. I cursed my folly. I had thought myself safe, but Kernolde had dug another pit – probably the previous night. No doubt she'd been aware of my forays into the dell and had waited until the last moment to add another trap.

A witch assassin must constantly adapt and learn from her own mistakes. Even as I lay there, facing my imminent death, I recognized my stupidity. I had been too confident and had underestimated Kernolde. If I survived, I swore to temper my attitude with a smidgeon of caution. *If* . . .

The witch assassin's broad moon-face appeared above and she looked down at me without uttering a word. I was fast and I excelled with blades. I was strong too – but not as strong as Kernolde. Not for nothing did some call her Kernolde the Strangler. Once victorious, Kernolde sometimes hung her victims by their thumbs before slowly asphyxiating them. Not this time though. She had seen what I had achieved already and would take no chances. She would soon put her hands about my throat and squeeze the breath and life from my body. I knew that I would die here.

She began to climb down into the pit. I was calm and ready to die if need be, but I had already thought of something. I had a slim chance of survival.

As Kernolde reached the bottom of the pit and began to weave her way towards me through the spikes, flexing her big muscular hands, I prepared myself to cope with pain. Not the pain she would inflict upon me; that which I chose myself.

My hands were strong; my arms and shoulders

capable of exerting extreme leverage. The spikes in the pit were thin but sturdy; flexible, not brittle. But I had to try. From where I lay I could reach only the one that had pierced my leg, so I seized it and began to bend it. Back and forth, back and forth, I flexed and twisted the spike, each movement sending pain shooting down my leg and up into my body. But I gritted my teeth and worked away at the spike, until it finally yielded and broke, coming away in my hands.

Quickly I lifted my leg clear of the stump and knelt to face Kernolde, my blood running down to soak the earthen floor of the killing pit. I held the spike like a spear and pointed it towards her. Before her hands could reach my throat I would pierce her heart.

But the witch assassin had drawn much of her stored magic out of the tree, and now she halted and concentrated, beginning to hurl shards of darkness towards me. First of all she tried *dread* – that dark spell a witch uses to terrify her enemies, holding them in thrall to fear. Terror tried to claim me and my teeth began to chitter-chatter like those of the dead on the Halloween sabbath.

Kernolde's magic was strong; but not strong enough. I braced myself and shrugged aside her spell. Soon its effects receded and it bothered me no more than the cold wind that had blown down from the arctic ice when I slew the wolves and left their bodies on the snow.

Next she used the unquiet dead – the 'bone-bound' – against me, hurling towards me the spirits she had trapped in Limbo. They clung to my body, dragging my arm down so that it took all my strength to keep hold of that spike. They were strong and fortified by dark magic – one was a strangler, who gripped my throat so hard that Kernolde herself might have been squeezing it. The worst of them was an ab-human spirit, the ghost of one born of the Fiend and a witch. He darkened my eyes and thrust his long cold fingers into my ears so that I thought my head was about to burst, but I fought back and cried out into the darkness and silence:

'I'm still here, Kernolde! Still to be reckoned with. I am Grimalkin, your doom!'

My eyes cleared and the abhuman's fingers left my ears with a *pop* so that sound rushed back. The weight was gone from my arms and I struggled to my feet, taking aim with the spike. Kernolde rushed at me then – a big ugly bear of a woman with strangler's hands. But my aim was true. I thrust the spear right into her heart and she fell at my feet, her blood soaking into the earth to mix with mine. She was choking, trying to speak, so I bent and put my ear close to her lips.

'You're just a girl,' she croaked. 'To be defeated by a girl, after all this time . . . How can this be?'

'Your time is over and mine is just beginning,' I told her. 'This girl took your life and now she will take your bones.'

After taking what I needed, I lifted Kernolde's body out of the pit using her own ropes. Finally I hung her up by her feet so that at dawn the birds could peck her bones clean. That done, I passed through the dell without incident: the dead witches kept their distance.

Grim Gertrude was on her hands and knees, still rooting around in the mouldy leaves, trying to find her head. Without eyes it would prove difficult.

When I emerged from the trees, the clan was waiting to greet me. I held up Kernolde's thumb-bones, and they bowed their heads in acknowledgement of what I'd done; even Katrise, the head of the coven of thirteen, made obeisance. When they looked up, I saw the new respect in their eyes; the fear too.

Now I would begin my quest to destroy my enemy, the Fiend. The spikes in the pit had given me an idea. What if I crafted a sharp spike of silver alloy and somehow impaled the Fiend on it? What if it went right through his heart? And if that didn't work, there had to be some other way . . .

One day I *will* find a way to destroy him.

My name is Grimalkin. I am the witch assassin of the Malkins and I fear nobody.

ALICE AND THE BRAIN GUZZLER

CHAPTER 1
MY NAME IS ALICE DEANE

My name is Alice Deane and I was born into the Pendle witch clans. Didn't want to be a witch, did I? But sometimes you've no choice and things just happen.

I remember the night my aunt, Bony Lizzie, came for me. Like to think I was upset, but I don't remember crying. My mam and dad had been cold and dead in the damp earth for three days and I still hadn't managed to shed a single tear – though it wasn't for want of trying. Tried to remember the good times, I really did. And there were a few, despite the fact that they fought like cat and dog and clouted me even harder than they hit each other. I mean, you should be upset, shouldn't you? It's your own mam and dad and they've just died so you *should* be able to squeeze out one tear at least.

I was staying with my other aunt, Agnes Sowerbutts. She'd taken me in and wanted to bring me up proper and give me a good start in life. Fat chance of that!

The day had been a scorcher and there was a bad summer storm that night – forks of devil-lightning sizzling across the sky and crashes of thunder shaking the walls of the cottage and rattling the pots and pans. But that was nowt compared to what Lizzie did. There was a hammering at the door fit to wake the rotting dead, and when Agnes drew back the bolt, Bony Lizzie strode into the room, her black hair matted with rain, water streaming from her cape to cascade onto the stone flags. Agnes was scared but she stood her ground, placing herself between me and Lizzie.

'Leave the girl alone!' she said calmly, trying to be brave. 'Her home is with me now. She'll be well looked after, don't you worry.'

Lizzie's first response was a sneer. They say there's a family resemblance and that I'm the spitting image of her. But I could never have twisted my face the way she did that night. It was enough to turn the milk sour or send the cat shrieking up the chimney as if Old Nick himself was reaching for its tail.

'The girl belongs to me, Sowerbutts,' Lizzie said, her voice cold and quiet, filled with malice. 'We share the same dark blood. I can teach her what she has to know. I'm the one she needs.'

'Alice needn't be a witch like you!' Agnes retorted. 'Her mam and dad weren't witches, so why should she follow your dark path? Leave her be. Leave the girl with me and get about your business.'

'She's the blood of a witch inside her and that's enough!' Lizzie hissed angrily. 'You're just an outsider and not fit to raise the girl.'

It wasn't true. Agnes was a Deane all right, but she'd married a good man from Whalley, an ironmonger. When he died, she'd returned to Roughlee, where the Deane witch clan made its home.

'I'm her aunt and I'll be a mother to her now,' Agnes retorted. She still spoke bravely but her face was pale, and now I could see her plump chin wobbling, her hands fluttering and trembling with fear.

Next thing, Lizzie stamped her left foot. It was as easy as that. In the twinkling of an eye, the fire died in the grate, the candles flickered and went out, and the whole room became instantly dark, cold and terrifying. I heard Agnes scream with fear; I was screaming myself and desperate to get out. I would have run through the door, jumped through a window or even scrabbled my way up the chimney – I'd have done anything, just to escape.

I did get out, but with Lizzie at my side. She just seized me by the wrist and dragged me off into the night. It was no use trying to resist. She was too strong and she held me tight, her nails digging into my skin. I belonged to her now and there was no way she was ever going to let me go. And that night she began my training as a witch. It was the start of all my troubles.

* * *

That first night in her cottage was the worst. Lizzie started off by showing me the crone she used as her servant. The old woman was standing outside the front door, leaning back against the window ledge, and didn't look too friendly.

She was old all right, but big and ugly too, with long grey hair hanging almost to her waist. She wore a dirty smock, but her short sleeves showed big, muscly, hairy arms that could easily have belonged to a man. Didn't like the look of her one bit. She just stared at me – didn't say a word.

'Her name is Nanna Nuckle and she's a very useful servant,' Lizzie told me. 'Only problem is, she can't go outside in daylight. So she sleeps then. Good at lifting big iron pots and at keeping disobedient girls in check, though. Best do as you're told, girl. She'll be watching you.'

Soon as we got inside, she locked me in a room without a window. Ain't many times in my life I've been as scared as that. It was so dark I couldn't see my hands in front of my face. Didn't smell good either. Something had died in there recently. Not sure if it was animal or human – maybe something in between. But it had breathed its last, slowly and in great pain. Didn't take much sniffing to work that out.

Sniffing is a gift. Born that way, I was. Always been able to do it. But I didn't know then that you could be trained so that it would become a powerful sense, almost as useful as the eyes in your head. That was the first lesson Lizzie gave me. Dragged me out of that stinky dark room well before dawn and took me outside. There were three small fires burning, and above each, a black bubbling iron pot with a wooden lid.

'Well, girl,' Lizzie said, that sneer on her face again, 'let's see how strong your gift is. In one of those pots is your breakfast. Find it and you'll eat well. Lift the wrong lid and you'll eat what's inside anyway. Either that or it'll eat you!'

After the storm the air was much cooler and, shivering with cold and fear, I stared at the three pots for a long time, watching the lids twitch and jerk as the water bubbled and the steam rose. At last Lizzie lost patience and gripped my shoulder hard, pushing me close to the pot on the left.

'Get on with it, girl, if you know what's good for you!'

I was scared of Lizzie and she was hurting my shoulder, her sharp nails pressing right into the flesh as if searching for my bones, so I did what she said. I sniffed three times.

Didn't smell good. Something wick in there, I felt sure; something alive when it ought to be dead; something thin and twiggy but still moving in that bubbly, boiling water.

Lizzie dragged me along to face the centre pot. Sniffed three times again and didn't like what was inside that one either. Something soft and squishy, it was. Something that once grew in the ground – but not fit to eat, I was sure of that. One bite of what was inside would boil your blood, make your eyes swell and pop right out of your head. Didn't want to eat that any more than what was in the first pot.

The third pot contained rabbit – tender, delicious pieces of it melting off the bone and almost ready to eat. One sniff and I knew that for sure.

'This one,' I said. 'I'll eat rabbit for breakfast.' I lifted the lid to prove that I was right.

'That was easy enough, girl, but you're right – this morning you'll enjoy your breakfast,' Lizzie said. 'Now, let's see what's in the middle pot. What do you think it is?'

'Something poisonous. Just one mouthful and you'd be dead.'

'But what kind of poison?' demanded Lizzie. 'Can you tell me the ingredients?'

I shook my head and sniffed again. 'Maybe toadstools . . . not sure.'

'Lift the lid and take a look!'

I replaced the lid on my breakfast and lifted the one over the centre pot. Stepped back right away, I did. Didn't want to breathe in that poisonous steam. There were pieces of toadstool churning in the boiling water.

'Nine different toadstools in there,' Lizzie told me. 'By the end of the month, with just three sniffs you'll know every one by name. You've a lot of work ahead of you, girl, but the gift is strong inside you. Just needs developing, that's all. Now try the third lid . . .'

This pot really scared me. What lay within? What could survive in that boiling water? As I hesitated, Lizzie dug her nails deeper into my shoulder, hurting me so much that, despite my fear, I reached for the lid.

As I slowly lifted it, Lizzie released me and stepped back. I got the shock of my life. Almost wet myself, I did. A small evil-looking face was watching me from within the pot. The head of the creature was just above the boiling water but I couldn't see its body. Suddenly it leaped straight at my face. I dropped the lid and ducked.

It went straight over my head. I turned and saw that it had landed high on Lizzie's chest, its ugly head nestling at her throat. It convulsed and burrowed down into her dress, hiding.

'This is Old Spig, my familiar,' Lizzie said with a fond smile. 'He's my eyes, nose and ears. Doesn't miss much, does Old Spig. So you do as you're told, girl, or he'll find you out. And once he tells me, you'll be in real trouble. Then I'll teach you all about pain . . .'

That was my first sight of Lizzie's familiar. Mostly she was a witch who used bone-magic, but for Lizzie, Old Spig was well worth his keep. He was scary, and from that first time I set eyes on him I knew he'd give me trouble.

After tucking into that delicious rabbit I felt a bit better. And for the rest of that day all I had to do was a few household chores; it wasn't so different to what I'd been doing while staying with Agnes. I had to lay the cooking fire, wash the pots, pans and cutlery, and prepare a lamb stew for our evening meal. Nanna Nuckle didn't help; she stayed in her room all day because she couldn't stand daylight. She wasn't a witch, so I couldn't understand why this was. But when I asked Lizzie, she just told me to mind my own business.

Didn't do much cleaning though, except in my own room. It seemed that Lizzie liked the cottage to be dirty. Made her feel comfortable. There was one room I wasn't allowed inside – I reckoned it was the one where Old Spig spent most of his time, and I didn't like the sounds that were coming out of there. Couldn't hear Spig, but something was whining like it was in pain, so I kept well clear.

But, looking on the bright side, I'd survived Lizzie's first test. Old Spig scared me rotten, but apart from him, maybe living with Lizzie wouldn't be quite as bad as I'd expected.

'Are you brave, girl?' Lizzie asked me once I'd finished my work. 'A witch needs to be brave! I've got something in mind that only a really brave girl can cope with.'

I nodded at Bony Lizzie. I didn't want to admit that I was scared, but my teeth were chattering with fear, and she smiled at my discomfort as if it gave her pleasure. The sun had been down about half an hour and we were standing in her small front room, which was very gloomy. A single candle made from black wax was flickering on the mantelpiece, filling the corners with strange shadows.

'Are you strong, girl?'

'Strong for my age,' I told her, nodding again, my voice quavering.

'Well, all you have to do is go down into Witch Dell and bring me back a special jug. You'll find it buried close to the trunk of the tallest oak there. Dig where the moon casts the tree's shadow at midnight!'

My whole body began to shake then. The dell was full of dead witches. They came out at night, looking for blood.

'Are you going to be a witch, girl?' Lizzie asked. 'Is that what you want?'

I didn't really want to become a witch, but to say no would have made Lizzie really angry, so I nodded for the third time.

'Then don't be afeard of dead witches. Besides, those

down in the dell won't do you much harm. They're all sisters-in-death. They don't bother each other much and they won't bother you. Get ye gone but be sure to be back afore dawn. What's in the jug will spoil in daylight!'

CHAPTER
2
A WITCH YOU'LL ALWAYS BE

Witch Dell was north of the Devil's Triangle, the three villages where the Malkins, Deanes and Mouldheels made their homes. It was a clear night, the moon waxing to three quarters full. Pendle Hill to the west was bathed in silver light, and so bright was that moonshine that only two stars in the sky were visible.

When I reached the dell, it was less than half an hour before midnight so I couldn't afford to dawdle and walked straight in. It was gloomy, a patchwork of dappled moon-shadows, the gnarled roots like ogres' fingers clutching the ground. But last year's autumn leaves were heaped thickly around the trunks of *some* of the trees. That bothered me. They could have been blown there by the wind, but a dark alternative wormed its way into my head.

They could have been piled there by dead witches, couldn't they? Dank loamy beds to rest dead bones under on a chill night; leafy lairs from which to strike, grasping the ankles of unwary travellers before dragging them down for a blood-feast.

Had to trust what Lizzie had told me though – that they wouldn't hurt me; that the dead forgot clan enmities. But I'd not gone more than a hundred yards when I heard something heading my way, feet shuffling through the leaves. Something nasty was approaching . . .

So I sniffed her out. It was a dead witch all right, but there was something odd about her. It was only when she stepped into a shaft of moonlight that I saw that she didn't have a head. She was carrying it under her arm like a big pumpkin. So I knew who she was right away!

It was Grim Gertrude, the oldest witch in the dell.

Years earlier, the witch assassin Grimalkin had sliced off her head. Best thing to do in the circumstances. That had slowed her down all right! Story goes that it was almost a month before she finally found it again. So she wasn't going to let it go now. Gripping it really tightly, she was.

Gertrude turned so that she was facing me, her eyes watching me. The glassy, rheumy eyes glistened in the moonlight and the pale lips moved, but no sound reached my ears. The head wasn't connected to the neck so her voice-box didn't work. But I could read her lips and knew what she was saying:

'Who are you? What clan are ye from? Speak while you've still breath in your scrawny body!'

'My name's Alice Deane, but my mother was a Malkin.'

'As you're half Malkin, I'll let you live, but you're not welcome here, child,' mouthed the lips. *'The living don't come here – not if they know what's good for them!'*

I began to tremble. Lizzie had lied to me. She'd not

wanted to risk coming to the dell herself after dark so she'd sent me to risk my neck.

'Bony Lizzie sent me to get something, she did. It's a jug buried near the biggest oak in the dell . . .'

Gertrude stepped nearer to me and suddenly reached out to grab me by the arm. She pulled me close, and a damp, loamy, rotting smell filled my nostrils, making me want to retch.

'*Do you do everything that Lizzie tells you*?' she asked.

'She's my mistress and is training me to be a witch. Don't have much choice, do I?'

Gertrude sniffed me three times. '*You were born a witch and a witch you'll always be. Don't have to be Lizzie who trains you. You've got the makings of somebody really strong. You could find someone else to show you the way.*'

'Only been with Lizzie just over a day,' I told her. 'Might give her till the end of the week. Let's see how she shapes up.'

Couldn't lip-read what Gertrude said next. It

took me a few moments to realize that she was laughing.

'*You've got spirit, girl,*' her lips mouthed at last. '*If Lizzie don't suit, I can teach you all about the dark. Won't be the first dead witch who's trained a young girl and shown her what's proper. Can't do dark magic myself – been dead too long for that – but I do still remember how things are done, and I can see that the power's in you. Together, we could bring it out. We'd make a good team, me and you. Help each other. So think it over, girl. You know where to find me. Now go and get what Lizzie needs. I won't stand in your way.*'

I watched the dead witch shuffle off into the trees, her head still tucked underneath her arm. Dead and smelly, she was, but still nicer than Lizzie.

I went on till I reached the tallest oak tree in the dell, waited until exactly midnight, and then dug with my fingers close to the trunk in the shadow cast by the moon. Didn't take me long to find what Lizzie wanted because it wasn't buried very deep. It was a small earthen jug. The lid was fastened on tight so I didn't try to force it off. It was Lizzie's business anyway. So I took it back to her.

'Well done, girl!' she said, giving me a twisted smile. 'Now get yourself to bed. I've got work to do and it's not something you're ready to see yet. You'll need months of training afore you're ready for that.'

So I went up to my room and tried to sleep. It took me a long while because every time I closed my eyes I kept seeing scary Gertrude. The noises coming from downstairs didn't help either. I heard what sounded like a wild animal growling and then, a little later, a young child bawling its eyes out. When I finally nodded off, I slept for hours. Lizzie didn't bother to wake me and I didn't get up till late afternoon.

'Look what the cat's dragged in!' Lizzie said as I staggered downstairs. 'Now you're up at last you'd best get busy making supper. Fancy a good beef stew, I do. I'm going out and won't be back until after dark. Make sure that stew's waiting for me and that it's piping hot.'

Sleeping in late had given me a headache so I went for a stroll first to clear my head. Enjoyed my walk and got back later than I'd intended, so I had to rush a bit with the meal. The sun had set before I even got started. I chopped up onions, potatoes, carrots and beets, and added them to the big iron pot, where chunks of beef were already boiling away over the kitchen fire. Only really good at cooking one meal, I am – that's rabbit turned on a spit over an open fire – but though I say it myself, about half an hour later, when I took a sip from the ladle, that stew was quite tasty.

All I needed to do now was put the lid on and let it simmer till Lizzie got back. Had to root through her mucky cupboards and it took me quite a while to find the lid. While I was giving it a good scrubbing in the sink, I heard a noise behind me – what sounded like a splash. I turned round but could see nothing. Puzzled, I dried the lid, then carried it across to the pot.

What I saw next made me come to a sudden halt

and drop the lid, which fell onto the flags with a loud clang. Two eyes were staring at me from the pot. It was Lizzie's familiar, Old Spig – but only his ugly head was visible; the rest of him was hidden by the bubbling stew. His mouth was wide open and he was slurping up the boiling liquid just as fast as he could.

'That's Lizzie's supper! She ain't going to thank you for eating it!' I warned him.

Spig's eyes widened a little but he didn't bother to reply. He just kept on gulping down the stew as if he couldn't get enough of it.

I started to get angry. Soon there wouldn't be enough left for our suppers and Lizzie would be really annoyed with me, to say the least. Not that I fancied the stew much now that Spig had decided to swim in it.

'Get out of there, you dirty little thing!' I snapped.

Old Spig's head rose out of the stew so that I could just see the beginning of his narrow scaly neck. '*What* did you just call me?' he demanded.

His voice was harsh and surprisingly deep for such a small creature. There was something so malevolent about it that made the hairs on the back of my neck stand up.

'Called you a dirty little thing!' I said. 'It ain't nice, you crawling around in our supper like that. Lizzie won't like it. I'll tell her what you've done unless you get out of my pot right away.'

He leaped out towards me and I stepped back quickly. But he hadn't meant to jump on me. He fell short of where I'd been standing and perched on the edge of the mantelpiece. He was covered in soupy stew and it started to ooze from his body and form a puddle underneath him. Despite that, I was now able to get a proper look at him for the first time.

Old Spig was about the size of a small rabbit but he was almost all head – and an uglier one I'd never seen. It was covered with green scales, apart from the face. He had a hooked nose and pointy ears, with a very wide mouth which he never closed properly, and his teeth were very long and thin – more like needles really. Apart from a scaly body, which was not much bigger than a large potato, the rest of him was just legs. Triple jointed, they were. Four of them had sharp talons but the fifth was really strange: it was like a long thin strip of bone, but one edge was like the teeth of a wood saw.

'You won't last long in this house if you speak to me like that!' he warned, his voice almost a growl now. 'And as for telling Lizzie, you'd just be wasting your time. We're close and snug, just like brother and sister. If ever she needed to choose between you and me, *you'd* be the one whose bones would go into the pot! You're new and still wet behind the ears, so I'll give you just one more chance. But ever behave like that again and you are dead – make no mistake about it!'

That said, Spig leaped from the mantelpiece to the floor and scuttled across the kitchen, leaving a trail of gravy across the flags which I had to clean up after him.

* * *

Later, when Lizzie got back, I decided to tell her what Spig had done anyway.

'Eat up your stew, girl,' Lizzie commanded. 'Need to keep up your strength in our line of work.'

'Don't fancy it much. Old Spig jumped in it and ate some. Put me right off it.'

'Creature needs to eat too. Can't blame him for that. Not his favourite meal though. When he's not after blood, Old Spig likes to eat brains. Human ones are best but he'll make do with sheep and cows. Once he was so desperate he cut off the top of a hedgehog's head and tried to crawl in. Funniest thing you ever saw.'

I couldn't touch the stew; I left Lizzie eating her supper and went to bed early. At the top of the stairs I found someone standing outside my room. It was Nanna Nuckle, and she didn't look happy. She stepped to one side as I reached for the door handle, but then, when I crossed the threshold, gave me a slap across the back of my head so hard that it almost knocked me into the middle of next week.

'What was that for?' I asked angrily as I regained my balance.

'It's for giving me cheek, girl. I won't tolerate cheek!'

With that Nanna Nuckle stomped along the landing to her own room. I hadn't given her cheek, I thought to myself. What on earth was she on about?

CHAPTER 3
NANNA NUCKLE'S HEAD

The following morning Lizzie started to teach me all about plants and herbs. To my surprise, it wasn't just about stopping enemies' hearts or cankering their brains. She taught me about healing too. And some plants were both good and bad.

One of those was called 'mandrake': eating it could make you fall unconscious; too much and you'd never wake up; or it could drive you absolutely mad. But it could also purge poisons and take away the pain from a bad tooth. Lizzie said its roots were shaped like a human body and it shrieked when you dragged it from the ground. I'd have liked to see one of them, but Lizzie said they were rare in the County.

'You never know when this will come in useful, girl,' she told me, pointing to a black-ink sketch of an elder leaf. 'The plant has white flowers and red or blue berries, and can cure rheumatic pain and ease heart problems. It rallies the dying too, giving them new vigour. Once in a while some even make a full recovery. If you or another witch were suffering and close to death, this would revive you.'

I wasn't allowed to write any of this information down though – Lizzie said I had to develop my memory. She said a witch needed to keep most of her spells in her head so she didn't need to waste time looking things up in books again. Lizzie had to go out again that afternoon; she told me to use her library and learn what I could about toadstools.

It wasn't much of a library – just two shelves of mildewed books down in the cellar. I put my candle on the table and looked along the first row, reading the spines. Three of 'em were grimoires covered in cobwebs – books of dark magic spells. I found the book on toadstools and pulled it off the shelf – but then I noticed something else: *Familiars: Good Practice and Bad Habits*.

That sounded a lot more interesting than reading about toadstools. I wanted to find out more about Old Spig, and this was my chance! So I picked up the book and started to leaf through it.

The introductory section was all about the different types of familiar and their suitability for different purposes. I found out that toads were good familiars for old witches who were long past their best, but that water witches in their prime used them all the time because they were suited to a wet and boggy environment.

I also read about how a witch got herself a familiar. You had to tempt it with blood. Most witches started by feeding it from a dish, but some made a small cut on their upper arm and let it suck the blood out directly from their flesh. Eventually, after months of that, a small nipple developed, making it easier for the familiar to draw out the blood. It was a bit like a mother feeding her baby, but really weird. Didn't really want to be a witch, did I? But if it ever happened, I certainly wouldn't be one who used familiar magic.

I flicked through the book faster, trying to find out what Old Spig was. No sign of him at first, but then I came to the last chapter, which was very long. It was called 'The Highest and Most Dangerous Categories of Familiar'.

Lots of strange creatures there, including boggarts and water beasts which I'd already heard of. As for some of the others, I didn't even know that they existed in our world. Maybe some came through portals from the dark, but I didn't have time to read it all and find out.

The opening paragraph contained a warning:

These types of familiar are difficult to control and can present serious dangers to a witch who employs one in her service. Frequently the creature becomes threatening and, over time, the familiar often assumes the dominant role. The witch then becomes the servant.

Then I came to a whole page of sketches. Whoever wrote the book had done a little drawing of each category with the name underneath and a page reference.

Old Spig was there. He was what they called a 'brain guzzler'. I was just turning to the page to find out more when I was suddenly interrupted.

There was a tremendous anguished cry from somewhere upstairs. It sounded like someone had been hurt badly. Lizzie had gone out, so who could it be? Nanna Nuckle?

After the way she'd clouted me the previous night it wouldn't have bothered me if she'd fallen downstairs and broken her blooming neck, but I left the cellar and went to find out what had happened. She wasn't in the kitchen or the gloomy front room. Neither was she lying dead at the bottom of the stairs. A pity, that! So I went up to her room. The door was open and I could see her sitting on a chair next to her bed. I gasped in horror at what I saw. I couldn't believe what had happened to her. It was just too horrible . . . I started shaking all over.

The top of her head had been sliced off and was hanging forward over her face, held on by just a bit of skin. And the inside of her skull was empty. Old Spig had killed her! He'd guzzled her brains!

I ran down the stairs in a panic, desperate to get as far away as possible. What if Spig was still hungry and he wanted my brains too? I might well be next.

I ran out into the woods and hid amongst the trees, waiting for Lizzie to return. She'd know what to do. Soon it started to rain and I got soaked to the skin, but I was too scared to take shelter back in Lizzie's house.

Lizzie didn't come back until well after dark. I heard her coming through the trees towards the house and rushed to meet her. It was the nearest I ever came to being glad to see her.

'What ails you, girl?' she shouted as I ran towards her.

'Old Spig has killed Nanna Nuckle!' I gasped out. 'He's sliced open the top of her head and eaten her brains!'

Lizzie came to a halt, but instead of being shocked and outraged, she started to laugh. It was loud, wild laughter that could have been heard for miles. Then she grabbed me by the wrist and dragged me back towards the house. We went straight up to Nanna Nuckle's room.

To my surprise, the woman was sleeping in her chair, snoring away, with her head slumped forward onto her chest, her long grey hair hanging down like a dirty curtain almost as far as the floor.

'But I saw it!' I protested. 'She was dead and her head was wide open and her skull was empty.'

Instead of replying, Lizzie stepped forward and eased away the curtain of hair to show a red line around the top of Nanna Nuckle's head.

'Old Spig's inside her head now, fast asleep. I'd show you how cosy he is but it's best not to disturb him. Likes his rest, he does.'

'So he *has* eaten her brains?'

'That's true enough, girl, but it happened long ago. To be truthful, Nanna Nuckle didn't have many brains left to eat. She was getting forgetful and couldn't concentrate. But she was still strong, and that big body can do lots of useful chores for me, like lifting heavy iron pots when I mix up my potions and poisons. So I let Spig guzzle her brains. It's a good arrangement: he finds it cosy inside her head – once inside he can look through her eyes, hear what she hears and talk using her voice. So he uses Nanna Nuckle's body to do heavy work for me. It's a good arrangement. Old Spig spends about half his time in there.'

'But I heard her cry out in pain last night. That's why I went upstairs to her room.'

'Nanna Nuckle isn't there any longer, but when Spig opens up her skull to climb in or out, her body feels the pain and sometimes gives a gasp or even screams if Spig's a bit rough. Anyway, now you know, girl. So take care and do as I say. That big old body is starting to slow down and Old Spig will be looking for a replacement soon. Best make sure it's not you, girl!'

I went to bed, glad to take off my wet clothes. I'd a lot to think about, and I lay there in the dark for hours before finally dropping off to sleep.

That was why Nanna Nuckle had clouted me the other night, I realized. It had been Spig taking his revenge because when he was in the stew I called him a 'dirty little thing'. He was a nasty dangerous creature, and I knew that in order to survive I'd have to sort him out one way or another.

CHAPTER
4
BRAIN PLUGS IN APPLE JUICE

The next four days were uneventful and I was starting to get into a routine. Daytimes were the best because then I saw neither hide nor hair of Old Spig and Nanna Nuckle.

Lizzie liked to sleep in late, and after I'd made her breakfast I'd have a lesson – usually the only one of the day. A lot of it was memory work. She'd make me learn spells by heart and then recite 'em back to her. Later I'd go down into her little library and study the book she'd suggested.

After that I'd go and collect herbs and toadstools before making the main meal of the day. But then it happened . . .

I was making another stew. It was lamb this time. Lizzie had caught and killed one north of Downham and carried it over her shoulders all the way back to her cottage. Wasn't the only thing she'd killed either. I saw the thumb-bones she pulled out of the leather pouch she always wears. They were human, and small too. She'd probably killed a child. It was too horrible to contemplate. I could never do that so it stood to reason that I could never become a bone witch.

Anyway, I was making the stew when Old Spig jumped into it again. This time he didn't even wait until my back was turned. He came over my shoulder from behind and landed slap bang in the middle of it. Gravy splashed up onto my dress, face and hair. It was boiling-hot too and it hurt. And there he was, just his ugly head showing while he slurped away like there was no tomorrow.

I saw red, and before I could bite my tongue I really gave him a telling off.

'Get out of there, you ugly little thing!' I shouted.

153

'Get out *now*, you greedy, slimy piece of muck! Don't you mess with me!'

Old Spig got out, jumping onto the mantelpiece again. I could see him quivering with anger: his mouth kept opening and closing, showing those sharp little needle-like teeth. It was a long time before he spoke, and when he did, his voice was low and dangerous.

'You're as good as dead,' he told me. 'Brains are best eaten just before the full moon, and that's when I'll eat yours. Soon I'll be sawing the top of your head off. Can't wait to get inside!'

With that, he put the edge of that strange little bone-limb he had against the edge of the wooden mantelpiece. Back and forth he drew it, and that sharp-toothed edge cut through the wood like butter, with the sawdust falling into the hearth. Then he leaped down and was gone, leaving me trembling.

It was just a few days till the full moon. What could I do? I wondered. Tell Lizzie? I decided to do just that, even though I wasn't at all sure she'd help me.

'Old Spig said he's going to eat my brains,' I told

her, just as she was starting to eat her lamb stew.

'Is he now, girl. You must have done something to really annoy him then . . .'

'He jumped in the stew again and I called him names and shouted at him to get out. Threatened me, he did. Said I was as good as dead and that he'd kill me before the full moon.'

Lizzie never even looked at me. She just kept shovelling stew into her mouth.

'Can't you help me?' I asked her at last.

Finally she glanced my way, but her eyes were hard and cruel, with no hint of any kind of sympathy for my plight. 'I'm training you to be a witch so there's one thing you should get into your head now – and that's before Spig's teeth get there!' she said. 'A witch needs to be hard; she needs to survive. This is between you and Old Spig. You got to sort it out one way or the other. Either that or you're not up to the job. Understand?'

I nodded. I would get no help from Lizzie – that much was certain.

'Anyway, tonight you must take yourself up to the dell again. I've buried another little jug close to the roots of that tree. Make sure you have it back here well before dawn. Moon won't help you this time so the digging might just take a little longer.'

That much was true: there was indeed no moon that night. A storm was moving in from the west, the wind bending the tree branches, the whole dell groaning and creaking as if in pain.

Only halfway to the old oak, I was, when Grim Gertrude found me. Moved fast for such an old dead witch who was carrying her head under her arm. Got herself between me and where I wanted to go.

'*Left Lizzie, have you, and come to work with me?*' the pale lips mouthed.

'Ain't ready to do that yet a while,' I told her.

'*No time like the present, girl. You and me would be useful to each other. I could teach you much more than Lizzie – help you lots, I could.*'

It suddenly dawned on me that Gertrude might just be able to help me now. There was no harm in trying. Who else could I turn to?

'Trouble is, Gertrude, I may never be able to work for you. Going to be dead myself soon. Lizzie's familiar, Spig, is going to guzzle my brains. Told me he'd do it before the next full moon. And Lizzie won't help; said I needed to be strong and survive. But I don't know what I can do.'

'There's always a way, girl, especially when you've got friends like me to help you. Do you know what's in that little jug that Lizzie's sent you to get?'

'Wouldn't let me see into the last jug I brought her. Told me I'd need a lot of training before I could see into it.'

'Did she now? Well, inside are prime plugs of young brain, fermenting in apple juice. Whenever Lizzie kills somebody, she takes the thumb-bones but gets bits o' brain for Old Spig as a treat. Doesn't saw the tops off their heads though – got an easier method than that . . . has a special tool she uses. Plunges it right up through the nose and into the

skull and cuts out a few choice brain plugs. Brings them back and puts them in that jug with a good lashing of juice. Buries it close to the roots of that tree and leaves it for a few nights to ferment into alcohol. Old Spig loves it. There's lots of magic in this dell that's seeped out of dead witches. That's absorbed by the jug too and gives him extra strength so he can do Lizzie's bidding.'

'So when I take the jug back he'll be more dangerous than ever?'

'She won't give him the jug until tomorrow night. She'll be going out then so it'll keep him quiet. But what you say's true enough. At first it makes him really sleepy. That would be your time to strike. Kill him while he sleeps. That's your best chance. And it's you or him, so you can't afford to be squeamish. Kill him tomorrow night. That's what I'd do in your place!'

'What's the best way to finish him off?' I asked.

'You could use a sharp knife and chop his little legs off. Couldn't do much then, could he? He'd starve to death slowly. Burying him under a big stone would be best. A very heavy one would finish him off quicker.

'Another good reason to do it tomorrow, girl. Big meeting of the three clans then – could last several nights. They're going to curse a spook who works in the south of the County. They want him dead. Done a lot of damage to our sisters down there over the years, he has, so he deserves it all right. Bit of a loner, is Lizzie, but she certainly won't miss something that big. So she'll be out, leaving you alone in the house with Old Spig. So kill him then!'

I'd killed things before, mostly by wringing their necks – chickens, rabbits and hares; you've got to eat, and everybody does that. But killing something that talks – that's different. Didn't like the idea at all. But if I didn't kill Old Spig, then he'd kill me for sure. So I didn't have much choice.

When I got back, I gave Lizzie the jug, then went straight to bed. The following day it rained heavily and Lizzie was quiet and in a right mood. Didn't even bother to give me a lesson – just sat staring into the fire all afternoon, muttering to herself – so I went down to her little library and started reading about familiars again – that last chapter with the section on brain guzzlers.

It didn't tell me much about how to deal with Old Spig. I suppose that's the last thing that crosses most witches' minds. They want to befriend and control a familiar, not kill it. But there was one interesting section on guzzlers' likes and dislikes that told witches about their vulnerabilities.

Brain guzzlers can tolerate extreme temperatures but they love boiling liquids, in which they happily immerse themselves for hours at a time.

Although they can generally look after themselves, it is important to be aware of some weaknesses that may be exploited by a witch's enemies.

The hard, scaly head and body are tough and resistant to the sharpest of blades, but salt is corrosive and burns them. Even if there's insufficient to kill them, it saps their strength and affects their coordination.

A blade can also be used to remove their limbs and

immobilize them. They are also vulnerable to sunlight and rarely venture out during the day.

The line about cutting their limbs off told me that dead Gertrude knew her stuff all right. That was all the help I could find in that book, but it was useful to know about the salt. Not that it was of any immediate help. Lizzy didn't like the stuff and there wasn't even a pinch of it in the house.

'I'll be gone for a couple of nights – maybe more,' Lizzie said that evening as she paused on the doorstep, looking up at the waxing moon. 'It's the full moon in a couple of nights. Will you still be here when I get back, girl? Or will Old Spig be curled up inside your skull?'

With a wicked laugh she set off into the trees. Full of foreboding, I closed the door and went to the kitchen. There I sorted through the knife drawer and picked up the biggest, sharpest one I could find, then started to climb the stairs.

No point in dawdling. It was best to get it over with.

Lizzie had given Old Spig the jug about an hour before she'd gone out. I hoped he'd still be sleeping . . .

The door of Nanna Nuckle's room was slightly ajar. I opened it just a fraction of an inch and peeped in. She was sitting in her chair, illuminated by a shaft of moonlight, the top of her head hanging forward on that bit of skin. So where was Old Spig?

I heard him before I saw him. There were faint snores coming from the window ledge, so I eased the door open ever so slowly and carefully stepped into the room. There he was, curled up into a ball, most of his legs tucked underneath that ugly head and body of his. I raised the knife and began to tiptoe towards him, one cautious step at a time.

I raised the knife high and prepared to bring it down. Three legs were sticking out. All I had to do was chop them off. He'd probably jump up in pain and fright and then I could slice off the other ones. But I hesitated and my hand began to tremble. To do that in cold blood was horrible. I just couldn't force myself to bring down that knife.

Suddenly both Spig's eyes opened wide and he stared right at me. 'You'd kill me in my sleep, would you?' he said, his voice quiet and dangerous. 'Did you think it'd be that easy? Well, now it's my turn!'

He leaped straight at me. I twisted away but I wasn't fast enough. He landed on top of my head and I felt his claws dig sharply into my scalp. I screamed, dropped the knife and tried to pull him off, but he was tangled up in my hair – and then something even worse happened. I felt him draw that bone-saw across the back of my head; felt it bite into my scalp!

I screamed and fell to my knees. I was terrified. Spig was starting to saw the top of my head off. There was only one thing I could do. One last chance. I crawled over to the wall and butted my head against it as hard as I could. Spig cried out as I squashed his body against the stone. Twice more I did it, then he let go and dropped to the floor, twitching and gasping.

Knew that wasn't the end of him, so I stumbled to my feet and ran out of the room and down the stairs, then out of the house and into the trees. I halted then and looked back, watching the doorway to see if he'd follow me.

Didn't take that long before Spig came after me, but now he was inside Nanna Nuckle's skull. So I kept moving through the trees, further and further from Lizzie's house. Wasn't that worried though. She was big, strong and ugly, and if she got hold of me those big hands could kill me without a doubt; but she had to find and catch me first. Nanna Nuckle wasn't a witch so she couldn't sniff me out.

As long as I kept moving, I'd be safe. And she'd have to be back in her room before dawn. For now the worst was over. But Lizzie would be away for at least another night, and after dark I'd have to face Spig again.

CHAPTER 5
SEVEN BIG HANDFULS

Long before the sun came up, Nanna Nuckle's big body turned and lumbered slowly back towards Lizzie's house. But I was in no hurry to return. I had a lot of thinking to do.

One option was to run away. But where would I go? I'd be welcome at the cottage of my other aunt, Agnes Sowerbutts, but Lizzie would only drag me back again. There was a good chance that she would find me wherever I went. Did she want me dead? Did she want Old Spig to guzzle my brains? What had been the point of training me as a witch if she was going to let Spig kill me? I wondered. Or was that what she'd intended all along? Was I the replacement for

Nanna Nuckle's old body, which was slowing down now?

Get hard and survive, she'd told me. That didn't make sense and contradicted the rest. Did she want me to survive or not? Well, I would do just that. It was me or Spig – one of us was going to die, and it wasn't going to be me. He was vulnerable during the daylight hours and might not think I was brave enough to go back to the house.

That was to my advantage. But what else? *Think, girl!* I told myself. *Use everything you know . . .*

Salt! That would slow him down and affect his coordination. He wouldn't be able to leap onto my head again so easily. But where could I get my hands on some? It was no use looking in any of the local villages. Witches lived there and they were wary of the stuff. None of them used it. I was still only being trained – hopefully I could still touch it. So I needed to go south and get right out of the Pendle district.

Washed myself in a stream first. My hair was matted with blood at the back where Spig had tried to saw my head open. Sore too when I touched it, but the blade hadn't gone very deep. A few tufts of hair came away but I would mend eventually.

I'm not a thief. Never take stuff that doesn't belong to me. But I was desperate. Besides, salt's cheap and I didn't want that much. I saw a farmer and his wife in the distance, working in the fields, so I sneaked into their store. There were big sacks of salt, but I found a bit of cloth and wrapped what I needed in that – seven big handfuls. That done, I set off back towards Lizzie's house.

It was late afternoon when I walked into the kitchen – plenty of time to sort out what I needed. But I went upstairs first to see what was what. Took a knife and a handful of salt, just in case.

Eased open the door of Old Spig's room. Gloomy in there, it was, with the heavy curtains closed. I waited for a few moments for my eyes to adjust, then tiptoed in. Nanna Nuckle was in her usual position in her chair, the top of her head hanging forward, but there was no sign of Spig.

Wasn't daft, was he? He was hiding away somewhere until dark. So I had another think. I had to make the best of the situation, and after about half an hour or so I'd worked out what to do.

I went down into the kitchen, made myself a brew and had something to eat. Then I searched Lizzie's house to find the things I needed. She'd no idea of how to keep things tidy and organized so it took me ages. One of the things I found was a meat cleaver – heavier than a knife and just what the doctor ordered.

About an hour before dark I went back up to Spig's room and made my preparations. That done, I became nervous and kept pacing up and down; but then, as it started to get dark, I hid behind the door, the cleaver in my right hand, salt in my left.

Old Spig didn't make much noise when he approached. I could just about hear the tapping of his spindly limbs on the floorboards as he came to the door. I was scared and my hands were trembling, but I couldn't afford to miss. Make a mistake, and a minute later I'd be dead.

At the very last moment he saw me, but it didn't do him any good. I hurled the handful of salt at him. A good shot, it was, and he screamed and started to twitch and writhe, his limbs trying to go in different directions. Then I used the cleaver – but I didn't chop off his legs as Grim Gertrude had advised. He still needed them for what I had planned. I chopped off his bone-saw instead, bringing down the cleaver so hard that it went deep into the floorboards and I couldn't pull it out. Not that it mattered.

After Old Spig had screamed for about a minute he went very quiet and looked up at me. His mouth opened and closed a few times, showing his needle teeth. His legs were still twitching, but I was no longer worried about him jumping onto my head.

'You've maimed me!' he said, his voice all wobbly. 'I'll kill you for that.'

'You said something like that once before,' I told him, 'but I'm still here. Reckon I'll still be here when you're dead and gone! Can't saw my head open now, can you?'

'Not today, I can't, but it won't take long to grow back. Didn't know that, did you? All my limbs grow back eventually. And now I'll make you wish you'd never been born! I'm going to twist your head off your scrawny neck!'

That said, he leaped towards the top of Nanna Nuckle's head, which was exactly what I wanted. No doubt he wanted to use that big body to hurt me good and proper, but he missed and skittered off onto the floor again. Took him five attempts to get inside.

As soon as he managed it, Old Spig started screaming. I'd thrown just one handful of salt at him. That left six more, and I'd put them inside Nanna Nuckle's skull.

Once he was in there, I didn't waste any time. Had to work fast, didn't I? Took the needle and twine I'd found in one of Lizzie's mucky cupboards and stitched the top of the skull to the bottom. Wasn't a very tidy job but I used lots of stitches and made them really tight. Nanna Nuckle twitched a lot and saliva started to dribble down her chin while I did it, but she didn't groan as she had when I'd poured the salt in. Old Spig was trapped inside – I didn't think his bone-saw would grow back fast enough to save him.

When I went back the following morning, Nanna Nuckle was very still. She looked dead. Couldn't tell whether Old Spig was still alive inside her skull, but when I put my ear really close there were no sounds. Of course, it didn't help that I'd pulled the curtains right back and a shaft of bright sunlight was shining straight into her face. Wasn't over yet though, was it? I still had to face Lizzie and tell her what I'd done.

I was sitting on a stool in front of the fire when Lizzie came home. It was late afternoon.

'You still here?' she asked. 'Thought you'd be dead by now.'

'It's Old Spig that's dead,' I replied. 'I killed him.'

'Pull my other leg,' she said; 'it's got bells on it!'

'Ain't joking,' I told her. 'He's upstairs . . .'

Lizzie must have read in my face that I was telling

JOSEPH DELANEY

the truth because she sort of twisted her mouth like she does when she's angry, grabbed me by the wrist and dragged me upstairs. She peered closely at Nanna Nuckle, and then, with her forefinger, traced the jagged line of stitches across that broad forehead, then put her nose very close and, after sniffing three times, shook her head.

'What I can't understand is why he didn't just saw his way out,' she muttered. Then her eyes drifted across to the place behind the door and she noticed the cleaver still sticking out of the floorboards and Old Spig's little bone-saw lying on the floor. The stump was red with his blood.

'I threw salt at him and put more inside the skull. When he jumped into it, I stitched him up.'

Lizzie didn't say anything for a long time; she just kept staring at the top of Nanna Nuckle's head.

'It was him or me. You told me I'd to sort it one way or the other or I wouldn't be up to the job. Well, I sorted it, didn't I?'

'Get hold of her legs, girl. I'll take the shoulders,'

Lizzie said. 'Can't leave 'em here or they'll start to rot.'

So we buried them out in the woods. One grave, two bodies – not that you'd notice. After that I walked back to the house with Lizzie, not sure what would happen next. I was past being scared. At that moment, after all I'd done, I didn't care one jot what happened to me.

We sat in front of the fire and it was a long time before Lizzie spoke.

'In a way, girl, you did me a favour,' she said, staring into the flames. 'Using a familiar as strong as Old Spig is dangerous. The longer it goes on, the more they start to get the upper hand. In the end I was killing when I didn't need fresh bones. Just doing it to keep him happy and stocked up with his favourite tipple – brain plugs in apple juice.

'He was starting to control me, and when it gets like that it's best for a witch to put an end to it and get herself a new familiar. But me and Old Spig were close, and I just couldn't bring myself to do him in. So I was half hoping that you might do the job for me. And you did well, girl. You remind me of myself when I was a girl of your age. You could almost be my daughter . . .' she said, giving me a wicked smile.

So that was it. I'd survived my first two weeks with Bony Lizzie. And that was what I was going to do in the future. Wasn't going to drink people's blood or take their bones, but I was willing to learn all the tricks that would keep me safe from other witches – and anyone else who tried to harm me.

I'm going to survive. You can be sure of that. It's as certain as my name's Alice Deane.

THE BANSHEE
WITCH

CHAPTER 1
A HARD LESSON

The enemy before me was big, strong and ruthless. This was dangerous and I couldn't afford to make a mistake. He clasped a long knife in his right hand and a heavy club in his left and was eager to use them.

With a roar of anger, he charged straight at me, swinging his club in an arc from right to left. I managed to block it, but the force of the impact jarred my arm and shoulder so badly that I almost dropped my staff. I groaned and twisted away, retreating clockwise.

We were in a ruined building, an old tavern long abandoned to the elements. I'd been chased through the woods and, thinking I'd shaken my pursuer off my trail, had taken refuge here. It was a big mistake: now I was in serious trouble.

We were fighting in a confined space, down in a large, gloomy cellar with only one door. Steps led upwards, but he was standing between me and my escape route. I feinted with my staff, and when he responded to block it, I changed the direction of my swing and made contact with his right temple. It was a good strong blow and he dropped to one knee. I hit him again – a hard crack on his shoulder. Then I ran for it – up the steps and towards the open door.

There was a thud as the knife buried itself in the woodwork to my left, just a few inches from my shoulder. Then he was pounding up the steps after me, getting nearer with every stride. I almost made it through the door, but then he jumped on me from behind, bringing me down hard, flat on my face. His right arm came across my windpipe and started to press. I'd just time to suck in a quick breath before I began to choke.

I struggled, kicking my legs and twisting my body, but it was no good. I was still gripping my staff with my left hand, but from that prone position couldn't use it. My eyes were darkening. He was strangling the life out of me . . .

So I rapped three times on the top step with my right hand. Instantly my assailant relinquished the choker-hold and stood up. I stumbled to my feet, my head spinning, but feeling happy just to be able to breathe again.

'Not one of your best days, Master Ward!' he said, shaking his head. 'Never take refuge in any room that's only got one door! Mind you, you did get in a couple of good blows with your staff. But never turn your back on an enemy with a knife. I could have stuck it in the back of your neck with my eyes shut!'

I bowed my head and said nothing, but I knew there was no chance he would have put the knife into me from behind. His job was to train me, not kill me. I'd taken my chance of escape and had come close to succeeding.

I'm a spook's apprentice, being trained to deal with all manner of things that come out of the dark, such as ghosts, ghasts, boggarts and witches. Facing me was a large, shaven-headed man called Bill Arkwright. My master, John Gregory, had seconded me to him for training in the physical skills needed by a spook: fighting with staffs; unarmed combat; hunting and tracking.

Picking up my staff, I followed him out of the house; soon we were on the canal bank, heading back to the dilapidated old mill which was his home. Arkwright was the spook who looked after the County north of Caster. He specialized in things that came out of the lakes, marshes and canals of this region – water witches mainly, but there were also all manner of weird beasts, such as wormes, selkies, skelts and kelpies to contend with, some of which I'd never seen except in the Bestiary, the big book of creatures of the dark which my master, John Gregory, had illustrated with his own hand.

Recently we'd defeated the water witch, Morwena,

and now Mr Gregory had set off back to his house at Chipenden without me. The final months of my training with Bill Arkwright were proving to be the hardest I'd ever experienced. I was covered in bruises from head to foot. The practice sessions when we fought with staffs were brutal, with no quarter given. But I was sharpening my skills; slowly starting to improve.

Arkwright's mill had once been haunted by the ghosts of his mam and dad; trapped there despite all his efforts to release them. That had made him bitter, driving him to drink. But recently I'd helped him to liberate them and they had gone to the light. As a result, Arkwright had slowly changed, a lot of his pain and anger dissipating. Now he drank rarely and his temper was much better. I still preferred John Gregory as my master, but Bill Arkwright was teaching me well, and despite his rough ways, I was learning to respect him.

But Arkwright was still a very hard man. John Gregory kept live witches imprisoned in pits indefinitely. Bill Arkwright confined them as a punishment for a limited time. Then he killed them, cutting out their hearts so that they couldn't return from the dead. He was a good spook but I knew him to be ruthless.

It was misty on the towpath, and before we came within sight of the large tethering post on the canal bank outside the mill, we heard the bell. Three rings indicated that it was spook's business, so Arkwright picked up the pace and I followed close at his heels.

A middle-aged woman was standing beneath the huge bell. She wore a dark wide-brimmed hat pulled low over her eyes, black stockings and sturdy leather shoes with flat heels. I thought she looked like a servant from a big house and I was soon proved right.

'Good day to you, sir,' she said, giving a little curtsey. 'Would you by any chance be Mister Arkwright?'

I tried to keep a straight face. Bill was wearing

his cloak with the hood up against the damp and carrying his big staff with its twelve-inch blade and six backward-facing barbs. Quite clearly he was the local spook.

'Aye, I'm Bill Arkwright,' he replied. 'What brings you here on a cold damp winter afternoon?'

'Mistress Wicklow of Lune Hall has sent me. She'd like to see you as soon as possible. We've heard a banshee wailing two nights in a row and we're all frit to death! The gardener saw it on the lakeside near the narrow bridge. It was washing a burial shroud in the water – which means someone is going to die soon—'

'Let me be the judge of that,' Arkwright said.

'My mistress thinks it'll be her husband . . .'

Arkwright raised one eyebrow. 'Is he in good health at present?'

'Fell off his horse in the autumn and broke a leg. Got pneumonia soon after and it's left him with a bad cough. Mistress says he's not the man he was. Getting worse by the hour . . .'

'Tell your mistress I'll be there before dark.'

The servant gave another little curtsey, and with a muttered thanks turned north and set off down the towpath.

'It's a waste of time, really,' Arkwright said as we watched her disappear into the mist. 'There's nothing a spook can do about a banshee. They forecast deaths but don't bring them about.'

'Mr Gregory doesn't even think they do that,' I said. 'He doesn't believe anybody can see into the future.'

'Do you agree with him, Master Ward?'

'Witches are able to scry, I'm sure of it. The things they prophesy can happen. I've seen it with my own eyes.'

'Your master would just say it was coincidence,' Arkwright said, rubbing the top of his bald head, 'but I'm sure that you and I are both of the same mind. There's got to be something in it. Some people and some entities, including a banshee, can see what's going to happen in the future. So I think it's very likely that Master Wicklow or somebody else in that house will be dead before the end of the week. But it won't be the banshee that actually does the killing. It's sensed a coming death, that's all.'

'So why are we going then? Why get involved?'

Arkwright frowned. 'People expect us to help; they feel better if we're around in situations like this. Think how many times a doctor repeatedly visits the bedside of a dying man when he's unable to do anything – sometimes not even to relieve the pain. But he visits anyway because it makes the patient and his family feel better.

'And we have a second reason for going. We need the money. Clients have been few and far between recently. I've killed water witches, but nobody has paid me for it. Our larder is bare, Master Ward, and although they're easy enough to catch, we don't want to eat fish every day. Up at that big house they pay good money to local tradesmen. They can well afford it, so we might as well have our share.

'And there's a third reason if the first two aren't enough for you. An apprentice should see and hear a banshee if there's one about. It's part of your training to learn the limitations of a spook. As I said, we can do nothing about 'em!'

CHAPTER 2
THE SHROUD WASHER

Carrying our bags and staffs, we set off within the hour, heading north. Normally we would have taken Claw, the big wolfhound that Arkwright used to hunt water witches through the marshes, but she was expecting pups and would give birth any day now.

'Let's hope they give us a bite of supper and a hot drink,' Arkwright growled as we left the canal and headed north-east through the trees. 'It's a miserable damp night to keep watch.'

We hadn't been walking much more than half an hour when we saw a figure jump over a stile and head our way down the towpath. It was a red-faced farmer, striding towards us in big muddy boots. He looked very worried, as if carrying the weight of the whole world on his shoulders.

'Here comes trouble!' Arkwright said, keeping his voice low as the man approached. 'Not known for paying his bills, is Farmer Dalton. Half the tradesmen in the district are chasing him!'

'Thank goodness I've caught you, Mr Arkwright!' he said, blocking our path. 'Three sheep have been taken in one night. In the west pasture. The one next to the marsh.'

'Taken? Do you mean missing, eaten or drained?' Arkwright asked.

'Drained of blood.'

'Big wounds or small?'

'Deep puncture marks on their necks and backs.'

'Three in one night, you say? Well, it's not a ripper boggart or their bellies would be cut open – most likely a water witch is to blame. Though for them to take animals is rare. It suggests the witch is injured and can't get human prey. In that case she could be very dangerous – might even approach the farmhouse.'

'I've young children . . .'

'Well, they'll be safe enough as long as you keep all your doors and windows secure. I'll sort it but I expect to be paid.'

'Won't have money until after the first spring market . . .'

'I can't wait that long,' Arkwright said firmly. 'I'll take mutton and cheese in direct payment. A week's supply. Is that a deal?'

The farmer nodded but clearly wasn't pleased at having to cough up payment so soon.

'I'll be there soon after dark,' said Arkwright. 'I've another job to attend to first.'

The farmer soon left us, climbing back over the stile to head for his farm, now clearly really worried that his family might be at risk.

The mist thickened, hampering our progress, and we didn't reach the manor house much before dark. Lune Hall was big, with a fancy turret, and was set in extensive grounds. Approaching it from the west, I could see a lake to the rear, with a small island at its centre, connected to the main garden by a narrow ornamental bridge. Beyond the lake was what looked like an ancient mound.

'Is that a burial mound?' I asked. 'A barrow?'

'Indeed it is, Master Ward. Some say it's the last resting place of an important Celtic chieftain.'

The Celts were the race who arrived in the County as the native 'Little People' were starting to decline. Centuries later, they sailed west across the sea to the large island called Ireland and made that their home.

I turned my attention back to the large and imposing house. Only lords, ladies, knights and esquires would be admitted through the front door of such an establishment, so Arkwright led us round the back to the tradesmen's entrance. After he'd knocked twice, the door was opened by the same maid who'd made the journey to the mill. She showed us into the kitchen and, without being asked, brought us each a bowl of hot soup and some generous slices of bread, thickly buttered. We sat at the table and tucked in. When we'd finished, she led us along a gloomy wood-panelled corridor and out into a small flagged yard to the rear, where a small woman in a dark, well-tailored coat and sturdy walking shoes was waiting.

'This is Mr Arkwright, ma'am,' said the maid, who immediately turned and went back into the house, leaving us alone with her mistress.

'Good evening, Mr Arkwright,' said the woman, giving us a warm smile. 'Is this your apprentice?'

Her accent told me that she originated from Ireland. Long ago, when I visited the Topley market with my dad, there were lots of horse traders there from that country. They used to race their mounts up and down the muddy lanes.

'It is that, ma'am,' Bill Arkwright replied, giving a little bow. 'His name is Tom Ward.'

'Well, thank you both for coming so promptly,' she said. 'I do fear that my husband's life is in danger. His cough is worsening by the hour.'

'Has the doctor attended him?' asked Arkwright.

'To be sure, he comes twice a day but can find no

explanation for my husband's very sudden deterioration. He had recovered fully from the pneumonia. There's no reason for him to get worse now. I fear the banshee has marked him for death. I'm just hoping that you can do something to save him. Follow me – I'll show you where she appears.'

It was still winter, so the garden was not at its best. Even so, you could tell that in spring and summer it would really be something special. It was subdivided into many sections, the path weaving its way through wicker archways and bowers sheltered by stone ivy-clad walls. The shrubs and ornamental trees gradually started to give way to larger species of oak and ash as the garden merged naturally into a wood.

We followed Mistress Wicklow down the long garden path towards the bridge that crossed the lake to give access to the island.

'In my country, *banshee* means "woman of the fay folk",' she said, glancing back at us over her shoulder. 'A fay is what you'd call a fairy in the County . . .'

'We don't believe in goblins and fairies, ma'am,' Arkwright told her. 'We have enough to contend with without them!'

'I'm sure you do, Mr Arkwright, but this threat is real enough. Matthew, my gardener, has seen her and I've heard her. 'Tis a terrible scream, enough to curdle the blood. Anyway, here is Matthew – he is waiting for us now . . .'

Matthew stepped forward out of the gloom and touched his cap in respect. He was old and weather-beaten, long past his prime. It must have been hard for him to keep up the hard physical work of gardener to such a big house.

'Tell them what you saw, Matthew,' Mistress Wicklow commanded.

The gardener nodded and shivered. 'It was yonder,' he said, pointing towards the lake. 'I was standing on the narrow bridge thinking how the lilies wanted thinning out when I saw her kneeling on the bank—'

'On this shore or on the island?' Arkwright interrupted.

'This shore, sir. She was kneeling right on the edge of the lake, washing something in the water. It looked like a burial shroud to me. The moon was shining brightly and I could see that the material was covered in dark stains. I was scared; fixed to the spot. I couldn't tear my gaze away. She kept dipping the shroud into the water, then wringing it out, but the stains were still there. The water was darkening each time, but she couldn't wash it clean.

'Then she turned her head and looked straight at me. Gave a terrible wailing cry that almost killed me stone-dead on the spot. A second later she disappeared, but I'll never forget her.'

'What did she look like? Was she young or old?' my master asked.

'That was the surprising thing, sir. She was young and really pretty. It was hard to believe that such a terrible cry could be uttered by such a comely mouth.'

'Well, ma'am, we'll stay here tonight and keep watch,' Arkwright told Mistress Wicklow. 'I suggest that nobody approaches this part of the garden for at least twenty-four hours. By then we should know what's what.'

'Then I'll leave everything in your hands,' she said. 'I have faith in you, Mr Arkwright. You look strong and dependable. If anyone can save my husband's life, it'll be you.'

Arkwright bowed, and with a little smile for both of us, Mistress Wicklow turned and walked back towards the house.

I looked at my temporary master. I wondered if he had forgotten all about the farmer he'd promised to help with the water witch that evening. I was about to ask him about it when he looked at me and shook his head. 'I fear there's nothing to be done here,' he said sadly. 'If Mistress Wicklow's husband is going to die, he'll die, and there's nothing you or I can do about it. But there's no point me telling her that.'

I wasn't happy with Arkwright's attitude. John Gregory would have told her the truth, but it wasn't worth saying anything to him. My new master was a law unto himself. And he soon answered my question about the farmer.

'Well, Master Ward, I'll be off to deal with the water witch but should be back sometime tomorrow. Probably best if they think I'm keeping watch too. It means that when you go to the kitchen at dawn, they'll give you two breakfasts to bring back here. Aren't you a lucky lad?'

'Looks like being a long cold night first,' I grumbled. I didn't like the idea of misleading Mistress Wicklow.

But he simply shrugged and told me, 'You've got the easy job! Forget all that fairies and fays nonsense – a banshee is just an elemental, and a low-level one at that. And this one's pretty with it! What more could you want? She can't hurt you, so get as close as you can and see what she's about.'

With that, Arkwright gave me a wink, headed for the edge of the garden and pushed through the hedge to rejoin the lane.

* * *

Soon the mist began to lift and the large disc of the moon rose over the trees. It was waning, two days beyond full, but it cast a strong silver light over the garden.

I decided to keep watch from the bridge. At first I stood leaning against the wooden rail, but finally I grew weary and settled myself down cross-legged on the boards, my staff in my left hand, my bag close by me. I kept nodding off and waking up suddenly, so finally I lay down on my back and rested my head on my bag. Then I closed my eyes.

Had Bill Arkwright been here, we'd have taken it in turns to keep watch while the other slept. But what did it matter in this case? The banshee couldn't actually hurt anyone, and if it appeared on the lake shore, its cry would wake me up instantly. So I allowed myself to fall asleep.

But suddenly I awoke. Something was wrong . . . A cold feeling was running the length of my spine – the one that warned me when something from the dark was close. I seized my staff and got quickly to my feet.

Instantly I heard a terrible wail, which made me shiver and shake. No animal or bird of the night could utter such a terrifying sound – I knew it had to be the banshee.

That unnerving cry seemed to have come from the far side of the lake. I decided to go and take a closer look as my master had instructed, so I left the bridge and began to follow the shore anticlockwise, heading for the source of that chilling scream. There were lots of shrubs and trees close to the lake – mainly willows with long trailing branches. The ground was boggy underfoot so my progress was slow.

Again I heard the wail of the banshee, this time much closer. It stopped me dead in my tracks. Arkwright had said that a banshee wasn't dangerous, but that cry suggested otherwise, and the hairs on the back of my neck were beginning to rise.

And then I saw her . . .

She had her back to me and was kneeling in the mud right on the very edge of the water.

Arkwright had advised me to get a really close look.

Why not? She couldn't harm me, he'd said. So I took a cautious step nearer, then another one. Yes, she was washing something in the lake. And the gardener had been right. It certainly looked like the shroud they wrapped a corpse in before nailing it inside the coffin. I moved closer still. The figure had her back to me and I could see stains spreading in the water like black ink.

Blood from the shroud? It certainly looked like it. And what was it that I'd read in the Spook's Bestiary? Blood on the banshee shroud meant that a violent death was being foretold.

But Mr Wicklow was ill with worsening congestion of the lungs, perhaps resulting from pneumonia. So that didn't fit – unless someone else in the house was going to die violently.

I took another couple of steps. Then I became aware of something else . . .

Perched on a branch directly above the banshee I saw a large black crow. It seemed to be staring directly at me. I shivered. There was something baleful and malevolent about that bird.

Suddenly the banshee pulled the shroud out of the water and started to wring it dry. At the same time she wailed for a third time, a cry so terrible and intense that I held my breath until it was finished and felt myself trembling all over.

The cry stopped as quickly as it had begun, and she carried on twisting the shroud as if determined to wring every last drop of moisture from it. While she was thus occupied, I took another step towards her. That was a mistake. A twig cracked under my foot and the banshee turned her head and looked directly at me.

My mouth suddenly grew dry and my whole body started to tremble. The cold feeling down my spine was suddenly much more intense. The gardener had been right about the burial shroud but wrong about the banshee's face.

It was hideous – pitted and cracked like the surface of a dry lake bed in high summer. The eyes were just two dark holes. She opened her mouth wide, but instead of that blood-curdling wail, the banshee hissed at me like an angry cat. No doubt she meant to terrify me, but I stood my ground, gazing directly into that horrible face.

I expected the water elemental to disappear, but to my surprise, she got to her feet. And then she spoke.

'Be gone, boy! Don't linger here or you'll be dead!'

No sooner had she uttered those words than the black crow flapped its wings and took flight.

I didn't think banshees spoke. They were known only for their terrible wail. Now she began to move away from me along the lake shore, walking quickly. I followed, but as I passed the place where she'd been washing the shroud, a shaft of moonlight showed me footprints in the mud. She was barefoot. Not only that: I could hear the sound of squelching feet moving away from me. This wasn't a banshee, I was sure of it, because they weren't solid. But what exactly was I dealing with? Some sort of witch? Had that black crow been her familiar? Mouldheel witches went barefoot. Surely there wasn't one here?

She started to run and I gave chase. Now I regretted leaving my silver chain in my bag – I could have cast it ahead of me and brought her down. I hadn't thought I'd be dealing with something solid that ran so quickly. She was beginning to widen the gap between us. And there, directly ahead, right at the edge of the trees, was the burial mound. She made straight for it and was now out in the open, while I was still hampered by trees. There was a sudden flash of bright light directly ahead. It blinded me momentarily, and I almost ran into a low branch, grazing it with my head. Then I burst out of the trees. I was in the open too now, but there was no sign of the banshee.

I stopped and looked about me. Nothing. Then I approached the grassy mound cautiously. It was roughly oval in shape, and on the side nearest me rose up quite steeply in an almost vertical wall. I looked down and saw the footprints in the mud. They led right up to the earthen wall. It was as if the witch had suddenly disappeared. Either that or somehow run right into the mound . . .

Puzzled, I did one full circuit of the mound and then headed back through the trees towards the ornamental bridge. Once there, I settled down for the night again, wrapped in my cloak with my head resting on my bag. It was very cold and my sleep was fitful. I kept thinking over what had happened. What was going on? This certainly wasn't a banshee we were facing – not according to what I'd read. I had a lot to tell Bill Arkwright.

By dawn I was pacing back and forth across the bridge, deciding whether or not it was too early to go to the kitchen and ask for my breakfast. Perhaps I would get two as Arkwright had suggested. Why not? I was certainly hungry enough. Thinking I'd waited long enough, I was just about to set off for the house when I heard footsteps in the lane and Bill Arkwright forced his way through the hedge and back into the garden. I started – I hadn't expected him back so soon.

As soon as I saw his face, I groaned inwardly. He was leaning heavily on his staff and walking with a pronounced roll of his shoulders. He looked very angry. What was worse, his lips were stained purple. He'd been drinking red wine. He did so only rarely these days, but it never helped his mood.

'Shall I go and get us some breakfast?' I suggested as he approached the bridge.

'Breakfast? You can forget about that, Master Ward. It's the last thing I want. I should have gone straight to the farm instead of bringing you here to see this blessed banshee.'

'It's not—' I began, about to tell him what I'd discovered, but his face instantly darkened with anger.

'Shut your mouth! Just listen for once!' he roared. 'It was a worme, not a water witch, and a blooming big one at that. It got into the farmhouse and killed a child! Blood and bone!' he cursed. 'A child died because I came here.'

I bowed my head, not knowing what to say.

'We're going back there right away. It's holed up somewhere in an old boathouse and it'll take two of us to flush it out. A very dangerous thing is a worme. So come on, let's waste no time or it'll kill again.'

With those words he led us back onto the lane, and soon we were hurrying along towards the canal and the farm beyond it – the banshee far from our thoughts.

CHAPTER 3
THE WORME

A cold wind was blowing in from the sea, so I pulled up my hood to keep my ears warm. I lagged behind Arkwright for most of the way, knowing of old that he was not in the mood for company and that the only words I'd hear would be curses. But once we'd crossed the canal and were on the track that led to the farm, he beckoned me forward to walk alongside him.

'Listen carefully, Master Ward, because what I say might just save your life. I'm going to tell you what I know about wormes – which, as you know, are spelled with an *e* at the end to set them apart from ordinary earthworms. Some have legs, most have tails, and all are vicious and very bad-tempered. I saw the tracks the creature made in the mud: this one has legs *and* a tail. The legs'll give it speed, so watch out!'

The thought of facing such a danger made me feel nervous. Arkwright hadn't been prepared to risk tackling it alone, so this was clearly going to be a very hazardous job.

'Their bodies are eel-like but covered with very tough green scales like armour plates, which are very difficult to penetrate with a blade,' he went on. 'And as for their jaws, they're long, with a mouth full of razor-sharp fangs that can easily bite off a head or an arm. Wormes are very dangerous creatures, Master Ward – they can be the size of a small dog or as big as a horse. This one is bigger than me – surprisingly big to stray this far south, away from the lakes. That's where they are usually to be found.

'When they catch a human, they usually kill their victim by squeezing him to death before eating him, bones and all, leaving hardly a trace. But with animals such as cattle, they just bite deeply and suck out the blood. That's what this one did with the sheep – that's why I made the mistake of thinking it was a water witch. A mistake that cost a young boy's life. It got into the house and dragged him from his bed. When the farmer went upstairs to check on the boy before going to bed himself, it was already too late. The worme had eaten him. All that remained was blood-stained fragments of his nightshirt.'

What Arkwright had described was terrible and sad. I felt really sorry for the parents. No wonder my master was angry, but it was a mistake that any spook could have made.

'Some people call them dragons,' Arkwright continued. 'That's because they breathe out clouds of steam to confuse their prey. It hides them while they spit. That spit is poisonous and can kill a fully-grown man in just minutes. If it makes contact with your skin, you're as good as dead. If it even touched your breeches or shirt, it would soak through in seconds, still probably delivering a lethal dose. But with two of us on the attack it'll be confused. It won't know which of us to tackle first and that'll give us a better chance of dealing with it. Any questions?'

'Will I be able to use my silver chain against it?'

Arkwright shook his head. 'You'd be wasting your time, Master Ward. Despite those scales, it's sinuous and slippery and would soon wriggle clear of it. No, it's immune to silver and to salt. We use our staffs. That's the safest and surest way. Let me deal with it directly while you approach it from one side; keep some distance between us to confuse it – then it won't be absolutely sure where the main threat will come from. Hopefully I'll be able to get in close and finish it off before it can do me any serious damage.'

As we passed the farmhouse, we heard a woman wailing inside – no doubt the poor mother who'd lost her young son. We continued down the narrow muddy track, which led to a water channel and then ran alongside it. We were now passing through a marsh and approaching the sea. There was little water in the channel at that moment, but it was tidal and allowed small boats access to the sea. A number of wooden boathouses were dotted along its edges, and Arkwright stopped outside the largest. The building was as big as a barn but dilapidated and fallen into disrepair. I saw that the clasp on the small door was fastened with a coil of barbed wire.

'Well, here we are,' Arkwright said. 'This is the place I tracked it to. Let's hope it's still lurking in here. It's likely to stay here because it's fed recently and will remain under cover until it next goes hunting again – probably after dark tonight. Let's check before we go in . . .'

Arkwright circled the boathouse warily. Around us the marsh grass was bent and twisted; it danced to the dictates of the wind. The landscape was flat and bleak, with mudflats in the distance. It seemed totally deserted, but for the seabirds far above descending in long slow spirals out of the grey winter sky.

'There! Can you see the tracks? That's where it went in . . .'

On the channel side of the boathouse there was a mud slope that led from a huge door down to the water. This was where boats were launched. There were clawed tracks, smeared in places where the worme's tail had slicked across the mud. The door was rotten, with most of the planks broken away near the bottom, leaving a jagged lower edge. The creature had squeezed itself in underneath.

We completed the circuit and Arkwright nodded in satisfaction. 'No fresh tracks, Master Ward, so it's still here. Light a candle. It'll be dark in there . . .'

I pulled a candle-stub from my pocket and got the tinderbox from my bag. I had to crouch low near the door and shield both from the cold wind, but in moments I'd managed to light the wick.

'Ready?' Arkwright asked.

I nodded. It took Arkwright just seconds to twist the wire free of the clasp across the small door; then he stepped inside cautiously, his staff at the ready. I followed close behind, protecting the flickering candle as best I could.

The moment I entered, I knew that the worme was lurking nearby. The whole area was filled with a dense warm mist that had a noxious, acrid stink, making my eyes water. It was the breath of the creature. No wonder some people confused wormes with dragons, thinking that they breathed fire.

The rotting hulk of a boat filled most of the space inside. It was supported by wooden beams, three feet or more above the earthen floor, and something large scuttled out towards us from the darkness beneath.

I caught a glimpse of a wide mouth full of sharp, murderous teeth. Then most of the worme came into view. It was big all right. Had it been able to stand upon its hind legs, it would have been taller than Arkwright, and the tail trailing behind it added another third to that. But its legs were stubby and the large toes were webbed and armed with sharp curved talons, so that its body was almost scraping the earth.

As Arkwright had told me, it had green scales covering its long body.

With a sudden loud hiss, the worme breathed out, and a large plume of steam erupted from its nostrils, making it difficult to see. Arkwright jabbed downwards at it with his staff. He missed the head by inches and it scampered backwards until the rear half of its body was once more under the hulk of the boat. It snarled up at us, its small eyes glittering in the candlelight.

'Stand back, Master Ward. I'll deal with this,' Arkwright said, moving forward and readying the blade of his staff.

Suddenly the creature spat, and Arkwright quickly stepped to one side, just in time to avoid the large globule of dark liquid that had been aimed at his legs.

'Keep your distance,' he advised, gesturing me back with his right arm. 'Remember what I said about worme-spit! If the venom touches your skin, you could be dead within minutes. Pass me the candle, then move away to the left.'

I handed him the candle and he held it high. The worme seemed to move its head and stare towards the light, but then it twisted back to face Arkwright and breathed out another plume of mist. Next, hidden by that cloud, it hissed and spat again: a thick ball of slime landed on Arkwright's right boot. Luckily the boot leather would be too thick to be penetrated; it was a good job it hadn't landed on his trousers.

Again Arkwright moved the candle. 'The light fascinates it . . .' he said softly. 'It's a good idea to distract its attention. Now you move a little closer and threaten it with your staff. Not too close, mind!'

I did as he commanded, thrusting my staff towards it. Its eyes were on me now and then, in a fury, his staff raised, Arkwright suddenly rushed in to attack the ugly creature. He brought the blade down hard, three times in quick succession. The first blow missed as the beast twisted away, but the second and third blows struck home and the long blade went deep into its head and neck. It thrashed and writhed, sliding back into the darkness under the boat. Its blood was dark and thick, a viscous slime oozing out onto the ground.

Arkwright handed the candle back to me. 'Crouch down and give me as much light as possible,' he ordered.

Then he put down his staff, fished a long-bladed knife from his bag and crawled under the boat. By the light of the candle I watched him stabbing the creature again and again until it gave a great gasp and lay still.

'Not quite as difficult as I'd thought,' he remarked when, once more, he was standing beside me. 'Well, Master Ward, let's go and tell Farmer Dalton the job's done . . .'

In answer to Arkwright's triple rap, the farmer came to the front door. I saw that his eyes were red and swollen with grief.

'The beast's body is lying in the biggest of the boatyards yonder and soon it'll start to rot,' Arkwright said, gesturing towards the salt marsh. 'It'll need attending to. I have urgent business elsewhere now.'

The farmer nodded and gave a great sob that shook his whole body.

'I'm sorry for the loss of your son,' Arkwright said respectfully.

The man nodded but couldn't speak.

'Well, erm, we'd best be on our way,' continued my master.

'Wait! You'll want paying,' said the farmer. 'Forget the mutton and cheese – I do have a little emergency money in the attic . . .'

'No payment is required,' my master said. 'Put it towards the funeral expenses.'

With that, we were on our way east again, heading back towards the Wicklows' residence. For a while we walked in silence, keeping up a steady pace, but then I remembered the strange business of the banshee.

'The banshee, Mr Arkwright . . .'

'The banshee, indeed, Master Ward. We really do need to be seen to sort that banshee now. We must hope they pay us well for our trouble. I hadn't the heart to take anything from Dalton after what happened.'

'But it wasn't a banshee, Mr Arkwright. At least, I don't think so . . .'

Arkwright came to a sudden halt and glared at me. 'Did you see it?' he demanded.

I nodded.

'Was she as pretty as the gardener said?'

I shook my head.

'Well, he was an old man. To a man of his age any woman looks pretty!'

'She was hideous. Her skin was cracked and disfigured.'

'Was she washing a burial shroud?'

'It was covered in blood and there were big dark stains in the water – that predicts a violent death, doesn't it? Yet Master Wicklow is suffering from congestion of the lungs . . .'

Arkwright rubbed the top of his head and frowned. 'So what makes you think it wasn't a banshee?'

'She left footprints in the mud at the water's edge. Banshees don't leave footprints, do they? That type of elemental is just a spirit. And she spoke to me. Warned me off. Said if I lingered, I'd be dead. Then she set off through the trees . . .'

As I spoke, I heard her voice in my memory and I realized something that I'd thought nothing of at the time. 'She had the same accent as Mistress Wicklow. She was from Ireland, the big island across the water . . .'

'Was she now? So what happened then, Master Ward. Did you obey her?'

'No. I followed her. I was running as fast as I could but I didn't catch her. She sprinted towards the burial mound and disappeared. Her footprints went right up to it. It was as if she'd vanished.'

'Really?' said Arkwright, scratching his head. 'Well, that's interesting.'

'And just before that there was a flash of bright light,' I continued. 'I think she was a witch. There was a black crow on a branch just above her while she was washing the shroud. Could that have been her familiar?'

Arkwright looked thoughtful and perhaps a little worried. 'Come on, Master Ward, let's continue on our way. I'll have to think about this for a while . . .'

So we went on towards Lune Hall, my master silent and deep in thought.

CHAPTER 4
THE CELTIC ASSASSIN

It was getting dark again by the time we reached the hall, but the sky was clear and the moon would soon be up.

'Right, Master Ward, we need to talk,' Arkwright said, stepping off the track, placing his bag and staff on the ground and leaning back against a tree trunk. 'It's been a long day and our bellies must be thinking our throats have been cut. I *was* going to suggest we get ourselves a bite to eat, but we can't risk that now. We need to follow the advice that John Gregory gave us, and fast before facing the dark. Because I think we're about to step into unknown territory. Ever heard of the Celtic witches?'

220

I put down my own staff and bag and frowned, searching my memory. 'I'm not sure whether the Spook's Bestiary has an entry on them or not – if so, it's very short.'

'Exactly, Master Ward, because not a lot's known about them. They mostly come from the south-western region of Ireland. That whole island is shrouded in mystery. Some call it the Emerald Isle because it gets even more rainfall than the County and the grass there is just as green. But it has dense mists too, and treacherous bogs. In the south-west there are also malevolent goat mages. We know more about them than we do about the witches—'

'I *do* remember reading about them!' I interrupted.

'Aye, the goat mages worship the Old God, Pan. They're a force to be reckoned with but never leave Ireland. As far as records go back, there is no mention of these Celtic witches visiting the County either. But amongst our fragments of knowledge is the name of the Old God they worship – the Morrigan. She haunts battlefields, and some call her the Goddess of

Slaughter. When summoned to this earth by one of the Celtic witches, she usually takes the shape of a large black crow—'

'The big crow on the branch?'

Arkwright shrugged. 'Who knows? But there's one more thing that I've heard said about Celtic witches. There are lots of burial mounds in Eire – and I mean a lot. For every one we have in the County, they have at least another ten. It's said that those witches can get into burial mounds and take refuge there. And that's exactly what she did when you chased her – I'm almost certain of it. I think we're dealing with a Celtic witch, Master Ward, and because we don't know much about her or her powers, that makes her *very* dangerous!'

Before going into the garden to keep watch, Arkwright decided to pay his respects to the mistress of the house again, so we went round to the tradesmen's entrance. This time it was a long while before anyone answered the door, and Arkwright started snorting with impatience.

The same maid answered, but this time she didn't meet our eyes and merely beckoned us inside. We were led not into the kitchen but towards the front of the house and were shown into a large drawing room.

Mistress Wicklow was standing with her back to the fire, her face pale; she was dressed in black. To her right, beneath the curtained window, was a coffin positioned on a long low table draped with a purple cloth. Two large candles were burning: one at its head, the other at its foot.

'My husband died suddenly last night at the very moment that the banshee wailed for the third time. Where were you?' she demanded, a dangerous chill to her voice.

'A child was killed by a worme and I was called away urgently,' Arkwright said abruptly, bending the truth a little. 'But I left my very capable apprentice here on watch. And from what he tells me, I don't think we are dealing with a banshee at all . . .'

Mistress Wicklow lowered her gaze to the carpet and her hands started to flutter nervously. She clasped them together tightly in an attempt to keep them still.

'Ah, I see it now. You knew that already, didn't you?' Arkwright accused her. 'You *knew* there was a witch out there . . .'

She looked up to meet his gaze, her eyes brimming with tears. 'We've been here in the County almost five years and I thought we were safe. But they've sent a witch assassin after us. She's killed my husband and I'll be next.'

'*They?* Who? A witch clan?' demanded Arkwright.

'No,' she said, shaking her head. 'Celtic witches don't form clans. They always work alone. The goat mages sent her. They want revenge for what my husband did. Do you know of those mages? Do you know what they do?'

'We know very little about them, ma'am. Most of what happens on that island of yours is a mystery to us.'

'Each year the mages tether a goat to a high platform,' she explained. 'They worship it for a week and a day. Human beings are sacrificed until the animal is gradually possessed by one of the Old Gods called Pan. Soon the goat starts to talk, stands upon its hind legs and grows larger, dominating the proceedings and demanding more and more sacrifices.'

What she was telling us was already in the Spook's Bestiary – Arkwright would also have read it there, but he let her speak without interruption in the hope of learning something new from a native of Ireland.

'The power they gain during those days of blood-shed lasts the goat mages for almost a year. But some years things go badly wrong. If Pan doesn't possess the goat, the mages must flee the region, taking refuge in hiding places throughout Ireland. They're vulnerable then, and their sworn enemies, a federation of landowners to the south-west, hunt them down. My husband was part of that federation; at that time, eight years ago, when the mages were weak, he was its leader. The landowners managed to kill five of them.

'But, following that, there was a succession of good years for the mages, when their power was in the ascendancy. Then it was their turn to hunt and kill the landowners. So, in fear for our lives, we gathered what we could of our wealth and fled here. This house belonged to my husband's brother, a bachelor. He died in a riding accident last year and my husband inherited it. We thought we were safe here, but the goat mages and the federation are in a perpetual state of war. Somehow our enemies found out where we were living and sent the witch after us.'

'If you knew, why didn't you tell us? My apprentice could have been killed!'

'I thought if you found out what you faced, you might not take on the job. I was scared and desperate.'

'What *do* we face, then? You come from that land. What powers does a Celtic witch have – especially an assassin?'

This really was an area we knew nothing about; more material for my notebook.

'They are deadly with blades and spears. Sometimes they impale their enemies so that they die slowly. But their favourite method is the one used against my husband – the one that will soon be employed against me. They mimic banshees – that's why my people call them banshee witches; though instead of just fore-telling a death, they bring it about. When they lift the burial shroud from the water and wring it out, by dark magic they twist the heart and arteries of their victim. Last night, when the witch wailed for the third time, my husband's heart burst and blood spurted from his mouth to saturate the pillow. Tonight she'll begin the process again. This time *I'll* be the victim.'

'Not if we can help it. But it may take us more than one night,' Arkwright said.

'You have until her third cry on the third night. Then, if you fail, I will also die.'

Arkwright nodded, then turned to leave the room. 'I'm sorry for your loss,' he said.

'He wasn't a nice man,' Mistress Wicklow told us, an edge of bitterness in her voice. 'Ours was a marriage arranged by our families. I never loved him. He was a fool and he caused me nothing but trouble.'

Arkwright bowed his head, at a loss for words.

'Have you eaten?' she asked us.

'We fast when we face the dark,' Arkwright answered. 'But we'd appreciate a light breakfast tomorrow morning. We'll need to keep up our strength for what's ahead.'

Mistress Wicklow rang for the maid, who showed us out through the tradesmen's entrance once more. We began to walk down the garden, heading towards the lake.

'Well, Master Ward,' Arkwright commented, keeping his voice low. 'This is something new all right. We face a Celtic witch, so ready your silver chain!'

CHAPTER 5
THE BANSHEE CRY

Once more we settled ourselves down on the narrow bridge. My silver chain was now in the left pocket of my breeches, and I coiled it about my wrist, ready to throw. We didn't have to wait long . . .

Soon the terrible wailing banshee cry echoed over the garden. This time it came from further round the lake, near the burial mound. Immediately Arkwright set off at a run; I followed close at his heels.

The second cry came far more quickly than it had the previous night. Would the witch shriek for the third time before we reached her? She did, and I groaned

229

inside. Mistress Wicklow would already have been hurt.

Arkwright was now on my right, almost level with me and running towards the source of the cry. 'There she is!' he called out, pointing with his staff as he ran. I saw a female figure ahead, fleeing through the trees.

Suddenly something dark swooped down towards me, claws outstretched. I ducked and glanced to my right as it glided on silently towards Arkwright. It was the large black crow I'd seen the previous night. I heard him cry out; saw him stumble.

'Keep going!' he shouted. 'Keep after her!'

I kept running, but the moon had gone behind a cloud and all that told me the witch was still ahead was the slap-slap of her bare feet against the ground. We were coming towards the end of the trees and the mound lay just beyond the wood. This time I felt sure that I was catching up with her. I prepared to throw my silver chain, relying on my ears to guide me.

All at once, straight ahead, there was an explosion of light so bright that it hurt my eyes. It was like gazing directly into the sun. My vision instantly darkened and I stumbled to a halt. The light quickly faded in intensity; now it was just the silver of a full moon, but one that had fallen to earth.

It wasn't the moon though; it was a circular door in the grassy wall of the burial mound. I could see the black silhouette of the banshee witch against it. As the light faded, I glimpsed things beyond, within the mound; what looked like a table and chairs . . .

It was dark once again and I walked slowly forward to face the mound. Now there was no sign of a door at all – just grass. The real moon came out again; I looked down and saw more footprints.

Arkwright ran to my side. There was a cut on his head, just above his left eye. Blood was running down his face.

'Are you all right?' I asked.

'It's nothing,' he growled. 'Bit of a scratch. That bird did it. Probably her familiar. So the witch got away again?'

I nodded. 'She did go into the mound – I'm sure of

it. I saw a door this time, a circular entrance, and things inside. Looked like furniture.'

'Furniture? You'll be telling me next that she's got a bed in there and is going to settle down for a cosy sleep. Sure you weren't seeing things, Master Ward?'

'It really did look like a table and chairs.'

'Well, the eyes can play funny tricks in such situations, but I am inclined to believe that by use of dark magic she's somehow taken refuge in that mound.'

We spent the rest of the night on the bridge, taking it in turns to sleep. Not that we expected anything to happen again that night, but Arkwright wasn't taking any chances.

At dawn we washed our faces and hands in the lake, then went back to the tradesmen's entrance once more.

'Your mistress promised us a bite of breakfast,' Arkwright told the maid.

We ate a light meal of bread, cheese and ham, and were then shown through to the drawing room again. Mistress Wicklow was sitting in an armchair in front of

233

the fire, wrapped in a long shawl. She was shivering and her lips had a blue tinge.

'I've always had a fear of dying in my bed,' she said, her voice slightly breathless, 'so I prefer to sit in my chair until all this ends – one way or the other . . .'

'She escaped into the mound,' Arkwright explained. 'But don't you worry – she won't get away tonight.'

'You've hurt your face,' she observed.

'It was a black crow that seems to be around whenever the witch is – probably just her familiar. Though I reckon it *could* be the Morrigan. But if it really *is* her, I'd expect her to do more than just scratch my face . . .'

Mistress Wicklow shook her head. 'Not necessarily. They say that those who are cut or scratched by the Morrigan are marked for death. They always die within the year. Of course, that's probably just a foolish superstition – and it probably wasn't the goddess anyway.'

We thanked Mistress Wicklow for breakfast, took our leave of her and strolled back towards the lake. It was a nice day, but there was little warmth in the sun. It would be a long wait until nightfall. I just wanted to get all this over with and return to the mill.

'Quite a deep cut,' Arkwright said, kneeling down to gaze at his face in the mirror of the lake. 'Don't think it'll scar though. Wouldn't want it to spoil my good looks!'

I laughed.

He was on his feet in a flash and cuffed me hard across the back of the head, sending me reeling forward. I almost fell into the water.

'It's not *that* funny, Master Ward,' he said angrily. 'I'm your master and you're just the apprentice. I expect a little respect.'

'I thought you were making a joke!' I protested.

'Blood and bone!' he cursed. 'I was – but it was a very mild joke. You laughed too long and too loud.' He suddenly gave me a wolfish grin, showing a mouthful of teeth. 'Get yourself ready, Master Ward. We shouldn't neglect your training. Prepare to defend yourself!'

With that, he picked up his staff and attacked me, trying to drive me into the lake. We fought for almost an hour, and by the end of it, muscles I didn't know I had were complaining and I'd two more bruises to add to my collection. But Arkwright never did manage to force me into the lake, so that counted as some sort of victory.

'We'll do things differently tonight,' he said as we rested on the bridge once more. 'You chase her towards the mound. I'll lie in wait amongst the trees close to it and block her escape.'

It seemed a good plan – that is, if the witch didn't somehow manage to long-sniff the threat. Witches could usually do this to see danger coming. But as seventh sons of seventh sons, spooks were usually immune to this power – though with a witch about whom we knew little, nothing was certain.

That night, the first cry of the banshee witch told me that she was very close! This time she had further to run in order to reach the safety of the mound. I might even be able to catch her before the edge of the wood. So, putting my silver chain in my pocket and gripping my staff, I ran towards the sound.

There was often an edge of competition between my temporary master and me; it would be really pleasing to bind her with my chain before he could intercept her, I thought. So I ran just as fast as I could in the direction of the cry. She would hear me coming, but I didn't care. I was on the attack. My heart was pounding and I was filled with exhilaration.

The second cry came very soon after the first. The witch would be using some kind of curse that demanded a precise form of words. Surely there had to be a limit to how fast she could utter it? But, to my dismay, the third cry echoed over the lake before I reached her. I groaned, remembering Mistress Wicklow's blue-tinged lips and breathlessness. Now she would have suffered further pain.

I drove myself on even harder. I could hear the witch running through the trees ahead. I *had* to catch her. We hadn't managed to stop her uttering her third cry tonight – what chance had we of doing that tomorrow, when it would kill her victim? I wondered.

I could see her just ahead of me now and I was closing fast, readying my silver chain. As I was about to cast it, she swerved to the left so that a tree lay between me and my target.

Suddenly a burly figure rose up to confront her. Arkwright! They seemed to collide . . . he fell . . . she staggered and ran on. We were in the open now, beyond the trees, making straight for the mound. Just as I was about to cast my chain, the light blazed out again. Again I was blinded, but this time I kept going. The witch's silhouette came into view against the round yellow doorway. Then, all at once, darkness and silence.

For a moment I didn't realize what had happened. The air was warmer and absolutely still. Lights flared on the rocky walls – I saw black candles in brackets. And furniture! My eyes hadn't deceived me. There was a small table and two wooden straight-backed chairs. I was inside the burial mound!

I'd followed the witch through the magical door, and there she was, standing directly ahead of me, still gripping the rolled-up burial shroud, an expression of anger and bemusement on her face. I took a few deep breaths to calm myself and slow my pounding heart.

'What a fool you be, to follow me!' cried the witch.

'Do you always talk in rhyme?' I asked.

The witch didn't reply because, as I spoke, I cast my silver chain and it brought her to her knees, the links tight against her mouth to silence her. It was a perfect shot. I'd bound the witch – but now I had a real problem . . .

There was no visible door. How was I going to get out of the mound?

I searched the inside of the chamber carefully, running my fingers over the place where I thought I'd entered, but it was seamless. I was in a rocky cave without an entrance. Arkwright was on the outside; I was trapped inside. Had I bound the witch – or had she bound *me*? I looked at her. She was still gripping the shroud; despite the chain she hadn't dropped it.

I knelt close to her, staring into her eyes, which seemed to crinkle with amusement. Beneath the chain her mouth was pulled away from her teeth; half smile, half grimace. But her face wasn't that of the hideous hag I'd glimpsed as she washed the shroud. It could have belonged to any young country woman passed without a second glance at a market. Perhaps she'd used some spell to try and scare me off – a mild form of *dread* perhaps?

I eased the chain from her mouth so that she could speak. It was a dangerous thing to do, but I urgently needed to question her; make her tell me how I could get out. But I soon realized that it was a big mistake . . .

Her lips free of the chain, the witch was free to speak dark magic spells, and she began to do that immediately. She uttered three quick phrases, each in a language I'd never heard before, each ending in a rhyme. Then she opened her mouth very wide, and a thick black cloud of smoke erupted from it.

I sprang to my feet and staggered backwards. The cloud continued to grow – to the point where her whole face was engulfed. It reminded me of the blood from the shroud that had stained the water of the lake. Now the air between us grew dark and tainted.

The cloud was becoming even denser and taking on a shape. There were wings. Outstretched claws. A ravenous beak. It had become a black crow. The witch's open mouth was a portal to the dark! It was the Morrigan!

But this was no longer a bird of normal size and proportions; it was nothing like the seemingly ordinary crow that had swooped through the trees to attack Bill Arkwright. This creature was immense; it was distorted and twisted into something grotesque. The beak, legs and claws were elongated, stretching out towards me, while the head and body remained relatively small.

But then the wings grew too, until they reached out on either side of the monstrous bird to fill all the available space. They flapped violently, battering against the walls of the chamber and smashing the table so that it broke in half. Its claws struck out at me. I ducked and they raked the wall over my head, gouging deep grooves into the rock.

For a moment I was filled with panic. A spook has little chance of defeating one of the Old Gods. I was going to die here, I was sure. But then I took a deep breath and calmed myself. My master had taught me well, and I knew that the first and most important thing to do was control my fear. I'd faced great dangers from the dark before and survived. I could do so again . . .

So I concentrated hard, feeling the strength rise within me. And confidence began to replace fear. There was anger too.

I acted without conscious decision, with a speed that astonished even me. I stepped forward, closer to the Morrigan, released the retractable blade and swept my staff across from left to right. The blade cut deep into the bird's breast, slicing a bloody red line through the black feathers.

There was a tremendous scream. The Morrigan convulsed and contracted, shrinking rapidly until she was no larger than my fist. Then she vanished – leaving behind only a few black feathers smeared with blood that fluttered slowly to the ground.

The witch shook her head, her expression one of acute astonishment. 'That's not possible!' she cried. 'Who are you to be able to do such a thing?'

'My name is Tom Ward,' I told her. 'I'm a spook's apprentice and my job is to fight the dark.'

She smiled grimly. 'Well, you've fought your last fight, boy. There is no way you can escape this place. Soon the goddess will return. You will not find it so easy a second time.'

I smiled and looked down at the blood-splattered feathers littering the floor. Then I looked up and stared her straight in the eye, doing my best not to blink. 'We'll see. Next time I might cut off her head . . .'

I was bluffing, of course; trying to appear more confident than I felt. I had to persuade this witch to open the door of the mound.

'You're a fool, boy. She'll return, slay you, then carry off your soul to her kingdom in the dark!'

'In that case you may suffer the same fate!' I warned. 'You brought her into a dangerous situation that caused her pain. She might feel that should earn its own reward . . .'

I watched expressions flicker across the witch's face: anger, uncertainty, and then fear. The Old Gods could be vindictive and vengeful, even towards their own servants. There was some truth in what I'd just said, and the witch knew it.

'So why don't you open the door so that we can leave this mound?' I continued.

'What? So that you can kill me or bind me for ever? Which fate do you have in store for me?'

'Neither. Once outside I'll release you from the chain. But, in return, you must promise to stop cursing Mistress Wicklow and go back to Ireland.'

'Why worry about her? She and her man were landowners who cared nothing at all for their servants and tenants. Six years ago, when the crops failed, they let the people starve. They could have helped but they didn't . . .'

'I know nothing about that. But you've killed her husband. Isn't that enough?' I asked.

The witch frowned, but then she allowed the shroud to fall from her left hand to the floor. 'Help me to my feet!' she commanded.

I did as she asked, and she hobbled towards the rock wall and muttered words in the same strange language as before. There was a flare of pale light and the doorway opened before us. Gripping the chain, I pulled her forward into the cold night air. The moon bathed the mound behind us in silver light.

'Release me!' she commanded.

'Will you keep your word?'

'Yes, but will *you* keep yours?'

I nodded and, with a flick of my wrist, released

the witch from the chain. She smiled. 'Don't ever visit my land, boy. The Morrigan is much more powerful there. And she is vengeful. She would torment you beyond anything you can imagine. Whatever you do, stay away from Ireland.'

With that, the banshee witch turned her back on me and made a sign in the air, muttering under her breath. Beyond her, the door faded and became the sheer grassy wall of the burial mound.

I think she was about to turn back and say something to me, but she never got the chance.

Something flew through the air towards her and buried itself between her shoulder blades. She fell down in the mud, a knife buried to the hilt in her back. She groaned, twitched twice and lay still.

Bill Arkwright walked towards me from the edge of the trees, carrying his staff and bag.

'You did a deal with her, Master Ward? Can't blame you, I suppose. How else could you have got out of that mound?'

'She would have kept her promise!' I protested.

'She was going home. She wasn't going to complete the curse . . .'

'You've just the word of a witch for that,' Arkwright said. 'What I've just done makes things more certain. Now she *can't* complete the curse. Am I right?'

'But I gave her my word—'

'Blood and bone!' cursed Arkwright. 'Grow up, boy! This is what we do. We kill witches. We fight the dark. If you can't stomach the job, go back to your farm!'

I didn't speak. I just stared down at the dead witch.

'What's done is done,' said Arkwright, pulling the knife out of her back. 'If you're squeamish, don't linger here . . .'

So I walked back through the trees and waited for him on the bridge. Dead witches could scratch their way to the surface of their graves and go hunting for victims. He was cutting out her heart to make sure that she couldn't come back.

* * *

We went to see Mistress Wicklow, and Arkwright told her most of what had happened. She seemed even more breathless than the previous night, but felt confident that she'd now make a full recovery. My master told her where the dead witch was, and she made arrangements to have her buried close to the mound. Then she paid him and we took our leave of her.

We walked back to the mill in silence. I was far from happy with what had happened and couldn't bring myself to chat to Arkwright; he too seemed lost in his own thoughts.

At last we waded through the salt moat that protects his garden from water witches and other creatures of the dark, and headed for the side door. Before we reached it, Claw started to bark.

'Well, at least somebody's speaking to me!' Arkwright said. But when we went in, Claw didn't bound towards him as I'd expected. She was otherwise occupied . . .

'Good girl! Good girl!' Arkwright said, kneeling down to pat her on the head.

She was feeding her new-born pups. There were two of them.

'So what shall we call these two little beauties, Master Ward?'

I smiled. 'Blood and Bone?' I suggested.

Arkwright grinned up at me. 'Perfect!' he exclaimed. 'Couldn't have chosen better myself. That's what I'll call them.'

The pups had stopped feeding now. Arkwright got to his feet and reached down into his bag. 'Better safe than sorry,' he said. 'And a nice treat for a new mother!'

Then he pulled out the witch's heart and threw it to Claw.

I had other adventures with Bill Arkwright, but that's the one I'll never forget. It's because of what Mistress Wicklow said: that those cut or scratched by the Morrigan are marked for death – they always die within the year.

And Bill Arkwright did die less than a year later,

sacrificing his life in Greece so that the Spook, Alice and I could escape.

Perhaps we paid a high price for dealing with that banshee witch.

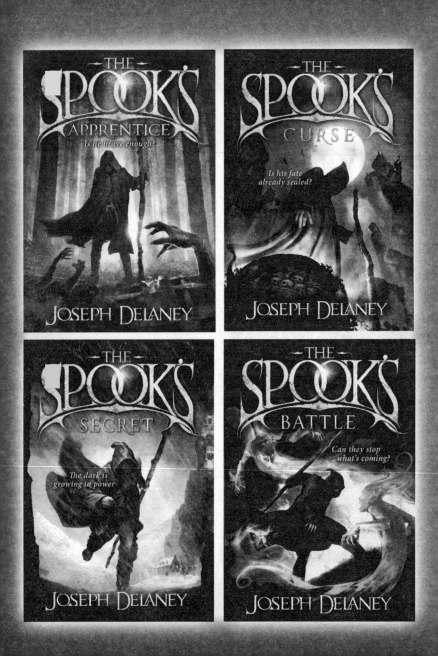

THE SPOOK'S

SERIES

Read more if you dare . . .

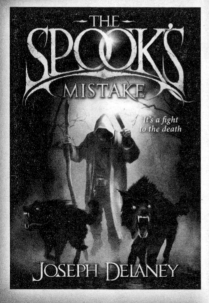

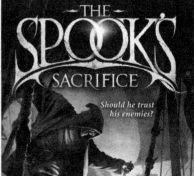

BOOK SIX

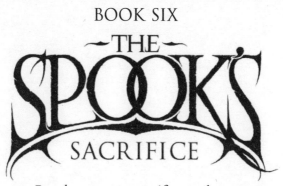

THE SPOOK'S

SACRIFICE

Read an extract – if you dare . . .

I'd taken no more than a dozen paces when there was a blood-curdling yell from my left and I heard the pounding of feet. Someone was running across the lawn, directly towards me. I readied my staff, pressing the recess so that, with a click, the retractable blade sprang from the end.

Lightning flashed again and I saw what threatened. It was a tall thin woman brandishing a long, murderous blade in her left hand. Her hair was tied back, her gaunt face twisted in hatred and painted with some dark pigment. She wore a long dress, which was soaked with rain, and rather than shoes, her feet were bound with strips of leather. So this was a maenad, I thought to myself . . .